**MA[...] [...]THE
WAY [...] [...]ALING
GLA[...] [...] HANDS—**

—even as she foc[...] on attaching the final few almonds to the wreath she was making. He plucked the two sides of the cornhusk figure upward into wings. A stray sprig of silk holly on the table inspired him to tuck it into the belt he'd formed with the wire. When he was satisfied with his creation, he handed it to her. "For you," he said.

Rosalyn's eyes widened with surprise. "An angel!" she whispered, turning the little doll this way and that. "How'd you *do* that?"

The amazement in her voice and her gaze touched him. "I used to make them for my nieces," he replied with a shrug. "When you live on a farm, cornhusks are easy to come by."

She was avidly studying the way the green floral wire formed a halo and also held the angel's neck in place, as though she'd never seen anything so clever. When Rosalyn dared to meet his gaze, her brown eyes reflected doubt and uncertainty even as she took pleasure in the angel. "This is for *me*? I—well, *denki*, Marcus," she stammered.

He blinked. Why did Rosalyn feel so undeserving? Had no one ever given her such a simple gift as a cornhusk figure? "Horses and women," he quipped. "I can have them eating out of my hand at the drop of a hat."

A SIMPLE CHRISTMAS

Charlotte Hubbard

ZEBRA BOOKS
KENSINGTON PUBLISHING CORP.

http://www.kensingtonbooks.com

ZEBRA BOOKS are published by

Kensington Publishing Corp.
119 West 40th Street
New York, NY 10018

All Kensington titles, imprints, and distributed lines are available at special quantity discounts for bulk purchases for sales promotion, premiums, fund-raising, educational, or institutional use.

Special book excerpts or customized printings can also be created to fit specific needs. For details, write or phone the office of the Kensington Sales Manager: Attn.: Sales Department. Kensington Publishing Corp., 119 West 40th Street, New York, NY 10018. Phone: 1-800-221-2647.

Zebra and the Z logo Reg. U.S. Pat. & TM Off.
BOUQUET Reg. U.S. Pat. & TM Off.

First Printing: October 2018
ISBN-13: 978-1-4201-3873-3
ISBN-10: 1-4201-3873-1

eISBN-13: 978-1-4201-3874-0
eISBN-10: 1-4201-3874-X

10 9 8 7 6 5 4 3 2 1

Printed in the United States of America

For Neal, always my guiding light

ACKNOWLEDGMENTS

Thank You, Lord, for sticking with me as I completed this series! Those ideas that come at me from out of the blue are from You, and I couldn't keep writing without them.

Thanks to you, as well, Neal for being a wise and patient man when I'm writing a book—and when I'm not!

Continued thanks to Alicia Condon, my editor, as we navigated this trilogy. My gratitude, as well, to my stellar agent, Evan Marshall, for your continued assistance with my career. It's a joy to work with both of you and I appreciate your enthusiasm, ideas, and support!

Special thanks to Vicki Harding, innkeeper of Poosey's Edge Bed and Breakfast, and to Joe Burkholder and his family, proprietors of Oak Ridge Furniture and Sherwood's Christian Books, both in Jamesport, Missouri. Your help makes my stories so much more authentic and interesting!

Matthew 2:2 (KJV)

Where is he that is born King of the Jews? for we have seen his star in the east, and are come to worship him.

Chapter One

As Rosalyn Riehl walked alongside the county highway pulling a cartload of Christmas wreaths, she gazed up at the sky in surprise. When she'd left home a few minutes earlier, the sun was shining, but now low, gray clouds were rolling in and the wind picked up—and for a brief moment tiny pellets of hail peppered her.

It's going to be a tricky winter, she thought. *The weather seems as crazy and mixed up as I feel.*

Rosalyn adored the holidays—Thanksgiving was only a week away—yet the thought of the approaching winter made her sigh. Her youngest sister, Edith, lived across the road with her husband, Asa, and their twins, and her younger sister Loretta was sharing the bedroom down the hall with her new husband, Drew, so Rosalyn felt like the odd woman out. All her life she'd longed for a husband and a family, yet at twenty-eight she saw no probability of fulfilling that dream.

Her cheeks tingled when the season's first snowflakes met her cheeks. *It's a* gut *thing I have my new job at Simple Gifts to look forward to*, Rosalyn thought as she made her way up the hill toward the store housed in a huge red barn. *Working for Nora on Wednesdays and Saturdays sure beats dealing with Loretta and Edith's moony-eyed gazes and happy chatter about being married to the Detweiler twins whenever we're all together.*

It wasn't that she begrudged her sisters their happiness. She just wanted some of her own.

When Rosalyn opened the door to enter Nora Hooley's shop, however, the merry tinkle of the bell above the door and the rich scents of bayberry and vanilla candles drove away her gloomy thoughts. It was impossible to feel grumpy as she carefully pulled her wagon between the beautiful displays of glossy walnut furniture, sets of pottery dishes, unique three-dimensional quilts, and the other lovely merchandise that had been handcrafted by Plain folks from around central Missouri.

Nora called out to her from the loft, where she was arranging an evergreen garland along the railing. "*Gut* morning, Rosalyn! I can't wait to see your wreaths and hang them around the store—not that we'll have them for long!"

Rosalyn couldn't help smiling. What a joy it was to work for Nora, whose encouraging words and freckle-faced smile always lifted her spirits. "I've got eight of them here," she replied as she stopped beside the office door. "We sisters had a work frolic on Monday, so Loretta will have another rug or two and Edith will have some baskets ready to sell in time for the open house on Saturday."

"You girls are amazing," Nora remarked. She fastened the end of the greenery garland to the railing and then started downstairs, her feet tapping a happy rhythm on the wide wooden stairway. Her deep-orange corduroy dress was set off with a paisley apron of earth tones, perfect for autumn and Thanksgiving. "And how's Cornelius? Is he accepting the way you and Loretta are trading off the days that you work for me?"

Rosalyn sighed. What good would it do to spoil Nora's cheerful mood by repeating the lecture Dat had delivered at the breakfast table . . . or to mention that yesterday's mail had brought them two more mysterious envelopes marked *Past Due*?

"He's still cranky about us working for you, and I suspect that'll never change," she hedged. "Dat's a man who hangs on to the past and the Old Order ways, after all."

Nora stopped a few feet away, her auburn eyebrows rising. "Puh! The trouble he's gotten himself into has nothing to do with proper Amish living," she said. "And I thought he was to begin some grief counseling with Bishop Tom this week."

"Oh, the two of them talked at Tom's place yesterday," Rosalyn murmured, "but I suspect the bishop's got a long row to hoe—uphill—before Dat lets go of his feelings for Mamm."

"It's one thing for him to love your mother, and another thing entirely for him to use memories of her to make you girls feel guilty," Nora put in quickly. "I'm really sorry he's thrown your family into such a tailspin with his deceptive activities, too. He'd be so much better off if he gave a full confession and made whatever amends Bishop Tom requires."

"Well, he hasn't made any more trips to Kansas City to buy clock parts," Rosalyn pointed out. As she held Nora's gaze, her curiosity flared like a piece of paper set aflame to kindle a fire. "Exactly what did he do—where did he go—that's gotten him into such trouble?"

Nora smiled sadly, grasping Rosalyn's shoulder. "I'm sorry I brought the subject up," she said. "Bishop Tom and Preacher Ben have asked Drew and me not to reveal all the details because they want your *dat* to come clean of his own free will, without folks around Willow Ridge pressuring him."

"That's not fair! We have to live with him," Rosalyn blurted out.

"You're right, it's not," Nora agreed. "But the truth will

come out in its own *gut* time, and right now we're leaving the matter in God's hands—and your *dat*'s. Now what've we got in this wagon? These bright red ribbons and greenery wreaths are just the ticket for our holiday open house, Rosalyn!"

With the blink of Nora's mischievous green eyes the conversation had been redirected. Rosalyn sensed it would do no good to ask any more questions about Dat's secretive wrongdoing, so she carefully picked up the wreath on the top of her pile. "I made a few of these fresh wreaths from evergreen clippings—and they should probably hang outside so they'll stay fresh until Christmas," she added.

"We'll tag them and put one on the front door," Nora said as she lightly ran her finger over a pinecone. "And the others can hang along the side of the door—or on the building where folks will see them first thing when they pull in to park." She inhaled deeply. "Wow, nothing smells nicer than a live wreath."

Rosalyn's spirits lifted. Nora's compliments bolstered her confidence and made the hours she'd spent making her wreaths feel worthwhile. "Here are two with silk holly and natural pinecones, and two made entirely of pinecones—"

"Oh, I love the way you tipped the pinecones with a little white paint and glitter," Nora put in with a smile. "Most English women like a little sparkle on their Christmas decorations."

"And this last one's covered in nuts, outlined with bay leaves," Rosalyn said, watching Nora's face. "It's not as colorful, so I only made one as an experiment—"

"A kitchen wreath! And look at the way the dark shells of the Brazil nuts contrast with the English walnuts and the pale almonds," Nora exclaimed as she studied the piece. "And I love that it's a star shape, too. I can tell you right now that you should load up on whole nuts next time you're at the bulk store, so you can make more of these, Rosalyn. My customers love items that are different from what they'll find at the other places where they shop."

Rosalyn's heart beat faster. "I bought a big bagful of those nuts last week, figuring we could always eat them if I didn't make any more wreaths with them," she admitted with a chuckle. "And I'm going to make a couple of wreaths from ribbon candies, too, because I love all the shiny colors—"

The bell jangled raucously as the front door flew open and hit the wall. "Hey—does anybody work here?" a young man called out. "You can't tell me this town doesn't even have a gas station."

Nora turned quickly toward him, her eyes widening in recognition as she handed Rosalyn the star-shaped wreath. "This could get interesting," she murmured.

Rosalyn watched as Nora took her time passing between the displays of handmade table linens and racks of hanging jackets, toward the fellow who'd entered with a gust of wind that had apparently blown the door out of his hand.

Or did he throw it open? Rosalyn wondered as she took in the man's black leather jacket and the rakish way his dark hair dipped over one side of his face. *Most English are at least courteous and they don't come in before the store opens. This fellow looks like walking, talking trouble—with a capital T.*

Rosalyn started slowly toward the front door, in case their unexpected guest caused Nora problems. She wasn't sure what she'd do if this brash young man behaved improperly, but she knew Nora would be coming to *her* assistance if the situation were reversed. She wasn't sure what to think, however, when the redheaded storekeeper walked quickly around the newcomer to shut the door against the wind. Nora faced their visitor, confidently crossed her arms, and gazed directly at him, unfazed by the fact that he stood head and shoulders taller than she did.

"Well, well, if it isn't Cousin Marcus from Lancaster

County, Pennsylvania," Nora said as she looked him up and down. "Did you finally show up to check out Wyatt McKenzie's job offer? Or did another girlfriend get smart and kick you to the curb for using her credit cards on the sly?"

Rosalyn gasped. Was this Marcus Hooley, the horse trainer Wyatt had called in October, hoping to hire an Amish man to manage the draft-horse farm he'd recently established? Everyone in Willow Ridge was wondering why the cousin whom Luke, Ira, and Ben had recommended hadn't bothered to provide the references Wyatt had requested. As Rosalyn looked more closely, she saw the resemblance this young man bore to Luke—and she couldn't miss the rebellious flare of his pale green eyes as he stared at Nora.

"And just how would you know who I am?" he challenged. "I've never met you or—"

"I'm married to your cousin Luke," Nora replied without missing a beat. "And so you'll know, I'd recognize the Hooley *attitude* from a mile away, Marcus. The first thing you'll learn about living in Willow Ridge is that news travels fast. Your reputation has preceded you."

Marcus tilted his head, his eyes narrowed. "Oh yeah? Folks here already know I'm the best horse trainer on the face of the earth? Or at least in America?" he challenged.

Nora shook her head, unimpressed. "Lots of men from around town were in the room when Luke and Wyatt talked to you on the phone a few weeks ago," she replied. "They know all about the references you haven't provided, and they know that Wyatt graciously offered to hire you on probation as well as to help you clear up the credit card debt you've run up. You're already off to such a bad start, maybe you should just gas up your car in Morning Star or New Haven and keep on driving. *I* certainly wouldn't hire you."

Marcus let out an incredulous laugh. "That makes us even, because I wouldn't work for you," he retorted. "When I see

Luke, I'll have to quiz him about why he ever hitched up with such a mouthy woman. Sheesh. Must've been desperate."

Spots of color rose into Nora's cheeks. "I suggest you talk to Luke at the mill store next door rather than showing up unannounced at Wyatt McKenzie's farm," she said in a voice tight with irritation. "But then, why should you listen to me?"

Marcus laughed, flashing even white teeth. He dismissed Rosalyn with a brief glance and turned toward the door. "I'll see myself out. I've had enough advice for one conversation."

The bell jangled loudly and Marcus shut the door behind him with more force than was necessary. Rosalyn let out the breath she didn't realized she'd been holding. "That was the rudest person I've ever met—even though I really didn't meet him, as such."

Nora shook her head. "Full of himself," she muttered. "Luke had an attitude when I met him, too, but he knew better than to shoot off his mouth and act like a spoiled brat—especially when he wanted things to go his way." When a car engine backfired next to the building, she glanced toward the window. "I predict we won't be seeing hide nor hair of Mr. Smart-Mouth after this morning. Wyatt won't give Marcus the time of day, much less hire him."

Rosalyn brushed off the front of her apron, as though wiping away any residue from Marcus's presence. As a member of the Old Order Amish church, she had absolutely no interest in a man who, according to his cousins, had jumped the fence—and who'd apparently used his English girlfriends' credit cards and hadn't paid his bills.

But did you see those dimples? And the way he filled out the back of those tight jeans?

Appalled at such thoughts, Rosalyn resolutely followed Nora back toward the office. After they tagged her wreaths and displayed them, she needed to dust and be sure the store was as tidy as Nora liked it before customers arrived. She was a twenty-eight-year-old *maidel*, but she wasn't nearly desperate enough to give Marcus Hooley another thought.

But what would it matter if you thought about him just a little, to pass the time? To Marcus, you're invisible, so nothing will come of it.

Chapter Two

Marcus backed out of the parking space, steered his car toward the road—and then stopped to take in the panoramic view of Willow Ridge from his hilltop vantage point. The farmland had a gentle roll to it, and he spotted black-and-white dairy cows in one of the pastures, along with a small herd of sheep on the acreage just south of it. The gardens behind the neat white homes had been cleared for the winter. Stacked, white beehives were visible among the trees of an orchard, and the deep orange and gold foliage of maple and sweet gum trees shimmered after the morning's brief bout of freezing rain. A few buggies and cars were parked at Zook's Market, which sported a blue metal roof. A café called the Grill N Skillet was doing a brisk business—and the aroma of roasting meat had made his stomach growl when he'd driven past it a short while ago.

But it's still a two-bit horse and buggy town—just a spot in the road. Even more rural and impossibly straitlaced than Bird-In-Hand, Marcus thought with an impatient sigh. *Maybe that redhead was right about gassing up and driving on. This place is already making you crazy.*

But where else can you go?

Marcus shifted into Park. When he pumped the accelerator hard to stop his old car from idling too fast, the engine back-fired and the tailpipe belched exhaust. He'd burned his bridges at the last horse farm he'd worked on, and it galled him that Luke's bossy wife had pegged him right: he'd worn out his welcome with his most recent girlfriend. He wanted to believe that living English was his ticket out of plodding along in broadfall pants and suspenders all his life, doomed to manual labor without electricity or technology. But opportunities for training horses were none too plentiful outside of Plain communities—especially considering how he'd been fired from his three most recent jobs.

Better to move on before Ben, Luke, and Ira get wind that you showed up. You don't need the Hooley brothers preaching at you about going straight to hell unless you join the Old Order.

Marcus gripped the shift knob, ready to roll down to the road, yet he paused. He could see Ben's farrier shop a short distance away, tucked behind one of the nicest, newest houses in town. And from all appearances, Luke and Ira's mill on the Missouri River was thriving only a couple of years after they'd come to Willow Ridge with little more than the clothes on their backs and some big ideas about growing specialty grains.

Truth be told, when Luke and his younger brother had still been living in Pennsylvania, they'd raised a lot of Amish eyebrows because in their late twenties they'd shown no sign of giving up *rumspringa*—yet they'd come to Missouri and made good. And Ben had been roaming the Plain country-side in his farrier wagon at thirty-five. He'd joined the church before that, but he'd been blowing around like dandelion fluff until he'd landed in this little town and taken root.

See there? They can't say a thing about your refusal to settle down just yet. All three of them were older than you—

and bucking tradition—when they came here. And Luke went
Mennonite rather than joining the Old Order!

Marcus reconsidered his options. His online research—
and the fact that several of the local Plain businesses had
websites—had suggested that there was more to this town
than met the eye. The new barns and stretches of white plank
fence pictured on Wyatt McKenzie's website had made
Marcus's pulse race, and seeing the place from the road this
morning had been the closest thing he'd had to a religious
experience in years. McKenzie obviously had big bucks to
spend, so why not make nice and play the game? Introduce
himself to Wyatt and apologize profusely for not emailing
the references he'd requested . . .

But McKenzie sounded way too nosy and superior during
that phone call, delving into your credit business—and
saying you'd have to bunk above the stable until you proved
yourself. Really? Who does he think he is, acting like he'd be
doing you such a big favor?

Marcus despised sitting in a car that rattled and shook,
with the sum total of his earthly belongings in a suitcase in
the trunk. He was a top-notch trainer—everybody he'd
worked for was impressed by his ability to make their horses
behave . . . at least until they chastised him for boozing it up
too much and asking for advances on his pay.

Clean up your act, Hooley. Three strikes and you're out,
his last employer, Enos Keim, had ranted. So Marcus hadn't
stayed around long enough for old Keim to hear about his
most recent brush-up with the county sheriff. He'd left Lancaster County at sunset and driven all night to reach Willow
Ridge. Wasn't that a sign of his commitment to starting
fresh? To turning over a proverbial new leaf?

Marcus laughed at himself, aware that he was exhausted
from the long drive. *Who are you kidding? When these*
Amish guys—especially your cousins—learn of all the stuff
you've pulled, they'll want you roped and tied, bound and

gagged by all their rules, and sitting on a pew bench for three-hour church services—

But McKenzie's not Amish.

Marcus shifted the car into gear and eased it toward the road. The longer he sat in the parking lot, the more chance his cousins had to spot him. He at least wanted to see the McKenzie place—the training facilities as well as where he'd be bunking—before he decided to drive away for good. He'd stayed awake all night by talking himself into coming here, practicing all the right lines to use with McKenzie, so it'd be a waste of his time and effort if he didn't at least scope the place out.

At the bottom of the hill, Marcus turned left toward the county highway and jammed his foot on the brake. A chill went up his spine when a sea-green sedan pulled away from the shoulder of the road and sped down the blacktop—a car he'd occasionally seen in his rearview mirror as he'd crossed Ohio, Indiana, and Illinois. It couldn't be coincidence that someone had driven such an odd-colored car along the exact route he'd taken.

Could it?

"So who are you and what do you want?" Marcus muttered. He shook his head to clear away the cobwebs of sleep deprivation that curled in his brain. If he'd been *thinking*, he would've followed the sedan to get its license plate number. But thinking didn't seem to be one of his dominant personality traits—*which explains why you're usually out of a job and out of money. Time to fix that.*

Marcus rolled down his window and inhaled deeply to bolster himself. Once again he caught the aroma of the meat roasting in the huge grills behind the café, and he decided to check out the restaurant after he'd seen what McKenzie had to offer. Folks there might notice his resemblance to Luke and figure out who he was, but maybe that wasn't such a bad thing. Maybe if they associated him with the Hooley brothers, whom they apparently respected, they'd give him a chance.

Most of these people have no idea what you left behind you, Marcus reminded himself with a smile. He turned and drove slowly along the county highway. *You're the top-notch horse trainer McKenzie's bringing in from Lancaster County, so you must be one special dude. Live up to that rep, and show these yokels how fabulous you really are.*

After he passed the picturesque gristmill that was churning the river with its wooden wheel, he spotted an opening in the white plank fence that marked the McKenzie property. He was surprised that there was no gate with a code to punch in—nothing to keep curious folks from entering at will, the way he was. Marcus drove slowly along the packed dirt track, visualizing how impressive the place would be once the private drive was paved and the lawn was landscaped and McKenzie's mansion was built.

When he spotted a fancy double-wide trailer, he instinctively followed the trail that led toward the barns instead. *No reason for McKenzie to know you're here until you've looked around. If you don't like what you see, you can be on the road and gone before Wyatt's any the wiser.*

Instinct told Marcus to park the car behind some cedar trees that had grown wild around an outcropping of rock. Missouri farmland was more rugged and untamed than the manicured farms where he'd come from, and he liked that. He walked past a large pond where a few migratory Canada geese floated, watching him. By following the tree line toward two of the largest barns he'd ever seen, he figured he'd avoid detection.

In a paddock near the barn farthest from him, five sleek bay Thoroughbreds came to the fence to follow his progress. He'd read on McKenzie's website that he planned to train retired racehorses to pull Amish buggies, and the beautiful animals would bring top dollar once Marcus had finessed them into their new purpose. The muscled black Percheron foals he spotted near the other barn would take more effort, but he'd soon have the massive horses pulling wagons, plows, and other farming equipment—and they would be the envy of their owners' neighbors.

Marcus smiled as he drew near to the corral where the young draft horses stood munching on hay. "Hi, guys," he called to them, delighted by the way their ears perked up. "You and me, we're gonna be real good friends."

Wyatt pulled his cell phone from his pocket and smiled at the name he saw on the screen. "Nora, how's your day going?" he asked. "If I remember correctly, you've got a big open house coming up this weekend."

"I do," Nora said. "Say, Wyatt, my day got off to an interesting start. Marcus Hooley breezed in about ten minutes ago and did *not* make a good first impression, so I thought I'd give you a heads-up. I suggested he talk to Luke rather than just showing up at your place, but he didn't impress me as the sort who'd take a hint from the *mouthy* woman his cousin Luke must've married because he was *desperate*."

Wyatt's eyes widened. "He said that to your face?" he asked as he walked toward the console of the security system sitting on his office credenza.

"He did—a real charmer, Marcus is, and quite impressed with himself," Nora put in. "But then, why wouldn't he be, when he's the greatest horse trainer on the face of the earth?"

Wyatt groaned inwardly as he focused on the screen that was split into quadrants. More than once in the past couple of weeks he'd been tempted to call Marcus and tell him to look elsewhere for employment if he couldn't supply three references or follow the simple instructions Wyatt had given him. "And there he is, approaching the Percheron barn. Thanks for your call, Nora. I'm on it."

"You're welcome. We can hope he's matured since he left my store—but I wouldn't count on it." *Click.*

Wyatt watched the screen for a few moments, considering his course of action and waiting for the alarm to sound on the console and his cell phone. Within moments a duet of insistent *beep-beep-beeps* filled his small office, reassuring him that his previously untested security system worked the way it was supposed to. Marcus appeared unaware that he was on camera, and the alarm didn't sound around the stables or paddocks because Wyatt didn't want the horses to be spooked.

"But you, young man, are about to find out who you're dealing with," Wyatt muttered.

By the time he was stepping off the deck and walking toward the barns, a car bearing a Home Security sign was turning in from the highway—with a cruiser from the county sheriff's department following close behind it. Wyatt waved at the drivers, gesturing for them to proceed toward the Percheron barn. The cruiser's siren was silent but its flashers were on. When two uniformed men hopped out and hustled toward Marcus, the expression on the kid's face was priceless.

"State your name and your business!" Sheriff Banks ordered as Officer McClatchey and a rep from the security company joined him to form a barricade around Marcus.

Wyatt took his time, allowing the local law enforcement team to do its job. Considering how quickly they'd arrived, he guessed they had probably been having coffee at the Grill N Skillet when the alarm went off—but Marcus wouldn't have known that. The kid's arms shot up into the air as though he assumed he was under arrest . . . as though he'd been in this position before.

"Hey, ease up! I'm Luke Hooley's cousin, and I work for Wyatt McKenzie, training his horses," he spouted off.

A name dropper—and mighty presumptuous about landing a job here, Wyatt noted. *Quick with an answer, but if he was my employee, why would the alarm go off?*

"Is that your red Chevy behind those cedar trees? If you work for Mr. McKenzie, why'd you park it clear out there?" Officer McClatchey asked without missing a beat. "Once we run a check on your license plate, we'll have your identity—and your record—in a matter of minutes. Want to reconsider your story before we do that?"

Marcus's eyes widened but he recovered quickly when he caught sight of Wyatt. "No need to check my plates," he blurted out. "Here's Mr. McKenzie to explain everything—and I didn't misrepresent the situation, right? I'm Marcus Hooley, Luke Hooley's cousin, and you asked me to come train your horses. So here I am. I just wasn't expecting such a—a flashy welcome."

Wyatt stopped a few feet short of Marcus, stepping into the semicircle of power when the other men made room for him. As the red and blue cruiser lights flashed behind him, he took his time assessing the tall, muscled kid whose winsome, earnest expression invited Wyatt to play along, to follow his script so the officers would get off his case. The dark hair draped over one side of Marcus's lean, handsome face was longer than Wyatt preferred, but at least he saw no piercings or obvious tattoos. His clothes smelled a bit ripe and were creased as though he'd been wearing them for a long time—and the worn black leather jacket was cut in a vintage style that suggested he'd found it at a thrift shop. The kid was accustomed to using his looks and his easy charm to get what he wanted—

Just like you did at his age, right? But he doesn't need to know that.

Wyatt didn't smile. Marcus, like the horses he worked

with, needed to understand who would lead and who would follow. He extended his hand, pleased that young Hooley had sense enough to give him a good strong grip that wasn't more forceful than it needed to be. "Welcome to Willow Ridge, Marcus," he said. "May I see the list of references I requested when we spoke on the phone, please?"

Marcus coughed. "Yeah, well—"

"So you know this young man?" Sheriff Banks asked.

"We've spoken on the phone," Wyatt clarified. "Thanks for coming so quickly, gentlemen. I can take it from here— but do run the check on his plates and send me what you find out, please. We might as well all be on the same page, considering Marcus's unconventional way of framing the truth."

Marcus appeared ready to protest but stifled his retort— a point in his favor, Wyatt thought.

Officer McClatchey nodded. "Nice to see how your new place is coming along, Wyatt," he said. He assessed Marcus again before he headed up the hill. "I hope our next occasion to meet will be under more positive circumstances, young man."

The security rep shook Wyatt's hand. "Your new system appears to be functioning properly," he remarked. "Are the sensors and cameras set the way you want them? We could still install a gate with a keypad—or an electric eye at the entry to your property—considering how far Mr. Hooley got before he was detected."

"We could," Wyatt agreed, "but I trust my Amish neighbors implicitly, and I don't want them to think otherwise. Thanks for asking, though."

As the rep headed to his car, the sheriff was scribbling on a notepad. Clyde Banks was a burly, barrel-chested fellow— congenial, but his size and no-nonsense bearing gave most lawbreakers pause. "Wyatt, I'll let you know what we find out about Mr. Hooley," he said with a nod. "It's to everyone's benefit to be aware of past incidents and activities that might color our impression of him."

Sheriff Banks studied Marcus for a moment. "If you're associated with the Amish hereabouts, you'll have every opportunity to do well—to make a go of training horses, or whatever you've come to do," he said earnestly. "But we don't tolerate folks who take advantage of our Plain residents—or who give our English residents trouble, either, for that matter," he added. "Do your best not to attract my attention, and we'll get along fine, Marcus. See you around."

Wyatt noted a flicker of resentment and rebellion tightening Marcus's face, but once again the kid kept his smart remarks to himself. After the cruiser followed the security rep's car off the property, Wyatt remained quiet to make the young man in front of him squirm a little. Marcus turned to observe the two-year-old Percherons in the nearby paddock. He seemed ready to chitchat, to break the pressure of the silence that was stretching between them, but he refrained.

"Let me guess. You don't have any references because you've offended—or cheated or lied to—the previous employers who've fired you," Wyatt began in a low voice. "And last night you hightailed it out of Pennsylvania before you got caught doing something else objectionable or maybe illegal. How am I doing so far?"

Marcus released the breath he'd been holding. "Nailed it."

"Is Sheriff Banks going to tell me you've got a criminal record? Or that he needs to extradite you to Pennsylvania to serve time in jail?" Wyatt continued, crossing his arms. "Will I find out that in addition to your credit card escapades, you have a drug problem or a habit of driving drunk?"

Marcus's dark eyebrows flickered as he remained focused on the horses. "I've been known to drink too much, yeah. Got a couple of DUIs a while back, but I did my community service and jail time for them. No drugs."

Wyatt believed he was being truthful, so he continued.

"Nora Hooley tells me you shot off your mouth in her store this morning, making offensive remarks and claiming to be the best horse trainer on earth. Was she misrepresenting the situation?"

The kid's shoulders dropped as though he hadn't anticipated the lightning-strike rapidity of the grapevine in Willow Ridge. He exhaled, looking totally exhausted. "Nope."

Knowing better than to believe the kid's display of humility would last more than ten minutes, Wyatt continued grilling him. "So far, I haven't heard one thing to recommend you for this training job, or that would allow me to trust you. Why should I even consider hiring you, Marcus—especially when you came sneaking around my property instead of knocking on my door?" he asked softly.

Marcus swallowed so hard his Adam's apple bobbled. He gazed at Wyatt with wary eyes that were an arresting shade of pale green. "Because I'm a lot better at handling horses than I am at handling myself?" he suggested in a hoarse whisper. "Or maybe because if I don't get this job, I don't know what I'll do . . . or where my next meal's coming from?"

The kid's voice throbbed with raw emotion that rang true—not that such honesty inspired Wyatt's confidence about his ability with horses. But he'd believed Marcus was the trainer he needed from the moment the Hooley brothers had unanimously agreed that their younger cousin was uniquely qualified. *Now there's a fellow who could train a horse to stand on its head, if you paid him enough*, Luke had declared.

Wyatt had searched online and had asked other men from Willow Ridge whom they would recommend, but candidates were as rare as hen's teeth and he hadn't felt compelled to contact any of them. He wanted Marcus, plain and simple—but he couldn't allow the kid to think he was a shoo-in, or that he was above Wyatt's basic behavioral expectations.

"Tell you what, Marcus," he said. "We can get better acquainted over brunch at the Grill N Skillet, and then you can rest in the apartment in the loft of the Percheron barn or spend the rest of the day however you want. We'll resume this interview tomorrow."

Marcus blinked as though such leniency surprised him. "Really? You're gonna give me a chance?"

"We'll see what the sheriff finds out and go from there." Wyatt held the young man's gaze a moment longer. "Is there anything you want to tell me straight out before I hear it from Banks?"

Marcus thought for a moment. "Naw. I was stupid for buying that last case of beer and for telling my most recent boss, Enos Keim, what I thought of him while I was plastered. Nothing illegal, though."

"And your most recent girlfriend?"

The kid rolled his eyes and looked over at the horses again. "Not a good scene. She accused me of taking cash from her wallet and said her credit card was missing."

"Did you take it—the cash or the card?"

"Nope. Not this time."

Wyatt let the statement stand. Such matters tended to resurface if they hadn't been resolved. "Let's get a bite to eat, and give you a taste of Willow Ridge and the folks you'll be spending your time with," he suggested. "Eventually, we'll both figure out if you belong here."

Chapter Three

As Marcus entered the Grill N Skillet, hunger and exhaustion slammed into him with brute force. Aromas of cinnamon rolls, fresh coffee, and frying bacon made him inhale deeply, desperately, and he was grateful that a table near the door was empty so he and Wyatt didn't have to cross the crowded dining room before sitting down. He kicked himself for assuming that he could slip onto the McKenzie property—into the tiny town of Willow Ridge—and remain invisible for any length of time. He felt grungy and gritty-eyed with fatigue and he'd blown his first impression, big-time.

But things are looking up! he thought as an attractive young woman came to their table with a carafe of hot coffee. She wore a cape dress of deep red and a pleated white *kapp* that proclaimed she was Old Order Amish, but her sparkling brown eyes and flawless complexion made Marcus sit up straighter and smile.

"*Gut* morning, gentlemen," the waitress said in a lilting voice as she deftly filled their mugs. "What'll you have?"

Sit yourself down, babe, and let's talk about that.

"Savilla, this is Marcus Hooley from Lancaster County, the man I'm considering as a trainer for my horses," Wyatt said with a smile. "Marcus, Savilla Witmer and her brother, Josiah, own this café—which is known for miles around as the best possible place to feed your face. The Witmers took the place over when your cousin Ben's wife, Miriam, had their first child."

"Great place," Marcus murmured. If Savilla was working with her brother, it meant she wasn't married, so he tried not to say anything stupid. "What do you recommend? I'm starved out of my mind."

Savilla's laughter teased at him. "The buffet still has biscuits and gravy, homemade rolls, the makings for hash-brown haystacks, and an assortment of sausages and bacon—or you can order pancakes and eggs from the menu," she replied, nodding toward the laminated pages in the table rack that held the ketchup and other condiments. "We're easing into the lunch menu with hot veggies, ribs, and pork steaks fresh off Josiah's grills, so you're sure to find something you like."

Oh, I already have, sweetheart. I could listen to you talk all day—

"We'll go for the buffet," Wyatt put in. "Thanks, Savilla. I'm always amazed at how many folks are in here no matter what time I show up."

Savilla's pretty face lit up. "*Jah*, we're doing better than we ever figured on. *Denki* for coming in, Wyatt—and it was *gut* to meet you, Marcus."

As she began refilling coffee mugs and chatting with other folks nearby, Wyatt leaned across the table. "Just so you'll know—before you step in a pile of it again," he said in a low voice, "Savilla's sweet on the fellow your cousin Luke has hired to manage his farming operation."

"Maybe I'll change her mind about that," Marcus shot back. He found it vaguely irritating that they couldn't seem to discuss anything without mentioning his cousins, but he knew better than to say that. Luke, Ira, and Ben had recommended him for McKenzie's training position, after all. "Let's eat, and then I'll crash for a while, all right? It'll save both of us some trouble, I suspect."

Wyatt nodded, gesturing for Marcus to head to the buffet. McKenzie greeted several folks seated at tables along their way, and Marcus was grateful that his prospective employer didn't insist on introductions. He picked up a warm plate and covered it with hash browns before spooning on a thick layer of cubed ham and fried peppers with onions—and then he covered everything with a generous coating of cheese sauce and sausage gravy. On a second plate, Marcus placed a cinnamon roll oozing with frosting, two large biscuits, and a large helping of fried apples. He was glad McKenzie returned to their table quickly, because with so much hot, enticing food in front of him, it would've been difficult to wait politely.

"Dig in, Marcus," McKenzie said as he sat down. "I envy your ability to devour all that food without thinking about the calories. I could do that when I was your age, but not anymore."

Marcus jammed a forkful of his hash-brown haystack into his mouth, considering McKenzie's remark. The man across the table looked to be forty-something, wearing a plaid shirt tucked into well-cut jeans that displayed a firm, fit physique. His face appeared as pleasantly weathered as the other male faces around them, yet his understated elegance set him apart from the crowd.

McKenzie could buy this entire town, Marcus realized. *But he doesn't let on. He blends in . . . seems to get along with these Amish guys just fine.*

"Seems we came to the right place, the way you're tucking away your food," Wyatt remarked pleasantly. "No need to rush—and there's plenty more where that came from."

"Really hungry," Marcus murmured. He wanted to pick up the cinnamon roll and jam it into his mouth, but he took

Wyatt's hint and cut into it with his fork. "Didn't eat on my way out here."

He realized that he'd left a conversational loophole open, yet McKenzie didn't quiz him about why he'd been in such a rush to leave Pennsylvania. Wyatt was savoring a mouthful of ham steak as though he had all day to eat his meal—as though he was patiently waiting for Marcus to unwittingly reveal more about his habits and his past.

"Oh my God, this cinnamon roll is like nothing I've ever tasted," Marcus groaned. "Am I just way too tired, or is the food here always this fabulous?"

Wyatt smiled. "You've got it right. Savilla—and Naomi Brenneman, the gal in the kitchen—make all the breads and side dishes and Josiah mans the smokers and grills," he said. "Their combination of good, basic food and friendly service attracts people from all over the area. On weekends you often have to wait for a table."

Chewing a mouthful of his cheese-drenched hash browns, Marcus took a moment to observe the people around them. "The places around Bird-in-Hand tend to be full of English tourists, but I see a lot of Plain guys here. Doesn't anybody eat at home with their wives and kids like they're supposed to?"

McKenzie smiled. "In the short time I've lived in Willow Ridge, I've learned that the Plain folks here are a bit more progressive and open to change than in other communities—and I believe that eating here is a way for them to show their support of the Witmers' business," Wyatt added. He gazed briefly at something behind Marcus and lowered his voice. "Just so you'll know, here comes Luke and the fellow who farms for him."

Marcus stopped chewing his mouthful of warm, buttery biscuit. He suddenly realized that McKenzie had a kind, generous nature despite his tendency to come on as a tough guy—and the wealthy horseman already *understood* him better than most folks. "Thanks, man," he murmured.

Before Marcus could brace himself for the lecture he was expecting, Luke yanked out the empty chair to his left and sat down, playfully swatting Marcus's arm. "It's been too long, cuz," he declared. "Welcome to Missouri! This is Will Gingerich, my farmer. Will, meet my cousin Marcus Hooley from Pennsylvania."

As Will nodded and sat down, Marcus quickly assessed the fellow Savilla was supposedly sweet on. He seemed quiet. Looked pretty average in his broadfall pants, blue shirt, and suspenders.

"Will's finished harvesting the popcorn and buckwheat crops, and he baled the last of the hay yesterday, so we're taking a day off," Luke said with a big smile. "So what've *you* been up to, Marcus?"

It sounded like a trick question, a trap Luke was setting. Marcus stabbed the soft, moist center of his cinnamon roll with his fork, figuring his food was a good excuse not to reply right away. Should he be honest? *Well, I went on a bender and told my boss he was so narrow-minded and old-fashioned I couldn't stand the sight of him anymore . . .* except he'd used a lot stronger language than that. Or should he fudge and let Luke carry the conversation? Marcus closed his eyes in total enjoyment as he put the last big bite of his cinnamon roll in his mouth.

Luke watched him, his expression tightening with the passing seconds. "My beautiful, delightfully independent and outspoken wife says you want to ask me why I ever hitched up with her, and that you believe I must've been desperate."

When Marcus swallowed before he'd chewed, the soft pastry formed a big lump in his throat. He sucked down some coffee, and began to cough. His gaze went fleetingly to the steam table, where a man who resembled Savilla was setting out big pans of sizzling pork steaks and sauced ribs. *So this is how it feels to be grilled*, he thought as he struggled to clear his throat of the sugary dough.

"You're speechless at the sight of me?" Luke challenged in a low voice. "Or has Wyatt actually taught you how to keep your mouth shut? Don't think I haven't noticed that you went to see *him* before you let *me* know you were in town."

Marcus coughed helplessly, and drank more coffee.

McKenzie smiled. "Let's just say Marcus made a grand entrance. Set off the alarm system, and moments later the sheriff and his deputy came to meet him with their lights flashing. It's been an eventful morning."

Luke raised one eyebrow. "I was wondering why Banks and McClatchey shot out of here a little while ago." He watched Marcus take another swallow of coffee, shaking his head.

"Let me tell you about my wife, Marcus. The first time I saw Nora she was climbing out of a bright red BMW convertible, wearing a tight T-shirt and shorts that left nothing to my imagination—and she'd just bought that big white house on the hill," Luke recounted as he leaned his elbows on the table. "She was my new neighbor. I immediately decided I was the man who should show her around town—show her a really fine time—and she shut me down so fast, I didn't know what hit me. Was I desperate?"

Marcus finally swallowed the dough in his throat, but he knew better than to answer that question.

Luke's expression softened. "I *was* desperate. I wanted that redheaded, freckle-faced woman in the worst way," he admitted. "I was gobsmacked when I learned she'd grown up Amish in Willow Ridge—a preacher's girl, no less—and that her *dat* had condemned her for having a baby out of wedlock, and that she'd married an English fellow who left her for another woman."

Marcus blinked. Could Luke possibly be talking about

the gal he'd seen in the store? The one who'd worn a small black Mennonite *kapp* and calf-length dress?

"And after all that, Nora had the guts to come back and reconcile with her family," Luke continued in a voice that thrummed with admiration. "She had the backbone to make her own way by opening a consignment shop featuring items from Plain crafters. And by not putting up with my adolescent attitude, Nora convinced me that I should finally grow up and get over myself."

Marcus couldn't miss the devotion that shimmered in Luke's deep green eyes. Once again, he sensed he should remain quiet.

"For Nora, I changed—I even joined the Mennonite church. Can you believe it?" Luke asked, playfully snapping his suspenders. He focused on Marcus, his gaze unwavering. "I hope someday you'll find a woman who convinces you to change your ways, cuz—somebody who makes you see the bigger picture—because I have a feeling you'll keep right on messing everything up until somebody gives you a reason not to."

Marcus's head was spinning with the details of Nora's incredible past, but he couldn't miss Luke's point. There was no denying his cousin's sincere desire for him to make something of himself, either, despite the uncomplimentary truths he'd pointed up. "Okay, so I'm sorry I shot off my mouth at Nora—"

"Tell *her* that," Luke interrupted quickly. "I don't need your apology. I also don't intend to clean up your credit messes or cover for you when you drink too much, and I hope I don't come to regret recommending you to Wyatt."

Marcus set down his fork. An uneasy silence settled around the table, and he didn't know what to say to start the conversation rolling toward a more relaxed, less embarrassing topic than his penchant for finding trouble.

Will shifted in his chair, smiling. "I got the same sort of

pep talk from the fellow who told Luke I should be farming
for him," he admitted. "The men in Willow Ridge expect
you to toe a high mark—but it was certainly worth my while
to follow Asa Detweiler's advice and come here."

"Asa and his brother run a furniture refurbishing business," Wyatt explained as he cut into his ham steak again.
"And frankly, every one of us at this table has endured some
tough talk about people's high expectations—usually at the
times we least wanted to hear them. Ben has told me a few
tales about Luke and Ira's running-around days—"

"*Jah*, and now that Ben's a preacher, he pays even closer
attention to what we Hooley boys are up to," Luke said with
a laugh. He gazed at Marcus and then stood up. "I'll leave
you to finish your food. We're all pulling for you, cuz. Anything you need, just let us know."

"Sure thing. *Gut* to see you," Marcus murmured. He
watched Luke and Will walk toward the door, noting the way
everyone they passed had a greeting or a teasing remark for
them. When he glanced at his smeared, empty plates he felt
so tired that he wondered where all his food had gone. "I
usually go back for a second round at a buffet, but I've sorta
lost my appetite," he admitted with a sigh.

McKenzie smiled, folding his napkin on the table. "Luke
wants the best for you—we all do," he added matter-of-factly.
"I fully believe that you'll rise to our expectations, Marcus.
Ready to check out the apartment in the barn?"

A few minutes later they were headed back up the road
to the McKenzie place, set apart by its white plank fences
and majestic red barns. Wyatt didn't chitchat a lot, and
Marcus appreciated it. When they reached the top of the
wooden staircase that led to the apartment in the barn, he
nodded as McKenzie pointed out the front room, a kitchen-
ette, the towels in the small bathroom, and the basic double
bed in a room that wasn't big enough to hold much additional furniture.

"Nothing fancy—no cable or Internet connection—but you've got hot water, heat, and electricity," Wyatt remarked. "As time goes by, we'll see about adding some improvements."

"This is great. Thanks for letting me stay here," Marcus murmured.

"See you tomorrow. Come on up to the house when you're ready for breakfast in the morning," Wyatt said, and then he left without any further ado.

The sparsely furnished apartment echoed with the closing of the door, and for a moment Marcus wondered if he'd been locked into another cell to sleep off his liquor after the cops had hauled him in for starting a fight in a bar.

Most of us live in prisons of our own making, one of his former Amish bosses had said when he'd bailed Marcus out. *And we decide how much time we'll spend there, or if we'll move on.*

Marcus had bristled at the old man's lecture, yet as he glanced out the bedroom window overlooking Luke's mill and Nora's gift store with the rest of Willow Ridge as a backdrop, he sighed. He was really tired of screwing up.

"Tired of being told what a mess I am, too," he muttered, "so maybe moving on is the best idea. Why do I want to hear this crap again? Why do I want to live under a small-town microscope with people knowing every little thing I do and say?"

Marcus dropped onto the bed without undressing or pulling down the plain denim bedspread. His last thought before he fell asleep was that he should shower and hit the road before McKenzie or anyone else woke up in the morning, figuring to pin him down and keep track of him. They all meant well, but he was starting to understand that his road to hell was indeed paved with their good intentions.

Chapter Four

Rosalyn quickly crossed the parking lot of Zook's Market and made a beeline toward the backyard and the white house she called home. While she'd been working in Nora's store, the temperature had dropped enough that she could see her breath as she walked. Her shoes were getting soaked by the light snow that nestled in the clumpy grass, but she was too happy to care. She hurried past the chickens pecking in the fenced part of the yard, and she was soon at the edge of the large garden, tilled and empty with the onset of winter. She entered the mudroom, hung up her black coat and bonnet, and inhaled the fragrances of the pot roast and baked potatoes her sister Loretta was fixing for supper.

"We sold three of my wreaths today!" she blurted out as she stepped into the kitchen. "I can't believe how customers were snapping them up. Nora wants me to make more as soon as I can!"

Loretta smiled from the stove, where she was stirring gravy in a skillet. "I'm amazed at how much merchandise she moves in her store—especially because she sells so many things that *we* make," she added with a laugh. "Were there a lot of customers, or do you think folks will wait until the big open house this weekend to do their shopping?"

"We were fairly busy, but I'm guessing there'll be quite a crowd on Saturday." Rosalyn glanced at their *dat*, who sat at the table reading his newspaper, seemingly oblivious to their conversation. "The store looks so pretty, Loretta. Nora's hung a greenery garland along the upstairs railing, and the candles make the place smell so *gut*. She's going to have hot spiced cider and a big tray of Lena Witmer's decorated Christmas cookies to serve on Saturday. It'll be more like a Christmas party than a job!"

"Christmas." Dat spat the word as though it tasted like a bitter pill. "Don't get any wild ideas about decorating the house or exchanging gifts this year. With your mother gone, I have nothing to celebrate."

Rosalyn turned to study their father. "You've said that for the past five years, Dat," she murmured sadly. "We were all hoping that for our first Christmas in Willow Ridge, we could at least put out the Nativity scene—"

"Forget it," he muttered.

"And we'd like to send Christmas cards to our friends in Roseville," Loretta put in as she removed the skillet from the stove.

Dat stared at Loretta as though she'd sprouted a second head. "Do you know how much postage that would cost us?" he demanded. "I warned you both that working in Nora's store would give you extravagant ideas about spending money for *things*. We do not need more *things* in our lives."

"But the Nativity set's been in Mamm's family for generations," Rosalyn pointed out. "And it won't cost a cent to clip some evergreen branches from the trees across the road—"

"Case closed!" Dat declared as he slammed his paper to the tabletop. "It's going to be a very simple Christmas this year, girls. We'll spend the day quietly remembering the Lord's humble birth without all the trappings and trimmings.

And don't plan anything or figure on a big fancy dinner on Second Christmas, either. End of discussion."

Rosalyn pressed her lips together to keep from protesting again as Dat strode toward the basement door, headed for his clock repair shop. When the tattoo of his descending footsteps on the stairs ended, she moved closer to Loretta. "Has he been this cranky all day?" she whispered.

Loretta shrugged in bewilderment. "You know how it is," she replied. "Only takes one wrong word to set him off. I'm glad I get to work at Nora's store tomorrow."

"His grief counseling sessions with Bishop Tom don't seem to be helping," Rosalyn observed. She picked up the bowl that contained the flour and other dry ingredients for biscuits, and added the milk her sister had already poured into a glass measuring cup.

"He's gotten worse, if you ask me," Loretta said under her breath. "Ever since Preacher Ben and Bishop Tom came here to confront him about whatever he was doing during his trips to Kansas City—besides buying clock parts—he's had a really short fuse."

"*Jah*, and Nora refuses to say what she and Drew caught him doing, that day they followed him and his driver." Rosalyn stirred the biscuit batter with rapid strokes of her spoon until it grew stiff. "Why is it such a big secret? It would be so much easier to understand if we knew the truth."

"Drew's not saying a word, either—not even to me," Loretta said, exasperated. "You'd think, since I'm his wife and we're Dat's daughters, he and Nora would fill us in so we wouldn't worry so much about it."

Rosalyn sprinkled flour on the countertop and began to knead the biscuit dough. She clearly recalled the day Ben Hooley and Tom Hostetler had appeared at the door and insisted that she and Loretta leave the house while they talked to Dat. Not long after that, the bishop had made a surprise visit and had carried away a long white contraption—an air conditioner Dat had secretly been running on his clock shop wall with power from the solar panel on the roof. She got a nervous stomach every time she tried to figure out Dat's mysterious situation. "Did you see the letter that came yesterday with *Past Due* marked on it?" she asked. "Why would we be getting those?"

Loretta's eyes widened. "I had no idea we were," she replied in a tremulous whisper. "He always takes the mail to his shop—"

"And with all the time he spends there—with all the clocks he's selling at Nora's and the repair work he's doing these days," Rosalyn put in earnestly, "I can't understand why he's so touchy about us spending money. All of the Christmas decorations we suggested are *free*, after all."

Loretta shook her head. "Can you imagine not having a big turkey and a ham for dinner on Second Christmas?" she asked. "Mamm surely must be shaking her head up in heaven, watching whatever's been going on with Dat."

"I miss her so much," Rosalyn said sorrowfully. "You'd think it would get easier after five years."

"She left a hole in our hearts that no one else will ever fill," Loretta whispered with a tremor in her voice.

They sighed together and kept cooking as a way to ease the pain of their mother's absence. After Rosalyn had rolled and cut the biscuits, she offered another idea. "Do you suppose Edith and Asa will host the Second Christmas dinner at their place, if we tell them what Dat has said?"

"Of course they will—and even if they didn't want to do that, you and I could buy all the fixings with the money we earn at the store," Loretta insisted, her smile returning. "Dat couldn't say a thing about *that*, now could he?"

"Oh, but he'd get mad," Rosalyn quickly pointed out. "I keep thinking that one of these days he'll barge into Nora's store and announce that we're forbidden to work there anymore because we're getting too many worldly ideas. He's never been keen on the idea of us earning money, even if we insist we're buying fabric to make our clothes, or supplementing the grocery money."

"He *hates* it when he finds out we've paid for groceries." With rapid flicks of her wrist, Loretta peeled carrots, clearly frustrated by how dull the old peeler had become after years of use. "But what are we supposed to do when the flour runs out or we've got no oatmeal for breakfast? It's not as though we can grow those things in our garden."

"I bet the Zooks wonder what's going on when we pop in with our own cash. Lydia's used to having Dat stop in every now and again to pay our account," Loretta speculated.

Rosalyn shrugged. "He's the deacon, so folks around the church district expect him to keep track of money," she said. "But I have to wonder if other women are limited to shopping every other week. Can it be such a sin to visit the market say, on a Tuesday, because we want chocolate chips for cookies—or because we've run out of toilet paper?"

Loretta giggled at this suggestion, but her somber expression returned. "All I know is that Dat seems to be working more yet he's pulling the purse strings tighter. And now you've seen something in the mail marked *Past Due*," she added with a sigh. "I don't understand it."

"It's a *gut* thing that Asa and Drew have been generous about bringing family-sized roasts when they come for dinner," Rosalyn said wistfully. "What would our life be like if you and Edith hadn't married them?"

"I don't even want to think about it."

As she opened the oven door, Rosalyn considered Loretta's response. Once again she envied her two younger sisters because they'd found attentive, affectionate husbands who truly loved them and respected their ideas—

But envy is one of the seven deadly sins, she reminded herself, *so it's wrong for you to want what your sisters have. Think about something else.*

Immediately Marcus Hooley popped into her mind. Rosalyn recalled the way he had entered the Simple Gifts store, and she frowned. Why should she spend any time thinking about such an arrogant, rude young man who was years younger than she was—in age and in mind-set, as well? She'd overheard Luke saying that Marcus had not only jumped the fence to avoid joining the Amish church, but he'd lived with his girlfriends instead of marrying them.

Even as Marcus's unthinkable behavior appalled Rosalyn, however, his handsome face and tall, muscular physique appealed to her. *What would it be like to go out with him? Just once in your life, wouldn't you like to break a few rules and find out about life on the wild side?*

Rosalyn blinked. *Puh! Wouldn't you just like to go out on a date, period?*

Her thoughts were so unsettling that the pan of biscuits slipped from her hands as she was putting it into the oven. "Oh!" Rosalyn gasped as she retrieved the pan from the floor. "I'd better pay closer attention to what I'm doing."

Loretta glanced at her, shrugging. "We've got a lot on our minds, thinking about Dat—and Christmas," she added with a sigh. "At least the pan stayed right-side-up and none of the biscuits fell off."

"*Jah*, there's that." Rosalyn rearranged the biscuits that had slid together and quickly shoved the pan into the oven. Her face felt flushed, and she knew it wasn't only because she'd set the temperature to four hundred degrees.

That's what comes of letting your thoughts wander where they shouldn't go, she chided herself. *Leave well enough alone—and Marcus, too.*

Chapter Five

As Wyatt sat at his table the next morning, he had eyes only for Rebecca Oliveri—except for occasional glances out the window. "Can't thank you enough for joining me, dear heart, and for bringing this breakfast casserole," he added as he reached for her hand. "If Marcus doesn't show up in a few minutes, we're going to eat without him. Actually, I'm surprised his car's still here."

Rebecca's blue eyes widened. "If you have such doubts about him sticking around, why do you want to hire him? The report Sheriff Banks sent you certainly doesn't paint a flattering picture."

Wyatt shrugged. "I was headed down the same path when I was Marcus's age, except I ran with a wealthier crowd," he said softly. "The Hooleys tell me he's the best horse trainer they've ever known—"

"But he hasn't given you the references you asked for? And he sneaked onto your property yesterday and set off the alarm?" Rebecca interrupted with a raised eyebrow. "I can understand your sentiments about helping a troubled young man find his way, Wyatt, but from what I've heard, I'm with Nora. I wouldn't touch him with a ten-foot pole."

"Will you at least listen with an open mind when Marcus—ah, he's coming out of the barn," Wyatt noted when he caught sight of the tall, lean figure starting up the path toward the house. "I trust the way you read people, Rebecca. I believe Marcus is just skittish, like a horse out of his own territory and surrounded by strangers. But if you think he's a bad bet after you've spent some time with him, I'll reconsider."

Rebecca's smile made butterflies flutter in his stomach. "I confess that after hearing Luke, Ira, and Ben speculating about the sort of life Marcus has been living, I'm curious," she admitted. "But then, I have no stake in this kid's future, while you're putting your entire new enterprise into his hands. Be careful, Wyatt," she warned him softly. "You might be assuming that anyone associated with the Amish is trustworthy and hardworking. After all, you fell for *me* way too fast."

"Within an hour of meeting you," he agreed. He rose from his chair and kissed her cheek. "Maybe I'm wearing rose-colored glasses, hoping to reform a kid because he reminds me of my younger self. But we won't tell Marcus that part."

From behind the curtain, Wyatt watched Marcus come up the steps and cross the deck. He had a sense that the kid was muscular from hard work rather than time at a gym. His swagger was subdued by a hint of hesitation—he started to knock, but then turned around as though he might leave.

Wyatt waited. Better to have Marcus take off now than later.

A few moments passed before the kid pivoted and knocked firmly, three times.

Wyatt opened the door with a smile. "Hey there, Marcus. You slept well, I hope?"

"Totally crashed," he said, gazing around as he entered.

"Wow, this is nice—but I'm guessing you're gonna build a big place on the hill to overlook your domain?"

"This double-wide's only temporary," Wyatt confirmed as he shut out the cold morning air. "I wanted to get the barns ready for the horses first. We've got a sausage and egg casserole and some fruit, compliments of someone I'd like you to meet. Rebecca Oliveri's the designer behind all the websites you may have seen for Willow Ridge businesses."

Marcus's eyes widened as he approached the table, which was set for three. The place mats and cloth napkins were colorful—elegant without being fussy—and the casserole's savory aroma made Wyatt realize how hungry he was.

"I was wondering how the Amish folks here could have so much presence on the web," Marcus said as he took in Rebecca's jeans and plaid flannel shirt. "You're obviously not one of them."

"Nope," Rebecca agreed, "but my mother's married to your cousin Ben."

Wearing an incredulous expression, Marcus slid into his chair. "You jumped the fence? And they let you live here?"

Rebecca handed Marcus a spoon and gestured for him to help himself to the casserole. "To make a long story short, I was washed away by flood waters when I was just a toddler, raised by an English couple, and then found out Miriam was my birth mother—and it's only by the grace of her loving heart that she and the other folks here understand why I'll never embrace the Plain life," she said in a voice that thrummed with emotion. "I'm very close to her and my two sisters, but I'm also a computer nerd through and through."

"Not to mention the way Rebecca has attracted a lot of customers to the Plain businesses here by designing their websites," Wyatt put in. "It's to everyone's benefit that she's English rather than Amish." He could almost see the cogs turning in Marcus's head as he considered the possibility of living in Willow Ridge without joining the Old Order.

Marcus heaped his plate with the steaming casserole of sausage, hash browns, eggs, and cheese. He took a large mouthful and savored it. "Wow, this is good," he murmured. "Glad I stuck around."

Wyatt shot Rebecca an *I told you so* glance. "You considered leaving before we talked this morning?" he asked nonchalantly. "Why are you having second thoughts, Marcus? Be honest. We need to speak our minds if we're going to work together."

The kid ran a hand through the longish, dark hair that was still damp from his shower. He let his fork drop noisily to his plate. "All right, here it is, man," he blurted resentfully. "During our *chat* about this horse training job, I got the feeling you wanted to take over my life. Oh, you want to *help* me, but you intend to call all the shots. Hey, if I need somebody else controlling everything I do and say, I can go back to being Amish."

Rebecca's eyes widened with dismay, but she kept quiet.

Wyatt filled his plate. It was just as well that Marcus was showing his true colors—he obviously had trouble dealing with authority and being held accountable. Wyatt had a copy of the sheriff's report on the kitchen counter, but he left it there and approached the conversation from a different angle.

"All right, let's think back to our phone call that day," he suggested. "Before Luke called you, he and Ira and Ben had assured me you had outstanding ability when it came to training horses—couldn't say enough good things about you. Then, after I told you about my state-of-the art facility, you said you wanted a sixty-inch flat screen TV, a computer, and a new car—and I replied that we'd negotiate for those perks after you completed a trial period of employment. I asked for three references. Is that how you remember our conversation?"

Marcus gazed at his plate as he took another large mouthful of food. "Yeah, pretty much."

"Good. You also told me you'd been working at an auction barn." Wyatt thought back to last month's phone call and continued. "When I asked why a man of your ability didn't have his own training business, you said you didn't manage money as well as you trained horses—and you mentioned that your ex-girlfriend had kicked you to the curb for spending more than you make. After that, the topic of spending her money on the sly—along with your credit card debt—came up."

Marcus's pale green eyes flashed as he glared at Wyatt. "How'd you know about the credit cards?" he demanded. "I never said a *word* about them belonging to my girlfriend! And then you went into this goody-goody spiel about paying me a decent wage and setting up a repayment program to clear my credit record, and—well *that's* what I see as you trying to control my life!"

Wyatt smiled. To his credit, Marcus had an exceptional memory—and he had just confirmed what had only been an assumption, about using his girlfriend's credit cards. Wyatt took his time reaching for a pen and a pad of paper on the kitchen counter.

"Come on, McKenzie! You can't just smile and keep your secrets—we're being honest and speaking our minds, remember?" Marcus challenged. "How'd you know I'd been using Kristin's credit cards?"

Wyatt looked at him, unruffled. "You said that, Marcus. I didn't."

The kid's mouth snapped shut.

Rebecca was toying with her food rather than eating it. Her lips were pressed together as though she wanted to give Marcus a piece of her mind.

Wyatt smiled at her. Rebecca was showing great restraint, considering the way she'd quickly vented her objections when she was talking to *him*. He poised the pen over the paper. "So let's talk about references. What's the name of the auction barn where you were working? And whom should I contact there?"

Marcus exhaled loudly. "Borntreger Auction Service in Quarrytown," he muttered. "I reported to Jake Borntreger, the owner. After that I was working for Enos Keim in Elizabethtown."

Wyatt stopped writing. "So in the three weeks since our phone conversation, you left the auction barn to work for Keim—and you've already quit that job?" he asked. "What do I need to know about that?"

Marcus rolled his eyes as though dismissing the situation—or Keim—as too stupid to talk about. "He's Old Order—older than God!—and he got on my case for not cleaning out the stalls just right," he ranted. "And he told me I shouldn't have a case of beer in my car, and that I shouldn't *have* a car—that I should get around with a horse and buggy!"

"So why'd you take the job with Keim in the first place?" Rebecca blurted. "You knew he was old—and Old Order—when you asked about the position, right?"

Wyatt winked at her, glad she was expressing the exasperation he, too, was feeling about Marcus's attitude and answers. The real question was why Marcus had been mucking out stables when he was supposedly a top-notch trainer who could pretty much choose his positions and salary. Once again Wyatt remained quiet, waiting for more information the kid might reveal after the silence made him antsy.

Resentment flashed in Marcus's pale green eyes. "Okay, so I sorta stumbled into the job with Keim because he needed a farmhand and I needed the money," he admitted. "And I left because I got pulled over by the cops. Again."

Wyatt gave him a point for honesty. "Sheriff Banks's report says the officer in Pennsylvania suspected you were drunk, but you passed the breathalyzer test so he let you go with a warning," he filled in. "So you left because you figured Keim was going to fire you anyway?"

"Yeah." Marcus set down his fork, probably figuring he'd be asked to leave.

Wyatt reached for the sheriff's report as he considered his next move. He still needed a trainer—and soon—but could he tolerate Marcus's arrogance? Did he really want to expend the energy it would take to turn this kid around—if indeed Hooley would cooperate? He didn't need to call Jake Borntreger or Enos Keim, because they would complain about Marcus's attitude rather than giving him a positive recommendation as a trainer.

When Marcus caught sight of the letterhead bearing the logo of the sheriff's department, his expression became more contrite. And he kept quiet.

"We've discussed your employment record, so let's move on to your personal qualifications," Wyatt suggested, tapping the letter with his pen. "Ben gave me the impression that you no longer live at home because your parents have sent you packing—which isn't all that common, from what I understand about the Amish culture's emphasis on forgiveness and family ties," he added purposefully. "And your girlfriend—or maybe more than one of them—kicked you out for using credit cards without their knowledge or permission. Correct me if I'm wrong, Marcus."

Marcus crossed his arms as though bracing himself for what came next. "You got it right. But how you learn about this stuff is beyond me."

Wyatt bit back a smile. The kid was admitting that he found Wyatt McKenzie more informed and intimidating than his previous employers. Would that inspire him to behave more maturely, to assume some responsibility?

"Seems to me you've burned all your bridges, Marcus—not to mention that you attracted the attention of the law yesterday before you were even in Willow Ridge an hour," he added. He held the kid's green-eyed gaze. "If you decide not to work for me—or if I decide not to hire you—where else can you go? What other kind of work can you do, if you're not training horses? How long can you keep running?"

Marcus focused on his plate. He seemed to be considering Wyatt's questions carefully. "Why do you care?" he finally whispered.

Again Wyatt gave the young man credit for expressing himself. Maybe it was time to share some personal experience so Marcus wouldn't think he took information without sharing any. Maybe he'd feel inspired enough by Wyatt's checkered past to believe that there was hope for his own future.

"Let's just say I know something about getting caught by a couple of girlfriends," he confessed softly. "I used my looks—and my air of having money—to get invited into their lives. Then I blew it by charging stuff on their cards just for the thrill of getting away with it. Stupid move, with serious consequences."

Marcus considered this. "*Did* you have money?"

"The dad who adopted me was one of the wealthiest Thoroughbred breeders in Kentucky," Wyatt replied with a nod. "When he found out what I'd done to those young women, he shut off my funds. Told me I'd be working for a salary until I cleaned up my act—and that I'd be totally cut off from my inheritance if I didn't," he added softly. "I don't want to think about where I would've ended up, had he not set me straight."

"So you're trying to work the same miracle for me, right?"

Marcus challenged without missing a beat. He gazed around the room as he dealt with his pride and his emotions—and as he figured out his options. He sat quietly for several moments, until the bluster had finally drained out of him. "Okay, so what's your deal? What do you expect me to do?"

Wyatt watched Marcus closely. Had he actually captured the young man's interest? Were his questions sincere?

"I'd like you to sign an agreement saying you'll work here for a probationary period of a month—which takes us up to Christmas," he replied. "I have five Thoroughbreds I've retired from the racetrack, and your first assignment will be training them to pull a rig. I want potential Amish buyers to be so impressed with these horses you've trained that they'll be outbidding each other for the privilege of owning them."

"I can do that," Marcus said matter-of-factly. "What else? What about those Percherons out in your paddock?"

"As you know, they're more of a long-term project because they need to mature before they're physically and mentally ready to be reliable draft animals," Wyatt pointed out. "I've got some Belgian yearlings coming in a couple weeks, as well, and because I have no experience with these breeds, I'll be relying on you to get them accustomed to halters and harnesses—"

"And they need to learn how to behave around people and kids and loud noises and car traffic so they won't spook while they're hitched to wagons and plows," Marcus put in quickly. "If they're not handled correctly at a young age and if they don't get worked every day, there'll be no controlling them once they're full grown."

"That's the way I understand it, yes. And you'll be teaching *me* to handle them, too."

"Truth be told," Marcus went on in a low voice, "unless those Percherons have already had some handling and paddock work, they'll need quite a bit of extra effort. They're already *big* suckers—"

"I'm relying on you to assess their level of competence," Wyatt said. "And I'll expect you to write up a proposed schedule for their training first thing, so I can build in pay bonuses as they achieve the levels of success you set for them."

"Fair enough." Marcus nodded, his handsome face alight with interest. After a moment, he looked at Wyatt again. "You gonna call Enos and Jake?"

"Why would I do that? We know what they're going to say, don't we?"

His lips twitched. "What happens if I screw up?"

"Define *screw up*."

Marcus cleared his throat. "What if I get hauled in for another DUI?"

"Someday you'll lose your license. I can't—won't—fix that for you." Wyatt leaned forward, hoping the kid realized the responsibility involved in what he was about to offer. "After your probationary period, if you've proven yourself to be the best horse trainer in America," he added lightly, "we'll set up a repayment plan for your credit card debt— and what you charged to your girlfriends—so you won't have that shadow hanging over you. If you put some of your money aside each pay period, you'll have a nice cash cushion one of these days."

Marcus's dark eyebrows rose. "*That* would be a first."

"What do you think, Marcus?" Wyatt asked earnestly. "You'll either succeed or you won't. You'll either stick with it or you'll go running down the road with your tail between your legs again."

Marcus's expression shifted between a hopeful smile and a somber stare as he focused on his plate. "All right," he murmured. "Where do I sign?"

"You're going to commit to staying at least until Christmas?" Rebecca asked. "Getting miffed or running off—or telling Wyatt he's too controlling—won't be options if you agree to what he's offering you."

"Yeah, I get that." Marcus's gaze went from Rebecca to Wyatt again. "What kind of pay are we talking about?"

Wyatt was pleased to hear this question. "Along with providing your apartment, I'll pay you a hundred dollars a day the first two weeks, and after that it'll double if you're behaving like a model employee and citizen around town," he replied. "Come Christmas, we can negotiate a living wage and some of those perks you were talking about earlier—like the TV and the computer and such."

Marcus counted with his fingers, doing the math. "That's potentially forty-two hundred bucks by Christmas."

"Yup."

"All right. I'm in."

Wyatt fought the urge to slap the table and shout *yes!* He had a long way to go, training Marcus in much the same way the kid would be working with his horses—step by patient step, with some allowances for backsliding. "I'm delighted you want to work for me, Marcus," he said as he reached for the agreement he'd written up. "This new enterprise is a total change from what I've spent most of my life doing, and I can't make this dream come true without your help."

Marcus skimmed the contract before signing it with a loopy, adolescent-looking signature. Wyatt signed on the line beneath Marcus's signature, and extended his hand. "Welcome aboard, Marcus," he said as the kid gripped his fingers. "It's a big moment—the beginning of a new career for both of us."

Relaxing in his chair, Marcus studied Wyatt. "So why'd you leave big-time Thoroughbred racing in Kentucky and New York to come *here*, of all places?" he asked. "I mean, I thought the towns around Lancaster County were pretty rural and behind the times, but Willow Ridge is . . . well, from what I've seen on your older website, you're taking a major step down."

Wyatt smiled at the astute question. "Maybe for me, down is the new up," he replied softly. "I got tired of the competitive back-biting in racing, and *really* tired of keeping up appearances with the social set who make that world go around.

"Let's face it, if Thoroughbred racing suddenly disappeared from the face of the earth, yes, a lot of wealthy folks would lose their livelihoods," he continued earnestly. "But racing is a sport, a pricey hobby. If there were no more draft horses, however, Plain folks couldn't farm or feed their families."

"Why does that matter to you?" Marcus asked with a shrug. "I'm guessing you could live out the rest of your life without working another day—"

"And what sort of life would that be?" Wyatt interrupted. "Why bother getting up in the morning? Willow Ridge and its people feel *genuine*. I can make a difference here—and so can you, Marcus."

The kid looked startled by that idea. "Right now I'll settle for having a job and a place to bunk, thanks," he said as he picked up his fork again.

"You're welcome." Wyatt smiled at Rebecca, who appeared slightly incredulous about how the interview had progressed. "After breakfast, I'll show you around the facilities and you can meet the horses. I have high hopes for what we'll accomplish together as time goes by."

Chapter Six

As Rosalyn cleared away used paper cups and napkins from the serving table at Simple Gifts on Saturday afternoon, her head was spinning. She picked up the nearly depleted tray of Lena Witmer's decorated Christmas cookies so Nora could place a fresh tray in its place. "This is the third big tray of cookies we've put out, *jah*?" she whispered in disbelief.

"Our open house is a huge success!" Nora replied happily. "I've called Lena, and she's bringing us another tray soon. If you'll refill the cider crock, I'll ring up the ladies who're waiting at the checkout."

Rosalyn nodded, happy to comply. Although she loved working in Nora's store, the afternoon's crush of customers intimidated her. She was delighted by the customers' enthusiasm, however, and by their sincere interest in the wreaths she'd made, and in Loretta's colorful rugs and Edith's baskets. She poured the steaming, fragrant cider into the crockery urn and wiped its spigot, looking up when the bell above the door jingled. Six more ladies came in together, exclaiming at the store's decorations and the array of pottery, walnut furniture, decorative linens, and Christmas items they saw.

"Oh, I have to have this star for my kitchen!" one of them cried out. "Have you ever seen anything like it?"

Rosalyn's heart hammered. Nora had encouraged her to mingle with the customers—especially to make conversation about the wreaths she'd crafted—so she made her way over to the lady who was admiring the star-shaped wreath covered with whole nuts. "Do you have any questions?" she asked shyly. "That's one of the wreaths I made—"

"Well, it's exactly what I've been looking for," the lady said as she held it out so her friends could admire it. "I don't want a lot of fussy red and green decorations in my kitchen, so this is just perfect—and it's such a treat to meet the young lady who made it, too!"

Rosalyn's cheeks went hot. "*Denki*," she murmured.

"Do you have any others?" one of the other women asked eagerly. "I bet the greenery wreath on the front door is yours, too—"

"*Jah*, it is," Rosalyn admitted.

"—but I'd rather have something I can store and use year after year."

"I'm with you, Sandi," a third woman in the group put in. "Live wreaths are beautiful, but you have to hang them outdoors. And when they're dead, they're dead."

"Well, I have a pinecone wreath on this wall," Rosalyn said as she led the group between the rack of patchwork jackets and the table covered with table linens. "And as you go up the stairs to the loft, you'll see one with silk greenery and gold pinecones—the one with the dark red bow. The wreath beside it is made from ribbon candy and sprayed with sealant, so it should last a long time, too."

"Oh, look at the silk one! It's the perfect size to hang above my fireplace," Sandi remarked eagerly.

"The bright colors in the candy wreath are so cute!" the friend beside her put in. "I want that one, please."

"Do you take orders, dear?" a fourth member of the group asked. "I don't want to be a copycat and get one just like

Rae's with the nuts on it, but could you make me a round one—maybe a little bigger? With a red bow?"

Rosalyn was so amazed she could hardly think. Her fingers trembled as she jotted the information she needed for the larger round wreath. When the bell above the door jangled again, she forgot to breathe. The tall, muscled silhouette in the doorway could only belong to one man.

Why would Marcus be coming into the store? Let's hope he keeps his attitude to himself.

Her cheeks prickled with heat as she stole glances at him, but she reminded herself about the business at hand. Several customers approached the cash register at the same time, so Rosalyn began removing tags and bagging items while Nora rang up purchases.

Nora leaned close to her. "I have the second cash register set up at the other end of the counter. Do you suppose you could run it?" she asked in a hurried whisper. "I know I haven't had a chance to show you how it works—"

"I'd mess up everything I tried to punch in," Rosalyn replied nervously. The cash register's keyboard and electronic screen reminded her of Rebecca Oliveri's computer—which might as well have come from Mars, as foreign as it seemed.

"Not to worry, dear, we'll be fine," Nora reassured her. Smiling at the purchase-laden customers in the line that snaked between the display tables, she called out over their chatter. "Thank you for your patience, ladies—and for making our open house such a huge success!" she exclaimed. "Please enjoy some cookies and cider while you wait for us to ring up your sales."

Moments later, Rosalyn looked up in surprise. Her hands paused on the Christmas banner she was rolling in tissue paper. Marcus had stepped behind the checkout counter. He set something slender and silver on the ledge beneath the counter as he studied the other cash register.

"Do I tap in the numbers and hit Enter?" he asked Nora.

When he touched a key, he didn't seem the least bit surprised that the screen lit up. "This looks similar to the one I used at the auction barn where I worked."

Nora beamed at him. "*Jah*, and once you've entered all the items, you hit the tax button, and then the total," she explained. "I'm right here if you need help. Bless your heart for jumping in, Marcus."

Rosalyn became much too aware of the tall young man in the red flannel shirt and tight jeans who smelled fresh from a shower. He seemed to take up more than his share of the counter space as he invited the next person in line to step in front of him. She tried to concentrate on removing the consignment tags from the items, but Marcus's effortless banter with the customers distracted her.

"These are nice-looking tooled leather wallets," he remarked as his fingers danced over the cash register's keys. "I'm going to have to shop here if they carry stuff for guys!"

The ladies in the line laughed, charmed by Marcus's teasing. Rosalyn noticed how *polite* he was as he thanked each customer and invited her to return—as though he'd had a personality transplant since he'd come into the store a few days earlier. Somehow she managed to keep up with bagging for both Nora and Marcus, so the lines moved faster for the next several minutes.

By the time the six ladies Rosalyn had helped made their way to the checkout counter, they'd chosen four of her wreaths and they'd also latched on to a set of Christmas dishes, two of Nora's Thanksgiving banners, an embroidered tablecloth, and a hand-carved Nativity set. Rosalyn found a sturdy box and carefully wrapped and packed the dishes, which were decorated with simple sprigs of holly. To her surprise, Marcus stepped up beside her and began rolling the wooden figures from the Nativity set in tissue paper.

"I've never seen a manger scene that had Amish folks in it," he remarked. He admired the wooden Mary and Joseph figures before wrapping them. "Wow, look at the detail in her dress. It's painted like a quilt—and the star on top of the manger looks like a quilt piece, too."

Rosalyn cleared her throat nervously. "Our bishop, Tom Hostetler, carves and paints these Nativity sets," she said. "He works at them during the winter between the morning and evening shifts of milking his cows."

"I think the wise men, holding an ear of corn, a chicken, and a pail of milk, are the cutest pieces," said the lady who'd bought the set. "My kids—and grandkids—will cherish this Nativity for years to come. I'm so glad I found it!"

"We are, too," Marcus said, flashing her a smile. He stuffed tissue paper into another large box, placed the stable in it, and gently arranged the wrapped figurines inside. "I hope your family will spend a lot of time together this Christmas, enjoying this Nativity scene. Thanks for shopping with us today."

"We're so glad we came!" Sandi said as Nora finished ringing up her purchases. "It was worth driving all the way from Chillicothe."

"We're delighted you took the time to visit us," Nora replied graciously. "All of our items are handcrafted by Plain folks who live in central Missouri, you know."

"We'll be back," Rae called over her shoulder as the six of them started toward the door with their bags and boxes. "And thank you, young lady, for showing us your wonderful wreaths."

Rosalyn gave her a little wave. "My pleasure," she replied shyly.

Marcus strode quickly along a side aisle so he could hold the door open for the ladies, and then he went outside to help them put their packages in their car. Only one customer remained at the checkout, so Rosalyn went over to tidy the refreshment table—and to catch her breath, after working alongside Marcus. She was amazed at the way he'd helped out, and he'd known about the computerized cash register. He'd done a very careful job of wrapping the Nativity scene, as well.

"What a nice young man," the customer in front of Nora said. "It does my heart good to know that in a world with gang fights and crimes involving fellows his age, we still have some around who help other people without being asked."

"Marcus hasn't been in Willow Ridge very long," Nora said as she placed the lady's items in a sack. "I was glad he came along in the nick of time and knew how to operate my cash register—and as you mentioned, his courtesy was a breath of fresh air, too. *Denki* for shopping with us today!"

As the lady walked between the display tables toward the door, Nora caught Rosalyn's eye. "What did you think of Marcus's astounding turnaround?" she whispered as she came to rearrange the cookies that remained on the half-empty tray. "When he first walked in, I was just praying he wouldn't shoot off his mouth while so many customers were in the store."

"Same here," Rosalyn agreed. When the bell jangled, she didn't have to look to know that Marcus had reentered the store. Was her imagination working overtime, or did he have a real sense of presence? He'd seemed so comfortable and competent among English folks.

Nora filled a cup with cider and picked up the biggest decorated cookie on the platter. "Marcus, I thank you from the bottom of my heart," she said as she offered him the refreshments. "I take back the critical things I said when you came in here the other day. If you have spare time to work here during the holidays, let's sign you on."

Marcus downed the cider. "I appreciate your offer, Nora, but I suspect Wyatt would rather I didn't work regular hours here," he said as he admired the large snowman sugar cookie. "On the other hand, maybe taking a second job would prove to him that I'm serious about working and paying down my credit card debt."

Rosalyn blinked. She hadn't expected him to admit that he owed money—*and it's just one of many reasons you have no interest in him*, the little voice in her head reminded her. When he approached the refreshment table, she stepped away to straighten the displays on the tables and shelves around the store.

"Did I understand correctly that you made the wreaths those ladies bought, Rosalyn?"

Her cheeks flared with heat as she focused on the table linens she was refolding. Marcus sounded sincerely interested in her handiwork—and she hadn't expected that. She hadn't thought he even knew her name. "*Jah*, I did," she said meekly. "You could've knocked me over with a feather when they bought so many of them—and ordered another one."

"Rosalyn's sisters, Loretta and Edith Detweiler, made the rag rugs and baskets you were ringing up, too," Nora put in as she carried another set of Christmas dishes from the storeroom. "And the walnut furniture in the front of the store was made by the Brenneman brothers, who also live nearby— and the fellow who made those wallets used to live down the hill, but he's moved to Morning Star."

"Your cousin Ben made the pretty fireplace doors," Rosalyn said, pointing toward the back of the store. "When he's not shoeing horses, he makes garden gates and other decorative metal pieces to sell here."

"A man of many talents, my cousin Ben is," Marcus remarked under his breath. He came to stand beside Rosalyn, studying her with eyes that were an unsettling shade of pale green. "Do you make the bases for your wreaths, or do you buy them and cut the greenery from all the evergreens around here?"

Rosalyn was suddenly stricken speechless. "Um, *jah*, I make them," she rasped. Why had she offered that information about Preacher Ben's welded items, thinking Marcus would be interested in what she had to say? The nearness of him—the shine in his pale green eyes and the way his dark hair dipped over his forehead—had her so *ferhoodled* that she would surely make a fool of herself if she said anything else. She focused on restacking some tablecloths and embroidered napkins, relieved when he moved away from her after several nerve-wracking moments.

"May I ask a favor, Nora?" Marcus said as he ambled toward the checkout counter. "I was hoping I could log on to your Wi-Fi and check my email. The apartment above McKenzie's barn doesn't have cable or Internet access."

"Be my guest," Nora replied. "Click on the Simple Gifts network, and the password is 'Redhead twenty-twelve.'"

Rosalyn didn't understand a thing they were talking about, yet she listened closely. Marcus took the slender silver object from beneath the checkout counter—it resembled Nora's laptop computer, except it was smaller—and opened it.

He seems awfully comfortable with electronic gadgets and email, her little voice warned. *Such attachments to the English life mean he'll never consider returning to the Old Order or joining the church, so why bother with him?*

She glanced at his handsome face, which was aglow from the screen he was watching raptly. "This is interesting, to see so many different Wi-Fi networks in the mostly Amish town of Willow Ridge," he remarked. "Here's McKenzie's trailer, and Luke's mill, and your store . . ."

Nora, who had begun checking sales on the main cash register, glanced over and then pointed toward his screen. "Oliveri Design is Rebecca, the gal who does all our websites—"

"Wyatt's *much* younger girlfriend?" Marcus asked.

"We all depend on her expertise when it comes to web presence," Nora put in quickly. "The nurse who runs our little clinic, Andy Leitner, has special permission from Bishop Tom to have Internet access for medical connections.

He used to be English and converted to Old Order Amish to marry one of our local girls."

Marcus's dark eyebrows rose as he considered this. "That's different—a male nurse who went Plain, eh? So who owns this network called Reel Money?"

Nora's brow furrowed. "I have no idea. I've never noticed that one before."

"Well, anyway—thanks for letting me access my mail," Marcus said. "It's handy that you Mennonites allow Internet access, so I can use my iPad to keep up with my friends and what's going on the real world."

"Consider it your pay for helping out today," Nora teased as she returned to checking the cash register.

The jangle of the bell above the door alerted them to the arrival of three customers, and Rosalyn was happy to greet them. Computers and other gadgets would forever remain a mystery to her, but talking face-to-face with folks—even if she was still a bit shy around the English—was something she could handle.

"*Gut* afternoon and welcome to our open house," she said with a hopeful smile. "Is there something we can help you find today? We've got cookies and hot cider, too."

The women inhaled the heady fragrance of the cinnamon and spices, nodding.

"Oh, this store's every bit as wonderful as I imagined," one of them said as she gazed raptly at the array of merchandise. "By the time we've looked around, I bet we'll need those refreshments—"

"To give us strength enough to carry our purchases to the car!" another gal chimed in.

"Take your time," Rosalyn said with a nod. "Let us know if we can answer any questions. All of our items are made by Plain crafters who live around this area."

As the ladies started down an aisle, admiring what they saw, Nora flashed Rosalyn a thumbs-up. It gave her a sense of accomplishment, to have the owner of such a wonderful shop appear to be proud of her—for the help she gave customers, and for the wreaths that were selling faster than Rosalyn could make them.

She took mental inventory of the supplies she had in her room at home. *After Loretta and I redd up the kitchen tonight, I can make the bases for those two wreath orders*, Rosalyn thought. *It'll be something to do besides wonder why the words* Real Money *make me feel prickly inside, even though I have no idea what they mean.*

Chapter Seven

As Marcus sat at Ben and Miriam's table on Thanksgiving, surrounded by his cousins, Miriam's daughters, and their families, he felt acutely aware of being the only unattached person present—which made him a target for speculative glances during the huge meal. In the week since he'd arrived in Willow Ridge, however, he'd learned a few things about most of the folks around the long, extended table, which had given him plenty to think about.

As he passed a large glass casserole containing brilliant yellow-orange slices of glazed acorn squash, Marcus's gaze wandered to Rebecca. From his vantage point at the end of the table opposite Ben, he had a clear view of all the women and kids on one side and all the men across from them. The fact that Rebecca was dressed Plain today piqued his curiosity. She'd stated that she had no intentions of joining the Old Order, so what was she trying to prove? And how did Wyatt feel about her dusty blue cape dress, white *kapp*, and the way her hair was pulled demurely back from her face?

When Rebecca nailed Marcus with her crystal-blue eyes, he felt like the proverbial deer in the headlights. With eighteen people present, the big kitchen rang with two or three ongoing conversations, yet he felt surrounded by a bubble of expectant silence.

"You might as well ask me whatever's on your mind," Rebecca finally said. "You're surprised that I'm dressed like my sisters, Rachel and Rhoda, ain't so?"

The lilt of her Amish accent caught him off guard. Was this the same attractive English woman—somewhere near his age—he'd met at Wyatt's place last week? "Well, yeah," he admitted as he accepted a basket of warm dinner rolls that smelled heavenly.

Across the table from her, Wyatt leaned forward to join the conversation. "Believe me, the first time I came here to meet all these Hooleys, Brennemans, and Leitners, I was *not* prepared to see Rebecca dressed Amish," he said. "But the look becomes her, don't you think?"

She could be wearing broadfall trousers, a guy's shirt, and a broad-brimmed hat and she would look good. Marcus blinked at this thought and knew better than to express it. "It's a little, um, unsettling to see *three* of her," he hedged.

Miriam, seated to Ben's left, laughed out loud. "What was really unsettling was the sight of Rebecca when she first returned to Willow Ridge to find us," she said above the conversation Luke, Ira, and Ben were having. "Can you imagine her in spiky black hair, wearing all manner of little chains and black clothes—and even black fingernails?"

Oh, yes, I can . . .

"But seeing my dear child alive after nineteen years of believing she was dead," Miriam continued in a voice that thrummed with emotion, "well, it was a gift I'll never stop thanking God for. The fact that she's English matters little, considering she's alive and she's come home."

"You said that just right, Mamma," one of Miriam's other daughters chimed in. Marcus wasn't sure if it was Rachel or Rhoda, because both of them were tending babies between putting food on their plates and passing the serving bowls. "And Rebecca's had a lot to do with how well our Plain businesses are doing, what with her being a website designer."

"Hear, hear," a dark-bearded fellow agreed with a nod. "I could run the clinic without Internet access, but a few times when patients were having complications, I was mighty glad I could contact the hospital in New Haven for assistance. Rebecca's a fine receptionist, too."

Marcus nodded, recalling from the initial introductions that this man, Andy Leitner, had been English—and divorced—before marrying one of Rebecca's sisters. It surprised him that the Old Order leaders here were progressive enough to accept such a man. Most Amish communities would've forbidden him to associate with one of their girls, much less marry her.

Rebecca waved off their compliments, seeming more interested in the platter of roasted meat she'd just received. "Your duck smells divine, Rhoda," she said, glancing at her identical sister.

"And we've got Mamma's baked chicken, too," her sister Rachel remarked, nodding at the platter she held. "This is truly a feast to be thankful for."

"All the better because it's a family effort," Miriam put in happily. She, too, was placing morsels of food on a small plate where her toddler, Bethlehem, sat humming as she stuffed a handful of noodle casserole into her mouth.

For a moment the whole big-Amish-family thing overwhelmed Marcus, because it had been a few years since he'd gathered at a table with his parents and siblings and their little kids. In some ways he missed the noise and conversations of their gatherings—but he'd grown *very* tired of his *dat*'s lectures and increasingly critical remarks. He took a heaping spoonful of green bean casserole, passed the pan to

Will Gingerich on his left, and then accepted a big bowl of glazed carrots from Luke.

Is it me, or does this scene feel too happy to be believable? Marcus wondered skeptically. He glanced furtively at Will, who seemed subdued compared to the others—but maybe that was because he was awfully young to be a widower. Marcus wondered if Will and Savilla had plans for later in the day. He didn't ask, however, so Will wouldn't suspect his interest in the attractive young woman.

He took a big spoonful of mashed potatoes and offered the bowl to Gingerich. "Where you from, Will?"

Will took his time putting potatoes on his plate, as though thinking about his answer. "Grew up near Roseville, several miles from here," he replied. "My two brothers squeezed me off the farm, so I don't go back much. Holiday dinners get tricky, you know? I'm thankful Miriam sets a place for me."

"I know something about that," Marcus agreed. He saw no need to mention that he was the *cause* of the tension at his family's table, because Gingerich had probably heard about his situation from the local grapevine—or directly from Luke and Ira. "Sometimes I think it's best to stay single to avoid the entanglements of a large family."

Will let out a humorless laugh. "*Jah*, you've got that right."

Marcus ladled gravy over his potatoes and passed the gravy bowl to Will, waiting for whatever juicy tidbit he seemed ready to share. Gingerich seemed lost in his own thoughts, however, so Marcus tuned in to the conversation near the other end of the table. He couldn't miss the intensity of Luke and Ben's male voices beneath the Leitner kids' answers to Miriam's questions about school.

"—can't believe Cornelius hasn't come clean," Luke was saying with a shake of his head. "Why hasn't Bishop Tom read him the riot act—ordered him on his knees? This has been going on for *months*."

Ben shrugged, cutting into a piece of duck. "You can't force a man to confess," he pointed out. "Cornelius is apparently obeying the bishop's instructions—ordering his clock parts through the mail, and attending grief counseling."

Luke waved him off. "Going through the motions, if you ask me."

"Well, can you imagine what a shock it would be for his girls—especially Loretta and Rosalyn—if they found out the extent of his wrongdoing at the same time everyone else did?" Ben shot back. "We're hoping he'll admit his mistakes to them first, so they'll be a step ahead of the guilt and humiliation their *dat*'s confession will bring down on the family."

Marcus's eyes widened. What sort of things had Rosalyn's father done, that Ben and Luke were speaking so harshly about him? Rosalyn impressed Marcus as a meek, mousy sort of daughter, of an age to remain a *maidel* forever if some fellow didn't court her soon. It wasn't that she was ugly or dumb. But she was so painfully shy she hadn't once looked him in the eye the day he'd helped in Nora's store.

"I hope Tom's not making a big mistake, allowing Cornelius to go about his business as though he's done nothing wrong," Luke continued with a frown. "A lot of people could get burned if your deacon hasn't actually reformed."

"Tom and I have prayed extensively over this situation, and we've put it in God's hands," Ben insisted. "What more can we do?"

Luke seemed to take this as his cue that the conversation about Cornelius Riehl was finished, but for Marcus the seeds of curiosity had been planted. *Maybe there's someone in this town who's played fast and loose even more than I have*, he speculated as he chewed a mouthful of buttery acorn squash. *And if he's the district's deacon, that makes the situation even more intriguing. Too bad I don't have a clock that needs repairing.*

For the remainder of the meal Marcus nodded and replied in the appropriate conversational places, but his mind was toying with ideas about Cornelius—how to meet the man, or find out more about what he'd done that would adversely affect so many people and heap shame and degradation on his daughters.

This can't be easy for Rosalyn. She's been raised to honor her father—to believe in him—even though the rumors are starting to circle like vultures . . .

Rosalyn quickly scraped the dinner dishes while Loretta hurried over to the counter to cut the desserts. *Lord, is it too much to ask that Dat keep his bitterness and critical remarks to himself so we can enjoy our Thanksgiving dinner?* she fretted. *Must we forever rush around trying to please him, to keep him from blurting out hurtful words?*

"Your pumpkin pies look yummy, Edith," Loretta said cheerfully. "And they smell nice and spicy with cinnamon and cloves."

Their sister Edith looked up from wiping the trays of the high chairs where her twins, Leroy and Louisa, were starting to fuss. "I hope I remembered to include all the right ingredients," she said with a laugh. "My little kitchen helpers were toddling around, opening cabinet doors while I was baking."

"They're growing so fast," Rosalyn remarked as she carried the stack of plates to the counter beside the sink. "Hard to believe they're already thirteen months old and—"

"Old enough to sit still and be quiet," Dat groused as he glared at the twins. "But frankly, Edith, you could've made something other than pumpkin pies. You know how I despise them."

Edith, bless her, had a response ready for their father's annual complaint. "See the slab pie Loretta's cutting now? I made it with lots of cherry and apricot filling, just for you, Dat."

"Not that we'll let you eat it all by yourself," Edith's husband, Asa, teased. He lifted little Leroy from his high chair before holding him high in the air to make him giggle. "Our boy here is developing quite a taste for pie, so maybe he could sit on your lap and share your piece, Cornelius."

"That child's not touching my pie," Dat retorted.

"I intend to eat my share of it, too, Cornelius," Asa's twin brother, Drew, chimed in as he rose to carry the desserts to the table. "We wouldn't want you to get sick—or fat—from gorging on all that sweet, fruity goodness by yourself."

"It's my pie, and my business how much of it I care to eat," Dat snapped.

The kitchen rang with her father's caustic remark as everyone gazed uneasily at the red-faced man who sat at the end of the table. Rosalyn wasn't surprised to hear little Louisa's whimper, for Dat's tone had been angry enough to upset *her*, much less Edith's tiny child. Louisa's face puckered and turned as pink as her dress, and her wispy dark hair began to quiver.

"Honestly, Dat, do you have to make everyone around you miserable?" Edith asked as she began swaying and holding her little girl close. "Aren't you seeing Bishop Tom about—"

"I'm doing everything he told me to do," Dat fired back. "Nobody seems to realize how your mother's death shattered me—and none of you care how miserable *I* am."

With that, their father scooted back from the table, fetched a dinner plate from the cabinet, and strode over to where Loretta had been cutting the desserts. He snatched the metal spatula from her hand and lifted four large squares of the cherry-apricot slab pie from the cookie sheet, piling them on his plate. Muttering under his breath about how disrespectful his family was—and how the girls had completely forgotten about their mother—he headed for the basement. The *wham* of the door behind him made both of the babies jump and gasp in surprise.

"That was just wrong, manipulating you girls with his hurtful words," Asa murmured. "I'm sorry I stirred up such a hornet's nest over pie."

"It wasn't your fault, Asa," Edith replied. "Truth be told, Dat seems to find any little excuse to be rid of us all. And who can tell what will set him off? We girls have known him all our lives and we still haven't figured him out."

"Surely he's not going to work in his shop on a holiday," Loretta said.

"It's best to just leave him be—and let him stew in his own juice," Drew suggested as he began placing the cut pies in the center of the table. "If he's happier when he's not in our company, well, at least we don't have to put up with his rude remarks."

With a sigh, Rosalyn returned to the table. Surely there was a way to clear the air of Dat's negativity, to raise their spirits in a manner that was appropriate for the Thanksgiving holiday. She helped herself to a slice of pumpkin pie and spooned a dollop of whipped cream onto it, glad that they'd made it from scratch rather than buying a tub of topping from the store.

"When all's said and done," she began quietly, "we're still a family, and I for one am very thankful to have the two best sisters on earth. I'm also grateful that you fellows have joined us—"

"And we're thankful to have Leroy and Louisa to make us smile," Loretta put in as she grinned at them in their high chairs.

"So true!" Edith said, her face alight. "As the years go by, we'll have each other, no matter what."

"*Jah*, you girls have it right," Drew said as he took a square of the slab pie. "It's all about family, today and every day."

"And we're thankful you girls love us enough to put up with us," Asa added. He closed his eyes over his first mouthful of the cherry-apricot pie. "Oh my, but this is tasty. I'm thinking a few more pieces of this slab pie have my name on them."

"It's a first-come, first-served situation," Drew teased. "Maybe there'll be some of it left for Cornelius when you folks go home this evening, and maybe there won't."

As everyone chuckled, Rosalyn's thoughts wandered ahead to Saturday, when she'd be working at Nora's store again. She had agreed with Nora's idea to bring the materials for more Christmas wreaths so she could work on them at a table where customers could watch her—which sounded scary yet exhilarating.

It's such a blessing to spend time with Nora, and to be where folks appreciate the time and effort I put into my wreaths, Rosalyn thought. As her sisters savored their mouthfuls of pie, their sweet smiles gave her another idea.

"What would you girls think about joining me at the shop on Saturday?" she asked. "Nora would be tickled to have us making our baskets, rugs, and wreaths when the store's sure to be busy with holiday shoppers. Maybe she wouldn't pay you, but—"

"But it would get me out of the house for part of the day," Loretta pointed out with a glance at the basement door.

"And it would be a chance to work on a couple of basket orders I need to complete," Edith put in. She deftly moved Louisa's small plate before the girl smashed her hand down onto her pumpkin pie. "I could put these monkeys in their playpen in Nora's back room—"

"And we could all take turns peeking in on them," Loretta offered brightly. "Nora wouldn't mind having them there—and if they get fussy, we'll take them outside to play."

"Drew and I have a load of furniture to deliver to Warrensville on Saturday," Asa said, "so why don't we go our way and you girls can do your crafty thing together, and we'll see you for supper? Let's go to the Grill N Skillet, since you'll all be working that day."

"You're on!" Edith replied happily. "It'll be sisters day at Nora's store, and we won't have to cook—except for whipping up a dish or two to take for the common meal after church on Sunday."

"The customers will love watching us," Loretta said. "And if Nora needs extra help at the checkout, we'll be there for her. What a great idea, Rosalyn! *Denki* for thinking of it."

Rosalyn's heart swelled as she helped herself to another slice of the rich, spicy pumpkin pie. She and Loretta could leave a pot of soup simmering on the stove for Dat's noon meal, along with some sandwiches in the refrigerator, and he could spend all the time he wanted in his shop without his daughters around to irritate him. Maybe he'd go to the Grill N Skillet for supper, and maybe he wouldn't. She decided not to worry about what he would eat that evening if he chose not to join them.

Sounds like a wonderful day for all of us.

Chapter Eight

Marcus entered Nora's store late Saturday morning and paused to read the room. Although the shop wasn't as busy as it had been during the open house, several customers were browsing—and obviously enjoying the ambience of the soft Christmas music, the scent of pine and peppermint candles burning on various display tables, and the carefully crafted items Nora offered on her shelves. Marcus was impressed with the variety of merchandise in Simple Gifts, and he headed over to the far front corner where tooled leather saddles and Ben's ornamental metal pieces provided a more masculine place to spend some time . . . spying.

From behind a tall ornamental metal garden gate decorated with welded sunflowers and hummingbirds, Marcus gazed up toward the loft and around the main level to locate Rosalyn. A burst of laughter caught him by surprise—and told him why she hadn't immediately approached him. All three of the Riehl sisters were seated at tables, chatting happily with customers who watched them as they worked on their crafts. McKenzie had told him that the two younger sisters were married, so their presence here in a store that catered to an English clientele surprised Marcus.

Isn't there an unwritten church law about married

women—especially those with children—working outside the home? Don't their husbands lay down the law and expect them to serve a noon meal?

The sister with a pixie face and sparkling brown eyes picked up a tiny girl in a lavender dress and bounced her against her hip, chatting with the English ladies who'd been watching her make a basket. Another sister was showing a customer how she created a rug from strips of deep green and burgundy fabric, with the plastic contraption she held in her hand. Rosalyn sat on a stool behind a table strewn with the components for the wreaths she was making, appearing a bit more subdued than her sisters. She was nodding and answering questions, however, as her nimble fingers attached dark, glossy Brazil nuts to a circular wreath already covered with English walnuts and pecans. Redheaded Nora looked on with the air of a proud mother hen whose chicks amazed and amused her, before joining two ladies at the cash register.

Although Marcus enjoyed the fact that he'd escaped the notice of the four women who were minding the store, he soon eased away from the handsome black leather saddle he'd been standing beside. He admired his cousin Ben's welding skill as he gave the garden gate one last look, and then meandered toward an entire bedroom set handsomely crafted from walnut and set off with a puffy Christmas quilt and a rug that Rosalyn's sister had probably made. When the hairs at the nape of his neck tingled, Marcus discovered that Rosalyn was watching him—until he met her gaze and she quickly focused on her wreath again.

She wants nothing to do with you, Hooley. She's probably a goody-goody who's already joined the Old Order, and she's scared of you—and that's just as well. Rosalyn's not your type at all.

Marcus approached her table anyway. Surely with her sisters nearby, Rosalyn wouldn't feel as threatened by his presence. Was he really so intimidating?

"You ladies seem to be having a great time," he remarked. He flashed a smile at all three of them and at the customers gathered around.

"*Jah*, we're happiest whenever we're together." Rosalyn gestured toward each of her sisters in turn. "Marcus Hooley, this is Loretta Detweiler, who makes toothbrush braided rugs, and Edith Detweiler, who makes baskets."

"And you all make such amazing items, too," remarked one of the ladies who was watching them. "I've bought a couple of Loretta's rugs over the past month or so, and I'm thinking that the one she's making now belongs in my entry-way when I put up my Christmas decorations."

Loretta's cheeks turned a pretty shade of pink. "This rug could be yours," she teased, as though she'd enjoyed working with this customer before. "It doesn't have a home yet."

"Fabulous!" the lady said as she dug out her wallet. "And I'd like this unusual wreath with the nuts to go with it, please."

Rosalyn appeared pleasantly flustered. "This one's already spoken for, but I—I'll take your name and number," she said, looking around for paper and a pen. "Do you have a certain size you want, or a shape? The last nut wreath I made was a star—not quite as big as this one."

Marcus ambled between the nearby display shelves to give Rosalyn a chance to get the information she needed. He'd heard from Luke that Loretta and her new husband had chosen to live in the Riehl home after their recent wedding, so he was even more intrigued about their *dat*, Cornelius the church deacon—about the secrecy that shrouded his reputation, and about the fact that he would allow his daughters to work in Nora's store. While Rosalyn chatted with her customer, Marcus looked at the various materials on her worktable, and he got an idea.

When the customer headed toward Nora at the cash register, Marcus made his way behind the girls' tables. He picked up one of the cornhusks Rosalyn had placed near some fresh greenery that would probably be worked into another wreath. He spotted some green floral wire, too—and he couldn't miss the way Rosalyn self-consciously scooted a few inches away from him.

"Um, can I help you?" she asked in a low voice.

"Oh, I'm beyond help, Roz," Marcus teased. He smiled at her as he deftly manipulated the cornhusk, using the slender wire to hold the head of his creation in place. "I'm really curious about how you ladies can work in Nora's store, what with your *dat* being the district's deacon—and two of you being married," he remarked. "Most Old Order gals don't have that option."

Loretta looked up from the rug she was making. "If Nora were still English rather than Mennonite, we wouldn't be here," she stated. "But I started this ball rolling before I got married, by defying Dat and working here against his orders that I stay home. I'm glad Rosalyn's helping here, too. Our father gets . . . *testy*."

"I suspect Bishop Tom realizes how unpleasant things can be at home, so he allows Rosalyn and Loretta a little time away," Edith put in softly. "Most bishops would flat-out forbid them to work here, as you suggested, Marcus."

"How's it going with Wyatt's horses?" Loretta asked, turning the interrogation around.

Marcus chuckled, recognizing her deliberate change of topic. "McKenzie gave me some time off for good behavior today, because I've already retrained two of his retired racing Thoroughbreds so they're reliable buggy horses. The other three will be ready by the end of next week," he added as he continued coaxing the stiff leaves of the cornhusk into place.

Edith's expressive eyebrows rose. "You sound mighty sure about that," she teased.

"I am," he shot back without missing a beat. "Horses

respond well to my instruction. I work them hard, I work them fast—and I'm *very* persuasive."

Marcus hadn't missed the way Rosalyn was stealing glances at his hands even as she focused on attaching the final few almonds to the wreath she was making. He plucked the two sides of the cornhusk figure upward into wings. A stray sprig of silk holly on the table inspired him to tuck it into the belt he'd formed with the wire. When he was satisfied with his creation, he handed it to her. "For you," he said.

Rosalyn's eyes widened with surprise. "An angel!" she whispered, turning the little doll this way and that. "How'd you *do* that?"

The amazement in her voice and her gaze touched him. "I used to make them for my nieces," he replied with a shrug. "When you live on a farm, cornhusks are easy to come by."

She was avidly studying the way the green floral wire formed a halo and also held the angel's neck in place, as though she'd never seen anything so clever. When Rosalyn dared to meet his gaze, her brown eyes reflected doubt and uncertainty even as she took pleasure in the angel. "This is for *me*? I—well, *denki*, Marcus," she stammered.

He blinked. Why did Rosalyn feel so undeserving? Had no one ever given her such a simple gift as a cornhusk figure? "Horses and women," he quipped. "I can have them eating out of my hand at the drop of a hat."

Rosalyn's gasp—and Edith and Loretta's dropped jaws—told Marcus it was time for him to leave. Was it his imagination, or had the entire store gotten quiet?

"*Jah*, well, have a great day," he muttered before he quickly made his way toward the door.

Jah? *When was the last time you said that? And what possessed you to make such a crude remark, idiot?* Marcus's thoughts challenged him. When he stepped outside, the chilly winter air was a relief after being in the store, which had grown stuffy. He half expected Nora to follow him and tell him exactly what she thought of his inappropriate remark, because she'd probably heard it from where she stood at the cash register.

Large, lacy snowflakes tickled his cheeks. In the short time he'd been inside, the grass had become coated with a thin layer of snow. Although the flakes weren't coming down fast, the gray sky and the low temperature suggested that the snow wouldn't stop anytime soon.

I hope it snows well into the night and keeps Rosalyn at home for a while, Marcus thought. An image of her trusting face and the hurt look he'd put on it accompanied him as he strode across the back lot of the store and past Luke's mill, toward the McKenzie place. *No point in me going to Nora's store to see her anymore. She'll always be a sweet, innocent Amish girl—way too sweet and innocent for a guy like me.*

"Oh, what fun it is to ride in a one-horse open rig!" Rebecca sang happily. She and Wyatt had been out in a courting buggy Luke had loaned them, and the snow had caught them by surprise. "Look how pretty the evergreens are with the white lace gathering on their branches."

Wyatt smiled, keeping a firm hold on the lines as the horse clip-clopped along the blacktop toward Willow Ridge. "I'm actually looking forward to some winter weather, after living in the South for so long," he remarked. "I can already tell, however, that I need to see Ben about some different shoes for these Thoroughbreds, now that they'll be negotiating the curves and hills of snowy blacktop roads. Brewster seems a little unsure of his footing."

"He's doing amazingly well, though," Rebecca said as she tucked her arm under Wyatt's elbow and sat closer to him. "And so are you, for a man who's only recently learned how to drive a buggy."

His handsome face creased in a smile. "Marcus may be

full of himself, but he's an excellent teacher," he admitted. He glanced behind them to check for traffic. "Let's see how Brewster and I do on this lane that's coming up. *Gee*, fella."

The horse's ears pricked straight up and after a moment's hesitation he made the right turn into the dirt-packed lane that led up to Atlee Glick's place, just outside of town.

Rebecca held her breath, not wanting to distract either the horse or the driver.

After they'd gone about thirty feet, Wyatt tightened his grip. "Whoa, boy."

Brewster stopped immediately. When he shook his head and exhaled, his breath came out in white wisps of vapor.

"Good job, Brewster."

They sat for several moments, waiting to see if the horse forgot his command and started moving. The bay with the black mane and tail remained stock-still, however, awaiting further instruction.

"Good boy, Brewster. Back now," Wyatt said quietly. "Easy, boy. Back up."

The obedient horse shifted in the harness and slowly reversed directions. When the rig reached the edge of the road, he awaited Wyatt's pressure on the leather lines to determine which way he should turn. "You got it, Brewster," Wyatt murmured. "Gee now, fellow. Back . . . back . . ."

Rebecca nipped her lip to keep from crying out in her excitement. The Thoroughbred was performing as though he'd been an Amish buggy horse all his life.

"All right, off we go, Brewster. Let's head home now."

The horse shook his head and picked up his pace, soaking up Wyatt's praise as he pulled them past Bishop Tom's dairy farm. Black-and-white Holsteins raised their heads from the hay they were munching, watching the rig go by. In the distance, a border collie raced along a pasture fence to bark out its greeting as a herd of woolly sheep looked on.

Wyatt slung his arm around Rebecca's shoulders and

hugged her close. "Every time I drive through this area, I feel as though I'm in a live picture postcard," he said. "I'm still waiting for reality to set in—for something to distort the absolute perfection of my new life. Do you have any idea how happy I feel whenever I'm with you, Rebecca?"

Her pulse raced and she snuggled closer to him. "I have a whole new definition of happiness these days," she murmured. "Must be the company I'm keeping."

As they continued along the road, Rebecca sensed Wyatt wanted to say something else, but she didn't press him. It was enough to let her heartbeat settle into the steady *clip-clop, clip-clop* of Brewster's hooves, and it didn't matter that her coat and jeans would be soaked through with the snow by the time she got home. Wyatt watched for car traffic at the intersection and expertly steered them onto the county highway. They passed Andy's clinic, and then the Schrocks' quilt shop, which shared part of the Grill N Skillet's building, directly across the road from Mamma and Ben's house. Once they'd crossed the bridge near Luke's mill on the river, Wyatt guided the horse between the distinctive white gateposts that marked his property. Moments later they were pulling into the barn where the Thoroughbreds would live until they were sold to new Plain owners as exquisite buggy horses.

With a gentle tug on the lines, Wyatt halted the horse. In the unlit dimness, his gray-blue eyes gazed all the way into Rebecca's soul. "I love you, Rebecca," he whispered. "I don't know why I've been so hesitant to say it out loud, because I've known how I feel about you practically since the moment we met."

Rebecca cupped his face in her hand and kissed him. His feelings for her had never been a secret, but she was glad she'd let him say the words first rather than stealing his thunder—or making him feel he should say them back to her. "I love you, too, Wyatt," she murmured. "It's not something either of us take lightly, or take for granted."

He rested his forehead against hers. "Never ceases to amaze me, the way you often say exactly what I'm thinking, dear heart."

They sat together in the shadowy barn for several long, lovely minutes. For Rebecca, it was the long-awaited beginning of a sweet dream that was about to come true.

Chapter Nine

As Rosalyn sat in church on Sunday, she was relieved that Marcus hadn't felt compelled to attend the service—even though he clearly needed to return to the ways of their faith. Every time she'd gazed at the cornhusk angel, she'd felt such delight that he'd fashioned the Christmas figure for *her*. But then she would recall the next words that had come rushing out of his mouth and she'd blush with discomfort all over again.

Horses and women. I can have them eating out of my hand at the drop of a hat.

Squirming on the pew bench, Rosalyn reminded herself that Marcus's embarrassing remark was the last thing she should be thinking about during Preacher Henry Zook's sermon. The storekeeper rarely delivered a Sunday message, so he wasn't as polished as Bishop Tom or Preacher Ben—

That doesn't matter. God chose him, and you're to follow his teaching.

Straightening her spine, Rosalyn noticed that other folks in the congregation appeared distracted, too. Preacher Henry spoke in a reedy monotone, and his reluctance to stand before a crowd was reflected in his murmured words and a sermon that seemed to ramble on pointlessly. On the preachers' bench, Dat gazed blankly at his knees while Preacher Ben fought a yawn. Bishop Tom stole a furtive glance at the clock on the Brennemens' mantel.

"In closing, we should never forget that the poor shall always be with us," Preacher Henry said. "Rather than feeling pity for them, we should stand ready to assist at a moment's notice—and we should give thanks that we don't count ourselves amongst them."

As the preacher retreated to the bench behind him, the women around Rosalyn were frowning, trying to figure out what the final sentence of the sermon meant. How were the poor related to the Scripture Dat had read before the sermon, about Nicodemus coming to Jesus under cover of nightfall to ask how he could attain everlasting life? A couple of fellows on the men's side across the Brennemens' front room coughed, and others shook their heads in bewilderment. Everyone seemed eager to sing the final hymn.

After Bishop Tom's benediction, the room immediately rang with chatter, as though folks were trying to put Preacher Henry's awkwardness behind them. Rosalyn and her sisters headed toward the kitchen with the other women to set out the meal.

"Naomi, is it true what they say about that Marcus fellow Wyatt McKenzie hired?" Preacher Henry's wife, Lydia, asked. "Somebody told me he could teach a horse to dance—and that he eats his weight in food when he's at the Grill N Skillet."

The ladies all laughed as they began filling baskets with fresh-sliced bread. Naomi Brenneman, the day's hostess— who helped the Witmers in the café's kitchen—pulled a large metal pan of baked chicken from her oven before she responded.

"I don't know anything about his way with horses," she said, "but *jah*, he has quite the appetite. We're glad he comes for his supper close to closing time, because he doesn't leave us much in the way of leftovers."

Rosalyn blinked. Where did a lean, lanky fellow like Marcus put so much food? She envied him, because it seemed that an extra helping of potatoes here or a second brownie there was all it took to make her clothes feel tighter. She focused on filling the water pitchers, determined not to think about Marcus any more.

"And why isn't Marcus here this morning, worshipping with us?" Nora's *mamm*, Wilma Glick, asked in a judgmental tone. "I'd think Preacher Ben would make it a priority to see that his cousin came to church."

"The way I hear it," Leah Kanagy put in, "that young man's socializing with English women got so out of hand, his Old Order *dat* sent him packing. *Five* of them he's lived in sin with—at his young age!"

Rosalyn's eyebrows shot up. Maybe what Marcus had said about his way with horses and women was true.

"Let's not stretch this gossip out of proportion, sister," Miriam challenged Leah above the other women's shocked whispering. "Marcus has indeed exasperated his family in Lancaster, and he's jumped the fence, *jah*. Ben and Luke have tried to talk to him concerning the salvation of his soul, but it'll take some time to win him over. Marcus has been in Willow Ridge just over a week," she added as she cut a sheet cake into serving pieces. "If you throw in a day of rest, it took God seven days to create the world, after all."

"And I've heard that he's already trained some of Wyatt's retired racehorses to pull rigs—and that he stepped in to help Nora at her store and was the perfect gentleman," Edith put in quickly. "Let's not be too quick to condemn him, or he'll find no *gut* reason to rejoin our faith."

Rosalyn was pleased that her sister and Miriam's remarks stanched the flow of gossip about Marcus, but she quickly carried the pitchers to the tables in the front room so she wouldn't have to hear any more about Wyatt's controversial new employee. She was grateful that her sisters didn't mention the cornhusk angel or the frightful things Marcus had said before he'd hurried out of the store on Saturday.

As folks sat down to eat, the three inches of snow they'd received overnight gave everyone something besides Marcus to talk about, and the crisp whiteness had put most of them in a festive mood. With Thanksgiving behind them, talk of upcoming Christmas visits from kinfolk who lived in other towns kept the conversation lively.

"I'm really looking forward to some of my family coming from Bowling Green," Miriam said brightly. "They plan to arrive early in the week—and they're hoping we'll put on another live Nativity this year, Bishop Tom."

From his seat a couple of tables away, the bishop smiled as all eyes focused on him. "We seem to have started a tradition that my bishop friends in other communities believe is rather radical," he remarked. "Ben and Henry and I discussed this the other day, and we still believe that an outdoor pageant shared with any English folks who care to attend is a wonderful-*gut* way to celebrate the miracle of Jesus's birth."

"As you'll recall, we first put on a live Nativity because, what with only six kids attending school—all of them still in the lower grades—Teacher Alberta has a hard time putting on the usual Christmas Eve program," Preacher Ben reminded everyone. "If none of you objects, Miriam and I are willing to host the pageant at our place again this year. Our big barnyard allows room for lots of folks to attend, and they can park along the county highway."

"I wanna be a wise man this year!" one of the six-year-old Knepp twins called out.

"Our brother Aden could be Baby Jesus!" Taylor Leitner, Andy's daughter, said excitedly.

As the grownups around Rosalyn smiled, she became fascinated by the idea of the children reenacting the birth of Jesus outdoors. What a way to celebrate her family's first Christmas in Willow Ridge! Their bishop in Roseville would never have allowed such a spectacle—yet Bishop Tom was offering to provide a couple of his Holstein cows for the manger scene while Ira Hooley volunteered a pair of recently born Percheron mules and Leah Kanagy's husband, Daniel, had lambs to bring.

As talk about the pageant continued, Rosalyn and her sisters couldn't help smiling. Even though Dat had told them their holiday preparations would be minimal again this year, they enjoyed hearing about the past Christmas Eves' live Nativities and other families' plans for fun on Second Christmas, after a Christmas Day of quiet reflection. With anticipation of holiday festivities fueling their conversations, the afternoon passed quickly.

Once they got home, however, time hung as heavily as a snow-soaked cloak. Rosalyn and Loretta tended the chickens while Drew did the horse chores, remarking about how much earlier darkness fell at this time of year. Because they'd eaten a large meal after church, supper consisted of cold cuts, cheese, and bread for making sandwiches, along with what remained of a chocolate cake Loretta had baked on Friday. Drew and Dat took their places at the table, in a kitchen that was dim because Dat kept the lamp wicks low to avoid burning too much oil. Loretta sat down with them, but Rosalyn wasn't hungry so she went upstairs to her room.

From her window on the back of the house, she had a view of the Simple Gifts store, the Hooleys' mill, and beyond that, the expensive white plank fencing that marked the McKenzie place. Maybe it was a reflection of a security light she saw in the upper-level window of one of Wyatt's barns . . . or maybe Marcus was in his apartment in the loft.

Rosalyn picked up the cornhusk angel from her dresser and gazed at it for the umpteenth time. How was it possible that Marcus, such a brash, mouthy young man, could effortlessly fashion a doll from a cornhusk and a strand of wire? Like the Amish cloth dolls Nora sold in her store, this angel had no facial features. Her wire halo—which also formed the neckline of her gown and defined her waist with a slender belt—and the lift of her wings gave her a serene, almost saintly, personality. The little sprig of silk holly in her belt added a festive touch of color.

Marcus made this just for me.

Rosalyn sighed. She was reading more into Marcus's gift than he'd intended, yet her lonely soul longed to believe that such a handsome, adventurous—*dangerous*—young man found her worthy of his notice. In mere moments he'd provided her imagination the material for endless romantic fantasies in which she won him over and he gave up his wild life to join the church and marry her.

That will never *happen*, the little voice in her head warned.

But what could it hurt to secretly adore Marcus from afar? With each passing week she came closer to being labeled a *maidel* who would never wed—some folks already believed Rosalyn, at twenty-eight, was beyond the age when men would consider courting her. It didn't help that Dat, a deacon who was expected to toe a higher line than other men, was a difficult father whose recent activities had cast a dark shadow of doubt over their household, rendering his eldest daughter even less desirable.

Marcus called you Roz yesterday, she recalled with a tremulous smile. The simple nickname set her apart as special—made her sound less bound by the rules and more likely to cut loose and have fun. Her father would *never* tolerate anyone calling her Roz—even at home—which made the nickname seem that much more exciting . . . a secret she and Marcus could share in their private moments.

"But then he had to go and talk about his way with women," she muttered as she turned her back to the window.

Rosalyn pulled her shawl more tightly around her and shivered in the chilly room. With five previous girlfriends, Marcus must know all there was to know about what went on between men and women. Because of Mamm's revelations years ago, fearful thoughts about the physical side of love made remaining a *maidel* seem like a far more comfortable option than the marriage bed. In a desperate moment, her mother had confided secrets that Rosalyn could never share even with Loretta or Edith—and certainly never with Dat, who would deny Mamm's words in a burst of fury.

Mamm realized what a burden she laid upon you when you were only twelve, and she begged you not to repeat what she said. For weeks afterward, she looked worried and guilty about heaping her fears upon you.

Rosalyn sighed. Their family and friends knew about the tiny graves of the stillborn Riehl babies in the Roseville cemetery, one of them buried ten months before Loretta's arrival and one of them ten months later. Rosalyn clearly remembered the babies' pale bluish faces and the eyes that had never opened—not to mention Mamm's pain and grief after carrying babies to full term, only to learn their cords had become wrapped around their necks.

What folks didn't know about were the miscarriages . . . and the night after one of them when Mamm had clung to Rosalyn, crying and confiding her abject fear of going to bed each night, having to submit to Dat's demands before her body had a chance to recover from her pregnancies. The muffled noises coming from her parents' bedroom took on a sinister meaning after Mamm's confession, and Rosalyn wasn't sure if she'd heard her mother crying in the night afterward, or if her girlish imagination had conjured the sound. But even at twenty-eight, with two sisters who absolutely glowed from the attentions of their new husbands, she became a knot of apprehension at the mere thought of lying with a man.

Not that you'll have to worry about Marcus wanting you, Rosalyn tried to reason. *He can't be a day over nineteen and acts even more adolescent sometimes, so to him you're already impossibly old and—*

"Why are you standing in the middle of your room in the dark, Rosalyn?" Loretta asked from the doorway. "Are you not feeling well? I missed you at supper."

Rosalyn pressed her lips together to keep from blurting out her fears about intimacy. Loretta, who had been open and flirtatious first with Will and then with Drew, couldn't possibly understand her misgivings.

Loretta slipped her arms around Rosalyn and hugged her. "I suspected that this morning's gossip about Marcus was getting to you—especially after he made that wisecrack about horses and women," she murmured.

Rosalyn shrugged helplessly, unsure of what to say. If her sister was reading her so easily, had all the other women in Naomi's kitchen figured out that she was *ferhoodled* about Marcus?

"Well, when Marcus said that, he sounded like a lot of guys who think they're God's gift to women," Loretta went on with a shake of her head. "And the fact that he's been living with English girlfriends has surely warped his perception of what sort of talk is acceptable, and what's not. At least he had the decency to *leave*," she added. "Maybe he embarrassed himself. Maybe there's hope for him yet."

"Maybe next time he shoots off his mouth, Nora will wash out his mouth with soap," Rosalyn put in quietly.

Loretta hugged her hard, laughing. "*That* would cure him of such inappropriate talk!" she said. "I'll never forget the time Mamm did that to me for calling old Bishop Ammon a fiddle-fart—even though neither of us knew what a fiddle-fart was."

Loretta's giggling was contagious and Rosalyn began to laugh despite her earlier bleak thoughts. As she wiped tears of mirth from her face, she realized again that her worries about Marcus were unfounded. A guy of his age, who'd had so much worldly experience with cars and computers and women, had a *rumspringa* mind-set that meant he'd never settle down, much less join the Old Order and marry an Amish woman.

"Loretta, I'm so glad you and Drew decided to live here," Rosalyn confided. "I can't imagine how lonely I'd be for your company if it were just Dat and me rattling around in this house like two dried peas in a shoebox."

"Rosalyn, you are nothing like a dried pea!" her sister shot back. "Drew will stand by his offer to provide you a room, come the day we find a place of our own. So don't go worrying about being stuck with Dat."

Rosalyn heard the hint of a move in Loretta's future, but she let it go by. "*Jah*, Asa has said the same thing."

"Don't go thinking you'll never marry, either," Loretta insisted, planting a fist on her hip. "God hasn't found you the right man yet, but He will. Keep the faith, sister."

Rosalyn's spirits lifted, even though she didn't fully believe she would ever marry. "You've got a *gut* point. When all else fails—when we lose everything and everyone precious to us—we still have our faith. Jesus will never forsake us."

Loretta tweaked Rosalyn's nose and started for the door. "That's not what I meant, but you're smiling again so I'm not going to disagree with your statement about faith. *Gut* night, Rosalyn. Sleep tight."

"You, too, Loretta," she said, even though *sleep* probably wasn't what her sister had in mind when she and Drew closed their bedroom door.

And isn't it nice that they're so happy together? Rosalyn thought as she pulled her flannel nightgown from the drawer.

Maybe she's right. Maybe God's hand-picking a husband for me and He hasn't yet found one who's as wonderful—and patient and understanding—as I deserve.

It was a good thought to ponder before she went to sleep.

Chapter Ten

Marcus pulled his car into the parking lot of the bank in Morning Star on Friday morning and looked around him with interest. The sidewalks were full of shoppers, a mix of English and Plain. It gave him a sense of hope that this town, only a few miles from Willow Ridge, had a car dealership, a pizza place, a couple of clothing stores—and even a pool hall—because he'd spent his first three weeks in Missouri working way too hard. After opening a bank account, he intended to look around town and maybe drink a few beers away from the prying eyes of his kin. He also hoped to find some girls to date.

He entered the bank with a sense of accomplishment that came from having twenty-eight hundred dollars of regular pay plus another five hundred—his bonus for training all five of Wyatt's Thoroughbreds to be reliable buggy horses before the deadline they'd set. McKenzie was a strict boss, but he was fair and he'd seemed as pleased to write those checks as Marcus had been to receive them.

Opening a bank account was a big step, which implied that he intended to stick around Willow Ridge for a while. Marcus planned to pocket a chunk of cash as his reward for working hard and behaving as a responsible adult—

Well, except for shooting off your mouth in Nora's store.

"How may I help you this morning, sir?"

The sight of an attractive young woman smiling at him from her teller station seemed like a good omen—even if he noticed a diamond on her left hand. "I, um, would like to open an account—for checking and savings," he said as he approached her.

"If you'll have a seat over there," she said, gesturing at the sleek wooden desk behind him, "I'll be with you in just a moment."

Marcus noticed a coffeemaker and a tray of chocolate chip cookies on a credenza near the entry. As he helped himself to breakfast, a gust of wintry wind came through the door along with a middle-aged man whose broad-brimmed black hat and austere black coat—and a dark beard with hints of silver—announced that he was Amish. The man strode toward the teller windows as though he had urgent—or secretive—business to conduct.

"How can I help you this morning, Mr. Riehl?" the other teller asked him.

Marcus blinked. *Mr. Riehl*? Could this be the Cornelius Riehl Luke and Ben had been discussing at Thanksgiving? The fact that he was carrying a thick leather briefcase seemed intriguing. As he took his seat at the desk, Marcus reminded himself not to let his imagination run amok. But the man bore a definite resemblance to Rosalyn, especially around his brown eyes and in the shape of his face, so he probably was her father—

"Got a deposit—for my business account," Cornelius replied as he unfastened the briefcase.

Marcus sipped his coffee, trying not to be too obvious about observing Riehl's transaction. He jammed a second cookie into his mouth, suddenly very hungry for the walnut chunks and gooey chocolate chips.

His teller sat down on the other side of the desk. "My

name's Carolyn, and I'm happy to be helping you set up your accounts, Mister—?"

"Marcus Hooley," he replied. He noticed how Riehl turned slightly to stare at him, as though he recognized his name.

"I'll need your driver's license or another form of photo ID, please," Carolyn said as she opened a document on her computer. "Won't take me but a few minutes to get this information filled in."

"Yeah, sure." As he took his wallet from his back pocket, Marcus wondered what sort of photo ID Cornelius had provided, as most Amish men of his age strenuously objected to having their pictures taken. "And here are the checks I want to deposit to open my accounts. I'd like to set up online access, too," he added. Wyatt had suggested online payments as a nearly painless way to begin repaying his credit card debt—and Marcus liked the sound of the *painless* part.

"I'll do that for you, yes. You'll be receiving an ATM card, too." Carolyn smiled at him as she took the checks and his license. While her fingers tapped the keyboard, Marcus glanced toward Cornelius again. Were his eyes fooling him, or had Rosalyn's father just placed three bundles of bills on the counter? Why would a clockmaker be handing over money in paper wrappers instead of checks or loose cash?

"Is this your current address, Marcus?"

The teller's question drew him away from his spying. He focused on Carolyn, answering her questions and explaining about how his new job had brought him to Missouri. He wasn't sure why, but he spoke just loudly enough that Cornelius could hear him, if he cared to listen—

Not that you intend to have anything to do with his daughter Rosalyn, he assured himself. *But if Cornelius is up to something—as Ben and Luke seem to think he is—maybe he'll realize I've been a witness to some of it.*

As Carolyn continued typing, Marcus couldn't let this

opportunity pass him by. He smiled, extending his hand as he approached the teller station. "Say, are you the Riehl who runs the clock shop in Willow Ridge?" he asked breezily. "I'm Marcus Hooley, your new neighbor at—"

"What if I am?" Cornelius snapped. "That's really none of your concern, is it?"

Marcus blinked. Riehl's glare and tone of voice were intended to shut him up—to cut him down to size—yet before Cornelius turned his attention back to the teller who was helping him, Marcus noticed a nervous paleness around his eyes. For a brief moment, Cornelius looked like a trapped animal.

You shouldn't have pushed his buttons, Marcus chided himself as he returned to his chair. *He's the kind of guy who'll take out his frustrations on his family . . . on Rosalyn.*

Marcus wasn't surprised that Rosalyn's father strode out the door a few moments later without making further eye contact with him. When Carolyn had completed the paperwork for his account and he'd signed on all the lines, he left the bank with a couple hundred dollars in his wallet. He felt very responsible, having money in the bank for the first time—not to mention a glimmer of hope that he could pay down the credit card debt he'd accumulated over the past couple of years.

When Marcus stepped outside, the aroma of pizza overwhelmed him. Thoughts of wolfing down a pizza with a pitcher of beer lured him toward the pizza place a few doors down from the bank, yet his steps slowed on the sidewalk. He became sadly aware that he'd left his drinking buddies behind, and that a pizza fresh from the oven tasted even better with friends.

He entered the restaurant anyway, and ordered a house-special pizza with five kinds of meat to take home with him. While he waited for it, Marcus sipped a cola—because the restaurant was a family-oriented place that didn't serve alcohol—and let his thoughts wander. Rosalyn's face popped into his mind and he imagined her sitting across the table from him, smiling shyly as she shared his pizza and his company.

That'll never happen, the voice in Marcus's mind mocked him. *She's not your type—and you're not the sort of fellow she'd be seen with, either.*

Marcus frowned. It had never occurred to him that a young woman might not enjoy his company or that her standards might exclude him.

It's a religious difference, not a personality conflict, he reassured himself as he finished his drink. *Rosalyn's been raised by a strict father—and Deacon Cornelius would no doubt warn her away from you because you're a threat to her reputation. Too dangerous.*

Marcus laughed so loudly that the folks at the next table looked over at him. Maybe he should cultivate a relationship with Rosalyn just to irritate her old man, and to prove he could entice her to set aside her straitlaced Old Order rigidity.

The thought made him pause. When he saw Rosalyn's face in his mind again, Marcus sensed her feelings would be deeply hurt if he befriended her for either of those reasons—and when had he ever worried about such a thing?

Wouldn't it be nice to see her smile—to hear her laugh? She's probably every bit as lonely as you are.

Marcus quickly tipped his glass and began crunching ice between his teeth—anything to dispel the notion that he'd lost his touch when it came to attracting female companionship. He'd thought about asking Savilla for a date—and it would be a real coup if Rebecca would go out with him—yet winning Rosalyn's affection seemed like the ultimate challenge . . . a way to pass the gray winter days and boring nights that stretched ahead of him.

That's the ticket. You'd be doing Rosalyn a favor, getting her out from under her father's thumb once in a while.

"House special ready for Hooley!" the man behind the counter called out.

Marcus paid his tab, his good mood restored. With a hot pizza box in his hand, he headed back to his bare-bones apartment to spend Friday afternoon planning his conquest of Rosalyn Riehl.

At their noon meal, Rosalyn couldn't miss Dat's scowl or the way he plowed through his hamburger and hash brown casserole so fast that he couldn't possibly taste it. As she and Loretta exchanged a quiet sigh, she was glad Mamm's empty place acted as a buffer between her and their moody father, and she was grateful that Drew sat across the table from them. She couldn't imagine how unpleasant her life would be had the newlyweds left her to deal with Dat alone.

When Dat tossed his fork onto his empty plate, its clatter rang in the kitchen. "This morning I saw that infernal horse trainer McKenzie hired—and I want you girls to steer clear of him!" he added as his eyebrows rose ominously. "The Hooley family is taking over this whole town, and this one's the worst of the lot."

Rosalyn wondered what had led to Dat's vehement statement. He'd left for a while this morning without mentioning where he'd gone—but he'd apparently run across Marcus.

"What don't you like about Marcus?" Drew asked as he took a second helping of casserole. "When Wyatt came into the shop yesterday, he had nothing but *gut* things to say about his new employee."

"Such as?" Dat fired back.

Drew took his time squirting ketchup on his casserole. "Well, Marcus may be full of swagger, but he's made *gut* on all his claims about being a fine horse trainer," he replied calmly. "Not only has he retrained five retired Thorough-breds to be excellent buggy horses—which have already sold for top dollar—but he's also taught Wyatt to drive a rig—"

"*Jah*, Hooley thinks he's *somebody*, all right," Dat groused. "McKenzie must be paying him too much, the way he was flashing his checks while the bank clerk was opening an account for him."

Rosalyn pondered this information, focusing on her food so Dat wouldn't suspect her interest in their topic of conver-sation. She felt a new respect for Marcus because he was putting money in the bank—and she was glad Drew was de-fending him, because Dat would be on her like a duck on a bug if *she* spoke up in Marcus's behalf.

"Hooley needs to mind his own business, too," Dat con-tinued in a rising voice. "The way I hear it, he should be repaying his own considerable debts instead of—well, never mind."

Loretta cleared her throat. "Instead of what, Dat?" she asked. "From what I've seen, Marcus's behavior has im-proved a great deal since he first came to town."

"Just get dessert on the table," Dat snapped. "I'm telling you girls again to stay away from him. He's bad news. A cor-rupting influence, what with jumping the fence and living in sin before he came here."

Her father's diatribe gave Rosalyn a lot to speculate about as she scraped their plates. Why had Dat been at the bank this morning? And what had Marcus done to inspire her father's tirade against him?

After they'd eaten their cherry cobbler, Dat stomped downstairs to his shop and Drew returned to Detweiler Furniture Works across the road, leaving the kitchen peace-ful again. As Rosalyn washed the dishes while her sister dried them, they talked quietly so their father wouldn't overhear them.

"What do you suppose Marcus did that got Dat so riled up?" Loretta asked. "You'd think that as a deacon, he'd be commending Marcus for banking his paychecks."

"*Jah*, from what we saw of Marcus a few weeks ago, I wouldn't have expected him to be acting so responsibly," Rosalyn remarked under her breath. She frowned as a new idea occurred to her. "Did you know Dat had a bank account? He used to tell Mamm that he would keep track of his money rather than trust an English bank with it."

Loretta's eyes widened. "You're right. I never knew him to set foot in the bank in Roseville," she said. "Maybe that's why he clammed up and demanded dessert when I asked what Marcus had done to upset him."

"Maybe he has to have an account to order his clock parts through the mail," Rosalyn said with a shrug. She peered through the window, which was fogged from the steam coming off the dishwater. "Looks like we're in for some more snow, so I'm going out to cut some greenery and gather more pinecones for my wreaths. It gets dark so early, I don't want to wait until after supper."

"I'll bake some bread with those overripe bananas in the fruit bowl, and stir up some dough for cinnamon rolls," Loretta said. "It feels drafty in here, so it's a *gut* day to run the oven."

Rosalyn pulled the plug from the sink drain. Dat had instructed them not to touch the thermostat, to conserve the propane in the big tank outside. They weren't to burn any more wood than necessary in the upstairs fireplace, either, so the house was cold even on days when the wind wasn't blowing. As she slipped into her old barn coat and high boots, she wondered again why they seemed to be falling so short of money this winter. Dat was spending every spare moment in his shop, so why wasn't his clock income covering their expenses anymore?

When she stepped outside, Rosalyn held her face up to catch the tiny white flakes that were falling. She fetched the high-sided pull cart and a small handsaw from the shed. Rosalyn crossed the road, over to her brothers-in-law's property, where a windbreak of evergreen trees would provide the materials she needed. Several of the neighbors had told her she was welcome to trim greenery from their pine and spruce trees—said she'd be doing them a favor if she picked up the pinecones and little seed balls from the sweet gum trees. The wind was blowing harder, however, so staying close to home seemed like the best idea.

As Rosalyn trimmed sprigs of greenery, the fresh scent of pine made her inhale deeply. On a whim, she sawed off a few boughs that would be large enough to decorate the fireplace mantel and some of the windowsills. How could Dat complain that she was being extravagant by decorating the house with greenery God had provided? She and Loretta could pull out the box of fat red candles—and Mamm's Nativity set!— and have the front room and kitchen looking festive before Dat emerged from his shop to protest their decorations. Surely it couldn't be a sin to freshen the rooms with the natural scent of pine and the fragrance of the bayberry candles they'd had since before Mamm had died.

When the thought of her mother brought tears to her eyes, Rosalyn resolutely thought about something happier— and then waved at the rig that passed by with a cheerful *clip-clop, clip-clop* of the fine horse's hooves. As Bishop Tom and his wife, Nazareth, cheerfully returned her greeting, Rosalyn wondered if the beautiful bay horse might be one that Marcus had trained.

Marcus. Now there's an interesting topic to ponder.

As she gathered the pinecones from beneath the nearest trees, Rosalyn once again wondered why Dat had grown so agitated about seeing Marcus at the bank. She imagined him striding confidently inside with his paychecks, probably flirting with the teller as he opened an account . . .

The sound of a car engine made Rosalyn look up—and then suck in her breath. As though God had been listening to her thoughts, an old red car stopped at the side of the road and Marcus got out of it. The wind teased at his dark hair and made the loose plaid scarf around his neck float like a banner. He was smiling at her, the way he did in her fondest fantasies. Rosalyn suddenly felt so flummoxed she couldn't think of a word to say, so she turned and began clipping greenery again.

Why on earth would Marcus be stopping to see me? If Dat gets wind of this, he'll be angry all over again—figuring that I must've encouraged this encounter to spite him.

Chapter Eleven

Marcus stood beside his car for a moment to assess the situation. When he'd spotted Rosalyn from his apartment window, the time had seemed perfect for coming on to her. But her fear gave him pause. It wasn't his style to coerce a woman into spending time with him—he'd never had to do that. Women seemed to gravitate toward him.

Easy does it, big boy. She's as skittish as a new foal and she'll bolt if you get too close too fast. Then she'll never speak to you again.

A smile eased across his face. He walked to the evergreen beside the one Rosalyn was clipping and slipped beneath its low branches. "Is it all right if I help you, Roz?" he asked gently. "A lot of pinecones land way in near the trunk and I can reach them with my long arms—unless you don't want me to."

When she turned toward him, her wide brown eyes took up her entire face. Her black bonnet made her skin appear pale—or had she been crying?

His conscience prickled. *Only a jerk would take advantage of her when she's upset. Who knows what her life must be like, living with a man whose own daughters call him testy?*

"That—that would be very nice," Rosalyn stammered. She smoothed the front of her old barn coat as though she wished he hadn't seen her wearing such a faded, timeworn garment. "*Denki* for your help."

Marcus nodded, proceeding slowly. When he'd gathered an armful of fat, perfect pinecones, he stepped from beneath the tree to put them in her cart. "As quickly as your wreaths are selling in Nora's store, I was wondering if you'd like some help with them," he ventured carefully. "I've been making evergreen wreaths for years—and pinecone wreaths, too. Maybe if I made some basic greenery bases, you'd have more time to attach the decorative stuff."

Rosalyn's mouth dropped open and she shut it, gazing at him like a deer caught in his car's headlights. "I—I wouldn't want you to go to any trouble—"

Marcus laughed. "Trouble? I cause trouble all the time, Roz," he teased her. "Maybe some wreath bases would make amends for some of the, um, inappropriate things I've said to you."

Her brows rose. "I suppose I—I could split the money when the wreaths sell—"

"No way!" Marcus interrupted. He sensed he was getting too close for her comfort, so he ducked beneath the tree to fetch more pinecones. "I'm not doing it for the money. I just get really bored in my apartment on these long winter evenings all by myself. I'd be happy to have something to do."

When Rosalyn's eyes widened in empathy, Marcus knew he'd snagged her. He waited patiently for her to respond, knowing he'd proposed a win-win situation with no apparent strings attached.

"I had no idea you liked to make wreaths, Marcus," she said with a tremulous smile. "Truth be told, I never dreamed Nora's customers would buy them faster than I could make them, so if you want to help me, I'd be—well, I'd be ever so grateful."

I'd be ever so grateful. Marcus swallowed so hard his Adam's apple hurt. When had a young woman ever expressed gratitude for his company or his help? Rosalyn's voice did funny things to his insides as he realized she'd strung together several words in a row instead of turning away from him.

"I have some wire and straw wreath bases at home, if you'd like to use them," she offered shyly. "I wouldn't expect you to buy supplies unless I could repay—"

"Sure," Marcus said. "I could stop by for them on my way home—or I could give you a ride—"

"Oh, that would never do!" Rosalyn's cheeks flushed with pleasure even as fear crept back into her voice. "Um, after I take this greenery home, I could put the supplies in my cart and—and leave it behind Nora's store for you."

Idiot, she's joined the church so she's not supposed to ride in your car.

Marcus quickly gathered his thoughts as he placed another armload of pinecones in her cart. "Seems silly for you to pull your cart halfway across town," he said softly. "What if I pull up in front of your place and load those wreath bases into my trunk—"

"Oh, that won't do, either," Rosalyn said with a nervous shake of her head. "Not after the way Dat's warned me against being seen with you. I mean—"

Her face flushed as though she wished she could take back her admission. Marcus had put her in an uncomfortable spot. "Ah. Your *dat*," he said softly. After all the time he'd been away from his family, the Amish word sounded odd as he pronounced it.

Rosalyn had nervously turned away—but then she faced him again. "Did you see Dat at the bank this morning?" she asked in a voice he could barely hear. "What was he doing?"

Marcus hesitated. Her question sounded oddly suspicious, coming from a young woman who'd been raised to obey her father without questioning him or his motives. From the troubled expression on her face, he surmised that Cornelius had returned from Morning Star to give Rosalyn an earful about him.

But she's still here with you. She could've gone running home, yet she's accepted your help with her wreaths and she's talking to you across the road from her house, where Cornelius could see us.

"I was opening an account when your father came in," Marcus said carefully. "I overheard the bank teller call him by name."

Rosalyn nodded, her wide-eyed gaze urging him to continue.

"He seemed to be making a deposit."

She nibbled on her lower lip, as though wondering if she should reveal anything further. Marcus found the sight of her teeth against her deep pink lip unexpectedly arresting. "Did he say anything to you?" she murmured.

Her question intrigued him. Was she checking up on her father—being nosy? Or had Cornelius's activities signaled that he was up to something she felt she had to know about? Apparently her father hadn't mentioned their very brief conversation, so Marcus decided not to tell her about it, either. What good would come of telling Rosalyn how rude—and secretive—her father had been? "Nope, just went about his business—although he did look me over as though he didn't approve of me," Marcus admitted. "Why do you ask?"

When Rosalyn turned away, as though wishing she hadn't brought up the subject, he kicked himself for asking her such a blunt question. She grabbed the handle of her cart and pulled it away from the windbreak, toward a trio of evergreen trees that grew at the side of the Detweiler Furniture Works shop.

Marcus followed her, wondering how he'd managed to botch their conversation—and feeling sorry that he had. Again he wondered about the atmosphere at the Riehl house, and what Cornelius must've said about seeing him at the bank this morning. His reputation had improved a lot since he'd come to Willow Ridge and trained those Thoroughbreds, so he felt compelled to pursue a meaningful dialog with Rosalyn. Wyatt had given him the weekend off, and a lot of unstructured hours loomed ahead of him . . . time he would spend alone, because McKenzie would most likely be with Rebecca.

"Roz, I'm sorry I've made you uncomfortable again," he said as he bent beside her to pick up more pinecones. "Can you forgive me for being so insensitive?" It was a line he'd used with great success on his previous girlfriends, to soften them up after he'd done something stupid.

Rosalyn, however, straightened and looked right through him. "Puh," she said lightly. "You *love* making me uncomfortable, Marcus. But I can forgive you, *jah*, because you're a kid and you're inexperienced with women who expect—well, why should I expect anything of you?" she asked with a shrug. "You've jumped the fence and left the Amish faith, so you can never be anything more than an acquaintance to me."

Was she teasing him? Or was she putting him down in no uncertain terms—calling him a *kid* and dismissing anything more than a casual relationship? *And why does that make you angry . . . and ashamed?*

"But if you'd still like to make wreath bases for me, I'd welcome your help, Marcus," Rosalyn continued with a shy smile.

He suddenly realized that the tables had turned, that Rosalyn had taken control of their conversation—and their relationship—by *allowing* him to work for her.

Marcus blinked. He'd had no trouble attracting older, more sophisticated women who'd considered him their equal—at least until they'd caught him using their credit cards. Yet this shy mouse of an Amish *maidel* had smacked him down and then agreed to let him help her. If she weren't acting so nervous, Marcus would've believed Rosalyn was manipulating the situation . . . the way he had intended to manipulate this not-so-coincidental meeting with her.

"What if I leave your share of the greenery in my cart and

park it behind Zook's Market in a little while?" Rosalyn asked pensively. "I have to pick up a few things there anyway, so it'll be no trouble."

"All right, that'll work." Marcus nodded in agreement, although he felt strangely disappointed that he wouldn't be spending any more time with her once they finished gathering materials. "When I've finished the wreath bases, I can take them to Nora's store for you."

Rosalyn's sudden smile lit up her face, and for a few moments she appeared much younger and more carefree—maybe even glad to be spending time with him. "That'll be just fine. It—it's awfully nice of you to help me this way, Marcus," she said happily. "I think Dat's all wrong about you. You put on a show, as though you're one tough customer, but inside you're as soft and sweet as a cream puff."

As though she'd embarrassed herself with that statement, Rosalyn grabbed the handle of her cart and moved away from him. She stood stock-still for several moments, wistfully gazing into the picture window of the Detweiler brothers' furniture shop.

She appeared so caught up, like a child longing for a Christmas gift, that Marcus's curiosity got the best of him. He approached the shop carefully, so as not to frighten her again, and peered through the window of the Detweilers' shop. He saw an assortment of rocking chairs, desks, and other pieces Asa and Drew had lovingly restored, but it was the old sleigh that caught his eye. The wood had been refinished so the carving around the curved seat glimmered in the afternoon light. The sleigh's padded seat was in bad shape—but the piece of deep red velvet fabric folded over it suggested that Drew would be reupholstering it soon.

"I haven't ridden in a sleigh in years," Rosalyn said with a sigh. "After Mamm passed on, Dat got rid of ours. Said he could never drive a sleigh again, because it wouldn't be the same without her sitting beside him."

Marcus's heart thudded in his chest. He sensed Rosalyn had just revealed part of the secret behind Cornelius Riehl's harsh demeanor, and—with a poignant tone no words could convey—she had also expressed her deep loneliness and the way she still missed her mother.

His heart went out to her. Marcus knew a lot about loneliness, even though he'd been the one to take leave of his family, his home, and the faith he'd grown up in. "*Jah*, there's nothing like the jingle of sleigh bells and the rush of the wind as you glide across the snow," he whispered.

Rosalyn blinked, as though he'd interrupted her reverie. "Well, then," she said, glancing hastily at the load of greenery and pinecones in her cart. "Dwelling on the past won't bring Mamm back—and it won't get my wreaths made, either. I'll head home, and then I'll pull the cart over to the market. *Denki* again for offering to help me, Marcus."

He watched her cross the road, treading carefully in the snow that was beginning to make the blacktop slippery. Her sadness touched him. Once again he had the overwhelming urge to make Rosalyn smile—or better yet, *laugh*.

When she disappeared around the back of the white Riehl house with her cart, Marcus stepped inside the shop for a closer look at the sleigh. It was old—*vintage*, in current terms—and its high curved seat and carving told him it was too decorative to have been made by an Amish craftsman. It appeared sturdy and sleek, however. The wood glowed and the runners had been restored, as well.

What girl can resist a ride in a sleigh? Once you get her out of town—out from under her dat*'s shadow—you can get to know Rosalyn for who she is . . . and she can figure out that you're not such a bad apple after all.*

One of the Detweiler brothers approached him, carrying a tray of upholstery tacks and a hammer. "How can I help you, Marcus? Welcome to our shop!"

"I'll take this sleigh when you've finished it," Marcus replied in a rush. "I hope you haven't already sold it!"

It was a crazy idea. Why did he want a sleigh, when he no longer owned a horse to pull it? And why did he care about making Rosalyn smile, when she'd told him in no uncertain terms that he didn't stand a chance with her—that she was forbidden to spend time with him?

But Marcus couldn't back down. In his mind, she was already sitting beside him beneath a blanket as they went gliding across the snowy fields on a moonlit night.

"It's a beauty," Detweiler agreed with a smile. "And now it's yours."

After Marcus paid a deposit on the sleigh, he chatted for a few minutes while Drew began tacking the red velvet upholstery on the seat. When he stepped outside, he felt ten feet tall and eager to see Rosalyn's reaction when he invited her for a sleigh ride—but he stopped short. The sea-green sedan he'd seen a few times since he'd left Pennsylvania sat idling alongside his car, as though the driver might be waiting for him.

When Marcus broke into a jog, the car shot down the road, picking up speed as it passed him. "Hey, wait!" he called after it. "*Talk* to me, you—"

The sedan's tires squealed as it turned onto the county blacktop, heading in the direction of the mill and the McKenzie place.

By the time he reached his car, Marcus was thoroughly spooked. As far as he could tell, nothing was missing—he didn't think the sedan's driver had gotten out—but he couldn't shake his suspicion that somebody was following him. Considering some of the stunts he'd pulled before he came to Missouri, whoever was checking him out might find plenty of dirt on him.

Is this Sheriff Banks's way of letting you know you're being watched?

Marcus didn't think so. Clyde Banks impressed him as a sheriff who would do his surveillance work in his marked county cruiser rather than sneaking around in such an odd-colored car. And the sheriff would've spoken to him rather than speeding away. Besides, Marcus had spotted the sedan before he'd even met Clyde Banks.

Did Wyatt hire an investigator after that first phone call?

He doubted it. And even if McKenzie had been checking him out, he would've called off a detective by now.

So what did this incident mean?

It means the car and its driver have been tailing you—it's no coincidence, as you assumed before.

Marcus lowered himself into his car and slapped the steering wheel. He should've gotten the sedan's license plate number—should've told Wyatt earlier that he was being tailed, so his new boss wouldn't think Marcus was hiding something.

Shoulda, woulda, coulda, his thoughts taunted him as he started the car. He'd spent the past few years avoiding the responsibility those words implied, and now he sensed the proverbial pigeons were coming home to roost . . . or to crap on his head.

As Marcus headed for the McKenzie property he saw no further sign of the sea-green sedan lurking around town. It was a relief, yet it gave him the sense that he'd be constantly looking over his shoulder until he figured out why he was being followed . . . and by whom.

Chapter Twelve

As Bishop Tom, Preachers Ben and Henry, and her *dat* entered the crowded front room of Adam and Annie Mae Wagler's place to begin the Sunday service, Rosalyn felt troubled—ready to go before God, hoping He would cleanse her lonely soul. The folks seated on the pew benches around her were singing the long, slow opening hymn, but she was merely mouthing the words because her thoughts were elsewhere.

You put on a show, as though you're one tough customer, but inside you're as soft and sweet as a cream puff.

Why had she spoken such flirtatious, misleading words to Marcus on Friday? For one thing, she barely knew him—except for the unflattering things she'd heard about his English lifestyle and the way he'd used his girlfriends' credit cards. And why had she compared him to a cream puff, of all things? From what she'd seen of Marcus—and she'd indulged in plenty of secretive gazes—there was nothing at all soft about his tall, muscled body or his attitude.

"As we enter into the season of Advent, we await a Savior," Bishop Tom intoned when the singing had stopped. "Let us pray now for God's peace, which passes all understanding, that we may better prepare our hearts and minds to worship Him and welcome Him into our lives anew."

Rosalyn clasped her hands and bent forward, closing her eyes tightly. *Lord, forgive me for my foolish behavior with Marcus, and for acting as though he and I could ever be more than acquaintances*, she prayed earnestly. *Guide me along the path You would have me follow with open eyes and an obedient heart—*

The creaking of the Waglers' front door announced a latecomer. Curiosity prodded Rosalyn to peek with one eye—and she sucked in her breath.

Marcus had come to church. To his credit, he appeared sorry that he'd disrupted their prayer, yet he seemed relieved to slip into the back pew of the men's side, where he could remain mostly unnoticed.

Rosalyn's heart pounded. Why would Marcus join them in worship? Her first hopeful thought was that he intended to become active in the Old Order again—so he could court her.

Don't be silly, she chided herself as she bent her head lower and tried to pray again. *Marcus must be tired of spending his weekends alone in his apartment. Or maybe Ben and Ira have badgered him so often about leaving his family and the Amish faith that he showed up so they'd stop pestering him.*

When Dat stood up to read from the big King James Bible, Rosalyn was grateful to have something worshipful to focus on. "Our Scripture reading today is from the fortieth chapter of Isaiah, beginning with the first verse," he said, holding his finger in place as he began to read. "'Comfort ye, comfort ye my people, saith your God. Speak ye comfortably to Jerusalem, and cry unto her, that her warfare is accomplished, that her iniquity is pardoned,'" he declared in a grand, confident voice.

When Dat glanced up at the congregation, however, his expression grew tight.

Rosalyn followed his gaze and held her breath. Dat was glaring at Marcus. Some of the women shifted for a better look and the men turned around to see what had captured the deacon's attention, which brought high color into Marcus's face. He had the presence of mind to give a little wave, however.

If I were in Marcus's place I'd feel so embarrassed, I'd slip out the back way, she thought.

"Welcome, Marcus," Preacher Ben said as he rose from the preachers' bench. "It's *gut* to see you amongst us, cousin. As we begin this holy season of Advent," he continued, encompassing the entire congregation in his gaze, "let's think about what it means that Jerusalem's warfare is accomplished—or finished, as such—and that her sin has been pardoned. But first, Deacon Cornelius, we'll listen to the rest of today's Scripture, which introduces John the Baptist as the voice crying in the wilderness to prepare the way of the Lord."

With Preacher Ben standing beside him, Dat had no choice but to refocus on the large Bible he was holding.

As he began reading aloud, however, Rosalyn felt anything but focused. She tried to concentrate on the verses, but her attention wandered to the opposite side of the room. When she sneaked a peak, Marcus was leaning slightly sideways on the end of the pew bench—so he could look at *her*.

What does this mean? Rosalyn wondered with nervous hopefulness. *If he keeps gawking at me, folks will think he's interested—or that he came to church for all the wrong reasons.*

Marcus reined in his wayward thoughts about Rosalyn, who appeared sweet and demure as she sat across the room among the women. He told himself to pay attention as Ben began the first sermon—which might last half an hour or more, even though it was traditionally the shorter sermon of the two he would have to endure. Such long-winded preaching was only one of the reasons Marcus had stopped attending church services, but he set aside his objections. If he was to become any more than Rosalyn's acquaintance—if she was going to take him seriously—he had to make a sincere effort to become a part of her world.

"As we consider today's Scripture, think on this," Ben said in a clear, resonant voice. "If God declared that Jerusalem's war and bloodshed were over, and that her sin had been forgiven, how easily can He free us from the turmoil we carry around inside us? Or the turmoil we cause with our careless words and deeds?"

Marcus noticed the men in front of him nodding comfortably. The women across the room were gazing raptly at Preacher Ben, hanging on his every word as though they had absolute faith that he stood before them as God's own spokesman.

"But for God's peace to prevail, we have to do our part—and that's the catch," Ben added earnestly. His face was alight with conviction, and his shining hazel eyes conveyed his utmost sincerity as he addressed his friends and family. "First we must listen for His voice until we truly hear it, and then we must *believe* that His peace and forgiveness can be ours," Ben added as he held everyone's gaze. "And then we must give up the sinful ways and thoughts that keep us from attaining the peace God's trying to grant us."

Marcus sat spellbound. This sermon was a far cry from the hellfire and damnation the preachers and bishop in his home church had expounded upon as he was growing up. The idea that God was benevolent, wanting to bestow peace and forgiveness—to somebody such as he—came as a huge revelation. And these stirring words came from the cousin who'd been born under a wandering star—a man who'd had the older Hooley generation in Pennsylvania shaking their heads.

The way Marcus recalled it from his childhood, Ben had

joined the Old Order when he was around twenty-five, but he'd roamed the countryside in a farrier wagon for nearly ten years, until he'd happened upon Willow Ridge and found Miriam Lantz, a widow. It was unheard of for a Hooley male—or any Amish man—to remain single and unsettled for so long, yet now Ben was married, with a baby, and God had chosen him as a preacher for this district.

Maybe there's hope for me, no matter what I've done, Marcus thought. Did he dare believe that God had led him to work for Wyatt McKenzie as a way to resolve his credit problem and find a fresh start? Had he made this last-chance trip to Willow Ridge not realizing that God had bigger plans than rebellious Marcus Hooley could possibly conceive? He sat taller, listening closely to his cousin and the good news he preached.

"Sometimes we can't believe that God will really forgive us," Ben continued, "so we don't come forward in confession, even though we know our secrets and our guilt are eating away at our well-being."

Marcus blinked. It had been a long time since he'd even prayed, much less confessed anything to God. And the reappearance of that sea-green sedan certainly had him thinking about his secrets, lies, and cheating ways.

"And sometimes," his cousin went on in a sharper tone, "we don't *seek* God's forgiveness—don't even consider confessing—because we foolishly believe that we *won't get caught.*"

Marcus squirmed, nailed by the words Ben had chosen to emphasize.

An ominous, airless silence filled the crowded room. A few folks glanced down at their laps, as though they wondered if Preacher Ben had somehow discovered their secret sins and was preaching directly to *them*. When

Marcus noticed Cornelius Riehl's pinched expression and pale face, however, his ongoing suspicions were confirmed.

The deacon of Willow Ridge was up to his eyeballs in guilt.

Marcus suddenly realized that Rosalyn's father resented him because he had indeed seen something at the bank that Cornelius wanted to keep hidden.

And what if that odd Wi-Fi network you noticed in Nora's store—Reel Money—is tied in with this questionable situation?

Reel money . . . Riehl money? Marcus frowned. It was one thing for Nora, as a Mennonite, to have Internet access in her shop, but an Old Order Amish deacon would be vehemently opposed to the presence of a worldly Wi-Fi connection—or even a computer—in his home.

All the more reason for you to spend time with Rosalyn as a way to ferret out what her dad's up to—so you can protect her when the truth hits the fan. What if there's a lot of money—real money—going to places it shouldn't?

Chapter Thirteen

Tuesday afternoon Wyatt checked the monitor of his security system, watching the views on the screen change every few seconds, but he wasn't the least bit concerned about an intruder—he was just fidgeting while he waited for Rebecca to arrive. The interior of the empty Percheron barn appeared peaceful, with sunlight pouring through a window and illuminating tiny motes of dust in the air.

When the camera out in the paddock kicked in, Wyatt watched Marcus putting one of the young Percheron geldings through its paces. Although the black horse hadn't yet reached its full growth, Marcus looked like a child beside it—yet when the gelding snorted and tossed its head, frisky and eager to play, the lanky trainer peered into its eyes and patiently said something to bring the horse back into focus. The Percheron continued circling the paddock then, its head held high and a disciplined spring in its step as it pulled a wagon loaded with hay.

Magic. Marcus Hooley possessed a power over horses that humbled Wyatt, even after he'd spent most of his forty years working with temperamental Thoroughbreds.

The shot from the next camera showed Wyatt the view he'd been waiting for: Rebecca's car was coming up the lane, passing between the solid white gateposts that marked the entry to his property. He switched off the monitor. He glanced at the table, where two places were set side by side so they could enjoy the view while they ate supper. Rebecca had been coming to his place for cozy, casual meals for months now, yet Wyatt felt oddly flustered on this wintry afternoon.

It was time to speak up, to pop the question. He and Rebecca had acknowledged their love for each other and it was time for him to move their relationship forward, but he felt as jittery as a kid asking a girl out for the very first time.

Rebecca jabbed playfully at the doorbell before opening the door, knowing it made him laugh. She entered with a gust of wind that blew a few snowflakes inside. They sparkled like tiny diamond chips in the halo the sunshine created around her shiny brown hair—yet another sign that a diamond ring was in order.

"Sorry I'm running late," she said, leaning against the door to shut it. "It was a day when half of my online clients wanted updates to their sites, like *yesterday*, and the other half called me to chat as though they—and I—had nothing else to do at three o'clock this afternoon. Sheesh!"

Wyatt smiled, drinking in the sight of Rebecca's wind-ripened cheeks as the cadence and timbre of her voice brought his quiet home to life. She was wearing an old red-and-black plaid hunting jacket that had belonged to her dad. It was baggy and worn, but she loved it and Wyatt thought it suited her perfectly. He kissed her, lightly at first, until she moaned her approval—and prodded him with the foil-covered casserole in her hands.

"This needs to be in the oven for about an hour," she said. "I put everything together last night, but didn't get home in time to bake it."

"Sounds like you could use some time to distance yourself from your work before you eat anyway," Wyatt suggested. "Three fifty for the oven setting?"

"That'll work."

Wyatt carried the cool glass casserole into the kitchen, his thoughts racing. Should he invite her to relax on the couch with a glass of wine? Or offer to massage her shoulders and neck? Or—

"Let's take a walk," Rebecca suggested. "The air feels supercharged with an energy I can't put my finger on— maybe a change in the atmosphere before we get a snowstorm. I just don't feel like sitting still."

Wyatt's eyebrows rose as he set the oven temperature. Could she sense his restless emotions? Was she feeling the same nervous anticipation he was, wondering if it was time to formally commit?

"Perfect," he said. "After a day of staring at the computer, hunting for more Belgian and Percheron yearlings, I could use the fresh air."

He slipped the glass dish into the oven, then shrugged into the hooded sweatshirt and lined denim jacket hanging on the coat tree—the outerwear he usually worked in. Rebecca wrapped her arm around his waist before burying her face in his coat.

"Mm. You smell like horses."

Wyatt laughed as he opened the door. "Is that good or bad? If you want me to change into—"

"Don't change a thing," she insisted as she gazed at him. "I like the rich scent of the leather jacket you wear when we go out, but to me, these work clothes smell like *you*, Wyatt. The you that gets his hands dirty and takes care of business."

He swallowed hard. Rebecca's blue eyes shone as bright as a summertime sky. "Thank you, dear heart," he said, guiding her outside. "I've known wealthy women who turned up their noses at the scent of work. That will never be you."

"Maybe because I'll never be wealthy," she shot back.

We'll see about that, Wyatt thought when she tucked her gloved hand into his. Plenty of men in his position would insist upon prenuptial agreements that limited a wife's access to bank and brokerage accounts, but he wouldn't be one of them. He trusted Rebecca implicitly. Any woman who could gaze up at a sky that was gray with impending snow and smile with such total delight would be his partner in sunshine and shadow, for the long haul.

"I'm glad you've tamed Marcus and that he's working out so well for you," she said, gesturing toward the paddock. "That big black horse seems to be totally under his control."

Wyatt stood close behind her on the deck. "I can't take credit for his attitude adjustment. I think he just needed some structure—and a paycheck with a few expectations attached to it," he remarked. "I suspect a young woman has caught his eye. Saw him pulling a cartload of evergreen clippings to his apartment the other day, and he transformed them into wreaths and took them to Nora's store."

"Hmm," she said, making her way to the deck stairs. "Who knew Marcus was the crafty sort? Or that he'd take a shine to Rosalyn Riehl? She's the shyest of the Riehl sisters. Shall we stroll?"

Snowflakes tingled on Wyatt's cheeks as the wind picked up, but he didn't feel the least bit cold. Rebecca was holding his hand, appearing invigorated by the winter weather as they crossed the snow-covered yard. It seemed the perfect moment to propose, yet their companionable silence was a balm to his soul.

"Your land is so rugged and beautiful, Wyatt," she said. "I'm glad you left so many trees when you built your barns. Now that Marcus is proving to be worth his salt, it's as though the last piece has fallen into place—like your dream has come true."

I need you to make this dream complete, he nearly blurted. Rebecca had created the perfect opening, yet all of his experience—with women, and with life in general—hadn't prepared him for asking the important question that burned in his heart.

What if she says no? What if she laughs in your face? She can whittle you down to size with one cutting remark—

Wyatt reminded himself that Rebecca was as deeply in love as he was. And the longer he waited to say something, the more she'd wonder why he wasn't keeping up his end of their conversation. Why was this so difficult? He'd spoken his mind with her since the day he'd met her.

He inhaled deeply, hoping he didn't sound painfully adolescent. "This—this dream I've been creating would be complete if you'd marry me, Rebecca," he said in a rush. "Will you be my wife? *Please*?"

Rebecca froze beside him. When she stared at him for several impossibly long moments, Wyatt wondered if the *please* had set the wrong tone—as though he'd been begging. *Why doesn't she say something? Did I sound desperate or—did I put in a wrong word without realizing—*

Rebecca grabbed him around the waist, sobbing—which worried him even more, because she was always in control of her emotions. He gingerly wrapped his arms around her shuddering shoulders, awaiting the worst when she finally found words for him. When he'd envisioned this moment, he'd anticipated a widening of her blue eyes, or perhaps a sucking in of her breath. But never a meltdown.

"Oh, Wyatt," she finally managed. She was still sniffling, her face buried in his barn coat. "I've dreamed of this moment—of being asked—since I was a schoolgirl reading romance novels. I always pictured how it would be—"

He braced himself, waiting for the other shoe to drop. He must've said something wrong.

"—and I practiced writing my answer—memorized it so I would say it just right when my true love proposed to me," Rebecca continued in a quavery voice. "But I saw myself wearing a gorgeous gown in the moonlight, with the scent of roses in the air—and he was wearing a tux. I marveled that when he opened the box from the jeweler, the ring was sparkly and splendid, and somehow he'd known the right size and the exact style I wanted."

Wyatt's heart sank. He'd done enough ring shopping to realize that the jewelry stores in Morning Star didn't carry the sort of diamond he wanted to give Rebecca. Why hadn't he waited until they were in the candlelit corner of a romantic restaurant? What sort of man proposed on a cold, windy day when neither of them was dressed for such an important moment?

Rebecca mopped her face with the sleeve of her plaid jacket. "After living among society women, you must be really disappointed that I'm such a plain Jane—that I don't wear dresses or makeup or—"

Wyatt's jaw dropped. He'd always found Rebecca's natural beauty refreshing, and he was surprised to hear her being so critical of her appearance.

"But I didn't ask any of those society types to marry me," he pointed out gently. "I love you for being you, Rebecca—and I'm glad you haven't redesigned yourself because you thought I wanted a different sort of woman. I'm glad I waited for you to come into my life . . . waited for *your* answer to the most important question a man can ask."

Rebecca's mouth formed an O. She started shaking again, but this time it was with quiet laughter. "You must think I'm a mindless twit, babbling on like a romance junkie or a— *yes*, Wyatt! Yes, I'll marry you."

Joy flooded his soul. Rebecca had agreed to be his wife! He grabbed her up in an exuberant embrace, laughing and kissing her and exulting in her equally enthusiastic response. Then he held her close, savoring the beat of her pulse and the white vapors of breath that rose around them in the crisp, cold air.

"I *have* looked for rings," Wyatt said apologetically, "and the jewelers nearby don't carry anything I want to give you, Rebecca. Maybe we should go to Kansas City, or St. Louis, or—"

"Oh, Wyatt." Rebecca's face glowed as she gazed at him in the fading daylight. "My romantic fantasy belonged to a starry-eyed girl who fell for gushy movies and fairy tales. Now that I've lived in Willow Ridge among Plain folks, I know a strong marriage has nothing to do with a ring. I'd feel really out of place going to Mamma's with a big diamond on my hand."

Wyatt's eyes widened. "You would?"

Rebecca shrugged. "Nobody I spend time with wears jewelry—except my English dad, and his ring's a simple gold band."

Wyatt considered this for a moment. Money was no object, so if Rebecca wanted a big, showy diamond he'd be delighted to have one specially designed for her . . . but maybe that was *his* fantasy. He'd always figured on having a wife to be seen with at racing events and social gatherings—but he'd left that lifestyle behind. Maybe he needed to rethink his vision of a trophy wife, because Rebecca would never be that sort of woman.

"But if you want to exchange rings, that's perfectly all right, Wyatt. We both grew up with that tradition, after all."

Rebecca's offer brought him out of his thoughts. He'd always admired her open-minded way of looking at life—it was just one more reason he loved her. Wyatt smiled as an idea occurred to him, thinking the fading daylight and falling temperature were good reasons to enjoy a warm dinner as they continued this conversation.

"I occasionally wear a ring that belonged to my adoptive dad, but when I'm working I prefer not to have anything on my hands," he mused aloud. "My sister kept our adoptive mother's rings, but she never had them resized because they're understated and no longer stylish. As you might recall, Vanessa has a flare for flashier accessories."

Rebecca laughed. "How can I forget the day I pitched a cobbler in your face because I thought Vanessa was your lover? Lucky for me, she understood that my jealousy meant I was serious about you."

Wyatt gently removed one of her gloves to study her hand. It was slender yet strong, with clipped fingernails devoid of polish. "What if I ask Vanessa to bring our mom's rings someday soon?" he asked softly. "My two favorites belonged to our grandmother, an opal and a garnet, both set in gold bands so narrow you barely see them beneath the stones. And if you don't want them, I'm fine with it."

Rebecca's smile softened. "I like that idea," she murmured. "It would *mean* something to wear a ring that belonged to your adoptive mom or your grandmother. My adoptive mom wore a plain band that matched Dad's, and we buried her in it."

Feeling very much in love, Wyatt slipped his arm around Rebecca's shoulders. "Let's go in and enjoy that casserole and we'll call Vanessa," he suggested. "She'll be delighted that I finally popped the question."

"We'll need to tell Mamma and Ben and my sisters—and Dad—our big news, too," she said as she walked alongside him. "All of a sudden, we have plans to make! And dates to set! And decisions to make about where we'll live and—well, life just got a whole lot more exciting, didn't it?"

Wyatt smiled. "Who knew what I'd be getting myself into when I sought you out to design my new website!"

"You were a big surprise, Wyatt," Rebecca replied fondly. "Only God could bring a man like you my way."

He stopped in the middle of the snow-covered yard to kiss her, because sometimes her insights left him absolutely speechless.

Chapter Fourteen

Wednesday morning, Nora eagerly awaited Rosalyn's arrival at the store. She found herself speculating as she set a dozen evergreen and pinecone wreaths on the table where Rosalyn had been working while customers watched her— they'd often purchased her wreaths before the sealant was even dry. Although Loretta was much more outgoing and comfortable dealing with the public than her older sister, Rosalyn was an invaluable employee, as well—dependable and mature, determined to learn about merchandising and to overcome her shyness around English folks.

The bell jingled and Rosalyn entered, quickly shutting the door against the snow that was blowing in. "*Gut* morning, Nora," she called out as she removed her black wraps. "Do you suppose we'll have many shoppers today, what with all this snow?"

"We won't know the answer to that question until the day goes along, dear!" Nora replied. "Sometimes bad weather keeps customers at home, and sometimes they'd rather shop than be cooped up all day."

"Ah. I hadn't thought of it that way. It's a *gut* thing Ira and Luke are shoveling the driveway and parking lot."

Rosalyn's sigh made Nora look more closely at her employee. Judging from her downcast eyes and somber air,

Cornelius had been in a foul mood before she'd left home. When Rosalyn passed the worktable on her way to the office, however, her eyes widened. "My word, where did all these wreaths come from?"

Nora laughed. "I think you know," she teased. "I was surprised to learn he had such a way with greenery and pinecones—and to catch a hint of *romance* in the air when he dropped them off for you."

Rosalyn gaped. "Marcus made all of these? I—I didn't leave him nearly enough evergreen cuttings to make so many."

Nora slipped her arm around Rosalyn's shoulders. "I suspect he enjoyed having something to do—and I sensed he was making them to please you more than to help you," she confided. "I could be wrong, but I think Marcus is coming around. Growing up."

Rosalyn looked away. "That's all well and *gut*, but Dat was on another tirade this morning," she said softly. "He was saying I should be grateful to have a home and a purpose—meaning that I should devote my life to looking after *him* rather than getting ideas about marriage. Especially with a bad apple like Marcus, he said."

Nora frowned. "Why does your *dat* say such harsh things about Marcus? I doubt the two of them have spent much time in the same room, let alone—"

"Marcus came to church on Sunday," Rosalyn explained with a shake of her head. "Dat accused me of getting all moony-eyed when he showed up. He believes Marcus wasn't sincere about worshipping God—that he had a hidden agenda for being there."

Nora's eyes widened. When Marcus had delivered the wreath bases, he'd mentioned how pale and nervous Cornelius had appeared when Preacher Ben had spoken about keeping secrets and not getting caught. She hadn't told Marcus that she and Drew had spotted the deacon entering a casino in September—just as she'd kept Marcus's suspicions about Cornelius's visit to the bank to herself. It sounded as if Rosalyn's *dat* was afraid of what Marcus knew, and he was lashing out at Rosalyn to keep her away from the handsome young man.

Life would be easier for a lot of people if you'd just come clean, Cornelius, she thought. Not that she could see him confessing of his own free will.

Nora set aside her dark thoughts as she watched Rosalyn at the worktable. Tenderly she lifted each wreath and looked it over, nodding her approval. "Marcus was right about being an old hand at this," she said. "Maybe *he* should be the one working in your store instead of me, considering—"

"Don't go thinking that way!" Nora joined Rosalyn at the table to reassure her. "You're doing a beautiful job of waiting on customers—and they love your work, sweetie," she insisted. "Don't put yourself down just because your *dat* said hateful things this morning. It's *you* I want working here, Rosalyn—"

Rosalyn's sigh suggested that she had more on her mind. Nora stood quietly beside her, waiting for whatever she wanted to get off her chest.

"I've spent my entire life living by the rules, being a *gut* girl," Rosalyn said sadly. "I—I've held the family together since Mamm died—"

"*Jah*, you have," Nora agreed.

"—and I kept the checkbook balanced, at least until Dat insisted he would do it," she continued in a faraway voice. "The clothes have been laundered and the meals have been cooked, the eggs have been gathered and the garden's been tended, even as Edith and Loretta were courting and getting married."

"They couldn't ask for a more supportive, more loving sister," Nora put in gently. "You've been a model daughter, too, Rosalyn. I believe your *mamm*'s looking down on you from heaven with a pleased, proud smile on her face."

Rosalyn blinked rapidly, trying not to cry. "Why isn't that enough?" she whispered. "Is it so wrong for me to want more—like a husband and a family? Am I a bad person if I want to live somewhere other than with Dat, or—or if I just want to have some *fun*?"

Nora's heart clutched with sympathy. She couldn't imagine how lonely and desperate Rosalyn must feel, reaching the age of twenty-eight with both of her younger sisters married, and feeling she had nothing happy to look forward to. "You're not a bad person, Rosalyn—"

"And am I blind and stupid to have . . . ideas about Marcus?" Rosalyn asked sadly. "*Jah*, he did some bad things before he came here, but does that make him a bad person? Are we not to forgive him, and give him a chance to do better?"

"He *is* doing better," Nora put in quickly. "Marcus told me he'd opened a bank account and is paying down his credit card debt, with the intent of paying back what he stole from his former girlfriends, too."

Rosalyn's brown eyes widened with surprise. "He's told you all these things?"

Nora shrugged, her cheeks heating with pleasure. "He and I had a nice little chat when he brought these wreaths in," she admitted. "Sometimes folks feel they can confide in me, I guess—"

"*Jah*, like I just did."

"—but while Marcus was taking these wreaths out of his car," Nora continued quickly, "I got the impression that he thought *you* were changing, too. And I think he likes you, Rosalyn. A lot."

Was she wrong to say such a thing? Was she giving poor Rosalyn false hope? It wasn't as though she'd lied, because Marcus had been wearing a telltale grin while he'd spoken with her—much like the love-struck smile that was brightening Rosalyn's face.

Nora thought twice, but decided to reveal one more little detail. "He mentioned something about a cream puff, too."

"Oh, no! I—" Rosalyn's face turned crimson, yet she was laughing. "Marcus is anything but a cream puff in his tight jeans and leather jacket. But those clothes are all for show, you know?" she asked demurely. "He looks like he should be roaring down the road on a motorcycle, covered with tattoos, yet I suspect he's as lonely as I am. He just doesn't want to admit it."

"Not many men do," Nora said. She sensed a big improvement in Rosalyn's mood, so the jingling of the bell above the door was a good reason to turn the conversation to a lighter mood. "*Gut* morning—and thanks for braving the snow to visit our store today!" she called out to the trio of women who were shaking snow from their coats.

"When your husband's retired, you look for all sorts of excuses to get out of the house—no matter what the weather's like!" one of the ladies teased.

Nora laughed. She saw that Rosalyn was bringing spools of ribbon and other materials to her worktable. "If you're in the market for a live Christmas wreath, you'll not find any fresher than what Rosalyn's decorating today," she told the women. "And if you tell her how you'd like it customized, she can probably have it finished by the time you've done the rest of your shopping."

Rosalyn smiled gratefully at Nora and held the ladies' gazes as they approached her table. "*Jah*, I can do that! I've got all sorts of ribbon candies and shiny little balls and silk poinsettias to dress them up," she said cheerfully. "I can make you a special wreath that won't look like anyone else's."

Nora smiled. With a bit of reassurance, Rosalyn was becoming quite a salesperson.

That afternoon Marcus stood in the Simple Gifts parking lot, checking his watch, only to find that the hands hadn't moved since the last time he'd glanced at it. Should he go in to speak with Rosalyn as soon as the last car left? Or should he stay outside? He didn't want her to think he'd been hanging around like a school kid—or stalking her—yet he didn't want to embarrass her in front of Nora or the day's last customers, either.

No, it's you *who'll be embarrassed if she shuts you down, Hooley,* his thoughts taunted him. *Stay out here. Since when have you felt so nervous about asking for a date?*

He'd worn the wrong shoes for standing in the snow that was accumulating on the lot only half an hour after Luke and Ira had cleared it. He was getting cold feet in more ways than one, and his leather jacket wasn't nearly warm enough to handle the dipping temperature, so he quit waffling and stepped inside the shop.

The infernal bell above the door sounded like a fire alarm to a man who was trying not to draw attention to himself. Marcus stomped his snowy feet on the doormat, relieved to see that Rosalyn and Nora were talking with the day's final two customers as they rang up a tall stack of pottery plates and serving pieces. Rather than helping Rosalyn wrap each dish in heavy paper, he waved at her and Nora and headed to the loft as though he intended to shop.

Marcus realized immediately that the creaky wooden floor would give away his nervousness if he paced. He sat down in a handsome upholstered chair, not surprised to see Drew Detweiler listed as the consignee. From his seat, he commanded an awesome view of the floor's main level, so he watched the seamless way Nora and Rosalyn wrapped and packed each piece of pottery.

Marcus almost offered to carry the boxes to the customers' car, but he thought again. He was jumpy enough to drop a box and cause a major disruption in everyone's afternoon. Only two wreaths remained on Rosalyn's worktable, and that tickled him. Marcus hoped she'd given him extra points for gathering enough additional greenery and pinecones to complete a dozen wreath bases rather than just six—

"Marcus, what a nice surprise to find you here. How can I help you?"

He sat bolt upright. How had Rosalyn reached the loft area without his being aware of her approach? Had he been daydreaming—or had she sneaked up on him by knowing which creaky spots on the steps to avoid?

Rosalyn asked you a question, dummy. Don't act as though you've never realized how low and pleasing her voice is, or how wide and soft her brown eyes look in the shadows—

"Hey there, Roz! Guess I got so comfortable in this chair, I didn't hear you come up here," Marcus blurted with an adolescent-sounding laugh. "Just, uh—just thought I'd stop by and see how your wreaths are selling."

Rosalyn began straightening a stack of embroidered tea towels. "Thanks to you, I've had enough wreaths to stay ahead of the folks wanting to buy them," she replied graciously. "How can I ever repay you for making more of them than I gave you materials for?"

How can I ever repay you . . .

Half a dozen totally inappropriate replies raced through Marcus's mind as heat rose under his collar. She'd given him the perfect opening for the question he'd been rehearsing, hadn't she?

"How about if you join me for a sleigh ride Saturday night?" Marcus said in a rush. "There's enough snow on the ground to make it, well, *perfect,* so I was thinking—"

"A sleigh ride?" Rosalyn whispered. "Oh, Marcus. You—you have a sleigh?"

Her wide eyes and pink cheeks—the childlike wonder in her voice—stopped his heart. Hoping to regain control over his responses, Marcus rose from the chair. "I do now," he said, congratulating himself on his purchase. "And Wyatt just acquired a Percheron mare that should be perfect for pulling a sleigh!"

"I'd love to go," she murmured, glancing away. "But if you come to the house and Dat sees that I'm going out with—"

"I could pick you up right here, after you get off work on Saturday," Marcus suggested. "If you tell Loretta you won't be home for supper—"

"What'll I tell Dat, though? He'll know it in a minute if I don't tell the truth—it's not like I ever go anywhere of an evening," she admitted with a shake of her head.

Marcus had anticipated this problem, and he wasn't about to let Cornelius call a halt to their date. "What if you don't tell him anything?" he suggested breezily. "Sometimes it's best to sin first and confess after the fact. It's more fun, and it saves a lot of explaining."

Rosalyn's eyes widened in disbelief, and Marcus thought he'd blown any chance of getting a positive answer. Then she covered a soft giggle with her hand, as though he'd shared his juiciest secret with her. Her face turned a girlish shade of pink and she straightened a few more towels while she considered her response.

"Just this morning I was wondering if I'd *ever* have any fun again," she said in a voice that quivered with excitement, "and now Mr. Fun himself is asking me to ride in his sleigh. And *jah*, I'm going, too! I have three days to think of a story for Dat . . . or not."

Marcus had the sudden urge to kiss her—but Nora might see them. His body was twinkling like the string of lights along the loft railing, even as he reminded himself that Rosalyn was his means of getting more information about her dubious father's secrets. "I can't wait," he said. "We'll grab some supper somewhere and ride around the countryside—"

"And laugh with the jingle of the sleigh bells, and catch

snowflakes on our tongues," Rosalyn put in wistfully. She appeared deliriously happy. "It'll be like old times, but with a—a *boyfriend*. Oh, Marcus, this is so exciting!"

Marcus held his breath. In the blink of an eye he'd gone from being forbidden fruit to becoming Rosalyn's boyfriend. She was already seeing them as a couple—in a long-term relationship—as though she'd been thinking about him in a romantic way all along. This hadn't been part of his plan at all.

When Rosalyn saw his expression, her smile faded immediately. "Oh dear," she whispered. "I'm making too big a deal out of a simple invitation to—"

"It's all right," Marcus reassured her. "Truth be told, I bought that sleigh in the Detweilers' shop mostly because you seemed so . . . well, you were yearning for something you'd lost—something you thought you'd never have again. And so was I."

Oh, now you've done it—smeared it on so thick you'll never get out of this mess without seriously hurting her feelings. What was it about being with Rosalyn that made him say things he couldn't possibly live up to?

Marcus didn't have a clue. But Rosalyn was gazing at him as though he'd hung the moon and stars.

"How did you know—well, you've read me like a book," she said in awestruck disbelief. "I never figured you for a fellow who could express such deep thoughts so perfectly, so poetically—and I thought you were too young. I was wrong about you, Marcus."

You're still wrong about me, sweetheart. And I was wrong to lead you into this predicament with pretty words, knowing you'll catch trouble from your dat. *But here we are.*

"I'm twenty-one—I'll turn twenty-two the day after Christmas," he protested with a laugh. Then he sobered. "I hope I won't get you into trouble, Roz. Maybe with you I need to confess first in hopes that I won't commit the sin—which would be a big switch for me."

Marcus sensed Cornelius would give his daughter no end of grief if he found out she planned to go riding around in a sleigh with him—or learned of their ride after the fact. If things went wrong because of their date, it wouldn't be such a big deal for him to leave town, but for Rosalyn there would be no such escape. She would always be her father's daughter.

If you leave Willow Ridge, you should take Roz with you, the voice in his head pointed out. *She'd go in a heartbeat. It's written all over her pretty face.*

Rosalyn's tremulous smile made her look years younger, heartbreakingly happy. "Dat's already lectured me about you, but I'm going sleigh riding anyway," she said in a voice he could barely hear. "For once in my life I'm going to defy my father—maybe do something that needs confessing—and I don't regret it, Marcus. I'm ready to face the consequences."

It had taken a lot of courage for Rosalyn to say such a thing, and he could only hope she would find the risk of dating him worth those consequences she'd mentioned. Maybe he should back out now, before he broke an innocent heart and did irreparable damage to a late bloomer's confidence . . .

But Marcus smiled and lightly touched her cheek. "See you Saturday afternoon, Roz. Let's go have some fun."

Chapter Fifteen

"Have a wonderful-*gut* time with Marcus tonight," Loretta whispered as Rosalyn donned her bonnet, coat, and boots on Saturday morning. "I'll let on to Dat as though I don't know a thing. I'll have to keep a big smile from my face while I'm imagining the adventure you're having."

"You're the best sister ever, Loretta," Rosalyn replied as she picked up the canvas tote with her shoes in it. "I keep telling myself this is only a one-time thing—not to be disappointed if Marcus brings me home early, or—"

"Puh! He's showing signs of better judgment just because he's asked you out," Loretta countered playfully. "Live for the moment, sister. Have a *gut* time tonight, and the days ahead will take care of themselves. And *denki* for delivering my rugs to the store."

Live for the moment. As Rosalyn stepped out the back door, her sister's words shone like a beacon on a dreary day. The sky was gray and heavy with clouds, but she refused to let the weather dampen her dancing spirits as she slogged along the slushy shoulder of the road to Nora's shop. Loretta's rugs were heavy, rolled into a bundle beneath her arm, but her spirits were so light she didn't mind. As snowflakes kissed her cheeks, Rosalyn held her face up to welcome them.

If it's too snowy tonight, Marcus will find a cozy place for us to escape the cold, she thought happily. She tingled all over with the mischief she was making, going on a date with the most daring, dangerous young man she'd ever met. She hadn't had to fabricate a story for Dat, because he'd retreated to his workshop after every meal for the past few days. He'd been so preoccupied with his clock repairs, he hadn't even protested the greenery and candles she and Loretta had arranged on the mantel and the windowsills.

After Rosalyn stepped inside the Simple Gifts shop, she removed her wraps and slipped into her shoes. "*Gut* morning, Nora!" she called out as she approached the office. "Do you figure we'll have a busy day, what with this snow?"

"With only three Saturdays left until Christmas, *jah*, I'm expecting a lot of shoppers," Nora replied. She was arranging a tray of Lena Witmer's decorated sugar cookies to go with the spiced cider that already filled the store with its delectable scent. "I'm glad you and Loretta are helping me four days a week, Rosalyn, or I'd never get all the new merchandise tagged and displayed—not that merchandise is on your mind today!" she teased. "Are you ready for your big date?"

Rosalyn nodded eagerly. It was a blessing to share her excitement with a friend who gave her such sincere encouragement. "I hope I won't be making silly mistakes because I'm all *ferhoodled* about going out with Marcus," she said. "I almost put shoes from two different pairs in my tote this morning, so I'm going to apologize right now for anything goofy I do—"

"As though you're the only one who ever gets goofy," Nora interrupted with a laugh. She reached for the rolled bundle beneath Rosalyn's arm. "I'm amazed at how many rugs and wreaths you and Loretta have made these past few weeks. You're a fine employee, Rosalyn, and I'm delighted that you're going out to have some fun with Marcus this evening."

When the bell above the door jingled, their business day began. The constant flow of shoppers made the hours fly by. Somehow Rosalyn helped customers, wrote out consignment tags, and wrapped the purchases Nora rang up without losing her focus—even though thoughts of Marcus simmered in her mind while she worked. Late in the afternoon when she was in the loft straightening the displays, something outside drew her to the window.

Rosalyn held her breath. At the McKenzie place, Marcus was in his sleigh, putting a beautiful black Percheron through its paces—urging the horse forward, stopping it with voice commands, and instructing it to back up. What a picture it made, with the red velvet sleigh seat and the ebony horse moving through the gently falling snow. Soon she'd be part of the wintry scene, caught up in the magic of a December dusk . . .

It was the driver who held her attention, however. Marcus appeared so competent and in control of the massive horse, it made her pulse thrum to watch him. When he turned the sleigh toward the road, her heart began to hammer. After a day of waiting, it was almost four thirty.

This is really happening, she thought as she quickly finished tidying the shelves. *I'm going out on a date with a fellow who could be seeing any girl he chose, yet he picked me!*

Rosalyn went downstairs and busied herself at the back of the store as the last of the customers were heading to the checkout counter. When the bell jingled, she held her breath, determined not to seem overeager for fear Marcus would think she was silly. The tread of his sturdy boots on the wooden floor made her so light-headed, she took several deep breaths so she wouldn't pass out from anticipation.

And then Marcus was standing beside her, carrying the chill of the evening on his leather jacket even as his body's warmth and masculine scent overwhelmed her senses. When she looked up at him, his pale green eyes shimmered in his handsome face.

"Ready, Roz?" he whispered. "Your sleigh awaits you."

Rosalyn sensed her life was about to take a wild detour that would forever alter her mind-set—and her *maidel* assumptions about the world. She nodded, unable to breathe, much less speak.

"You two need to skedaddle before you set my shop on fire," Nora teased. "It's the perfect evening for a sleigh ride, so enjoy every moment of it. I've got a major case of sleigh envy, Marcus."

His face lit up. "You and Luke can borrow it whenever you want—if Roz and I ever stop riding around in it, that is."

Marcus helped her with her coat and waited patiently as Rosalyn put on her bonnet and boots. She felt like a princess when Marcus helped her into the sleigh. As he tucked a blanket around them, she couldn't stop gazing at the beautifully carved woodwork, the fine velvet upholstery, and the magnificent Percheron that shifted her weight in expectation, making the harness bells whisper with a hint of joy.

"Let's go, Sophie!" Marcus called out.

When the sleigh lurched forward, Rosalyn closed her eyes with the excitement of it all. She was sitting so close to Marcus, her arm brushed his beneath the blanket. The heavy *clip-clop, clip-clop* of the mare's huge hooves made the harness bells jingle with each step. Rosalyn held her breath so she wouldn't laugh out loud, filled with the same exhilaration that came from swooping and swirling on carnival rides at the county fair.

"From the look on your face, you're either overjoyed or scared spitless," Marcus said once they were gliding alongside the county highway.

Rosalyn opened her eyes to find him gazing at her. Gazing at *her*. "This is so—so awesome!" she gushed. "You probably think I'm a silly goose, acting so ga-ga over a sleigh ride with you, but—"

"I think *you're* awesome," he interrupted softly. "The way I see it, if you can't get excited about this sleigh and this horse and this perfect snowy evening, you might as well be dead. Hang on!"

Marcus steered the Percheron up the hill toward the entry to the McKenzie place. "Thought I'd give you a quick tour, and then we'll ride across open land, away from traffic. There's the Thoroughbred barn, where my apartment is," he put in, pointing as they rode past it. "The second barn is for the Percherons I'm training."

Rosalyn nodded, taking in the grandeur of the new red barns and the rolling, snow-covered pasture beyond them. "I'm surprised Mr. McKenzie hasn't built a new house that's as stunning as his horses' homes," she remarked as she glanced at the double-wide trailer they were passing. "Nora says he and Rebecca are engaged, *jah*?"

"Yup," Marcus replied as he deftly steered the mare toward open pasture. "Considering how much time she spends here—or he spends at her house—it surprises me that they return to their own places at night rather than sleeping over."

"As well they should," Rosalyn said emphatically. "Her *mamm* has accepted the fact that she'll never join the Amish church, but to Miriam, it would be a big slap in the face if everyone in town knew Rebecca was doing, well—*you know*—before she was married."

When Marcus focused silently on his driving, Rosalyn realized that a fellow who'd lived with a couple of different women would take sexual relations for granted. She'd caught herself discussing an inappropriately intimate topic with him, too. Her cheeks tingled with embarrassment as she changed the subject. "What's for supper tonight?"

Marcus's smile returned. "Do you like the pizza place in Morning Star? Or if you'd rather go someplace a little more upscale—"

"Oh, pizza, please!" she said without missing a beat. "We rarely have that at home because Dat's a meat-and-potatoes man. Doesn't consider pizza a real meal." A sigh escaped her. "Anyplace you take me will be a treat, Marcus. It's not as though I've gone to any restaurants other than the Grill N Skillet since we moved to Willow Ridge. And we've only gone there for Edith and Loretta's wedding dinners."

Was that pity in Marcus's eyes? Rosalyn looked out over the snowy fields, wondering if everything she said to him would incriminate her as a hopeless *maidel* . . . an invisible homebody who'd only gone on two dates in her entire life.

"At least you've eaten at the best place around," Marcus assured her. "I've heard that Mother Yutzy's and Mrs. Nissley's Kitchen in Cedar Creek are both good, but they only serve breakfast and lunch, so I haven't been to either of them."

Rosalyn nodded, allowing the rhythmic jingle of the bells and the mare's footfalls, muted by the snowy earth, to lull her into a gentle sense of euphoria. Marcus had slowed Sophie's pace to extend their ride, she sensed, because just over the upcoming rise she saw the lights of Morning Star. When the sleigh made a wide curve so the lights of town were behind them, however, the lush evening enveloped her. She sighed contentedly as she gazed up at the moon and stars shining in the deep blue canopy of night.

"So besides making wreaths—and riding in a sleigh with me—what do you really, really love to do, Roz?" Marcus asked softly.

Rosalyn sensed he was teasing a bit, but hadn't he nailed it? When she realized that his handsome, moonlit face was only inches from hers, she forgot how to speak. "You've pretty well summed it up," she admitted after a few moments. "Working in Nora's store has become my favorite way to spend time, but . . . well, this sleigh ride we're sharing ranks right up there as a major highlight of my quiet life, Marcus. You probably think I'm really dull and boring and—"

"I think you're the sweetest, most authentic person I've ever met, Roz," he whispered.

She lost all track of time and space and reality when Marcus stopped the sleigh and took her in his arms. Then he kissed her.

As Marcus lifted his lips from Rosalyn's, her soft gasp went straight to his heart, like an arrow of honesty. With her moonlit face uplifted and her eyes still closed, she appeared angelic, and it struck him that she'd entrusted him with her entire being—with her innocence and her reputation. Going out with him would bring her nothing but trouble, when her father found out.

Yet she'd come willingly, joyfully. Rosalyn wore her heart on her sleeve—and with a careless slip of his tongue or a stupid move he could destroy the beauty of this enchanted snowy evening, not to mention cause her personal pain that would haunt her long after he left her behind.

Marcus suddenly realized that his motives were all wrong. Using Rosalyn as a way to satisfy his curiosity about Cornelius Riehl was one of the most selfish things he'd ever done—and he'd pulled more than his share of self-centered tricks with the other women he'd known.

Truth be told, none of those girls could hold a candle to Roz. The bills you ran up on their credit cards are nothing compared to the damage you'll do if you play fast and loose with this woman's trust, his thoughts warned sharply. *She has more integrity in her long eyelashes than you've shown in your entire life, Hooley.*

Marcus swallowed hard. It scared the daylights out of him that Rosalyn might be making an honest man of him—might make him feel accountable for his actions, after numerous family members had tried the same thing and failed.

"Did I do it wrong?" she asked in a tiny voice. "I—I've never—"

"It was perfect," he whispered. "You're making me rethink what our kiss might mean, Roz."

Her dark eyes glimmered with relief, and maybe mischief. "Maybe you should kiss me again," she hinted. "I got so twinkly and light, I almost floated away. I might've missed something."

Marcus smiled at her endearing way with words. How many hundreds of times had he kissed the various girls he'd been with before? Yet not a one of them had ever confessed to feeling twinkly or light. He cupped Rosalyn's sweet face in his hand, and kissed her as though she were the most precious, beautiful soul with whom he'd ever connected.

Because she was.

Marcus parked the sleigh at the far end of the restaurant's lot, where there was a hitching post for Plain customers. Rosalyn helped him fasten a large horse blanket over the massive mare's back before they went inside. The place was noisy with kids and families enjoying an inexpensive Saturday night outing, but Marcus barely noticed. As Rosalyn sat across the well-worn booth from him, her clear, low voice penetrated the fracas while they talked about a surprising number of interests they had in common—besides pizza and sleigh rides and making wreaths.

"I hope you'll show me how to make a corn husk angel someday," she said wistfully.

As she took a long sip of her cola—another treat she rarely indulged in, and never at home, she'd admitted—

Marcus found her charming. She'd worked at Nora's store for most of the day, yet in a pleated white *kapp* that framed her face and a home-sewn cape dress of deep green, she appeared as fresh as the evergreens in their snow-white finery. She wore no makeup, yet her dark brows and lashes, soulful brown eyes, and deep pink lips set off a pleasantly proportioned face that was much more attractive than he'd thought when he'd first met her.

"As nimble as your fingers are, it won't take you long to make an angel," he remarked. "I've been impressed with how many wreaths you've put together these past few weeks, yet no two have been alike."

Rosalyn shrugged modestly. "It would be boring to make them all the same," she pointed out. "Truth be told, a lot of them have been decorated with leftover scraps of this and that—ribbon and silk Christmas flowers and whatnot. I can't duplicate them because I use up my scraps as I go."

Her remark reminded Marcus of his mother, and that sent a pang of regret and wistfulness through him. His *mamm* didn't waste *anything*, whether she was cooking or sewing or crafting, because she had no spare money. Such a frugal lifestyle was a far cry from the mind-sets of his former girlfriends—

So is Roz your girlfriend?

The question startled him, yet his heart already held the answer. Marcus reminded himself to go slowly, because a lot was at stake for Rosalyn—

Don't kid yourself, Hooley. You're more invested in this relationship than you want to admit.

He was grateful that their pizza arrived just then so he didn't have to delve too deeply into feelings that were threatening to embrace him and never let him go. Rosalyn ate with the delight of a child, laughing when the cheese hung suspended between her slice of pizza and her mouth . . . a mouth Marcus found himself watching as she chewed. After they'd finished eating, he almost hated to leave the restaurant for fear the ambiance they'd woven like a magical web might get blown away once he drove her home.

His thoughts became more serious when they stepped outside, however. "Uh-oh, the snow has some ice in it now," he said as he offered Rosalyn his arm. "Walk carefully. The parking lot's turned into a skating rink."

"It's a *gut* thing you put a blanket over Sophie," she remarked as she baby-stepped over the slick surface. "I'm glad she's a Percheron rather than one of the fine-boned Thoroughbreds you've trained. She's a much heavier horse with bigger hooves. Better on snowy roads."

"We'll turn on our lights and the flashers," Marcus said. He reached under the seat to flip the switch of the car battery that powered the sleigh's lights, hoping they would shine brightly enough to be visible to cars.

They'd only traveled a short distance on the icy street when Marcus realized they were in trouble. "We'll take the same way back as we came, across the pastures rather than alongside the road," he said. "Let's hope Sophie keeps her head. I haven't been working with her very long—"

"She'll be fine, and you're just the man to be driving her," Rosalyn quickly assured him. She pulled the spare blanket from beneath the seat and draped it over their heads and shoulders to keep the sleet from freezing on their wraps.

Her confidence in his driving touched Marcus deeply and made him even more aware of his responsibility to get her home safely—to *protect* her. It was a new emotion for him, wanting to be Rosalyn's guardian rather than just a guy showing off his prowess as a horse trainer and a driver. As he steered Sophie across the ice-crusted stretches of snow, he prayed for their safety.

I haven't talked to you for a long, long, time, God, but if

You could get us back to Willow Ridge . . . well, I'll strongly consider being more faithful.

Marcus knew God didn't like folks playing games with Him, promising to improve their behavior if He gave them what they prayed for, but he was asking for Rosalyn's safe return home, so that made his plea more legitimate, didn't it? He focused intently on the pasture they were crossing, allowing Sophie to instinctively choose the best path as she paced herself. He didn't admit it aloud, but he was scared. Had he been by himself, he would've pulled into somebody's barn for the night rather than drive in such treacherous conditions. The sleet was still pelting them and the trip home was taking a lot longer than their drive into Morning Star.

But we've got to get Rosalyn home, God, because—well, You know how much trouble she'll be in if we don't.

Even if they slept across the barn from each other—or if Rosalyn slept in someone's house while he slept in their barn—Marcus would never convince Cornelius that he hadn't compromised her. Amish fathers tended to jump to that conclusion, and he suspected Riehl would lash out with accusations rather than listen to reason.

Rosalyn shivered beside him, peering out from beneath the sleet-encrusted blanket. "Oh, but it's *gut* to see the lights of Willow Ridge," she whispered after they'd been traveling nearly an hour. "I've never been so aware of how dark it gets in the countryside, or in Amish towns where there aren't streetlights."

Aware. She hadn't said she was frightened out of her mind—hadn't once whimpered about the possibility that they might not make it home. Marcus didn't dare let go of the leather lines, but he quickly kissed her cheek. "Thanks for not carrying on, Roz," he said. "Other women would be—well, it doesn't matter what they'd be doing. You're a rock, and you've been kind enough to keep your doubts to yourself."

"I didn't want Sophie to pick up on my fear," she said softly. "And truth be told, I've been too busy praying to fuss at you, Marcus."

He chuckled despite how tired his tense muscles were getting. It was a sure bet that God was paying more attention to Rosalyn's prayers than to his.

"You're driving a lot better than I could," Rosalyn went on. "We'll make it. The lights at Wyatt's place are just down the way now—and I can see lights in the upstairs windows at Luke and Nora's house, too. We're almost there, Marcus."

Her encouragement meant the world to him as the sleigh crossed the big yard that surrounded Wyatt's house. Just as he dared to feel confident, however, Sophie headed down the snow-packed lane toward the road. The sleigh began to slide sideways behind her.

"Easy girl. Side to side," Marcus called to her. "Please, please don't let us turn over and pull you down," he murmured before he realized he'd said it out loud.

They were helpless as the sleigh skidded farther downhill on the ice-covered snow—heading toward a tree in what seemed like suspended animation. "Brace yourself, Roz," Marcus whispered.

"Poor Sophie—hang on, girl!" Rosalyn said as the Percheron struggled to step forward and sideways—anything to keep the sliding sleigh in place without losing her footing on the icy hillside.

The side of the sleigh struck the tree trunk hard, jolting the vehicle and Marcus's body. At least they'd stopped, and Sophie was still standing. He didn't want to think about the broken legs or muscle damage the mare might've suffered, had she been pulled down by the sleigh's weight—not to mention the repairs his sleigh was going to need—so he pondered his options.

"Maybe I should walk home," Rosalyn offered.

"Too slick. You'll fall and get hurt," Marcus quickly insisted.

He inhaled deeply to settle his nerves as he peered at the side of the sleigh where it rested against the tree. "I'm not going to ask Wyatt to come get us in his truck, either, because it's likely to slide off the lane just like we did. Then he'd be stuck, too."

He leaned forward to get a closer look at the county highway. The sleet was letting up. He was tempted to pull the heavy, saturated blanket off their shoulders and heads—but who knew how much longer it would take to reach the Riehl place?

"Sophie seems to be gathering herself, getting ready to pull again," Rosalyn observed as the mare stomped tentatively on the ice-coated snow. "Our lights and flashers are still working, so maybe we're safest if we stay in the sleigh and let her pull us out of this, *jah*?"

Marcus smiled in spite of his worries about the weather. "Your instincts are spot-on, Roz," he replied. "It's usually better to trust the horse—and Percherons can pull an amazing amount of weight and overcome a lot of resistance. They love the challenge of a heavy load."

He looked toward the county highway again, relieved that the sleet was changing over to snow. "The road looks like it's been plowed recently, so if we stay in the yard until we reach the pavement—instead of trying to reach the lane again—we stand a better chance," he murmured. "With Sophie pulling and you praying for us, I think we can make it. I'll steer as best I can. Geddap, Sophie."

The sleigh's wooden side made a sickening sound as it scraped against the tree, but they were moving again. Sophie picked her way across the yard, slowly pulling the sleigh to the road without further mishap.

When they reached the road, Marcus tugged the blanket from their shoulders and stuffed it beneath his feet. "Help me watch for cars, all right?" he asked as he steered Sophie into the plowed center section of the pavement. "I doubt we'll see many, but if this storm took us by surprise, other folks might be trying to get home, too."

Rosalyn turned sideways in the seat so she could look behind them. "All clear," she called out.

Marcus let the mare have her head as they passed the mill and the Grill N Skillet, which were closed and dark. At the next intersection, he carefully steered Sophie onto the east-bound road where the Riehls lived. Rosalyn faced forward again, peering through the darkness as she looked for lamp-light in the windows of her home. "I have no idea what time it is," she said. "Everyone must've gone to bed—"

Marcus fished his cell phone from his shirt pocket. "Just past ten o'clock. Took us an hour and a half to get here."

"But we made it—and you must be exhausted," she put in. "Why not park in the barn so Sophie can eat and get warm? Meanwhile you and I can have some hot chocolate and whatever dessert might be left from supper."

"Now there's an offer I can't refuse," he replied. "By the time I'm ready to head home, maybe the snow will have stopped."

After Rosalyn directed him to the barn, she hopped out of the sleigh to slide the big door open—and then she closed it after he'd pulled inside. When she lit the lantern, the light made her face glow—made him think of other ways to spend time in the hay. Instead, they quickly put out some feed for Sophie and covered her with dry blankets. Clutching each other's hands, he and Rosalyn walked cautiously across the yard and entered the door at the back of the house.

Marcus stood in the mudroom and listened for several seconds. All was hushed and dark. "Roz, I hope you know—"

"Marcus, you were wonderful tonight," she blurted at the same time.

His heart warmed—until the *fffft* of a striking match made them both jump.

Rising from the kitchen table, holding a lamp in front of him, Cornelius glared at them. "Hooley, you dog, where have you been with my daughter?"

Chapter Sixteen

Rosalyn sucked in her breath, but after a wonderful evening and Marcus's valiant effort to get her home safely, she wasn't going to let him take the heat—nor did she appreciate the accusation lurking beneath Dat's words. "We went to Morning Star for pizza, and then—"

"I didn't ask you," Dat interrupted brusquely. "But I'm highly disappointed in you, daughter. You're known by the company you keep—and once again you've defied me."

"I'm sorry we're so late," Marcus said, stepping into the kitchen. "We got caught in the sleet, so it took us—"

"The weather has nothing to do with the fact that I've forbidden Rosalyn to spend time with you," Dat said in a rising voice. "You've obviously slithered into my naïve daughter's romantic imagination, and you were planning to take advantage of her innocence—most likely upstairs in her bedroom. Get out of my house. You're not welcome here."

"Dat, you've got it wrong!" Rosalyn protested. "It wasn't as though Marcus took me for a sleigh ride against my will. I *wanted* to go—"

"We'll discuss your fall from grace—the way you threw yourself into the face of temptation—later," he snapped. "Go to your room."

Rosalyn's eyes widened. After all of her years as a chaste, dutiful daughter, why would her father believe she had such lustful inclinations? The child inside her wanted to duck her head and hurry upstairs to cry—*but you're twenty-eight years old. You can't let Marcus bear the burden of Dat's wrath alone.*

She crossed her arms, refusing to move from Marcus's side.

Dat's eyes widened, but he focused again on Marcus. "You've done enough damage for one night, Hooley. Move on!"

Marcus, too, stood fast. "Your accusations are unfounded, sir," he insisted. "Please let me explain—"

Rosalyn heard rapid footsteps descending the stairway, and a few moments later Loretta entered the kitchen, clutching her bathrobe around her. "I'm so glad you two made it home," she murmured.

Drew, also in his robe, came in behind her. He assessed the situation. "Hey there, Marcus. Glad you made it safely through the storm and—"

"Don't encourage him!" Dat cried out. "Now get a move on, Marcus, before I forcibly remove you from the premises!"

Marcus stood taller, studying the man whose face was growing ruddier in the light of the lamp he held. "We've barely even met, Cornelius, so why do you act as though I'm not fit to be in the same room with you or Roz?" he asked calmly. "If you'll let me explain—"

"I've heard all I need to know about your sins with women!" Dat spouted, pointing at Marcus. "Her name is *Rosalyn*. And now you've led her into temptation, dragging her down to your level of—"

"Do your feelings have anything to do with the time I introduced myself in the bank?" Marcus asked. He seemed unruffled, as though he was prepared to deal with Dat on a different level. "I thought it was *interesting* that you were depositing wrapped bundles of bills that day, and I bet you didn't want me to see that. Am I right?"

Rosalyn's heart stopped. Why hadn't Dat said anything about speaking with Marcus at the bank? Why did Marcus think it was important that Dat's money had been bundled—and what did it mean, that the money had been wrapped?

And why was Dat putting a bunch of money in the bank when we have so many past-due bills that need to be paid? He told Loretta and me not to buy groceries this week.

"That's none of your business!" Dat blustered. "I see no reason to answer such an impertinent—"

"Maybe this is another chance for you to come clean, Cornelius," Drew said in a low, purposeful tone. "Maybe you're only going through the motions of grief counseling and repaying—"

"Don't *you* start on me!" Dat interrupted. He had a frantic look about him, like a cornered animal, until he regained control over his emotions. "This conversation is finished, and what's been said tonight is to go no farther than these kitchen walls. Do I make myself absolutely clear?"

Rosalyn exchanged a puzzled glance with Loretta while Marcus and Drew said nothing. The measured *tick-tick-tick* of the battery clock on the wall marked a long, strained silence.

Drew exhaled loudly. "We've heard what we've heard."

"Okay, so I won't say another word," Marcus put in. He turned to Rosalyn with a resigned smile on his face. "I had a really nice time tonight, Roz. I'm sorry I've gotten you in hot water."

Rosalyn's heart clenched. Between his lines, she heard *goodbye.* She had visions of being trapped in this house with Dat for the rest of her life.

"I'm not one bit sorry," she countered. "We have nothing to be ashamed of, Marcus. It was a wonderful evening, and I thank you for getting me home safely. I'm sorry your beautiful sleigh was damaged and I—I'll never forget our moonlight ride or our fun supper together."

Rosalyn hurried through the dark front room to go upstairs before Marcus could see her cry.

The next day was a visiting Sunday when there was no church service, and Rosalyn prepared herself for a long day of lectures from Dat. It was a surprise when her father poured a mug of coffee, put a square of warm coffee cake on a plate, and headed downstairs to eat his breakfast. At the basement door he paused, however.

"Ponder your wrongdoing, Rosalyn, so you'll be prepared to confess your sins at church next Sunday," he warned her. "We'll discuss your situation further at a family meeting when Edith and Asa come for the noon meal."

He closed the door behind him so forcefully that Rosalyn and Loretta both jumped.

"Why on God's *gut* earth does Dat think you and Marcus behaved improperly?" Loretta whispered. She poured coffee for herself, Rosalyn, and Drew as he entered the kitchen. "When you weren't eating in a public restaurant you were fighting your way through a sleet storm. It wasn't as though you had a chance to—"

"Marcus was right," Drew put in as he sat down at the table. "Your *dat*'s tantrum has more to do with his own secretive behavior at the bank than with anything you two did last night."

"Dat's going to remind me again and again that I've broken the fifth commandment by not honoring his order to avoid Marcus's company," Rosalyn said with a sigh. She sat down and looked at the pan of coffeecake Loretta had baked. It was fragrant with sugar and cinnamon, but she had no appetite for it. "I can't believe he accused us of being ready to sneak upstairs—and said Marcus was taking advantage of me. Does he think I have no moral sense at all?"

Loretta reached for her hand. "The rest of us know better, sister."

"It was all a smoke screen," Drew insisted. "And why has he gone downstairs to his shop rather than joining us for breakfast? Working on the Sabbath is as much a breach of God's commandments as not honoring your parents, after all."

Rosalyn felt numb, weary from lack of sleep and frustration. She focused on Drew, keeping her voice low in case Dat was lurking behind the basement door. "What does it mean that Dat had wrapped bundles of money?" she asked. "And why would he be putting them in the bank instead of paying our bills—"

"Or letting us go to Zook's," Loretta put in. "Our Sunday dinner's going to be casserole—again—because he's forbidden us to shop."

Rosalyn frowned. "Do you suppose he's run up such a tab that Preacher Henry's not letting us charge anything else until Dat pays him?"

Loretta's eyes widened. "If that's the case, Dat wouldn't want us to find out about it, so he's making us stay home," she said softly. "I've half a mind to take my money from working in Nora's store to buy what we need—and ask Lydia about our account while we're there," she added in a rebellious tone.

Drew chuckled and took a second piece of coffeecake. "Save your money, honey," he quipped, "because I'll be happy to cover anything we owe the Zooks. Maybe Asa and I can compare notes and figure this out. Meanwhile, I'm glad it was Marcus who bought that fine old sleigh—and that you got to ride in it, Rosalyn," he added in a more upbeat tone. "Did you have a *gut* time?"

Rosalyn's heart thrummed. She'd been awake most of the night because Dat's harsh accusations had upset her, but she'd soothed her soul by calling up every wonderful moment of her evening with Marcus. "We did," she replied. "He drove us to Morning Star for pizza, and we talked and laughed—it was just perfect until the weather kicked up. Even after the sleigh slid down an icy hill and hit a tree at Wyatt's, the Percheron mare pulled us through," she pointed out with a touch of pride. "I felt safe and . . . well, I knew Marcus would take care of me."

A little thrill went through her when she recalled their kisses, but she kept them private. "I think he would've asked me out again, if Dat hadn't lit into him," she said sadly, "but now I couldn't blame him if he wanted nothing more to do with me."

"I don't think Marcus will give up on you, *Roz*," Loretta teased lightly. "He seemed genuinely glad that he'd spent the evening with you."

Rosalyn absently broke apart her coffeecake with the tines of her fork, pleased that her sister saw some hope for her future with Marcus. "We'll see," she murmured.

Edith and Asa arrived just before noon with a pot roast and a big pan of the mac and cheese the little twins loved so much. Leroy and Louisa toddled around the kitchen babbling to each other while Rosalyn and her sisters set the table. Drew and his brother went to the front room to chat.

Edith pointed to Dat's place, looking around with a question in her eyes.

Loretta and Rosalyn silently gestured toward the basement door.

As Edith's expressive eyebrows rose in surprise, Dat emerged from his hideout as though nothing out of the ordinary had been going on. He checked the kitchen counter to see what desserts they'd be having, and then looked at the platter of pot roast and the two glass casserole dishes on the table.

"Well, I see *my* dinner," he teased. "Maybe there'll be some left for the rest of you after I fill my plate."

Rosalyn and Loretta watched him carefully, unsure of how to respond. Edith, however, spoke right up. "Has working on Sunday morning made you especially hungry, Dat?" she asked, matching his light tone. She pulled two white envelopes from her apron pocket. "The mailman put these in our box yesterday by mistake. What with all the overtime you've been working lately, it's surely another mistake that they're marked *past due, jah*?"

Anger flashed in Dat's eyes as he snatched the envelopes from Edith's hand. "We have more pertinent things to discuss today," he snapped. "Your sister defied me by spending the evening with Marcus Hooley—"

"Oh, but he's cute!" Edith exclaimed, grinning at Rosalyn. "When Asa told me he'd bought that old sleigh, I was hoping he'd take you out—"

"He took her for a ride, all right," Dat interrupted. He went to the doorway of the front room. "Are you men going to yack all day, or can we eat already?"

Rosalyn's heart thudded dully. Dat only called family meetings when he wanted to grill someone, and she dreaded whatever he'd dreamed up to say about her and Marcus. If Mamm were still alive, she'd find a way to buffer his confrontational attitude—and to turn the conversation to something more constructive.

Rosalyn sighed. It was useless to wish for her mother's intervention.

I'd be grateful if you'd watch over our dinner anyway, Mamm, she thought as they all bowed in silent prayer before the meal. *Guide our hearts and minds and our talk, Lord, because without Your grace, not a one of us stands a chance.*

Dat cleared his throat to end the prayer. He looked

ominously at each adult seated at the table, and when his gaze lingered on Rosalyn, her heart shriveled. She didn't dare pass the casserole in front of her to break the tension that hung like an invisible noose over the table.

"We must not only keep watch over Rosalyn to prevent her soul from sinking further into depravity after her evening with Hooley," he said gravely, "but we must also see to it that she's on her knees confessing her sins next Sunday—to insure that her chances for our Lord's salvation have not been lost."

Across the table from Edith, Asa crossed his arms. "How'd you happen to be depositing bundled money at the bank, Cornelius?" he asked calmly. "Wrapped money has been counted, and each bundle is fifty or a hundred or a thousand dollars—or more—depending on the denominations of the bills."

"And bundled money is generally taken *out* of a bank rather than deposited," Drew said, continuing the thread of his twin's inquiry. "Merchants and business owners bring in their loose checks and cash deposits, and the bank later bundles the paper money by denomination to insure that it's counted accurately. They keep it in the vault."

"So where'd you get bundled money to take to the bank?" Asa asked again, in a tighter voice.

Dat's face remained a mask of composure, but the color was draining from it. "See there?" he asked in a dramatic whisper. "Hooley has bamboozled you men as surely as he's insinuated himself into Rosalyn's hopes and fantasies. That's how the devil works. He's slick, like a snake. He plays upon a shred of truth we want to believe, and then he weaves an entire scenario of falsehood around us, like a spider spins her web . . . to catch her innocent prey."

Rosalyn sat motionless alongside her sisters, sensing this talk of spiders and snakes was an extension of the smoke screen Drew had spoken of earlier.

"Are you saying you didn't make that deposit?" Drew demanded. "If Marcus saw you at the bank—"

"*If Marcus saw me*," Dat repeated in a mocking tone. "Are you saying you believe Hooley's word over mine? That's the question, isn't it?"

When Louisa and Leroy began to fuss in their high chairs, Edith spooned some macaroni and cheese into their bowls to quiet them. Rosalyn didn't dare look at her sisters' expressions to see how they felt about the men's conversation. She was grateful that their husbands didn't shrink away from Dat's confrontational attitude, but it still made for a very uncomfortable time at the table.

Dat leaned toward Asa and Drew with a deepening scowl. "Answer me!" he demanded. "Who do you believe? Marcus Hooley, or me?"

"Tell us your version of the story, Cornelius," Asa replied smoothly.

Dat raked his hand through his graying wavy hair. "That's not what we're talking about!" he declared testily. "Why do you believe a thing Hooley says, knowing what we do about his past? He made up that story about seeing me in the bank to divert my attention from what he and Rosalyn had been doing last night! Why on God's *gut* earth would I go to the bank in Morning Star—with bundled bills, no less—when my business account is in the New Haven bank?"

A foxlike expression overtook Drew's face as he reached for the platter of pot roast. "Marcus didn't say you were at the bank in Morning Star," he replied quietly. "But *you* did."

When Dat's mouth clapped shut, Rosalyn got a sudden queasy feeling. As she reviewed the previous evening's confrontation in her mind, she realized Drew was correct: Marcus hadn't named the bank where he'd seen Dat.

But why would her father—the man she'd grown up believing and trusting—deny taking money to the bank in Morning Star? Did he have accounts in two different banks?

And why would a deacon of the church be untruthful about anything—much less about matters involving money?

Why would Dat be asking questions and making accusations that cast doubt upon Marcus's integrity . . . unless he's trying to divert our attention away from his own lack of integrity?

The thought made her throat so dry she couldn't swallow. Rosalyn was grateful that she was no longer the topic of conversation, but deep in her soul she knew that as surely as Dat had a wavy gray beard, he'd just been caught in some bald-faced lies.

Chapter Seventeen

As Rebecca stepped into Mamma and Ben's house Sunday morning with Wyatt, she was keenly aware that although everything appeared the same—the furnishings, the voices coming from the kitchen, the heavenly aroma of the food they'd be eating at noon—a lot had changed. *She* had changed. Arriving with her fiancé in tow, wearing English clothes, instead of showing up alone in a Plain dress that matched her sisters', would set the tone for the day—and for the remainder of her life.

Rebecca gripped her pan of brownies. She felt nearly as nervous as she had on that fateful morning a couple of years ago when she'd entered her Amish mother's Sweet Seasons Bakery Café to demand answers about who she really was, after her adoptive English mother had died. Discovering her Plain roots had changed her life dramatically, yet she sensed her upcoming marriage would bring a more profound emotional readjustment. Rebecca quickly prayed that Mamma would be as gracious—and excited—about her engagement as she'd been about the return of the daughter whom she'd believed had drowned in the flood of 1993.

"Relax, dear heart," Wyatt whispered near her ear. "You're

bringing your family tidings of great joy. Or I *hope* you see our announcement that way," he teased.

Rebecca smiled at him gratefully. The love in his gray-blue eyes steadied her racing pulse. "I know that, but even though they're probably expecting—"

"Expecting?" Ben called out as he came from the kitchen. "Who's expecting—besides Rachel?"

Rebecca's cheeks burned. "Not me!" she blurted out before she realized Ben was teasing. "But I—we—"

"Well, here's the happy couple now!" Mamma declared as she, too, emerged from the kitchen with little Bethlehem toddling behind her. Her eyes sparkled as she looked expectantly from Rebecca to Wyatt. "I see a new glow on your faces, as though you're bursting with your own *gut* news—ain't so?"

Rebecca laughed loudly. Why had she imagined she could keep a secret from her perceptive mother?

"Matter of fact, we are," Wyatt replied as he slipped his arm around her. "Rebecca has agreed to be my wife, and I couldn't be happier."

"Glory be to God!" Mamma cried as she embraced them both.

"What a happy day! First Rachel's announcement and now yours!" Ben chimed in as he joined them. "Congratulations, you two."

Other family members poured out of the kitchen and Rebecca was engulfed by hugs from her sisters, Rachel and Rhoda, while Nora and her daughter, Millie, crowded in to express their joy, as well. After Luke and Ira pumped Wyatt's hand, Rhoda's husband, Andy, and Rachel's husband, Micah, took their turns—and even Marcus greeted them with his congratulations. The front room echoed with their combined voices, and for the next several moments Rebecca was surrounded by delighted smiles.

See how much love you would've missed had you limited yourself to your English parents' world?

Rebecca's heart swelled when Bethlehem reached for her. She scooped the little blonde to her hip, sharing a noisy kiss as her family ushered her and Wyatt into the kitchen. Her English dad would be delighted to hear of her engagement when they visited him in the afternoon, but his reaction couldn't compare to her Amish family's outpouring of love and excitement. The large table in Mamma's kitchen, set with more than a dozen plates, was the ultimate symbol of Plain life and hospitality—and Rebecca suddenly realized how blessed she was that she and Wyatt would always have places at this table.

When the men headed for the front room, Rebecca turned to her sisters. Rhoda was lifting her little son, Aden, into one of the high chairs positioned at the table while Rachel playfully summoned her toddler, Amelia, from playing hide-and-seek in Mamma's pantry. "Congratulations on your *gut* news, sister," Rebecca said. "How are you feeling? When's your due date?"

Rachel and Rhoda flashed her identical smiles. "Late summer, early fall, best we can tell," Rachel replied. "I'm feeling better this time around, thank *gut*ness."

After casting a glance over her shoulder, Rhoda leaned closer. "Could be another wee one showing up about a month after that—but that's not for anyone else to know just yet," she whispered happily. She squeezed Rebecca's hand excitedly. "And before we know it, *you'll* be setting up a nursery—"

"Probably in a new house at Wyatt's farm," Rachel put in with a knowing nod.

Rebecca shrugged, keeping a smile on her face. Having a career and a future husband who was nearly forty-one had put an English spin on her expectations, so having kids would be a conscious choice rather than letting nature take its course, as her Amish sisters did. "We'll be living at my place after the wedding, which will give us time this winter to draw up plans for a house on Wyatt's property," she hedged.

When Mamma took a blue enamel roaster from the oven, Rebecca placed a couple of thick kitchen towels on the counter for the hot pan. As her mother lifted the lid, salty-sweet-smelling steam rose from a ham that was baked to perfection. Pineapple slices and bright red cherries added a festive touch, and Rebecca realized how ravenous she was.

"This looks fabulous, Mamma," she remarked as she snatched a sliver of ham that had fallen back into the roaster. "You went to a lot of trouble."

"After Preacher Henry's lecture last Sunday about ladies bringing hot food for the common meal, Preacher Bennie might put up a flap about the *work* that went into this dinner," Mamma confided as she began carving. "But I decorated this ham yesterday, so I figure that getting it out of the fridge and turning the knob on the oven isn't any more work than Rhoda or Rachel put into carrying their food across the road."

Rebecca chuckled. Mamma's remark came as no surprise, for Henry Zook kept a tight rein on his kids and his wife when they were working in the local market. "I doubt that Ben will refuse to eat this meal—or any other food you fix for him," she teased, placing the slices of ham on a platter.

"This time of year, we all crave something more substantial than the cold sandwiches some church districts eat on the Sabbath," Mamma said. "And when the aunts, uncles, and cousins from Bowling Green get here for their Christmas visit, we're going to pull out all of our favorite recipes! I hope you and Wyatt will join us whenever you can."

"We'll be glad to, Mamma. I still have lot of catching up to do with those folks, considering all the years I wasn't around them." Rebecca's heart swelled as she placed the platter of ham on the table. Once again she was aware of how blessed she was to belong to such a wonderful Amish family.

Nora and Millie were setting the side dishes on the table—a cheesy hash-brown casserole, a huge bowl of four-bean salad, baskets of dinner rolls, a fruity gelatin salad, and a relish tray—while her sisters filled the water glasses. When the food was all in place, Millie called the men. Everyone took a seat and bowed their heads to pray.

"As we say our grace, let's remember my mom, who stayed home today with a nasty cold," Andy requested.

"And we're grateful that Taylor and Brett wanted to be with her," Rhoda put in, pleased that their children were so devoted to their grandmother.

Rebecca had wondered where Betty and the Leitner kids were. When she closed her eyes, she asked for God to be a healing presence with Betty—and then she sensed that Wyatt was peering at her. Sure enough, he was watching her from across the table with one eye open even as his head remained reverently bowed. When he smiled boyishly, it was all Rebecca could do to keep from giggling.

After a few moments, Ben reached for the ham platter. "By the looks of this food, you must've known we'd have plenty to celebrate today, Miriam," he said with a wink.

Rebecca smiled as a girlish bloom rose to Mamma's cheeks. Would she and Wyatt still be flirting after they'd been married for a while? She snatched a soft, warm dinner roll from the basket Mamma passed her and couldn't resist taking a big bite of it.

"God is *gut*—all the time," Mamma added with a nod. "Every day He gives us is cause for celebration—but *jah*, some days are more joyous than others."

"So when's the big day?" Nora asked. From her place a few seats down, she smiled at Rebecca.

"And where will the ceremony be held?" Mamma asked

as she accepted the bowl of bean salad from Ben. "I haven't heard you mention which church you've been attending."

Rebecca's bite of roll formed a lump and sank into her stomach. She glanced nervously at Wyatt, knowing he didn't have an answer, either. Although Mamma had asked the question in a nonchalant tone, she probably realized that Rebecca spent Sunday mornings in her pajamas—or with Wyatt, until they came to this table on Sundays when Mamma's family didn't have a church service. As an incriminating silence passed with each tick of the battery wall clock, guilt burned in Rebecca's cheeks.

"We haven't talked about that yet," Wyatt finally replied. "But we will."

Mamma and Ben's unspoken disappointment made Rebecca feel like a little girl who'd been told to stand in the corner with her nose to the wall. "I—I'm sorry," she whispered. "I know you want me to get married in a church, even if it's not *your* church—"

Mamma grasped her hand under the table, waiting for her to go on.

"At least you're not making excuses or promises you don't intend to keep," Ben said. "But your *mamm* and I are concerned about the state of your faith in God—about your souls' salvation—"

"And we worry about a marriage that's not built on a firm foundation of trust in our Lord Jesus," Mamma said softly. "Without faith, what will you have to fall back on when you face difficulties or disaster? How will you raise your children without the support of a church family?"

Rebecca swallowed hard. She should've anticipated these questions—should've kept attending church with her English dad after her adoptive mom died. It would've been easier to bear Mamma's probing questions if she'd asked them in a sharp, lecturing tone of voice.

Mamma, however, was gazing at her with eyes the color

of strong coffee and a face that radiated patience and love. She wasn't asking these questions to shame Rebecca. Mamma was asking them because a life without faith in God as its highest priority seemed totally foreign—and frightening—to her.

"You'll have the support of *our* family," Rachel insisted from the other end of the table.

"*Jah*, we know you'll never be Plain," Rhoda put in earnestly, "but you're our sister for *gut* and forever, and nothing will change that, Rebecca."

Tears dribbled down Rebecca's cheeks as she gazed gratefully at her identical sisters. She shared a miraculous bond with Rhoda and Rachel despite the fact that she hadn't grown up with them—and she was thankful that they'd never kept her at an emotional distance because she wasn't Amish.

"Rebecca and Wyatt's hearts are in the right places," Luke said as he passed the potato casserole. "With all due respect to matters of faith, we know that church membership doesn't guarantee a person's integrity. After all, Bishop Tom's first wife ran out on him—and there's a certain fellow in town who's been seen entering a casino."

"That's not really the issue here," Ben pointed out. "And the part about the casino is still privileged information that's not to go any farther than these kitchen walls, please."

Nora had mentioned Cornelius Riehl's deception to Rebecca, but it wasn't her place to ask why he hadn't been pressed into a confession. As she put a big spoonful of lime gelatin on her plate, she was relieved that this serious discussion hadn't interrupted the meal her dear friends were sharing with her. In more conservative Amish households, parents didn't allow any wiggle room when talking to their children—even their grown children—about the necessity of joining the church and attaining their salvation.

"A few of us are prime examples of folks who grew up with our butts on pew benches but who avoided church membership until certain girls convinced us we wanted to get married," Ira put in with a chuckle. He smiled at his wife, Millie, and then at Rebecca. "So, see there? You and Wyatt aren't so different from the rest of us—except you wear trendier clothes."

As everyone around her chuckled, Rebecca relaxed. *Thank you*, she mouthed at Ira. He had matured a lot since he and Luke had come to Willow Ridge as free-wheeling bachelors. Eyebrows had raised when Luke had dated Nora and Ira had fallen for Millie, the daughter she'd conceived out of wedlock, but their marriages were as solid as the bedrock they'd built their mill upon.

"Your points are well taken," Wyatt said with a nod. "In the English world, it's all too easy to get out of the habit of going to church—although I was raised by adoptive parents whose faith in God and service to their church were integral parts of their lives. Next time this topic comes up, we'll have better answers for you."

Mamma smiled as though she was greatly relieved. Soon all the bowls and platters had been passed, and folks began eating in earnest. Rebecca smiled at Wyatt, pleased that he still seemed comfortable with Ben and Mamma despite their talk of religion.

"If you two go to English services every week, I guess you won't be here for dinner with us on our visiting Sundays," Marcus remarked. "Maybe I'll take pity on you and bring you some of our leftovers."

Nora laughed. "Luke and I make it to the Mennonite church in Morning Star every Sunday and get out in time to come here for dinner," she pointed out. "Rebecca and Wyatt might find a church with an early service and they'll arrive ahead of us."

"*Jah?*" Marcus raised an eyebrow as he looked at Luke. "How long's your service?"

"About an hour, hour and a half," Luke replied. "It's one

of the perks of going Mennonite—*not* that I'm luring you away from the Old Order," he added emphatically. "Our cousin Ben is one of the most compelling reasons to remain faithful to Amish ways. He's a lot more progressive than our preachers and the bishop back in our Lancaster district."

Ben smiled, cutting into a slice of ham. "Marcus will be an inspiring, energetic addition to whichever congregation he joins."

"And we're all pleased that he's come to Missouri to join *us*," Mamma put in without missing a beat.

"Hear, hear," Wyatt said, raising his water glass in Marcus's direction. "Without Marcus, my draft horse business wouldn't have gotten out of the barn."

Rebecca caught a hint of pink in Marcus's face as he focused on his plateful of food. Could modesty be making him blush? She recalled his swagger—the way he'd boasted about his ability to train horses—when she'd first met him, and the change in his personality was nothing short of amazing.

The meal progressed at a leisurely pace, with occasional outbursts from little Aden or pleas from Amelia and Bethlehem, who wanted to get out of their high chairs so they could play. After everyone had enjoyed Rachel's cherry cobbler and Rebecca's brownies, the women began clearing the table. The men bundled up the kids to head outside, so they could discuss the live Nativity that would take place in Ben's barn on Christmas Eve. As newcomers, Wyatt and Marcus were asking a lot of questions about the event, so when the mudroom door closed behind them, the kitchen got a lot quieter.

Rebecca ran hot water into the sink—and slipped her arm around Mamma's shoulders when she came over with a stack of dinner plates. "What would I do without you, Mamma?" she asked quietly. "Where would I be if you hadn't taken me back into your family?"

Mamma kissed Rebecca's cheek. "Why speculate about

such a thing?" she asked. "Even when you showed up wearing all that dismal black clothing, with your hair and fingernails colored black, I could see beneath your disguise— your despair—and I knew you were my child, come home at last."

"And look at you now!" Nora put in happily. "The better question is, where would Willow Ridge be without *you*? You've kept our Plain businesses alive by advertising online, where thousands of shoppers find us."

Rebecca shrugged as she shut off the water. "It's what I do."

"Ah, but it's who you *are* that matters to us, honey-bug," Mamma insisted. "Your clothes and computers mean you're part of the English world, but to me you'll always be the little Rebecca Lantz who played harder and ran faster—and got her dresses dirtier—than her two sisters."

Mamma's expression waxed nostalgic as her thoughts went back in time. "While Rachel and Rhoda clung to my hands, terrified by the storm and the rising river that fateful day, *you* were fascinated by the churning waters—ran to get a closer look even though I was hollering at you.

"And then," she continued with a snap her fingers, "you were gone. In the blink of an eye you'd slipped down the muddy bank to be swallowed up by the river. It was a scene that tortured me night and day for years," she added in a whisper. "Praise be to God for bringing you back, daughter. For you see, only God could've saved you from that flood."

Rebecca could barely imagine the shock and grief her mother had suffered because she'd been an adventurous, headstrong toddler. "I don't recall a thing about that day," she murmured. "Until I found the little pink Plain dress in the bottom of my English mother's chest after she died, I had no idea I hadn't been born Tiffany Oliveri."

"It was God who brought you back to us," Rachel insisted.

"How else would you have known to come to Mamma's café with that dress in a bag?"

"The dress that matched the ones we'd been wearing the day we lost you," Rhoda put in softly.

"God is *gut* all the time," Mamma said once again. She beamed at Rebecca. "I'm not preaching at you, understand. I just want you and Wyatt to be happy, honey-bug—and happiness hinges on being right with our Lord. I can only tell you what I know to be true in my own life."

Feeling immensely blessed and cherished, Rebecca nodded. The very best example of the happiness found in God's love was the woman standing beside her.

Chapter Eighteen

Marcus's heart hammered as he and Wyatt entered the Simple Gifts store on Wednesday afternoon. The cars in the parking lot attested to the crowd of shoppers that would be keeping Rosalyn busy—and he didn't intend to distract her, or embarrass her by flirting with her in front of English folks.

But he had to see her. He wanted to be sure Rosalyn was okay after the blistering accusations her father had made on Saturday night . . . and he wanted to hear her voice. Make her smile.

It was a lucky coincidence that his boss wanted to shop for Rebecca's Christmas gifts on a day when Rosalyn worked.

"No wonder Rebecca loves this place," Wyatt said, gazing toward a dining room table and chairs the Brenneman brothers had made. "I'd better move faster on plans for the house, considering that I can buy all the furniture for it right here. And look at these pottery dishes—and those quilts hanging from the loft railing," he added as his gaze encompassed the store.

Marcus, however, was focused on the young woman wearing a pleated white *kapp* and a cape dress of deep cranberry.

"*Jah*," he said softly, "money can't buy you happiness, but the stuff in this store can put a smile on your woman's face."

"*Jah*?" Wyatt teased. "Since when are you speaking the local lingo—unless maybe the young lady standing beside Nora has been working her magic on you?"

Marcus waved Wyatt off, but didn't deny what he'd said.

"You have excellent taste in women," Wyatt continued in a low voice. "She appears modest and hardworking and cheerful—all good qualities. Look at her smile as she's handing that shopping bag to her customer. She's a looker, son."

Marcus stuffed his hands in the pockets of his jeans. "You've pegged her just right, but her old man's a piece of work," he added with a shake of his head. He caught a twinkle in Wyatt's blue-gray eyes. "How do you figure this stuff out, anyway? I haven't told you a thing about Roz—"

"People talk. And I've been around the block a time or two, remember?" he asked with a wink. "It took the right woman to make me give up my freewheeling bachelor ways, and I suspect it'll work the same way for you."

Marcus caught a movement in the office behind the checkout counter and let out a low laugh when a familiar brunette waved at them. "So you knew Rebecca would be here today? Probably working on Nora's website?" he teased.

When he saw the way Nora was smiling at him—and at Wyatt—he realized she'd probably told Wyatt about his date with Rosalyn—and he was fine with that. "Let me guess," Marcus said. "You're going to mosey around the store with Rebecca, and you're going to gauge her reaction—or ask her opinion—about pieces you'd consider putting in your future home. And you're going to buy all the stuff she likes for her Christmas presents."

Laugh lines bracketed Wyatt's mouth. "You catch on fast, Hooley," he said, watching Rebecca make her way between the displays. "Keep hanging with me, kid, and you'll be a pro at this relationship thing in no time."

As Rebecca joined them, she held out a decorated sugar cookie in each hand. "You fellows could surely use a snack—and there's hot cider, too," she added with a big smile for Wyatt.

He slipped an arm around Rebecca's shoulders as he took the snowman cookie she'd offered him. "Bribe me with sugar, and you can ask for anything you want," he said suavely.

Marcus fought the urge to roll his eyes, yet he envied the easy way his boss romanced Rebecca—and the way she responded, as though she was totally head-over-heels for him. *Considering the scene Rosalyn's dad made Saturday night, it might be years before she'll go out with you again—if Cornelius ever allows her to leave the house.*

Marcus bit the head off his frosted reindeer cookie, trying not to be too obvious about watching Rosalyn chat with a customer as she snipped tags from a tooled leather purse Matthias Wagler had probably made.

It's amazing that her dat*'s let her keep her job here, considering the temptations he believes English shoppers might lure her into.*

When Rosalyn looked at him from across the store, all signs of her previous confrontation with Cornelius were gone. Marcus saw pleasure on her face and a light in her eyes—positive signs that she was still interested in him. He started slowly toward the checkout counter, allowing her time to wrap the purse before he spoke with her.

The bell jangled behind him. When the door banged shut as though the wind had caught it, Marcus jumped, along with some of the customers—and when he turned, he braced himself.

What are the odds of Cornelius showing up just as you were thinking about him?

Rosalyn's father stood near the entrance. His expression could've curdled milk, and when he caught sight of Marcus, he seemed even more intent on whatever errand had brought him to Nora's store. As Cornelius stiffly made his way between the displays of merchandise toward the checkout counter, Marcus sensed the clockmaker's visit wasn't going to end well.

Nora's eyes widened. Rosalyn focused nervously on the pottery she was wrapping—and even the handful of ladies waiting at the cash register shifted closer together to stay out of his way.

"I've come to take you home, daughter," Cornelius announced loudly. "You defied me by coming to work here in the first place, and now—" He turned to point at Marcus. "Now it's obvious to me that you and that *Hooley*-gan are using this place as your meeting point despite the fact that I've forbidden you to see him!"

"Cornelius, please," Nora said, gesturing toward her office. "If you'll wait until I've finished with these customers, we can talk this out—"

The bell above the door jangled again, but it was such a common occurrence in the busy store—and folks were following Cornelius and Nora's conversation with such interest—that nobody paid any attention to it.

"Marcus Hooley?" a businesslike male voice demanded. "I believe we have some serious business to discuss about using a young woman's bank card to withdraw money from her account—without her consent."

Marcus nearly choked. Except for the soft Christmas music playing in the background, the store was totally quiet. Everyone was gawking at him, curious because he'd been singled out by two men who'd called his character into question. He couldn't miss the frightened frown that furrowed Rosalyn's forehead—the doubt in her eyes as she glanced at the stranger behind him and then went back to her wrapping, as though still trying to avoid her *dat*.

The man who'd just entered appeared to be about Wyatt's

age, but his thick glasses, thinning hair, and trench coat gave him a nerdy look—like a detective from the old shows Marcus watched when nothing better was on TV. The guy was clutching a briefcase that had seen better days.

Marcus didn't like the way his body trembled, as though this man had the ability to arrest him—or to disgrace him in front of Rosalyn, Cornelius, and so many other people. But he faced the stranger head-on, hoping to put a quick end to the guy's incriminating query. "I'm Marcus Hooley," he said quietly. "What can I do for you, Mr.—?"

"Boston Mendenhall, private investigator," his challenger replied boldly. "You've been a busy man, Hooley, stealing money that's not yours. I'm here on behalf of a client who's taking you to court."

Marcus's throat felt as dry as a dead Christmas tree. He couldn't think straight with Cornelius and so many other curious people witnessing this confrontation. "But—but I've been sending payments to—"

"Mr. Mendenhall, let's step into the back room to discuss this in a more private setting," Wyatt said as he and Rebecca joined the conversation. "You have no reason to intimidate my employee—and before we say another word, I need to see some identification."

Mendenhall pushed up his glasses. "This is none of your affair, sir. I've come to—"

"Oh, but it *is* my business when a total stranger accuses my employee of credit card theft in front of so many people," Wyatt insisted in a no-nonsense tone.

"We can move this conversation right back there—to the office," Rebecca said, pointing behind the checkout counter. "I'm sure this is a misunderstanding, so let's settle it quickly and get on with our day."

Although Marcus was extremely grateful that Wyatt and Rebecca had stood up for him, he still felt like a criminal being paraded in front of Rosalyn, her dad, and a gaggle of

other onlookers as the four of them made their way back to
Nora's office. Rosalyn remained focused on the purchases
she was wrapping, but her cheeks had turned a nervous
shade of pink. Maybe she wondered if the investigator's accusations would be further ammunition for her father—who
was watching Marcus with a knowing smirk.

"Help yourself to more cookies and cider, ladies!" Nora
called out cheerfully. "With less than two weeks remaining
before Christmas, if you see something you want, you'd best
latch onto it now. My crafters won't have time to make you
a similar item in time for holiday gift giving."

Marcus appreciated Nora's attempt at drawing attention away from him, but as he stepped into the office, it
reminded him of the times when he'd been interrogated in
small, windowless rooms in police stations. Since moving
to Willow Ridge he'd lived a remarkably legal life, without
any traffic violations or being pulled over for driving under
the influence. He'd made a real effort to straighten up and fly
right.

*But maybe those Pennsylvania pigeons are returning to
roost—and maybe you should be asking some questions of
your own*, the voice in his head advised him.

When Wyatt had closed the door behind them, Marcus
gazed closely at the investigator. "You wouldn't happen to
be driving an old green car, would you?"

Mendenhall's eyes widened behind his glasses. "That has
nothing to do with the matter at—"

"Yeah, it does," Marcus interrupted. "If that's your car,
you've been tailing me since I left Pennsylvania. You
could've spoken to me about this matter any number of
times—like last week when you parked beside my car—but
instead you drove off like a shot. Now you're showing up
where you can have an audience, right?"

Wyatt scowled, holding out his hand. "Even more reason
for us to see your ID," he stated. "We also need to know who

hired you, and why—specific charges your client has made, rather than idle threats about taking Marcus to court."

Sighing theatrically, Mendenhall pulled a wallet from his pocket and opened it to show his private investigator's license. "And who are *you*?" he demanded.

Wyatt briefly flashed his driver's license. "Wyatt McKenzie, Marcus's employer. State your case and let's see some documentation," he said impatiently.

"Did your client tell you to confront Marcus in the most public place possible, or was that *your* idea?" Rebecca chimed in, crossing her arms. "I have zero tolerance for people who depend upon intimidation to conduct their business."

Marcus's eyes widened with an idea. Had Rosalyn's father hired this guy to embarrass him in front of her—to call him out in public when Cornelius, too, was in the store, so she'd never want to associate with him again?

Nah, Mendenhall's been tailing you all the way from Lancaster County. And considering the many opportunities he's had to nail you, he's either a really incompetent investigator—or he knows he's got a lame case. Or he's running up his billable hours to make more money from his client.

This line of logic helped Marcus to regain a sense of perspective. He breathed easier as the investigator pulled some papers from his briefcase.

"Here is the record of withdrawals you've made with a bank card that belongs to Carrie Hoskins," the investigator said with a flourish. "*Thousands* of dollars—"

Marcus snatched the papers, becoming angry and suspicious at the mere mention of Carrie's name. "That's nonsense!" he snapped as he skimmed the first page of the credit card statement. "As of last Monday, I've repaid Carrie in full—and look at this! Most of these withdrawals were made in the past week, long after I left Lancaster County—"

"You still have her card number and her PIN," Mendenhall pointed out, sneering in Marcus's face. "Carrie believes the only way to stop you is to take you to court—"

"Wait just a minute," Wyatt interrupted, placing his hands on both men's shoulders. "This is escalating beyond reason. Marcus did indeed repay Ms. Hoskins. He has the checkbook register and bank statements to prove it."

"Yeah, they're back at my apartment," Marcus put in. He inhaled deeply to settle himself, regretting that he'd allowed Mendenhall's accusations to upset him. Even with the office door closed, he sensed the folks at the checkout counter—including Rosalyn and her *dat*—were hanging on every word the investigator was saying as they watched through the glass.

"That's *nonsense*!" Mendenhall mocked him. "If you've repaid Ms. Hoskins, why would she have advanced my fee on Monday morning—for another two weeks? She's not letting up until she sees you in court, Hooley."

The question jarred him. Marcus thought back to his rocky relationship with Carrie—kicked himself for getting sucked in by her looks and sweet talk, and for staying in the relationship after he'd realized her habits had taken control of her life. "Carrie kicked me out in a fury," he muttered, "because her recreational drug use was getting way out of hand. I paid her off as fast as I could so I could put her behind me. Her habit—and the friends that came with it—were starting to scare me."

Rebecca's eyebrows rose. "Why do I have a feeling she received your money, blew it on drugs, and then decided maybe you were good for *more* money?"

Wyatt cleared his throat, eyeing Mendenhall. "We might be able to say the same thing for you, considering how long you've been on Marcus's trail without closing in on him," he pointed out. "It's not as though he's been hard to find. I can vouch for him working with my horses every day since he's arrived in Willow Ridge. May I see that transaction record, please?"

As Marcus handed the pages to Wyatt, the investigator bristled. "That's all conjecture!" he blurted. "You have no proof, whereas *I* have the log of my hours to—"

"And *you* have no proof that Marcus made these withdrawals," Wyatt countered, tapping the pages with his finger. "The money was taken from ATM machines in various places in Pennsylvania—while Marcus has been in Missouri—so the person using the ATM would've had the card in her hand. Ms. Hoskins has sent you on a wild-goose chase, Mendenhall—"

"I can't even believe you took her case," Rebecca put in as she, too, perused the transaction record. "Maybe Carrie— and you—figured that because Marcus grew up Amish, he wouldn't know about ATM records and he'd fall for this flimsy setup. For all we know, Carrie herself—or a new boyfriend—took this money out of her account," she added in a disgusted tone. "These papers don't prove *anything*."

"Maybe we should have Sheriff Banks take a look at these papers—and call the bank that issued the card," Wyatt continued, glaring tersely at Mendenhall. "While we're there, we'll have him run a check on you, as well, Mr. Mendenhall. The more I hear, the more I wonder if you've printed out a bogus investigator's license on your computer."

Mendenhall got very quiet.

Marcus let out a disgusted sigh. "So what's your real story? Have you actually *met* Carrie Hoskins?"

The investigator shoved his glasses into place as he considered his reply. "I spoke with her on the phone, and she emailed me these account documents," he admitted under his breath. "She was quick to cover my fee with a PayPal deposit. Considering how hard it is to get some clients to pay me, I didn't ask many questions."

"So you have no idea how erratic her behavior is—how she talks in circles and changes her mind from one minute to the next," Marcus said. "You just followed the money and took her at her word."

Mendenhall shrugged. "Most people who hire investigators for jobs like this one are a little out of balance, and they don't usually tell the whole truth," he admitted with a sad laugh. "I went with the evidence she gave me."

"Well, when you're in contact with her again, you can tell her I didn't fall for it, and I'm not paying her another cent," Marcus stated. "Carrie was fascinated with me because I grew up Amish, and yeah, maybe that's why I didn't figure out her personality quirks and her habits sooner—I was naïve. But I've repaid her. I'm done. Got it?"

Mendenhall fastened the clasp on his worn briefcase. "Fine by me," he murmured. "I'll leave you folks alone now."

As the investigator preceded them out of Nora's office, Marcus felt exonerated—ready to announce to the customers milling around in the store that he'd met his responsibility honorably. But the expression on Rosalyn's face broke his heart. She was standing a short distance from the cash register, her head bowed and her hands clasped tightly in front of her, as Nora spoke to Cornelius in a low, urgent voice.

"What you assumed about Marcus and your daughter meeting here is absolutely untrue," she insisted to Rosalyn's burly, bearded father. "Marcus came in with Wyatt not two minutes before you showed up—"

"Ah, and here he is now," Cornelius said as he glared at Marcus. "A bad apple, rotten to the core. I'll not have him dragging my Rosalyn's reputation any further through the mud."

At these words, Wyatt stopped to address Cornelius. "We've cleared Marcus of the wrongdoing of which he was accused, Mr. Riehl," he said, loudly enough that the nearby customers could hear him.

"The way I hear it," Rebecca murmured as she stood beside Wyatt, "you have no room to be pointing a finger at anyone concerning fiscal integrity."

Although Marcus appreciated her support, he wished Rebecca hadn't made such a remark. Cornelius's face reddened as he brusquely took hold of Rosalyn's arm. "You English!" he muttered, looking askance at Wyatt before glaring at Nora, Rebecca, and Marcus. "And you who have forsaken the Old Order, constantly flaunting your lack of faith and respect, and now undermining my parental authority! Get your coat, Rosalyn. We're going home."

Blinking rapidly, Rosalyn headed to the storeroom. Marcus knew better than to follow her or say anything, but his heart ached for her as she emerged a few minutes later wearing her black coat with her black bonnet tied tightly beneath her quivering chin.

She might as well be dressed for her own funeral.

The thought startled Marcus, because he'd grown up among Amish women and men who often wore black—the color that signified respect for God and the communal conformity that allowed no one to appear different or special. "I'm sorry, Roz," he whispered as she passed a few feet in front of him.

She gave no sign that she heard him. He hadn't really expected her to.

When the Riehls had gone, Marcus sighed. "I wish that had turned out differently," he murmured. "Maybe if I hadn't taken her out on Saturday—or if I'd paid closer attention to the weather report—"

Nora shook her head sadly. "Cornelius was intent on his own mission today, no matter what you had or hadn't done,

Marcus," she said. "I'm really sorry to lose Rosalyn—and Loretta, too, no doubt—during the busiest season in my store. But we knew their father might make a scene, considering he'd forbidden them to work here in the first place."

The three ladies closest to the cash register appeared confused. "I've chatted with both of those girls when I've shopped here, and they're delightful young women," one of them said.

"You have a lovely store that supports Plain crafters, Nora," another of the ladies chimed in. "Why could that man possibly object to his daughters working here?"

Nora turned to them with a resigned sigh. "The way Cornelius sees it, I've corrupted his daughters by exposing them to the worldliness of the English," she explained. "He believes I've encouraged them to be disobedient and disrespectful."

"Old Order women live in a tightly confined world. I could never pour myself into that mold again," Rebecca said softly.

"Neither could I," Nora agreed. She smoothed the bright red apron she wore over a dress made of red and green paisley fabric, reclaiming her smile as she stepped over to the cash register. "Thanks for your patience, ladies, while we dealt with a couple of local dramas. I'll ring up whoever's next."

One of the ladies in line held up a colorful wreath Rosalyn had made from ribbon candy. "Does this mean we won't have any more wreaths to choose from? I think I got the last one—and I'd like another one to give as a gift."

"I'm afraid not," Nora replied ruefully. "I don't want to get Rosalyn in hotter water with her dad by asking if she'll make her wreaths at home."

Marcus agreed. Nodding at Wyatt and Rebecca, he left the Simple Gifts store in time to see the Riehls' black buggy turning onto the road that ran past their house. He stood in the cold air to follow its progress, wishing he knew how to apologize to Rosalyn. Even if he joined the Old Order Amish church, Cornelius would never feel he was good enough to associate with his eldest daughter.

It was startling, to think about changing his life in order to meet with someone else's approval. *It's even scarier that you considered, for the briefest moment, taking your vows. Do you realize what that means? What you'd be giving up?*

Marcus buttoned his leather jacket and started off across the parking lot, headed for his lonely apartment.

The scariest thing of all is that Rosalyn's being held hostage by a father who's up to his eyeballs in something a lot more serious than I've ever tried. I wish I could figure out exactly what he's involved in . . . or catch him at it.

Chapter Nineteen

Early on the following Monday morning, Rosalyn opened the door to go tend the chickens and discovered several inches of fresh snow—and it showed no signs of stopping. It was an hour before sunrise. As her eyes adjusted to the darkness, she could make out the shapes of the barn, the chicken house, and the snow-capped fence, all of them a shadowy gray behind a curtain of falling snow.

"We'd better shovel a path as we go, or we'll get snow inside our boots," she told Loretta. "My word, *look* at it!"

Her sister gasped as she poked her head out the doorway. "It's like the song—like a winter wonderland!" she said. "But *jah*, we're asking for cold, wet feet if we tromp out to the chicken house without pushing the shovels ahead of us."

Once they'd put on their work coats and bonnets, each of them grabbed one of the lightweight plastic shovels they'd been keeping by the mudroom door. The snow was light and feathery, so they made a race of it to see who got to the chicken house first.

"I'm still the fastest!" Loretta crowed when she reached the door a few steps ahead of Rosalyn.

"But my shovel's bigger, so I was scooping a wider path," Rosalyn pointed out. She dipped her shovel blade into the snow and playfully tossed some onto her sister, who returned the favor. By the time they stepped inside, they were laughing loudly. As Loretta lit the lantern, Rosalyn closed the door to keep the snow from blowing inside.

"It feels *gut* to laugh again," she remarked as she caught her breath.

"*Jah*, the past few days have been rough," Loretta said. "Thursday, when I would've been working for Nora, the time passed so slowly I thought the kitchen clock's battery was dead. At least Dat has stopped yammering at us."

"His silence—and all the time he's been spending downstairs—don't feel right, though." Rosalyn's eyes had adjusted to the unlit corners of the chicken house, beyond the lantern light. It was a comfort to see the hens settled in the wooden roosts built along the walls, and to hear the muted rustling of their feathers as they shifted on their nests. At least out here, life seemed normal. "I'm glad Dat accepted it when Preacher Ben said that you and I didn't need to confess at church yesterday."

"That was a blessing," Loretta agreed. "Did you notice that once Ben had pardoned us for defying Dat's orders by working at Simple Gifts, he seemed mighty interested in how things were going at home?"

Rosalyn nodded as she scooped cracked corn into a bucket. "It was nice of him to say that Marcus has matured a lot, too—and to point out that my date with him didn't go against the *Ordnung* just because he hasn't joined the church yet."

Loretta hung the lantern on a big nail that stuck out from a center support pole. She joined Rosalyn with the bucket she'd filled with water, and together they went to the feeding and watering station in the nearest corner. A few of the hens hopped from their roosts to approach the fresh feed in the metal trough, pecking at the floor for stray grains along the way. The daily chicken ritual soothed Rosalyn even as her poignant thoughts dampened her mood.

"Even though we only went out the one time, I—I miss Marcus," she admitted softly. "I knew how it would turn out before I even got into the sleigh—how angry Dat would be, no matter what time we got home. But I'm not sorry I went," she insisted in a bolder tone. "I had a wonderful evening, and I'll cherish the memory of it."

"Don't write him off just yet," Loretta said sympathetically. She poured water into the galvanized metal dispenser, careful not to let it overflow. "He's been coming to church—"

"Dat will never accept Marcus, even if he gets baptized," Rosalyn said ruefully.

"Puh! Did Dat accept Drew?" Loretta challenged. "Did that stop us from courting and marrying? And moving in to live under the same roof with him?"

"I'm glad you did that, too," Rosalyn murmured. "I realize Dat won't really like *any* man I would choose, but he has such a chip on his shoulder when it comes to Marcus. I'm not sure I could endure his daily confrontations the way you and Drew do."

Loretta slung an arm around Rosalyn's shoulders. They stood together, giving and accepting comfort in a way that was difficult when they were in the house, where Dat would probably accuse them of scheming. "It'll all work out, sister," Loretta said. "Marcus will find a way to break through the barrier Dat's put up."

With a catlike smile, Loretta went to fill the watering container in the opposite corner. "Drew says that once Dat's big secret gets out, he and I will be building a house—and you can come live with us, Rosalyn."

Rosalyn's eyes widened. This was the first she'd heard that the newlyweds were definitely planning a new home. "I wish we could settle this whole mysterious mess Dat's created," she said, pouring the last of the chicken feed into the feeder. "I'm *tired* of living under such a cloud. Why do we have to be the last to know what's going on with our own *dat*?"

When they'd put away their buckets, they gathered the eggs and returned to the house to start breakfast. Soon the salty-sweet aromas of bacon and pancakes filled the air, mingling with the scent of coffee that had percolated on the stove. Although it was a more pleasant meal because Dat wasn't saying much, Rosalyn felt uneasy about his silence.

Drew was talking about the weather and how the snowfall would affect his day. "Before we start work at the shop, Asa and I will hitch up the horses and plow," he said as he drizzled syrup over his second stack of pancakes. "I suspect the county snowplow has driven past our intersection, so we'll have quite a pile of snow to remove before anyone on our road can get into town."

"Smart folks will be staying at home," Dat remarked gruffly.

Rosalyn fetched the plateful of fresh pancakes Loretta had made. "Eat your breakfast, sister, while I start cleaning up," she said. "With Christmas just a week from today, it seems like a *gut* morning to bake some cookies, don't you think?"

"Something chocolate!" Drew called out. "And sugar cookies with lots of frosting. Lena Witmer's decorated cookies are cute, but Asa and I have always preferred our cut-out cookies totally covered with frosting. Just sayin'."

Loretta laughed. "You think you have an inside track to the cookie baker, *jah*?" she teased as she sat down to eat. "How about you, Dat? What's your favorite Christmas cookie?"

Rosalyn turned from running dishwater into the sink to hear his answer. She'd been watching him eat cookies all her life, yet she couldn't recall him ever stating a preference.

Dat's face fell. "Any cookie your mother made," he replied

morosely. "I told you we're having a simple Christmas this year. Don't go overboard with the baking—and don't think you'll get me to be more cheerful."

As he went to the stove to pour more coffee into his mug, Rosalyn blinked back tears. Why did their father jump at every opportunity to ruin a conversation with his grief?

Drew rose from the table with his dirty dishes. "On that note, I'll go help Asa hook up the—"

A loud pounding on the door made them all look toward the front room.

"I'm on it," Drew said. "It's probably Asa, a couple steps ahead of me."

When he opened the front door, however, Bishop Tom's urgent voice made Rosalyn stop washing dishes to listen. "Cornelius is at home, I hope?" he asked loudly. "We've got a crisis on our hands."

"There's been a terrible accident on the road," Preacher Ben explained as they entered the kitchen. The church leaders nodded quickly at Loretta and Rosalyn before focusing on their father. "Miriam's kin were on their way to Willow Ridge and a delivery truck came up behind their driver's van too fast," he continued quickly. "The truck skidded into them, and the van flipped into the ditch. They've been taken to the hospital in New Haven—"

"Why on God's earth were they on the road in this weather?" Dat demanded. "Weren't they coming from Bowling Green? They must've left in the middle of the night!"

Ben sighed glumly. "They were to stay with cousins in Boonville over the weekend—"

"We haven't heard the whole story yet—just got word about the accident from Miriam's uncle, calling from the hospital," Bishop Tom put in quickly. "The eight Amish folks and their English driver are going to need quite a chunk of change to cover their time in the emergency room—or maybe a stay in the hospital for some of them—so we've come to get money from our aid fund, Cornelius."

"Why would we cover folks who've never paid into our district's fund?" Dat challenged. "Our bishop in Roseville wouldn't have even considered covering hospital expenses for out-of-town guests."

Bishop Tom frowned. "That might be so—every bishop has the prerogative to decide whom his district's aid fund will cover," he replied in a tight voice. "Far as I'm concerned, however, Miriam's kin are more than mere guests and we're going to help them. Why are you asking me these questions, Cornelius?"

When Dat's face turned chalky white, Rosalyn's stomach sank like a rock. Her father appeared unable to speak, and for the longest time he just stood in front of the stove. The way his hand was shaking, it was a wonder he didn't drop his coffee mug.

Ben and the bishop's eyebrows rose in suspicion. "Shall we go on downstairs?" the preacher prompted. "You lead the way, Deacon."

Dat slowly set his mug on the counter. He moved toward the basement door like a man being marched at gunpoint—as though he feared he might never come upstairs again. Tight-lipped and somber, Bishop Tom and Preacher Ben followed him, leaving the door open behind them.

Rosalyn didn't close it, even though Dat always insisted the colder air from the basement would make the main floor feel chilly—and would be a waste of their propane heat. Her heart was pounding double-time as the men's footsteps echoed on the wooden stairs.

"This doesn't look *gut*," Loretta murmured beside her. "What an awful accident—but why is Dat so pale and nervous?"

Rosalyn glanced at Drew. He and Nora had followed Dat to Kansas City several weeks ago—and had seen something they'd only shared with the bishop and Ben. "What's going on? Why is Dat so upset about getting money from the aid fund?" she demanded in a loud whisper. "We have a right to know—"

"I suspect it's going to hit the fan any minute now," Drew replied softly. "It's just a matter of how deep a hole your *dat*'s dug."

Rosalyn listened intently. She heard a muffled conversation coming from Dat's workshop but couldn't understand the words. Unable to stand still, she cleared Dat's breakfast dishes. Drew sat down, silent and alert. Loretta wiped the table, remaining quiet so they could catch any clues of the conversation downstairs.

Several minutes later, the men's boots beat a tattoo on the stairs. Was it her imagination, or did their footsteps sound louder, heavier, than when they'd followed Dat down to his shop?

Bishop Tom entered the kitchen first, his eyes wide with stress and disbelief. Preacher Ben came next, clutching something that resembled Rebecca's laptop computer. Dat stumbled to his chair as though he could walk no farther. He clasped his hands on the table and stared straight ahead, as though he anticipated a scathing lecture.

"You—you have some tall explaining to do, Cornelius!" Bishop Tom cried out. He slapped the edge of the table with the bundles of money in his hand—four of them, Rosalyn counted. "When Reuben moved to Roseville—traded houses and deacon positions with you—our fund was worth hundreds of thousands of dollars that our members had contributed over the years, and now we have only this! *What am I supposed to tell our congregation?*"

When the bishop's outcry filled the kitchen, the ringing of his voice apparently made him realize where he was. He exhaled loudly, glancing at Rosalyn and Loretta. "I'm sorry about this, girls," he said in a thin voice. "I must ask you not to say a word about what you've just seen and heard. Drew, your continued silence will be appreciated. We have to handle this matter appropriately. Prayerfully."

Drew nodded solemnly. Rosalyn clutched Loretta's hand, too startled to do anything but nod and nip her lip.

Preacher Ben's face was flushed as he glared at Dat. "You are not to leave this house, Deacon," he said in a low voice. "When Tom and I get back from the hospital, we're going to get to the bottom of this, understand me?"

Dat's head dropped and a sob escaped him.

"I should've heeded Ben's advice the first time we counseled you, Cornelius—should've called for your confession," the bishop muttered. "But I gave you the benefit of the doubt, so now I'm as much to blame for this *unthinkable* situation as you are. But we'll deal with that after we help Miriam's family."

The agony on Bishop Tom's face tore at Rosalyn's heart. The two church leaders departed quickly, leaving the atmosphere in the kitchen even more strained than it had been before they'd arrived.

Rosalyn knew better than to ask Dat about what Ben and Tom had said—hundreds of thousands of dollars that had apparently disappeared? The amount boggled her mind. Dat was resting his head against his hands on the tabletop, breathing very shallowly. He appeared even more forlorn than he had after they'd returned home from Mamm's funeral.

Baking Christmas cookies is out of the question now. Does Bishop Tom expect us to stay here with Dat, to be sure he doesn't run off?

"After we get the dishes washed," Loretta said, "I'm going to shovel the sidewalk out front—"

"I'll help you," Rosalyn put in, eager for something to do. "We can go over and clear Bishop Tom's sidewalks, too. He probably got the call from the hospital on the phone in his barn, while he was doing his milking."

"Asa and I will get started on the plowing," Drew said as he rose from his chair. "Hearing about that accident makes me even more inclined to keep our road cleared off."

Dat grunted, keeping his head on the table. "Fine. Just leave me here to suffer alone," he whimpered.

Loretta scowled at him in disbelief. "*Jah*, I believe I will," she muttered as she threw down her dishcloth. "Sounds like you have plenty to think about, Dat, and I wouldn't want our presence to distract you. Feel free to wash the dishes and redd up before Ben and the bishop come back. Come on, Rosalyn. Let's go."

Chapter Twenty

Marcus jogged alongside the dapple-gray Percheron, loosely holding the leather harness lines as the young horse pulled a large, heavy tree trunk behind him. The gelding was feeling frisky, wanting to play in the snow—which was the perfect opportunity for teaching him to focus on the work at hand.

"Easy, boy," he encouraged the horse. "Let's head for the barn, Herc."

Hercules, aptly named, perked his ears up at the word *barn* and broke into a canter as though the ten-foot tree trunk attached to his harness was merely a twig. He was figuring on being fed when he got to his stall.

"Whoa! Stop!" Marcus called out, tugging on the lines. He'd been debating about walking the Percheron along the highway—a chance to accustom the horse to traffic—and then asking the Detweilers if he could hitch Hercules to their V-shaped snowplow, but he decided against it. The horse was progressing nicely, but he wasn't yet ready to handle the distractions that might take him by surprise when they left the paddock. His attention span would improve as Marcus kept working him every day.

"*Gut* boy, stand steady," he said, reaching up to brush

snow from the horse's broad, muscled neck. "Now we'll *walk* to the barn. Slow and easy."

Herc shook his head impatiently, but he paid attention to the subtle change of pressure when Marcus tugged on the lines. When they stopped inside the barn door, Marcus unfastened the thick chain that held the tree trunk and then freed Herc from the harness. With a happy whinny, the Percheron trotted across the concrete floor of the barn, his huge hooves creating thunder that echoed in the rafters.

Marcus shook the snow from his scarf and stocking cap. He spoke to the other Percherons as he passed their stalls, considering which horse to work next. He was pouring a bucketful of grains into Herc's feeder when he heard the barn door slide open.

"Marcus, you in here?"

His eyebrows rose at the sound of a female voice—Nora's, he thought. But why would she be here? "*Jah*, back here! Center aisle and to your right," he replied loudly.

He emptied the bucket and started toward the barn door. Nora, wearing a bright red coat with a thick green scarf around her neck, peered around the wooden stalls at him with a mysterious smile. "Welcome to the Percheron barn," he said. "You're one of the last folks I'd expect to see out here amongst the horses."

"The Simple Gifts shop was the largest, fanciest horse barn in Willow Ridge before I turned it into a consignment store—and I dealt with horses when I was growing up Amish," she pointed out quickly. "Bishop Tom came over a few minutes ago and asked for my help, so I closed up shop—and suggested that you come with us."

Marcus's eyes widened. "As a Mennonite and a guy who's been avoiding membership in the Amish church, we make an odd couple to be hanging out with Bishop Tom," he hedged. "What's going on?"

"Tom and Ben are waiting for us at Wyatt's house, and

he's giving you the rest of the day off to tend to some, uh, *interesting* business. At the Riehl place."

Marcus's pulse rate shot up. "Is Roz all right?" he blurted out.

Nora smiled knowingly. "She's in for some startling surprises, but it's her father we'll be dealing with. Because you and I *know* things, Tom wants our help with the computer he found in Cornelius's clock shop this morning."

"Cornelius has a *computer*?" Marcus slid open the big door, his thoughts whirling like the snow as he and Nora stepped outside. He shoved the door shut again, frowning. "Does this involve that Reel Money network we saw the day I checked my email in your store?"

"Bingo," Nora replied. "See there? You're savvy about tech stuff, so you and I can help explain it to Bishop Tom. More importantly, we can keep Cornelius from wiggling out of the truth when Tom and Ben interrogate him this afternoon."

"Interrogate?" Marcus murmured as they strode along the snow-packed road toward Wyatt's house. "This sounds pretty serious."

Nora's freckled face tightened. "I might as well tell you this, since you're about to find out anyway," she said. "On a hunch, Drew and I followed Cornelius one morning in September when a driver was taking him to Kansas City, supposedly to buy clock parts. But he changed into English clothes at a rest area and—and then he went to a casino. With a briefcase that we assumed held money."

Marcus nearly choked. "Probably the same briefcase he carried into the bank in Morning Star," he said, shaking his head. "Cornelius didn't like it one bit when I challenged him about why he'd pulled wrapped bundles of money out of it— especially because I quizzed him in front of his girls and Detweiler."

"The more I hear, the worse this sounds." Nora focused on the snowy steps of Wyatt's deck, climbing carefully.

"Bishop Tom swore Drew and me to silence about where Cornelius had been going, so Rosalyn and her sisters don't know the details of their *dat*'s secret," she explained. "I don't have to tell you that things will get nasty when Ben and the bishop confront Cornelius this afternoon. The Riehl girls will need our support more than ever when the truth about their father gets out."

When they heard pounding on the front door, Rosalyn went to open it while everyone else remained in the kitchen. Dat had fussed when Asa and Edith had shown up with the twins after their noon meal, but Drew hadn't given him the option of talking with Bishop Tom and Preacher Ben alone.

"I'm calling a family meeting," Drew had said in the same tone Dat used when he said those words. "It's time your girls found out why Ben and the bishop are on your case, Cornelius. Soon, everyone else in Willow Ridge will hear about your activities, too—and it won't be pretty."

That hadn't set well with Dat at all. As Rosalyn, Edith, and Loretta had percolated a fresh batch of coffee and put some cookies on a tray, they'd exchanged worried glances. Waiting for the bishop and Ben to return had frazzled her nerves, so when Rosalyn opened the door and saw that Nora and Marcus had come with their church leaders, she felt even more puzzled about the nature of her father's misbehavior.

"Oh my," she murmured as she gestured for their guests to enter. "This looks worse than I'd anticipated. I can't imagine—"

"We're in this together, Rosalyn," Nora assured her as she reached for her hand. "Nothing you girls could've done would've made the situation come out any different—"

"And what your *dat* is involved in doesn't affect the way we feel about *you*," Marcus put in solemnly. His dark eyes held Rosalyn's gaze. "Afterward, if you have questions or need to talk, I hope you'll let me know, Roz."

His words made her heart dance—Marcus was still interested in her! She could only nod, because she had no idea what they would be dealing with around the kitchen table. For weeks, she and Loretta had wanted to hear about Dat's secrets, yet she was fearful of what would be revealed. They were serving coffee, cocoa, and goodies, but this would *not* be a Christmas party.

"*Gut* afternoon, everyone," Bishop Tom said as he and Ben hung their black hats and coats on pegs. The bishop sat down in the empty chair to Dat's left—the seat reserved for Mamm's memory—and placed a closed laptop computer on the table. He gazed expectantly at her father.

Dat was too startled to protest about where Tom was sitting, but he wasn't pleased. He crossed his arms tightly across his chest, pressing his lips into a tight line. Ben took the chair beside Asa's, while Nora and Marcus sat opposite each other.

"Coffee, anyone?" Loretta asked from the stove.

Her offer was met with the shaking of heads, so she and Rosalyn took their usual seats—which put Rosalyn beside the bishop. Although she liked Tom Hostetler a lot, it made her uneasy to sit so close to him during such an intense encounter. The lines on his weathered face had deepened. The dark circles beneath his eyes suggested that he'd lost sleep over the matter they were about to discuss.

As though they sensed the gravity of the situation, Leroy and Louisa sat quietly in their high chairs with animal crackers Edith had brought for them. After several moments of silence heightened by the sound of everyone's breathing, Bishop Tom murmured, "Let's pray for God's wisdom and guidance. We're going to need it."

Rosalyn bowed her head. When Loretta grasped her hand under the table, she felt her sister trembling. *Lord, we're confused and scared and we need help only You can give us*, she prayed nervously. *We thank You for the support of our friends and ask You to be with us all no matter what happens to—*"

"Amen," Bishop Tom said with a sigh. He seemed unsettled and disgusted—unsure of what to say—when he looked at Dat.

Preacher Ben, however, jumped right in. "Cornelius, why do you have a computer?" he demanded, pointing at the laptop. "You, as a leader of the Old Order, certainly know that such devices are forbidden—just like that air conditioner we took from your workshop this past summer."

Rosalyn held her breath, awaiting Dat's response. But he seemed at a loss for an answer.

"*My* question," Bishop Tom put in harshly, "is about what you've done with the money in our aid fund. I don't know anything about computers, but I suspect this one's connected to our money's disappearance. Am I right? *Answer me!*"

Rosalyn jumped at the sharpness of the bishop's words. He was ordinarily a compassionate, easygoing man, so his tone of voice said as much about his emotional state as his taut facial expression.

Dat cleared his throat. "I—in my grief, I may have made some unwise decisions," he mumbled.

"Your supposed *grief* has nothing to do with this, Cornelius," Ben shot back. "The first time we confronted you about money missing from the vault, we went along with your pleas that we not call you up in front of the congregation to confess your gambling habit—"

"And that was a big mistake on *my* part," Bishop Tom interjected with a shake of his head.

"—but this morning we discovered that thousands more dollars have disappeared since that day—hundreds of thousands of dollars, all told. *You* were responsible for that cash," Ben continued in a rising voice. "If you've stopped going to the casino, how have you lost so much more of our money, Cornelius?"

Rosalyn gasped. Apparently Dat's numerous trips to

Kansas City last spring and summer had actually been gambling flings. But why had Dat gone to a casino? And how could he have been gambling in recent weeks, when he'd been spending so much time in his clock shop?

Her throat got so dry she couldn't speak—not that she knew what to say. Marcus, Drew, and Nora were gazing at her with sad understanding in their eyes . . . as though they knew the answers to Tom and Ben's questions.

Dat closed his eyes, swiping at tears. "You have no idea how my wife's absence has affected me—how hollow I've felt ever since her—"

"How can you blame Mamm's passing for your behavior?" Loretta demanded in a terse whisper. "I'm appalled that you're connecting her to your—your *gambling* habit! Using her as an excuse to lose the church's money."

"I'm glad she's not here to witness this disgrace to our family," Edith declared in dismay. Her shoulders shook as she turned toward the twins to give them more cookies.

Rosalyn was amazed that her sisters had spoken out against their father so vehemently—and in front of Bishop Tom, too. Dat appeared shocked by their outbursts, but for once he didn't launch into a tirade about them disrespecting him or Mamm's memory.

Bishop Tom looked at them sadly. "You girls have nailed it. I'm sorry you've had to learn of your *dat*'s transgressions today, but there's no dancing around them any longer." With a sigh, he continued. "I'll be calling a members' meeting after our next church service for the purpose of your *dat*'s confession, and you should be prepared for his shunning. Of course, after I also confess to letting his behavior continue for so long, folks may well call for my shunning, too. Willow Ridge may soon be looking for a new bishop."

Rosalyn swallowed hard. Everyone around her appeared stricken by Tom's words. Even Dat seemed taken aback, as though he hadn't considered all the consequences of his deceitful behavior.

Preacher Ben rose to look at the calendar on the kitchen wall. "We'll be holding church at my house on December thirty-first," he said glumly. "Not a very auspicious way to end this year or to begin the new one."

"Puts a damper on Christmas, too," Drew remarked. "It's a shame we'll have this issue hanging over our heads for nearly two weeks before folks hear how seriously Cornelius has betrayed the church district."

Dat's eyes flashed angrily at Drew, but the fact that he didn't protest—or offer more excuses—told Rosalyn that he finally realized he couldn't escape punishment for what he'd done. She shook her head, embarrassed and confused. How had her father, the deacon of the church, fallen so far?

"I don't understand," she whispered. "How could Dat gamble if he wasn't leaving home? I—I don't know enough about casinos or computers to fathom how he lost so much money. Money that wasn't his to spend."

"Ah, but some of it *was* his money," Loretta pointed out somberly. "This explains those letters about bills that haven't been paid, *jah*? And lately he's told us not to buy groceries, too, because he can't afford them."

Across the table, Marcus cleared his throat. "Do you see that little silver gadget sticking out the side of the computer?" he asked gently, gesturing toward the laptop. "It's a hot spot that creates Internet access, so your *dat* could use online gambling sites without leaving the house. The day I saw him deposit money at the bank in Morning Star, he was funding an account connected to an online casino. When he placed bets on this computer and lost, the online casino deducted money from that account."

"Marcus and I noticed a new online network the day of my Christmas open house," Nora added softly. "But because of the different spelling, we didn't realize that Reel Money was connected to Cornelius. We had no idea he had a computer, you see."

When Dat quickly looked away, Rosalyn knew the truth: her father was guilty of all the horrible misdeeds the bishop and Preacher Ben had accused him of. Her stomach knotted. For the past several months, her father had been deceiving his family and their neighbors . . . hiding behind lies while insinuating that she and her sisters didn't respect Mamm's memory.

Preacher Ben's eyes widened. "Is that how it worked, Cornelius?" he asked in disbelief. "You stopped traveling to the casino, as you promised us you would—"

"But you were here at home gambling all the same," Bishop Tom summarized. "Why didn't you stop sooner? How on God's *gut* earth did you figure on paying back what you lost?"

"And how will you explain this to our church members?" Ben put in without losing a beat. "Some of them have been sharing a portion of their earnings for more than sixty years—all of their adult lives—and now they're going to learn that their money's gone to a *casino*. I hope you're ready to face their questions, Cornelius. Their outrage."

Dat's mouth moved but it took a while for any sound to come out. "I—I couldn't stop," he rasped. "I knew it was wrong, but I kept winning just enough to believe I could recoup my losses. I'm sorry. I hope folks will find it in their hearts to forgive me."

"*Sorry.*" The bishop grasped the edge of the table so tightly that his knuckles turned white. "I doubt your friends will feel too forgiving when they learn what you've done, Cornelius. I'm removing you from the office of deacon immediately. We'll take the vault and what little remains of the church's money someplace else for safekeeping."

"We were barely able to cover the hospital expenses for Miriam's kin this morning—even though the doctors discounted their rate when Tom explained that Amish folks don't carry insurance," Ben said in a low voice.

"*Jah*, God surely softened their hearts toward us," the bishop put in with a shake of his head. "I'm hoping He'll help us through this situation and provide ways to rebuild our aid fund, too. We've got a long row to hoe, to regain any sort of financial stability."

The weight of the church district's situation stifled conversation for several moments. Rosalyn still had a hard time understanding how her *dat* could have gambled away hundreds of thousands of dollars—especially because they'd lived in Willow Ridge for less than a year.

Preacher Ben broke the uncomfortable silence. "How much is left in that bank account, Cornelius?" he demanded.

Dat looked away. "I don't know. Haven't checked the balance lately," he mumbled.

Bishop Tom scowled as though he didn't believe Dat's answer. "I'll be taking you to Morning Star first thing tomorrow to close out that account. Why do I suspect there'll be very little money left to claim?"

As silence filled the kitchen again, Rosalyn hung her head. What a nightmare this was—so humiliating. And it wasn't nearly over.

"I'm not a member of the church yet, but if I were," Marcus said pensively, "I'd want to know about this crisis sooner rather than later. And I'd want to be working on plans to raise money, too, rather than letting nearly two weeks go by before the next church service."

"Folks generally have deeper pockets at Christmastime," Nora put in. "I can think of several of my customers who'd donate to the aid fund—even English folks—but once January sets in, they'll be paying off their credit card bills from Christmas."

Bishop Tom considered their ideas before rising to his feet. "I appreciate your help today—and your thoughts about rebuilding our fund—and I'll pray on them," he added wearily. "Right now, though, I'd like some help getting the vault out of the workshop downstairs."

Preacher Ben stood up. "Won't be nearly as heavy now that it's empty," he remarked sadly. "I'm thinking three of us fellows can get a *gut* hold on it and bring it up the stairs."

"I'm in," Drew declared as he started for the basement door.

"Me too," Marcus said. He smiled solemnly at Rosalyn before he got up from the table.

"I'll go fetch my horse and wagon," Asa said, turning toward the coats hanging on the wall. "Might as well get this done."

"I don't know how large your vault is, but if it'll fit in my van, I'm parked right outside," Nora offered quickly.

Ben and Tom paused on their way to the basement door, considering her idea. "*Denki*, Nora, but I'm thinking it might be too tall to lay in your van," Ben remarked.

"As I recall, we brought it in through the downstairs door years ago when Reuben became our deacon," Bishop Tom mused aloud. "It'll be a lot easier to carry it outside that way than maneuvering it up the stairs—especially if you can back your wagon around the house and toward that door, Asa."

Asa nodded as he pulled his black stocking cap firmly over his head. "My Percheron can handle that, but somebody might want to shovel a path so the guys carrying the vault won't have to deal with snow up around their knees."

"I'm on it." Loretta crossed the kitchen to get her wraps and a shovel from the mudroom.

"I'm with you, sister," Edith said. "Let me just get my coat on and—"

"You'll be needing somebody to open and close the doors," Nora volunteered as she, too, fetched her coat from a peg.

Edith sighed as though Dat's situation were weighing

heavily on her. "Rosalyn, would you mind looking after the kids while I grab the other shovel?"

It seemed her family and friends were leaving the scene like rats abandoning a sinking ship, but Rosalyn nodded. Ben and Tom grabbed their coats, and then the bishop picked up Dat's laptop.

"I'm sorry we've put you and your sisters through this, Rosalyn," he murmured. "I'll keep you girls in my prayers as we decide how to move forward. And I'll pick you up first thing tomorrow, Cornelius."

Dat crossed his arms, scowling as though Bishop Tom had said something particularly disgusting. When Ben and Tom closed the basement door behind them, the tattoo of their boots echoed in the narrow stairwell. The kitchen took on a prickly, tight silence.

Rosalyn didn't want to be the only adult left in the kitchen with Dat. She couldn't look him in the eye—didn't want to hear whatever he might say—so she smiled at Louisa and Leroy. "Let's go out and play in the front room," she suggested as she released the children from their high chairs. "Your wooden train and the cloth dolls are out there—"

"So you're deserting me, too, Rosalyn?" Dat demanded.

Rosalyn blinked against sudden, hot tears. What could she say to the man whose secret thievery had wiped out the funds their neighbors had been steadily, trustingly donating over the years—not to mention the way Dat's gambling had also put her life into a bind? If he was shunned for the customary six weeks, his family wasn't supposed to eat with him or touch him or accept anything directly from his hand . . . and Rosalyn sensed her father was going to milk that situation for all it was worth. Rather than acting penitent, her *dat* would probably lay guilt about his separation on her and Loretta. He was already trying to make her feel guilty—feel sorry for him—with the question he had just asked her.

And she was tired of taking the blame.

"Seems to me it's not a case of us deserting you, but rather of you driving us away," Rosalyn replied tersely. "Ever since Mamm passed, you've been accusing us of not loving her, and now you've used her memory as your excuse to gamble. You've created a chasm in our family—a huge, gaping wound that won't soon be healed."

Dat stared at her as though gearing up for a lecture, but after living in fear of his punishment for twenty-eight years, Rosalyn suddenly felt as though she'd been sprung from an invisible prison.

"After all these years of telling us girls that as we made our beds so we'd have to lie in them, you'll have to take your own medicine," she said bluntly. "Don't be surprised if you find yourself living here alone, cooking your own meals and doing your laundry after you're shunned. Once they've heard what you've done, not a soul in Willow Ridge would blame Loretta, Drew, and me for moving out."

"Hah!" Dat mocked her. "You have no place to go—and you wouldn't have the gumption to go there if you did."

Rosalyn's eyes widened—and indeed, she felt as though her eyes had just been *opened* by Dat's apparent assumption that she would never marry or move out on her own. Who did he think he was, implying that she was only good enough, only capable enough, to remain at home as his servant?

"Watch me," she heard herself mutter. "Just you watch me go, Dat."

Rosalyn quickly scooped a twin into each arm. Then she went upstairs to pack.

Chapter Twenty-One

Tuesday morning after breakfast, when Asa had left the house to work in the furniture shop, Rosalyn set down the dishes she was scraping. "Be honest with me, Edith," she implored her youngest sister. "Are you sure it's all right for me to stay in your guest room? I—I feel like I've barged in on you and Asa without asking you—"

"Nonsense," Edith insisted. She lifted Leroy from his high chair. "Asa and I have told you time and again that you had a room in our home if you wanted one. After what we learned about Dat's gambling habit yesterday, why *wouldn't* you and Loretta and Drew move out? What he did was unthinkable."

Rosalyn exhaled slowly, allowing Edith's words to soothe her unsettled soul. The pale yellow walls and fresh white cabinets in her sister's kitchen were such a cheerful improvement over the faded paint and curtains at home—a lift to her spirits even though she felt weary from a restless night. Rosalyn couldn't help smiling when Louisa reached for her after Edith released her from her high chair. The world was a brighter place when she held the blond toddler against her hip, her little face mere inches away.

"Bah, bah, bah?" Louisa babbled.

"Bah, bah, black sheep, have you any wool?" Rosalyn joined in softly.

"Bah, bah, back seep!" the year-old girl mimicked with a giggle.

Rosalyn hugged Louisa close. Maybe her life would be different in many positive ways, now that she'd be around Edith's kids all the time. She set the little girl on the floor. "Here, you can help clear the table," she said as she handed the girl two spoons. "Carry these to your *mamm*, sweetie."

As the little girl toddled toward the sink, Rosalyn refocused on the conversation. "I think Loretta and Drew were tickled to move into the apartment above the shop," she speculated. "It must be like playing house when we were girls—such a small space. Won't take her long to clean it, either."

Edith turned on the faucet, waving at someone she saw through the window. "Here comes Loretta now. We can ask her."

Moments later, Loretta burst through the mudroom door. "How is everyone this morning?" she asked as she stomped the snow from her boots. "It's been an eventful several hours since we left Dat."

"How so?" Edith asked. "Rosalyn and I were just talking about how much less time it'll take you to redd up the apartment—almost like you're playing house."

"Well, there's that," Loretta agreed with a chuckle. "The fridge was empty, so Drew and I made a trip to Zook's Market yesterday, right before they closed. Preacher Henry watched us like a hawk while we put our groceries in the cart, let me tell you."

Rosalyn sighed as she plucked the plates from the hot rinse water. "What did he say? Did Lydia get that long-suffering expression on her face when you checked out?"

"She was pressing her lips into a tight line, *jah*—until Drew pulled out some cash," Loretta added as she removed her wraps. "We paid for our stuff and put the rest of the money toward Dat's bill. I couldn't believe it. According to Lydia's ledger sheet, he still owes them almost two hundred dollars."

Rosalyn's eyebrows shot up. "No wonder Dat was telling us to stay out of the store."

"I'll have Asa give them some money, too," Edith said. "It's not right that the grocer's going unpaid."

Loretta brightened as she entered the kitchen to help them. "On a happier note, Nora was coming into the market as we were leaving," she said. "I told her we'd moved out— and asked if we could work in her store again, since Dat has no say about it anymore. She lit up like Christmas, Rosalyn! I'm going to resume working my usual Tuesday and Thursday hours, so I'll go in as soon as she opens this morning—"

"Oh, I'd love to work for Nora again!" Rosalyn exclaimed. She felt immediately better, as though her days would once again have purpose. "If she still wants me on Wednesdays and Saturdays, well—I'd even be glad to help on other days, what with Christmas being less than a week away."

Loretta smiled as though she'd anticipated Rosalyn's answer. "Well, Saturday's Christmas Eve, so she won't be open—and we have another, um, *event* to attend tomorrow. But I'm sure she'd be glad to have you on Thursday and Friday to handle her last-minute shoppers."

Rosalyn got a funny feeling in her stomach. "What event?"

Loretta began drying the plates in the drainer. "Bishop Tom stopped by this morning," she replied. "He and Ben have decided to hold a special church meeting tomorrow at Ben and Miriam's, rather than waiting for our regular church Sunday. They want to get this matter before the members so they can admit their own bad decision, about not insisting that Dat confess earlier," she added with a shake of her head.

"Poor Tom's afraid folks are going to hold him responsible for so much money getting gambled away, and shun him and Ben along with Dat. He's asked Bishop Vernon from Cedar Creek to come, so the meeting will proceed properly during his confession—and afterward."

"What a mess," Edith whispered. "Dat's been weaving a tangled web ever since we moved to Willow Ridge, by the sound of it."

"I still don't understand how he could lose so much money," Rosalyn murmured. "Why would a casino—in a real building or on the computer—allow someone to keep playing if they weren't winning?"

"Oh, the whole purpose of gambling—for a casino—is to make money on people's belief that they'll win a boatload of money, or at least win back what they've lost. That's how Nora explained it, anyway," Loretta replied. "The *real* question is why Dat would gamble with the church district's money."

"And why wouldn't he stop when he was losing instead of winning?" Edith demanded sharply. "What really irks me is that he was blaming the whole thing on his grief—and that he pretended to be in his shop working all those extra hours. It takes a special kind of liar to get caught in a loss of that magnitude and then blithely say he hoped folks would *forgive* him. As though his kneeling confession and six weeks of being shunned would make everything right again."

Rosalyn blinked. The three of them had lived in Dat's shadow all their lives, tiptoeing around his whims and moods, but she couldn't recall sweet, kindhearted Edith ever speaking so harshly of *anyone*. "I suspect we'll find out more than we want to know at the meeting tomorrow," she said ruefully. "Folks might wonder if we girls are also guilty by association—if we knew what Dat was up to but didn't tell anyone. Why would folks who haven't known us all that long assume we're innocent bystanders?"

Edith pulled the stopper from the sink drain. "I guess we'll find out where we stand tomorrow, ain't so?" she asked softly. "Depending on what Dat says and does—and what folks vote to do about him—we might find ourselves wishing we could move back to Roseville."

Chapter Twenty-Two

Worms of worry squirmed in Rosalyn's stomach as she, her sisters, and their husbands entered Preacher Ben and Miriam's home Wednesday morning. Folks were removing their coats with whispered conversations and concerned expressions—and why wouldn't they? Their questions buzzed like bees in the big front room.

What's so urgent that Bishop Tom couldn't wait until after the service on December thirty-first? Why didn't he call a meeting after church three days ago?

Rosalyn remained silent, nodding as Savilla and Lena Witmer greeted her. Miriam's identical daughters, Rachel and Rhoda, holding their toddlers against their hips, preceded Loretta into a pew bench on the women's side. Rosalyn sat down between her sisters, happy that little Louisa was beaming at her from Edith's lap—Leroy was sitting with his *dat* so the little twins' chatter wouldn't disrupt the meeting. Across the large room, Asa and Drew appeared somber, as though they anticipated a lot of unpleasantness before all was said and done.

Because this wasn't a church service, they didn't begin with the usual singing of a hymn. When white-haired Bishop Vernon entered the room, his hands clasped before him, all talking ceased. Bishop Tom and Preacher Henry took their places on the preacher's bench alongside Vernon, their faces somber as they surveyed the crowd.

"Where's Dat?" Edith whispered.

"What if he doesn't show up?" Loretta shot back.

Rosalyn shifted uneasily. The Hooleys' front room was too warm and stuffy. The wooden bench felt unusually hard, probably because she'd gone a second night without getting much sleep.

When Marcus entered the room, however, Rosalyn's heart fluttered. He searched her out, his smile telling of his support—his belief that she was still worthy of his attention. She reminded herself to breathe. She sat up straighter, despite the tension that tightened the faces around her.

Bishop Tom stood up to speak, scanning the crowd one more time—looking for Dat, no doubt. It was odd, seeing the bishop dressed in broadfall pants and a blue shirt rather than the black suit and white shirt he wore on Sundays. By the expression on his taut face, however, his everyday clothing wasn't making him feel any more comfortable about the day's topic.

"Folks, let's quiet our hearts and minds," he intoned, raising his hand for silence. "We'll begin with a word of prayer to ask for God's guidance—"

Footsteps in the kitchen made folks look toward the doorway. Everyone's eyebrows rose when Dat entered the front room with his head bowed and his shoulders slumped, just a few steps ahead of Preacher Ben, who appeared unusually stern.

One look at them tells the story, Rosalyn thought, clasping her hands tightly in her lap. *If Ben hadn't gone to fetch him, Dat wouldn't be here.*

When she saw her father's woeful expression, a different thought occurred to her. *He's putting on that forlorn look so folks will feel sorry for him! Instead of appearing penitent, he's playing the victim—planning to weep and wail about his overwhelming grief.*

As though they were thinking the same thing, her sisters let out disgusted sighs. They watched closely as Dat and Ben sat in two of the three folding chairs that faced the congregation, which was the customary place for members preparing to give a confession. Ben appeared somber, sitting with his hands folded in his lap. Without looking at anyone, Dat quickly wrapped his arms around his knees and laid his head on them. His dejected moan accompanied the shuddering of his shoulders.

"I may have to leave," Loretta muttered under her breath.

"So help me, if he doesn't speak the truth—if he puts on an act—I'm going to stand up and call him on it," Edith whispered vehemently.

Rosalyn's eyes widened. As she took her sisters' hands, she was relieved when Bishop Tom bowed his head and began to pray.

"Father God, we come before You today imploring Your presence and Your wisdom as we discuss a very difficult situation," he said earnestly. "As the truth is revealed, have mercy on our human frailties yet hold us fully accountable—just as You will on the judgment day that lies ahead for each of our souls when You call us home. Amen."

As folks lifted their heads, they also sucked in their breath when Bishop Tom took the third folding chair rather than returning to his spot on the preacher's bench. When Bishop Vernon rose to speak, Preacher Henry appeared apprehensive—vulnerable and lonely—being the only church leader who remained on the preacher's bench.

"As a godly man of conscience, your bishop has asked me to oversee this meeting while we address issues of a very serious and unusual nature," Vernon began in his resonant voice. "Because Tom and Ben are more aware of the questions that will elicit a full response from Deacon Cornelius, they will conduct his confession before going to their knees to give their own."

Folks gazed at the three leaders in the folding chairs with widened eyes, now painfully aware of the seriousness of the meeting's purpose.

"This is an unfortunate and unprecedented situation—yet even so, our Lord has been present all along. If we listen, He will guide us to the proper conclusions," Bishop Vernon continued calmly. "During these proceedings, we must maintain the same respect and reverence we would display if we'd just finished a church service. First, I wish to attune our hearts and minds to what Jesus taught His followers concerning the proper stewardship of the gifts God has bestowed upon each and every one of us."

The white-haired bishop paused, gazing at the crowd with earnest blue eyes. "Although it may seem irregular— perhaps too progressive—I wish to paraphrase the parable of the talents rather than reading it from the Bible," he said solemnly. "My intention is to render Jesus's teaching in clear, unmistakable language, because the situation we face today calls for all the *clarity* we can muster."

The room rang with silence. Rosalyn glanced around— and saw that everyone else was doing the same thing. Folks seemed stunned by the magnitude of the apparent wrongdoing that involved three of their four church leaders. She was grateful that Bishop Vernon was handling the day's situation with the same compassion and discernment he'd shown on Edith's original wedding day, when Drew had drugged his twin brother so he could marry her in Asa's place. Folks had since forgiven Drew and accepted him as a valuable member of the community—but Dat's gambling habit would rock the foundations of Willow Ridge a lot harder than Drew's deceit had.

"The parable of the talents—like most of the parables— begins with Jesus saying, 'the kingdom of heaven is like—'"

Bishop Vernon began in a resonant voice. "In this case, the kingdom of heaven is like a man who's traveling to a far country, and before he goes, he's entrusting his money to his servants. The Lord is instructing us in the way our current everyday lives serve as preparation for the everlasting life He has promised to those who confess and find their salvation in Him."

Bishop Vernon paused, allowing his words to sink in.

"In this story, you'll recall that the man gives five talents to one servant—a talent being worth several thousand dollars, as best we can tell," Vernon explained patiently. "To a second servant he gives two talents, and to a third servant he gives one talent. For whatever reason, this man has entrusted quite a fortune to his employees, just as God has blessed us with spiritual and monetary riches beyond what we deserve."

The people in the room were listening closely, nodding as their understanding matched what the bishop was recounting for them. Rosalyn closed her eyes, wondering again just how many thousands of dollars her father had lost . . . and wondering how these neighbors would react when they heard Dat's confession.

"When the man returns from his journey and requests a reckoning of accounts," Bishop Vernon went on, "the servant who'd received the five talents reports that he's invested the money wisely and has earned five talents more—and the servant who'd received two talents has doubled those, as well. 'Well done, good and faithful servant,' the man declares. 'You were faithful with a few things, so I'll put you in charge of many more. Enter into the joy of your lord.'"

Bishop Vernon gazed imploringly at all in the room. "It should be the sincerest goal of every one of us to hear the Lord say those magnificent words to us someday—*well done, good and faithful servant. Enter into the joy of your lord.*"

Rosalyn swallowed hard. Every person present knew the

rest of the story. Folks were frowning as they glanced at their deacon, their bishop, and one of their preachers.

"But the servant who'd received one talent had hidden the money in the ground, claiming that he was afraid, and that his master had reaped where he hadn't sown," Vernon continued in a harsher voice. "The man rebukes the servant for his presumptuous attitude, saying that he could've at least put the money in the bank to earn some interest. 'You wicked and slothful servant,' the man says angrily. And he casts the servant into the outer darkness, where there would be much weeping and gnashing of teeth."

The bishop's shoulders sank sadly as he shook his head. "May God preserve us from such a bleak state of eternal damnation," he finished in a dramatic whisper. "And may God's will be done this day, as the men seated before you give a reckoning of accounts."

Except for the whisper of fabric against fabric as folks shifted uncomfortably, the room rang with a frightened silence. Even though Rosalyn knew the details that were about to be revealed, she quaked at the picture Bishop Vernon had painted with his words. Would Dat come clean? Would he be cast into the outer darkness by his enraged neighbors when they learned what he'd done?

Bishop Vernon turned to face the three men seated in the folding chairs. "Deacon Cornelius, because your unfortunate behavior is the root of the problem we're facing, and because you did not confess before your fellow church members several weeks ago when Bishop Tom urged you to do so, you will kneel before us first."

Rosalyn's throat got so dry she couldn't swallow. Her sisters' hands tightened around hers as Dat rolled forward out of the folding chair and onto his knees rather than walking to the center of the room. The sound of his rapid, shallow breathing filled the air, until folks probably wondered if he was going to keel over and die on the spot.

"I want to confess that I—I have failed," Dat began in a thin voice. It was the customary statement made by a member giving a confession, but the words sounded oddly out of kilter, considering the resounding tones in which Dat usually read from the Scriptures on Sunday morning. "I want to make peace and—and continue in patience with God and the church, and—"

Dat's voice cracked and he began to sob. "And in the future to take better care," he finished. He pulled a bandana from his pocket to mop his face.

If I didn't know what he's been up to—just how deceptively and thoughtlessly he's betrayed his neighbors, Rosalyn thought, *I would feel very, very sorry for the poor man kneeling before us.*

Folks were craning their necks to get a better look at their deacon. A few of the women glanced speculatively at Rosalyn and her sisters. Painful as it was, it seemed best to focus on her father rather than face the neighbor ladies' frowns. Even though she'd met them all at church services, Rosalyn hadn't spent much time with some of the women—and it was even more difficult to see the doubt-filled expressions of the ladies she considered her friends.

Bishop Tom stepped closer to Dat. "What is the nature of your failure, Brother Cornelius?"

Dat remained curled inward, shaking. "I . . . I have behaved irresponsibly with money."

The bishop sighed, as though he anticipated having to pry every word from Dat's mouth. "You must be more specific," he stated. "If your neighbors are to grant you the forgiveness you seek, they must know exactly what you've done wrong, Cornelius."

Rosalyn winced when her father's agonized groan filled the room. Folks shifted nervously on the benches.

"I have . . . misappropriated some of the district's money," Dat finally admitted in a theatrical whisper.

Preacher Ben rose from his chair to stand beside Bishop Tom. "Cornelius, you can either state your case and get your sin out in the open," he said sternly, "or you can prolong everyone's discomfort by forcing us to ask you the questions you'd rather avoid. This situation has gone on for far too long—"

"And you've compounded the problem by breaking the promise you made to Ben and me in September, to mend your ways—and repay your debt—when we allowed you to continue as our deacon," Bishop Tom continued sharply. "So, not only have you misspent the district's money, you've lied to us."

Several folks gasped, appalled by what Tom and Ben had said. The men across the room leaned forward, determined to catch every word from the deacon, who remained on his knees in a fetal position.

After a few moments of silence, Bishop Vernon stepped closer to Dat and cleared his throat. "What do you have to say, Cornelius?" he prompted. "The longer you wait, the more time you give your neighbors to imagine the worst."

Dat sighed dolefully. "I—I fully deserve your censure," he said. "May the Lord grant me mercy and peace and—"

"Tell us where you went and how much you've spent, Cornelius!" Preacher Henry blurted out from the preachers' bench. "The mercy and peace you crave will be a long time coming when everyone hears that you went to—"

"Let Cornelius say it," Bishop Vernon cut in, silencing Preacher Henry with his raised hand. "It's best if a sinner comes before God and his neighbors with a contrite heart, while we await the opening of his soul. Considering that your deacon's revelation won't change the situation your district faces, we can afford him some patience. However, Cornelius," he added, "folks will wonder about the sincerity of your confession if your leaders have to ask you for every little detail. Shall we proceed?"

Folks murmured more earnestly, exchanging troubled glances. Lydia Zook, seated a couple of rows in front of Rosalyn, flashed her and her sisters a worried frown. "What in the world's going on, girls?" she whispered. "It's one thing to run up a bill at the market, but—"

"Quiet, please!" Bishop Tom insisted above the rising chatter.

The room suddenly rang with an accusatory silence that made Rosalyn wish she could leave—and made her wonder if these people would make their lives in Willow Ridge so miserable that she and her sisters would have to live elsewhere because of Dat's transgressions.

But where could we go? Rosalyn wondered. *If the local folks stop buying Asa and Drew's refurbished furniture, we'll be unable to pay our bills—and we'll get the same embarrassing letters Dat's been receiving . . .*

"I was so consumed by grief after my wife's passing," Dat began in a quavering voice, "that I turned to gambling. I simply couldn't help myself—"

"Gambling?" Naomi Brenneman cried out. "I've never heard of such a thing amongst the Amish."

"How much money are we talking about?" Gabe Glick demanded from the front row of the men's side. He tapped his cane on the floor, his wrinkles deepening with his scowl. "When *I* was a preacher and Reuben Riehl was our deacon, our funds were accounted for down to the last penny—"

"Silence is in order," Bishop Vernon insisted, raising his hand to quiet the restless crowd. "Every member is entitled to a full rendering of his or her sins."

"Jesus taught that only a person without sin has the right to cast the first stone," Bishop Tom reminded everyone. "When Ben and I preached sermons back in September, urging guilty souls to confess, you might recall that Cornelius wasn't the only one squirming in his seat."

The room became quiet again, but it was the silence of

folks suppressing a bothersome cough. Rosalyn met her
sisters' nervous glances. As the eldest, she wished she knew
how to comfort Edith and Loretta, yet she was at a loss—and
grateful that they'd supported her when she'd moved out of
Dat's house. It was humbling, to feel so dependent upon the
younger women who'd looked up to her all their lives.

"Please find it in your hearts to forgive me," Dat bleated
like a lost lamb. "When Tom and Ben believed I could stay
away from the casino—when they counseled me and set up
a repayment plan—I failed them. I let them down."

"How much of the district's money did you lose, Cornelius?" Bishop Vernon prompted after a few moments.

Dat, still curled in on himself, let out another sob. "I don't
know. I—I lost count because I lost money of my own,
as well."

"That's no answer!" Naomi's husband, Ezra, blurted from
his wheelchair. "I've been paying into the aid fund all my
life—and my father before me did, as well."

"What are you saying?" Miriam asked in a strained whisper. "When my family needed their hospital bills paid this
past week, Ben wouldn't elaborate about how low the aid
fund had gotten. But I've never seen him so worried."

"Ben told me that if the hospital administrator hadn't
greatly reduced the bill because we Amish pay cash rather
than carrying insurance," Andy Leitner put in, "we wouldn't
have had enough money to cover the charges."

As their neighbors contemplated what Andy had said,
their restless silence became even more difficult to bear.
Rosalyn bowed her head, because she could no longer meet
the gazes of the women around her. *Lord, now that the truth
is coming out,* she prayed, *give us all the grace to accept it
and move forward in Your will for us. You're the only one who
can help us fix this mess Dat's gotten us into.*

"Are you saying we're broke—that *all* of the aid fund is
gone?" Josiah Witmer asked in a strained voice.

"How could this happen?" his wife Lena asked with a puzzled shake of her head. "There isn't a casino anywhere near Willow Ridge."

For several moments Dat didn't respond. Rosalyn wondered how long these folks would put up with his refusal to speak of the details. Dan Kanagy, who was married to Miriam's sister, Leah, stood up in the center of the men's section. The expression on his ruddy face was troubled.

"Although your prostrate position might symbolize your remorse, Cornelius," he said brusquely, "I, for one, prefer to see your face when you answer these questions. You have a lot of explaining to do!"

"*Jah*," Adam Wagler chimed in, "God already knows what you've done, so you might as well tell us. If it involves gambling and casinos and such, most of us have no idea how you've gotten us into this situation—"

"Or how you propose to get us out of it," Dan continued sternly. "We're talking about a *lot* of money."

"I agree," Bishop Tom said with a nod. "Your neighbors deserve your direct response, Cornelius."

Rosalyn's stomach churned. If her father couldn't pay his bills at Zook's Market, how could he possibly repay what he'd lost from the district's aid fund?

Very slowly Dat lifted his head. His face was as pale as poached fish. His graying hair and beard looked unkempt, and he was so rumpled, Rosalyn suspected he'd been wearing the same clothes for two or three days.

Was Dat truly distraught? Or was he playing upon these people's sympathy? She was appalled that such questions even occurred to her—but her world had been overturned like the proverbial apple cart when she'd learned the extent of her father's deceit. By the time he'd struggled onto his knees, with Tom and Ben standing on either side of him to help him up, Rosalyn was struck by how much he'd aged.

Dat looked quite different from the Deacon Cornelius who'd read the past Sunday's Scriptures with such gusto.

Rosalyn's heart grew painfully still when Dat finally stood at his full height and then gazed reproachfully at her, Loretta, and Edith.

"My family has abandoned me in the hour of my greatest need," he muttered, turning his head to include Drew and Asa in his accusation. "If they had been more supportive—more understanding of the depth of my grief after my beloved wife passed—perhaps I wouldn't have succumbed to the siren call of the casino."

Rosalyn's mouth went dry. Her sisters tensed on either side of her. Across the room, Asa and Drew rose to their feet with identical frowns on their faces.

"Your girls have taken *gut* care of you, Cornelius," Asa countered.

"*Jah*, let's not lay the blame for your gambling on them—or on my brother and me," Drew insisted. "We weren't the ones who called a driver to take you to the casino in Kansas City so many times."

"And we had no idea you were gambling on a computer in your workshop after you promised Bishop Tom you'd give up your habit," Asa added. "You've deceived your family every bit as much as you've betrayed your neighbors."

As folks took in this new information, they gawked at Rosalyn and her sisters—but their expressions hardened when they focused on her father again. What must these people be thinking now that the head of their family was admitting to heinous thievery only because the church leaders had compelled him to confess?

"Now that those two have spelled it out, what more do I need to say?" Dat spat.

"How much?" Dan quickly demanded.

"*Jah*, we have a right to know how much of our money

you lost!" Ezra snapped. "Seems we'd have been better off entrusting our funds to an English bank."

"But we didn't find out about this—this *astounding* betrayal by our deacon until it was too late to bank the money!" Adam pointed out as he stood up to glare at Dat. "Bishop Vernon and Bishop Tom, if you know these details to be true, I'm ready to vote on shunning Cornelius."

"*Jah*, what more do we need to hear?" Gabe Glick asked with a disgusted shake of his head. "I've witnessed a *gut* many confessions in my lifetime, but this beats all the previous ones rolled together."

A wave of sadness washed over Rosalyn. She'd known this moment would come, but nothing could've prepared her for the animosity some of her neighbors displayed. Ordinarily these folks took life's unpleasant surprises in stride, but as the enormity of Dat's betrayal sank in, fear and loathing hardened their expressions.

"Let's vote," Lydia echoed. "We have a lot of work ahead of us, figuring out how to rebuild our aid fund. Cornelius obviously can't pay us back."

Bishop Tom surveyed the agitated crowd before focusing on Dat again. "Cornelius, you know how this works. We'll call you back inside after we've voted."

With a dejected sigh, Dat hung his head. "I've been cast out into the cold—into the outer darkness," he lamented as he shambled toward the front door.

Rosalyn scowled when he left it open so that Preacher Ben had to shut it. The coldness that filled the Hooleys' big front room came as much from folks' chilly attitudes as from the brisk, wintry wind, however.

"Tom and Ben are recommending the customary six-week *bann* for Cornelius," Bishop Vernon said somberly. "I'll remind you that as he seeks to reconcile himself with God—and with you—you're not to deal with Cornelius except to encourage his repentance and return to the path of salvation. You cannot give him anything or accept anything directly from his hand," he continued in a hushed voice. "He will cover his face with his hand during church, and he's not to share the common meals after the services. He's to eat at a separate table in his home, as well. I ask your special consideration for his family, as these restrictions place a particular burden upon Rosalyn, Loretta, and Drew."

Asa stood up. "Bishop Vernon, because of the strain Cornelius's attitude has already caused in our family," he said sadly, "Drew and Loretta are now living in the apartment above our furniture shop and Rosalyn has moved in with us. Cornelius is now alone in his home."

Folks gazed at Rosalyn and her sisters with wide eyes. It was unheard of, to move out of a home rather than settling the differences between family members.

"Well, if his own family can't stand him, maybe we should send him back where he came from," one of the men muttered.

Bishop Tom raised his hand to still the whispering that filled the room. "I've already relieved Cornelius of his position as our deacon, and the vault has been relocated, so it behooves us to follow the *Ordnung*—to first prescribe a six-week separation," he reminded them. "Then, if Cornelius has shown penitence and he sincerely asks for forgiveness at the end of his *bann*—or if he does not—we'll proceed from there. Are we ready to vote?"

Everyone around Rosalyn nodded. The vote proceeded quickly along the rows of the men's side, each *aye* resounding clearly. As the older women in front of Rosalyn voted to shun her father, a sense of dread filled her soul. It was one thing to acknowledge that Dat had committed an unthinkable crime that affected the entire district of Willow Ridge. It was another matter entirely to cast a condemnatory vote as his eldest daughter. The *Ordnung* required a unanimous decision to shun a member, however.

Her sisters' hands tightened around hers as the vote continued down the row in which they were sitting. "Aye," said Lena and Savilla Witmer. Rachel and Rhoda's affirmative votes quickly followed theirs.

Edith sighed but then sat up straighter. "Aye," she said.

Tears slid down Rosalyn's cheeks. "Aye," she murmured, before Loretta added her muted affirmative vote. Annie Mae Wagler and her sister, Nellie Knepp, along with Ira's wife, Millie, completed the process.

"You have declared your unanimous decision," Bishop Vernon said. "Ben, if you'll ask Cornelius to come inside, we'll inform him of his *bann*. Then we'll proceed with Tom's confession and yours."

Rosalyn's heart clenched as Ben went to the door. Would Dat accept his fate, or would he make further accusations and excuses? He would know that his daughters and their husbands had voted to put him under the *bann*, so she couldn't imagine Dat hearing Bishop Vernon announce his punishment without taking a final verbal shot.

As Rosalyn braced herself for Dat's rebuke, she glanced over at the men's side—and felt grateful for the compassion that shone on Marcus's face as he gazed at her.

At least I have one friend who understands my difficult situation, she thought. Maybe, with Marcus's help, I'll get through this. Maybe someday he'll want to be more than just my friend . . .

Chapter Twenty-Three

Marcus longed to rush over and take Rosalyn in his arms, to kiss away her tears—but such behavior would be improper during this solemn public meeting. He held her gaze, however, while most folks were focused on her father's return.

"Cornelius!" Preacher Ben called as he stepped outside. "Where are you? Come inside now!"

Had the errant deacon left the premises rather than face his fate? All around the room, folks were craning their necks as they watched for Rosalyn's *dat*.

Marcus hoped life would be easier for the Riehl girls now that they no longer lived under their domineering father's thumb—and he vowed to see that Rosalyn and her sisters suffered no backlash from these neighbors who'd learned about Cornelius's gambling. It was highly unusual for Amish daughters to leave their father to fend for himself, so some of the more traditional folks in town—especially the men— might view the girls' departure as disrespectful.

Commotion at the doorway drew Marcus out of his thoughts. Because Cornelius had foolishly gone outside without his coat, Ben was brushing a lot of snow from his slumped shoulders. Had Cornelius burrowed in a drift or caught some snow as it slipped off the roof?

Why would he do that, unless he was trying for folks' attention—their sympathy? Marcus wondered. He hadn't known Cornelius long, but he was tired of the games Rosalyn's *dat* played—as well as the way he manipulated his daughters' emotions.

"Cornelius, the members have voted on a *bann* for a full six weeks—which is customary for an offense of such magnitude as yours," Bishop Vernon said. "Meanwhile, we'll be praying for your soul's recovery—and encouraging you to find a way to make restitution."

Cornelius's bushy eyebrows rose. "Did our Lord not teach his disciples to 'forgive us our debts as we forgive our debtors,'?" he demanded sourly. "I've been dealt a harsh blow by folks who claim to obey the Bible—"

"'Thou shalt not steal!'" Ezra exclaimed. "That's in the Bible, too."

"'Thou wicked and slothful servant!'" Gabe chimed in vehemently. "Why *wouldn't* we punish your crime?"

"You got off easy, Cornelius," Dan Kanagy put in with a shake of his head. "You've bankrupted our aid fund, and you don't even seem *sorry* for cheating us."

"You should go home now, Cornelius," Bishop Tom suggested quickly. "We have other matters for members in *gut* standing to decide—"

"You're not going to reprimand Rosalyn and Loretta for abandoning me?" Cornelius demanded. "They've repeatedly defied me by working in Nora Hooley's store amongst English, too—clearly going against our Old Order ways—yet you're allowing them to get off scot-free?"

Bishop Tom and Preacher Ben exchanged a look that suggested they were both tired of dealing with Cornelius. When Lydia Zook stood up, Marcus hoped she wouldn't suggest that Rosalyn, as the unmarried daughter, should return home to look after her *dat*. Rosalyn's tight-lipped expression told him that she, too, expected conservative Preacher Henry's wife to speak in favor of a Plain daughter's traditional role.

"Seems to me, Cornelius, that you should be grateful to your daughters and sons-in-law for paying off your bill at the market," Lydia said boldly. "*I* certainly am."

"*Jah*," red-haired Atlee Glick joined in. "The Detweilers paid off your horse feed bill at the sale barn yesterday, too. Seeing's how they were making the rounds, asking if you owed anyone else money, I'm convinced they had no idea you'd been gambling at a casino—and on a computer after that."

"Asa and Drew paid your bill at the mill, as well," Ira Hooley said as he rose from his pew bench. "Seems you dug yourself into this hole, Cornelius, so maybe it's best you dig yourself out—or at least show a little remorse for the way you've hoodwinked everyone in town. Frankly, I can't blame your girls for moving out."

Marcus relaxed. He'd been ready to defend the Riehl girls and their husbands, but it seemed everyone had figured out the truth.

Cornelius scowled, his fists clenched at his sides. "So that's the way of it?" he scoffed. "Why do I suspect that at the end of my six-week *bann*, not a one of you will believe I'm sorry and repentant? I might as well—"

"Actions speak louder than words," Atlee piped up again. "When the bishop tells us you've begun paying back the church's money, maybe we'll believe your plea for forgiveness is sincere."

"And meanwhile, not a one of you will buy my clocks or ask me to do repairs so I'll have an income, right?" Cornelius shot back. "I might as well go. I sense no Christian charity at all in this crowd."

When the door slammed behind him, everyone winced—and then remained very quiet. Bishop Tom walked to the center of the space between the men's and women's sides and went to his knees. As he clasped his hands in a gesture of prayerful entreaty, not a soul made a sound.

"I want to confess that I have failed," the bishop began softly. "I want to make peace and continue in patience with God and the church, and in the future to take better care."

"And I belong on my knees right here with Tom," Preacher Ben said as he knelt beside the bishop. "I have also failed, and I want to make peace and continue in patience with God and the church—with all of you folks who look to us for guidance—and in the future take better care."

Preacher Henry, alone on the preacher's bench, appeared self-conscious about being the only church leader who remained unscathed by this unusual situation. Marcus didn't know Vernon Gingerich very well, but he was glad the bishop from Cedar Creek had stepped in to assist them. Henry Zook was clearly more comfortable running his store than he was with the leadership role his neighbors had nominated him for, and for which God had chosen him by the fall of the lot.

"How about if you tell us why you feel compelled to confess, Tom," Bishop Vernon suggested. "I perceive some puzzlement on the faces of your church members, concerning your connection to what they've learned about Cornelius."

Bishop Tom nodded. "Nora Hooley told me in early September that she and Drew had become suspicious of Cornelius's frequent trips to Kansas City, so they'd followed him and seen him going into a casino," he explained. "When Ben and I went to the Riehl house to quiz him, we took Cornelius to task for having an air conditioner in his shop, and for placing his workbench across the doorway to the vault—"

"Because we'd asked him earlier to move it, in case we needed emergency funds and he wasn't at home," Ben added in explanation.

"When Cornelius finally admitted that he'd gambled away a chunk of the church's money," Bishop Tom continued ruefully, "he promised he wouldn't go near a casino again, and he agreed to some grief counseling and a repayment plan. He pleaded for a second chance—"

"Begged us not to tell anyone else about his habit," Ben added with a shake of his head. "Cornelius insisted that he could get beyond his grief and his gambling—"

"—and he asked us to forgive him, to have mercy because his wife's absence had gotten the best of him." The bishop closed his eyes in utter desolation. "I told Cornelius that confession would be the better path for him, but in the end I gave in to his plea for forgiveness . . . because we Amish believe so firmly in forgiving and moving forward in faith."

Bishop Tom paused, exhaling. "I should've listened to Ben. I should've insisted that Cornelius come before all of you back then—when most of our money was still in the safe," he added wearily. "I have failed you miserably. I wouldn't blame you a bit if you shunned me and asked me to step down as your bishop."

"And I was right there with him, knowing that Cornelius should be on his knees," Ben said earnestly. "But I wanted to believe that our deacon would change his ways and choose the right path."

Bishop Vernon nodded, observing people's reactions. Marcus was impressed by his air of patience and wisdom— his inclination to listen rather than to speak out in stern admonition, as the bishops in Pennsylvania tended to do. When Vernon's gaze lingered on Marcus, and his mouth curved in an approving smile above his snowy-white beard, Marcus felt he'd received a blessing directly from God.

"Ben and I agreed that Cornelius's confession would only be valid if he made it of his own free will," Bishop Tom explained further. "So here we are, in the week before Christmas, with scarcely a dime in the aid fund after paying off the hospital expenses for Miriam's family. The crime belongs to Cornelius, but I enabled him—when I should've followed the prescribed path and brought him before you earlier. I'm sorry, my friends," he murmured. "I accept whatever chastisement you choose for me."

"I do, too," Ben said as he looked out over the crowd. "I'm sorry I've let you all down—and that my lack of judgment has cost you so much of your hard-earned money."

A sad silence settled over the room as folks considered what Bishop Tom and Preacher Ben had confessed. Once again Bishop Vernon gauged the reactions of folks in the crowd, giving them time to process the unusual circumstances that had compelled two of their trusted church leaders to go to their knees.

"Does anyone have questions for Tom or Ben?" Vernon asked. "I've heard folks confess to having their hand in their boss's till—and I've asked a few members to put away electronic devices we Amish don't condone—but in all my years as a preacher and a bishop, I've never run across such a complicated situation."

Atlee Glick stood up. "So you're telling us that after Cornelius quit going to the casino in Kansas City, he began gambling on a computer?" he asked with a puzzled shrug. "How does that work? I've seen Mennonite and English fellows ordering and paying for supplies on computers, but how do you lose money with one? And how was Cornelius's computer getting money from our vault?"

"That's a *gut* question," Preacher Ben replied. "I asked my cousin Marcus to be here today because he understands this sort of thing. Will it be all right if he explains it? He's not yet a member of the church, but he's asked Tom and me about taking his instruction so he can join."

Marcus's heartbeat sped up as several folks nodded, looking at him. He hadn't anticipated Ben's public remark about his asking to join the church just yet . . . but maybe the congregation would have more trust in him now that they knew he didn't intend to remain an outsider. He reached under the pew bench for the laptop Ben had confiscated from the Riehls' basement.

"Marcus, can you show these folks what you showed us?" Bishop Tom gestured for him to come to the center of the room.

"Meanwhile, you men have made your confessions," Bishop Vernon put in. "You may stand."

With a prayer for confidence, Marcus strode to where Tom and Ben stood before the congregation. He felt uncomfortable being watched so closely by folks who'd only met him a month ago, yet he was pleased to put his computer knowledge to use for them. The encouragement and admiration in Rosalyn's eyes made him forget to be nervous, however. Knowing she supported him made him feel ten feet tall.

"Here's the laptop Cornelius was using in his workshop," Marcus said as he held it up. "I wouldn't have figured out what was going on if I hadn't seen him in the Morning Star bank, taking bundled money from his briefcase to make a deposit."

A lot of folks appeared puzzled, so Marcus explained further. "When there's a large amount of money—like, in a bank—it's easiest to count when it's been wrapped in paper bands—"

"In our case, we had bundles of hundred-dollar bills, some totaling one thousand, some ten thousand dollars, in the church's vault," Bishop Tom put in.

Marcus nodded. "Cornelius had a setup similar to the businesses Atlee described. He had opened a bank account in Morning Star that he could access with his computer—but instead of paying bills, he gambled at online casinos. The money he lost came from that bank account he'd opened with church money."

"I'm guessing he went through our funds a lot faster after he switched to gambling online, because he didn't actually handle the money anymore," Ben suggested.

As folks caught on to what Ben was saying, they began to murmur among themselves.

"I suspect you're right about that," Marcus said. "When I was in Nora's store to use her Wi-Fi one day, we noticed a network called Reel Money—not spelled like Cornelius's last name. Later we found out he had this gadget that creates a hot spot to let him get onto the Internet." He held up the metal attachment and then showed them how it connected to the laptop.

Gabe Glick speared his fingers through his white hair. "This computer stuff doesn't make a lick of sense to me, Marcus."

"It's complicated," Marcus agreed. "I have no idea how Cornelius got his computer or learned how to use it, but he knew that none of you folks would catch him at it because you're not on the Internet."

There was silence while folks thought about what he'd said.

Lydia Zook raised her hand. "So you're saying that Bishop Tom and Preacher Ben—and the rest of us—would've had no way of knowing Cornelius gambled away our money if you hadn't seen him at the bank?"

"Well, we'd caught him gambling a few months ago— when Nora and Drew tipped us off about his casino visits," Ben reminded her. "Tom and I checked the vault then to see how much of our money was missing."

"But Marcus's seeing Cornelius in the bank, and seeing that he was online, gave us the connection we needed to know he'd started gambling on a computer," Bishop Tom explained. "Without Marcus's help, we'd have been totally blindsided about how our money was disappearing so quickly. I'm only sorry we didn't figure this out sooner."

Marcus nodded. It occurred to him that God might've led him into the bank that particular day, but he didn't want to say that out loud.

"We were at the house when Ben and Tom came for money to pay the hospital bill for Miriam's kin," Drew witnessed as he stood up. "When they came up from the clock shop with the laptop and only a few bundles of money, we were appalled at how much Cornelius had gambled away—but no one was more horrified than Tom and Ben."

Gabe let out a low whistle. "Back in the day, we had hundreds of thousands of dollars in our fund," he murmured. "Sure, we spent some large lumps of it when we paid off medical bills—and when we rebuilt the Grill N Skillet after it burned down. But the fund got replenished each spring and fall when we took up our offering."

"Folks have been faithful about donating to the church's fund," Bishop Tom attested. "That's why I feel so horrible about not catching Cornelius faster—"

"Or not exposing his losses when we first heard about them," Ben added ruefully. "Unfortunately, we were wrong to take him at his word."

"Puh!" Dan Kanagy said, crossing his arms in disgust. "Seems to me we were wrong to accept him as our new deacon in the first place, back when his cousin, Deacon Reuben, traded houses with him. Cornelius has been a snake in the grass all along."

"*Jah*, it occurred to me that maybe Cornelius's being a deacon—being able to fit right into Reuben's place—was a little too convenient," Bishop Tom admitted. "But I thought it was one of those times when God had provided for our need before we even knew to ask for His help."

"Divine providence," Bishop Vernon murmured. "Who among us hasn't been saved by the hand of God catching us before we fell?"

A hushed silence filled the room. Some folks bowed their

heads even as they nodded at what Bishop Vernon had said. Once again Marcus wished he could kiss the tormented expression from Rosalyn's face, knowing that some of the comments about her father had stung her deeply.

"Are we ready to vote on Bishop Tom's penance, and then on Ben's?" Bishop Vernon asked. "I'll tell you now that after these men confessed to me, I decided they needed no further discipline—but they both insisted on coming before you, willing to be relieved of their leadership positions if you've lost your faith in them."

Preacher Henry cleared his throat nervously. "If we vote them out, does that mean I'm the only man eligible to become the district's new bishop?"

Bishop Vernon smiled kindly at him. "If that comes to pass, Henry, you'll have our prayers and our full support—as well as all the help I can offer you," he replied. "God will strengthen you, just as He does every bishop—all of whom have served despite their feelings of inadequacy . . . or their reluctance."

The folks around Marcus considered the consequences if Preacher Henry became their bishop—but not for long. Once again Dan rose to speak.

"Can we simply give a simple aye or nay to reaffirm our faith in Bishop Tom and Preacher Ben?" he asked earnestly. "It's clear to me that they acted in good faith, and that Cornelius is solely to blame for the financial mess we're in."

"Does anyone object to this procedure?" Bishop Vernon asked. "It's a little out of the norm following a confession, but I have no objection to a faster vote."

"Let's do it," Naomi Brenneman replied. "Tom and Ben took on the leadership of our district in the wake of the scandal with our previous bishop, and they'll get us through this crisis, too."

Marcus took his seat on the back pew bench, pleased that he'd helped these folks see their situation more clearly. After a unanimous *aye* resounded in the Hooleys' front room, Bishop Tom and Preacher Ben smiled gratefully at the folks who'd shown them such enthusiastic support. Preacher Henry appeared extremely relieved.

"*Denki* so much for your faith in us," Bishop Tom said humbly. "Although our monetary lot seems grim right now, we still have our God, we have our families and friends, our homes and our work, and a multitude of other daily blessings," he pointed out. "Ben, Henry, and I are open to any ideas for replenishing our aid fund—and to names of nominees, so we can choose our new deacon after church on December thirty-first."

"Meanwhile, we're putting on our Christmas Eve live Nativity this coming Sunday evening," Preacher Ben reminded everyone. "In this holy season of celebrating our Lord's birth, let's focus on God's greatest gift to us—His son, our Savior—believing that the other priorities of our lives will fall into place if we put Him first."

Bishop Tom nodded his agreement. His face had lost its haggard look, and he clasped Bishop Vernon's arm. "We owe special thanks to my dear friend Vernon for assisting us when we needed his wise counsel."

As everyone applauded, Vernon slung his arms around Tom and Ben's shoulders. "It's a special joy to be associated with you folks in Willow Ridge," he said. "I'm betting folks in Cedar Creek would be happy to contribute items to an auction, or any other sort of fundraiser you might have—"

"An auction!" Miriam exclaimed. "I can't remember the last time we held a big auction in Willow Ridge. I'll organize the food stand—"

"I bet the Schrocks would donate a quilt or two!" Rhoda blurted out.

"We'll contribute a roomful of furniture from our shop," Micah Brenneman put in.

Asa laughed, pointing playfully at Micah. "We Detweilers

can't let you Brenneman brothers show us up!" he crowed. "Count on us for several large pieces of refurbished furniture."

"I'll donate the painting or wallpapering of a couple of rooms," Adam Wagler called out. "Those services have sold really well at other auctions."

"The Grill N Skillet will be happy to contribute gift certificates for catering," Josiah added. "We'd also host the lunch during the auction, if you'd like us to."

Marcus smiled as he approached the two bishops and Preacher Ben. He'd figured on keeping his surprise private and low-key, but the enthusiasm for an auction filled the room with such a sense of hopefulness that he couldn't sit still. He handed Bishop Tom an envelope from the inside pocket of his coat.

"I'd like you to have this now," he murmured beneath folks' offerings of other items for an auction. "It might come in handy for covering the expenses involved with putting on whatever fund-raisers folks decide on."

The bishop's eyebrows rose in anticipation as he opened the envelope. When he pulled out three checks, his mouth dropped open. "My stars," he murmured. He excitedly held up his hand to get everyone's attention.

"Folks, here's yet another example of how help can arrive in unexpected ways from places we don't anticipate," he called out. He smiled at Marcus. "How about if you be the bearer of glad tidings and tell folks about these gifts, son?"

When the room got quiet, Marcus again felt self-conscious with so many folks focusing on him—but this time he saw smiles of acceptance and anticipation. "When my boss—your new English neighbor, Wyatt McKenzie—heard from Nora Hooley about the loss of the district's funds, he wanted you to know how much he appreciates the way you've welcomed him to the community."

Bishop Tom held up a check. "Wyatt's giving us ten

thousand dollars," he said in an awed voice. "Nora, too, sends a contribution from her Simple Gifts store, in the amount of six thousand dollars—and Rebecca's written a check for a thousand dollars, with an offer to design any advertising we might need. When you see these generous neighbors, tell them what a blessing they've been to our Old Order community."

"Luke and I will be giving you a contribution from the mill, as well," Ira chimed in. "Our business has grown beyond our wildest dreams since we came to Missouri, and we have you folks to thank for that."

Preacher Ben flashed his younger cousin a thumbs-up. "Who knew, back in the day, that you boys would grow up to actually amount to something?" he teased. "Your mill's been a real boon to this area by providing local farmers with a sales outlet for their grains and eggs—steady work they wouldn't have had otherwise."

"Are we in agreement that an auction would be beneficial?" Dan asked the crowd. "If so, why not set a date and get on with the planning, while we're all here?"

"I think that's a wonderful-*gut* idea," Miriam replied as she rose from the pew bench with little Bethlehem at her hip. "Let me fetch a calendar."

Several folks began talking, caught up in the excitement of having an auction in Willow Ridge. The positive attitude in this little town impressed Marcus, because neighbors and local businesses—even those who were Mennonite and English—were sincerely devoted to promoting the welfare of the entire area.

Bishop Tom called the meeting to order again. "As we consider the idea of an auction, I see a couple of factors to consider," he said. "It's to our advantage that other Plain communities tend to host their auctions in the summertime, so we'll have no competition. On the other hand, we're having a cold, snowy winter and we'll attract more of a crowd if we can hold the event indoors. But where could that be?"

"Let me make a call," Marcus said as he pulled his cell phone from his pocket. "A lot of our horses have gone to their new owners, so—*jah*, Wyatt?" he said when his boss answered. "First off, folks here at the church meeting are very grateful for your check, and for Rebecca's, too."

"Happy to help," Wyatt replied. "It sounds like you've moved beyond Cornelius's gambling losses to thinking toward the future."

"We have—so I have a big favor to ask." When Marcus realized everyone in the room was listening to his conversation, he wished he'd stepped into the kitchen to make this call. Was he being presumptuous, assuming Wyatt would go along with his idea? He hated to disappoint these people after gaining their confidence a few minutes earlier.

"What's your favor?" Wyatt asked. "Rebecca and I are jotting down ideas for our future home, so I'm in a mellow, open-minded mood."

Marcus smiled. Any time Wyatt was with his fiancée, his happiness tended to spill over onto whoever was around him. "The folks here are contemplating an auction—but it'll do better if we hold it indoors," he added. "Would you be willing to let our church use one of the barns?"

"We'll pay whatever sort of rent you'd want, Wyatt," Bishop Tom put in loudly enough for him to hear.

"And we'll leave the grounds clean and in *gut* shape after the crowd's gone," Preacher Ben added.

"An Amish auction," Wyatt murmured. "Just a sec."

Marcus could picture his boss putting his hand over the phone to discuss the idea with Rebecca. Meanwhile, Miriam had returned with the wall calendar from her kitchen.

"What about January sixth—the first Saturday after the New Year?" she suggested. "We could be ready by then if we get the word out to potential contributors right away. I see no benefit to waiting any longer—"

"Especially if Wyatt lets us use one of his barns," Ben said with a nod. "But we don't want to disrupt his business—or your training schedule, Marcus."

After a few moments Wyatt spoke again. "You and I are going to a big sale after the first of the year, remember, so we'll have more young Percherons then, as well as retired racehorses from my other farms. Any idea when they want to hold this auction?"

"Sounds like we're shooting for Saturday, January sixth," Marcus replied.

"We can make that work. If we dismantle the stalls—and put our current horses someplace else for the day of the sale—both of the barns would be available. No charge," Wyatt said cordially. "Rebecca will print and distribute posters as well as put out the online advertising for this event, soon as you give her the details."

"I'll call you back in a few." Marcus gripped his phone, amazed at how quickly his boss had come through. "Thanks a bunch, Wyatt—and thank Rebecca for me. This is huge. You're really doing us a big favor."

"Happy to help," Wyatt said again. "And I'm even happier that you've asked me such a favor on behalf of your church friends, Marcus. You've come a long way since you arrived, and only good things can come of your association with the Amish. Talk to you later, son."

Marcus pressed the button on his phone, grateful for the hopeful expressions on Ben and Tom's faces—and thankful that this friendly bunch of people wanted him to be a part of their faith and their fundraising. "Wyatt says we can use both of his barns free of charge—if we find a place for our horses to stay on the day of the auction."

"We've got room for your horses, Marcus," Dan volunteered immediately.

"*Jah*, so do I," Ben put in.

"And Rebecca will donate online promotion and put posters around the nearby towns for us, as well," Marcus added.

"Doesn't get any better than that," Bishop Tom said. "All right, folks, we have the use of Wyatt's two big barns and we have free advertising if we hold our auction fairly soon," he announced. "Miriam's suggesting Saturday, the sixth of January. Let's take a vote. A *no* means you'd rather have more time to consider another sale date—or another project altogether."

Everyone sat down to conduct the vote. Marcus couldn't help noticing the dramatic change in the facial expressions around him now the congregation had found an idea that moved them beyond Cornelius's betrayal.

"All in favor of having a benefit auction on the sixth, say *aye*," Bishop Tom said in a firm voice.

A resounding *aye!* filled the room so loudly that people started laughing.

"Anyone opposed?" Tom asked. "We've decided on this project very quickly, so it's not a bad thing if you know of reasons to delay an auction or to do something different. So—once again—does anyone think we should reconsider?"

Silence. Everyone was gazing eagerly at Bishop Tom, Preacher Ben—and Marcus—as though they were prepared to move into the planning stage immediately.

"You folks are amazing," Bishop Vernon said with a big smile. "Not half an hour ago you learned your aid fund had been drained, and now you've got a plan for restoring some of it—and you've received some sizable donations. God is *gut*—every day, all the time—and He's clearly at work among you."

"Amen to that," Bishop Tom agreed. "So we're set for Saturday the sixth at the McKenzie place. We've got a lot of planning to do, but we're on the forward path. Life in Willow Ridge—life in our God—is indeed *gut*, my friends."

Laughter and conversation erupted around Marcus, but when Rosalyn's gaze met his, he suddenly wanted to get away from the crowd. He moved between the women who'd clustered around Savilla and Lena Witmer to discuss baking pies and to organize an auction lunch menu at the Grill N Skillet. Loretta and Edith joined the chattering women—which left Rosalyn standing in the row of pew benches with her hands clasped, looking at him.

Marcus was struck by her singular beauty. Despite her red-rimmed eyes and weariness, Rosalyn didn't look away from him. Was that admiration lighting her pretty face? Was it his imagination, or had she shut out the excited hubbub around them to focus on him?

"Marcus, you're a wonder," she declared, beaming at him. "First you explain the fine points of computer gambling, and then you bring us checks—and then you arrange the perfect place to hold our auction. Are you the same fellow who burst into Nora's store full of ridicule and criticism because Willow Ridge didn't have a gas station?"

Marcus swallowed hard, unaccustomed to Rosalyn's praise. "How about if we talk about that after I pick you up in my sleigh—say, half an hour from now? I got it repaired, you know," he added. "I've just been waiting for the right time to take you out in it again."

"I'll be waiting at Asa and Edith's place," she replied breathlessly. "See you then, Marcus."

Chapter Twenty-Four

Rosalyn allowed Marcus to help her into his sleigh, delighting in the firm squeeze he gave her hand as she sat down on the velvet-covered seat. It felt like a special occasion—as though she was on a first date—because Marcus had changed so much that he was totally made over. He'd gotten his hair cut, so he'd lost the dangerous allure of having some of it draped over his face, but his dimples captivated her even more than before. The glow in his pale green eyes gave her hope that he intended to work as big a change in her life as he'd just brought about for the Willow Ridge church district.

It was a tall order. Rosalyn hoped she wasn't setting herself up for disappointment—believing the images she'd seen in her romantic imagination ever since she'd met rebellious, unpredictable Marcus Hooley. To her, he'd only gotten better looking—darker and bolder, despite the boyish appearance his blue stocking cap gave him and the way his attitude had improved.

As he clucked at Sophie, a few snowflakes drifted lazily in the cold air. The *clip-clop, clip-clop* of the Percheron's heavy hooves set the beat for the jingling bells on the harness.

Despite the fact that her father had been shunned for betraying their neighbors this morning, Rosalyn felt happy. Hopeful.

"*Denki* again for getting Wyatt's support for the auction," Rosalyn said, daring to clasp Marcus's hand beneath the blanket he'd draped around them.

"He was pleased to make both barns available," Marcus replied. "He was happy about, well—other things, too. It's all *gut*, and the auction should restore a big chunk of the district's aid fund."

Other things. Rosalyn grew immediately curious about the secret Marcus seemed to be keeping with those words. Could Wyatt possibly be as happy as she was about Marcus's involvement with the Old Order church? Did she dare ask what had prompted Marcus to request membership sessions from Bishop Tom—or would he think she was being nosy?

A lot of fellows join the church when they've found a girl to marry.

Rosalyn shivered with anticipation. Maybe Marcus was going to say he wanted to court her—

"Are you cold, Roz? Should we go back home?"

She felt a surge of longing. Rosalyn could think of nothing she'd like better than to go home with Marcus . . . to a home they would share forever. But she was pretty sure he was referring to Asa and Edith's house rather than his apartment or a more permanent arrangement.

"I'm fine. Just excited about having an auction," she insisted. "It amazes me, how fast these Willow Ridge folks jumped into such a large project at Bishop Vernon's merest suggestion. Back in Roseville, we had a contingent of very conservative families who took a long time to come to decisions," she added as she thought back to her previous home. "They talked on and on about the possibility that a new idea might not work, rather than believing that it would."

"*Jah*, that often happened where I grew up, too," Marcus

remarked with a nod. "Some fellows can talk the life out of an idea before it has a chance to succeed."

Silence settled between them as the sleigh glided along the snow-packed shoulder of the road. Marcus seemed lost in thought, miles away mentally, even as her own ideas bubbled like a freshly opened can of soda pop, ready to spew out. Would he ask her to help with preparations for the auction? Or suggest that they spend time together on Christmas or Second Christmas?

Is he figuring out a way to ask a much more serious question?

Rosalyn shimmered with a sense of anticipation—at least until the silence, punctuated only by the mare's hoofbeats, began to wear on her. Marcus had seemed so animated and full of ideas at the members' meeting, yet he'd grown preoccupied . . . as though he'd forgotten she was sitting beside him.

Rosalyn ventured into a new topic, hoping to draw him out of his thoughts. "I'm really curious about the live Nativity—"

"I'm sorry about your dat, Roz," Marcus blurted at the same moment. "And I'm sorry he tried to lay blame on you and your sisters for what he did."

Rosalyn's face fell. For a delightful half hour she'd managed to push aside the ordeal of her father's shunning, but she couldn't ignore Marcus's apologetic remark.

"I appreciate your thoughts," she mumbled. "We all saw it coming, after Bishop Tom and Preacher Ben confronted him the other day, but . . . well, I do wonder how he's going to get along all by himself. My decision to move out came so suddenly it surprised me as much as it did him."

"You did the right thing," Marcus quickly assured her. "Everyone could see he didn't intend to take responsibility for his actions—and he didn't seem the least bit sincere about confessing. Why did he think everyone in the church would immediately forgive him as though he hadn't stolen all the district's money?"

Tears stung Rosalyn's eyes. She looked out over the snowy hills so Marcus wouldn't see that she was crying again. "I don't know," she whispered. "It makes me wonder if he gambled away that money without any intention of paying it back . . . as though he thought the Old Order belief in forgiveness would be like a Get Out Of Jail Free card in a Monopoly game."

"What did he think would happen after he ran the district totally dry?" Marcus demanded angrily. "Once the money was gone, how did he figure to get his gambling fix?"

Rosalyn pressed her lips together, suppressing a sob. Dat's habit defied explanation—and it infuriated her that he'd named his grief for Mamm and his family's lack of understanding as reasons he'd lost so much money that wasn't even his.

Marcus sighed. "Sorry," he repeated. "I didn't mean to make you feel bad, Roz. Do you want to go home? Feels like it's getting colder."

Rosalyn's heart sank. She hadn't noticed a drop in the temperature, but Marcus's feelings for her had obviously chilled, if he was so eager to be rid of her. "*Jah*, that might be best," she whispered. "It'll take me a while to move beyond what happened with Dat today. I—I'm sorry if I'm not very *gut* company."

At the next intersection, Marcus steered the Percheron into a U-turn and they were headed up Asa and Edith's lane practically before they'd left—or so it seemed to Rosalyn. What had she said or done, that he'd lost interest in her? When he'd invited her for a sleigh ride, he'd seemed light-hearted and ready for some fun.

As Marcus slowed the horse to stop at the door, Rosalyn racked her brain for something to say—anything to make him smile and change his mind about dropping her off.

"Would—would you like to go to the live Nativity with me, Roz?" he asked hesitantly. "I have no idea what to expect, or—"

"I'll think about it," she blurted, wishing she didn't have to wipe her eyes in front of him. In her state of disappointment and confusion about his mood, she wondered why he didn't want to see her sooner than Christmas Eve, which was on Sunday. Was he planning to spend Friday and Saturday evenings with someone else? Rosalyn was aware that her mind had started spinning out irrational ideas and doubts about Marcus—fearful assumptions that had no basis—but she was too upset to stop her negative thoughts.

Rather than wait for Marcus to help her out of the sleigh, she shoved aside the blanket and hurried toward the door. She was relieved that Asa and her sister hadn't yet returned home so she could go to her room and cry in private.

Marcus slumped in the seat of the sleigh. Rosalyn's tear-filled brown eyes were a sight he wouldn't soon forget, because he was the one who'd made her cry. Of course she was upset! Why had he mentioned her father instead of talking about more pleasant topics? Why had he wasted the precious moments of their sleigh ride stewing over whether to say what was really on his mind?

Because you're scared. You spoke to Bishop Tom and Preacher Ben about church membership classes—and Ben's mentioned them publicly—so you've got no graceful way out.

"Geddap, Sophie," he said with a sigh. After years of attracting women without a thought for what he said to them, Marcus felt bewildered by his inability to tell Rosalyn that he wanted to court her . . . that he was pretty sure he was in love with her. He'd thought he was in love before, with both of the English women who'd invited him into their lives, but this time was different. His love felt strong enough that he was willing to forego the carefree pleasures of the English lifestyle to marry an Amish woman—within the framework of a faith that allowed for no escape.

It was exhilarating, the emotional and physical feelings he had for Rosalyn.

It was terrifying to realize that he could mess things up— send her away in tears—within moments, and without any apparent misunderstanding or harsh words.

And it was permanent, if he married her.

Better think about this some more, Hooley, he chided himself. *You have a steady job now, but it isn't as though you have a home to offer Rosalyn, or—*

And if you change your mind about marrying her, Willow Ridge is so small, you can't avoid seeing her—and her sad, disappointed eyes. That hopeful expression on her face meant she was waiting for you to pop the question.

"Well, fine," Marcus muttered as he steered his mare toward the McKenzie place. "Seems I'm doomed if I love her, and doomed if I don't."

After he parked the sleigh and brushed Sophie down, he threw himself into the day's training sessions. The three young Percherons that hadn't yet been sold were coming along even though they weren't yet ready for new owners. The cold weather made them frisky, but they responded well when Marcus harnessed them all to the large V-shaped snowplow he'd borrowed from the Detweilers. After pulling alone, it was a challenge for the horses to work as a team. Soon, however, they were negotiating the curves of the training paddock and even backing up smoothly as he drove them around and around with the blade lifted off the ground.

As Marcus worked the huge horses, however, his mind wandered away from the safety of the day's training routine into the more dangerous, desperate thoughts that had been chipping away at him. Ever since he'd dropped Rosalyn at her sister's house, he'd wondered if he was leading her on— leading them both along a path that would result in more unhappiness than he could imagine. Didn't she have enough misery in her life without him adding to her burdens?

Get out now, before you ruin two lives. You showed up in

*Willow Ridge without any warning or expectations, and you
can leave the same way.*

These thoughts set Marcus on edge as he steered the trio
of horses into the barn, yet he couldn't let them go. The
sight of his car, parked by the back barn door, was the ultimate reminder of what he'd be giving up if he joined the Old
Order—not just his freedom, but his access to the world as
he knew it. Did he really want to limit himself to the distance
a horse could take him, when he was accustomed to traveling as far as he pleased? If he started feeling trapped in
Willow Ridge, would he take out his frustrations on poor
Rosalyn?

Upstairs in his apartment, the iPad, cell phone, and laptop
on his kitchen table taunted him further. That morning he'd
finally proven himself truly *useful* to the Amish community
by answering folks' tech questions, so what good would he
be to his neighbors when he was no longer allowed to own
such devices?

Without a cell phone, how would he and Wyatt commu-
nicate from across big sale barns—or from opposite ends of
the McKenzie property? And how would he stay in touch
with the real world if he couldn't send Facebook messages
to his friends back east? If he couldn't go online, how would
he google answers to veterinary questions or check the lin-
eage of young horses and the price of supplies?

What if Wyatt no longer wanted him as an employee after
he shut himself off from the Internet?

*Maybe you should live English, like Rebecca. Everyone
around town—even her Amish mother and sisters—respects
her decision and depends on her computer skills. Willow
Ridge has stayed afloat financially because she helps the
businesses here advertise online.*

Marcus stared out the window into the gathering dusk,
truly troubled. What good would he be to Rosalyn if he was
so hesitant about being Amish? She deserved a dedicated

man of the faith who could provide her a home and the family she wanted.

What'll you do when the babies start coming? You can't raise them in this apartment—and you have no idea how to deal with them when they fuss and cry! You'll be a disastrous dat!

Marcus swallowed hard. The negatives were piling up a lot higher than the positives. Wasn't that a sign?

His heart began to pound. His palms felt clammy as he pulled a pizza from his freezer and popped it into the microwave . . . yet another luxury he wouldn't be allowed if he gave up living with electricity.

Get out now. You have some cash, so you could start over anyplace you want to. By the time anyone figures out you've left, you'll be far, far away and they'll have no way to trace you.

His mind was made up—but he owed Wyatt an apology and a wagonload of gratitude. McKenzie wouldn't like it that he'd bailed—and that he'd broken his agreement to stay at least through Christmas—but hopefully he would understand. Wyatt had lived on the wild side himself when he was younger. Marcus ate his pizza with his left hand while he scribbled a note.

> *Sorry to duck out on you this way, Wyatt, but Reality has slapped me in the face and I just can't stand the idea of being Amish for the rest of my life. Which means I can't stay in Willow Ridge, where Rosalyn will be disappointed every time she sees me.*
>
> *Thanks for all you've done for me, and for setting my credit record straight, and for steering me in a better direction. I owe you, big-time.*
>
> *Marcus*

He cleaned up the small kitchen and threw his clothes into his duffel bags, his mind racing as he thought about where to go. By five o'clock it was dark—and the surrounding countryside with its unlit farmyards was another reminder of how deep and long the winter nights would be, with only a flickering oil lantern to see by if he became an Amish husband.

With a last look around the apartment, Marcus hurried down the stairs into the barn. Moments later he was heading for the county highway as though he was driving to Morning Star for a few groceries—except he was never coming back.

Chapter Twenty-Five

It was a blessing to work in Nora's store on Friday, and Rosalyn lost herself in the excitement of the shoppers who were making their last-minute purchases before Christmas. When she and Loretta were wrapping pottery pieces at the checkout or straightening shelves or showing customers items they might enjoy, she could forget that her personal life—her entire future—felt so unsettled. The bell above the door jingled merrily when folks came in, and carols playing on the sound system made her hum along. The aromas of spiced cider and bayberry candles lifted her spirits, too.

"Merry Christmas, girls!" a customer said as she accepted a shopping bag of items Rosalyn had wrapped for her.

"You sisters have made this a holiday to remember with your rugs and wreaths," her friend chimed in.

"We're glad you've enjoyed our pieces," Loretta replied as she slipped auction flyers into their bags. "You won't want to miss the Willow Ridge auction on January sixth—"

"And it'll be held inside those big barns you see across the river behind my shop, with loads of furniture and quilts and one-of-a-kind items to bid on. The Grill N Skillet will be having a special auction lunch, too," Nora added as she handed them their receipts. "We hope you can come."

During a lull at the checkout counter, Rosalyn went up to the loft level to straighten the dwindling stacks of place mats and linens. Through the window she saw flakes of snow drifting placidly in the pale gray sky—but when she noticed a man loading a large truck across town, her pulse raced.

"Loretta, look—in front of the house! What do you make of that?" she called over the loft railing.

When her sister peered out the downstairs window, she sucked in her breath. "My word, there's Dat—and he's carrying tool cases out to that truck! Did he say anything to you about getting rid of his business?"

As Rosalyn hurried down the stairs, Nora joined Loretta at the window. "Do you think he's moving away?"

"I have no idea!" Loretta blurted. "He hasn't spoken to us since Sunday—"

"Maybe you should go check it out," Nora suggested with a worried frown. "I'd hate to think he would leave without telling you."

Moments later Rosalyn and her sister were hurrying along the shoulder of the county highway, tying the strings of their black bonnets as they went. She had a strange feeling in the pit of her stomach . . . a sense that they were about to receive yet another unpleasant surprise.

"What are we going to say?" Loretta asked breathlessly. "Surely Dat doesn't figure to duck out of town without letting us know."

"Or without serving the six weeks of his *bann* so he can get back into the *gut* graces of the church," Rosalyn added. "Do you suppose he's heading back to Roseville?"

"I can't begin to predict what Dat might be up to," Loretta replied sadly. "Oh, my—the driver is closing the back of the big truck. We'd better run along."

Heedless of the puddles and piles of snow along the roadside, Rosalyn broke into a sprint. Her heart contracted into a tight ball when they reached the lane and then bounded up

onto the front porch. She was glad Loretta was bold enough
to open the door and go in ahead of her.

"Dat?" Loretta called out. "Dat? What's going on?"

Rosalyn was relieved to see that the front-room furniture
was all in place—but the expression on their father's face as
he stepped out of the kitchen brought her to a sudden stop.

"What does it look like I'm doing?" he asked impatiently.
"If you can leave this house, well—so can I! Why should I
stay here when no one—not even the daughters I worked
hard all my life to support—bothers speaking to me?"

Rosalyn was struck dumb. Guilt niggled at her even as
Loretta stepped backward to stand beside her rather than
move any closer to Dat.

"We didn't think you would—where will you go?" Loretta
rasped.

"Why do you care?" their father challenged them bitterly.
"I'm as free as a bird and I'll be fine wherever I land. Don't
try to talk me into staying—and don't spend another moment
worrying about me, all right?"

The sarcastic edge to his voice warned Rosalyn against
making any protest. For once, maybe it was best to do as her
father said—to remain silent rather than coax him to stay . . .
which would give him more words to twist into arrows and
more time to shoot them into her heart. She almost suggested that he send them his new address, but the grim line
of his mouth stifled that idea.

"Why don't you go on back to playing store with Nora?"
he suggested brusquely. "I don't need you gawking after me
as I leave town. Shoo!"

When he started toward them with a malicious laugh,
waving his hands, Rosalyn bolted out the door. Loretta's footsteps clattered across the wooden porch and down the stairs
with hers, but instead of heading back into town, they hurried
across the road to Edith's house. They didn't stop running
until they reached the door and let themselves inside.

"Edith!" Loretta called out. "Did you see—"

"*Jah*, I'm here at the kitchen window," their sister replied. She turned toward them with a tear-streaked face, shaking her head. "I didn't have the nerve to go over there—didn't want to leave the twins, or take them, either. What did he say?"

"Oh, Dat's as free as a bird," Loretta began in a ragged voice.

"*Jah*, why should he stay here when no one—not even the daughters he supported all their lives—is speaking to him," Rosalyn recounted ruefully.

"It was awful," Loretta whispered. "He was so nasty—"

"He lunged at us and shooed us away," Rosalyn put in.

Only when the three of them shared an embrace, their arms around each other's waists and shoulders, did it feel safe to cry . . . to consider what had just happened in the house across the road. The pain felt so raw that she and Loretta didn't even remove their wraps as they clung to their younger sister.

"I—I'm so glad Mamm's not around to see what's happened to him," Edith murmured.

"Well, if she were still here, Dat probably wouldn't have gotten into gambling," Rosalyn pointed out between sobs.

"Or maybe he would have—or he might've found some other nasty habit," Loretta speculated with a sigh. "We'll never know. And truth be told, I've found out enough about our father this week that I don't want to learn any more. This is a terrible, unthinkable thing to say," she continued in a thin voice, "but our lives will be a whole lot easier without him. It's clear he doesn't intend to pay back any of the money he stole."

As the truth of Loretta's remarks weighed her down like a wet wool blanket, Rosalyn began to cry harder. She and her sisters had spent their entire lives trying to be model Amish daughters—struggling to be good enough, to measure up to Dat's expectations of them—and it seemed their efforts had

been for nothing. Their anguished tears flowed freely for a
few minutes, until little arms wrapped around Rosalyn's and
Edith's knees.

"Mama! Mama!" Louisa called out.

"Woof, woof!" Leroy chimed in.

Rosalyn and Edith leaned down to lift the twins to their
hips, but the three sisters remained in a close huddle. It was
hard to remain upset when she was cuddling her nephew,
who held his stuffed dog to her face. "*Jah*, we love Doggie,
ain't so, Leroy?" she asked after she'd placed a noisy pretend
kiss on the toy's head. "We love you punkins, too—"

"And we're glad when you remind us what's most important," Loretta said. She wiped her face with the back of her
hand. "We don't know what's gotten into your *dawdi*—"

"Who has ever really known him?" Edith asked softly,
shaking her head.

"—but we still have each other," Loretta continued with
a nod. "We'll figure out what to do about him and that empty
house, all in *gut* time."

Rosalyn drew a deep breath. Her thoughts about Dat were
now tainted by the image of him rushing at her and Loretta,
leering as he shooed them out. It would be a while before the
emotional wounds he'd inflicted in the past few days would
heal. "Do you suppose he really means to stay away?" she
whispered. "Or is he just . . . laying on more guilt—until
he comes back when we least expect him, begging for our
forgiveness?"

Edith shrugged. "Only God knows the answer to that."

"If he does show up, the folks around town will stand
by us," Loretta said in a more hopeful voice. "They've all—
especially Nora—made us girls welcome, and they've accepted Drew and Asa, as well. We've got a *home* here. That's
what matters."

Rosalyn felt strengthened by Loretta's faith in their
neighbors—and no matter what Dat did in the future, he

couldn't sever the bond she and her sisters shared. She clung to that thought as she wiped the last of her tears. "We left Nora to handle a store full of customers, on a very busy shopping day," she said. "After all she's done for us, we really need to get back."

"*Jah*, helping folks find gifts that make them happy will make us happier, too," Loretta said as she eased away from their huddle.

"I'm putting on a big pot of chili for supper," Edith said. "You and Drew should join us so we'll all be together tonight. We may be having a simple Christmas this year— different from the holiday we were expecting—but we still have plenty to celebrate."

Rosalyn nodded. "You said that just right, Edith. I'll be back in plenty of time to bake some cornbread—"

"And I'll bring dessert!" Loretta put in. "Many hands make light work of supper."

As she and Loretta left the warmth of Edith's kitchen, the wind felt cold and damp when it whipped at their bonnets. Rosalyn walked quickly along the shoulder of the road, with Loretta following behind her so they wouldn't get splattered by cars driving through the puddles on the blacktop.

The aroma of grilled meats tantalized her as they passed the Grill N Skillet, where the lunch shift was in full swing. Up ahead, the big wooden wheel of the mill spun slowly— which meant that Luke and Ira were grinding grain, taking advantage of another day before the surface of the river froze over. Plenty of vans, cars, and a few buggies were still parked at the Simple Gifts store, so Rosalyn composed herself. She felt grateful that the brisk business in Nora's shop would keep her too occupied to stew over the unsettling encounter they'd had with Dat . . . and the thought that they might never see him again.

As she and Loretta slipped through the store's back door, Rosalyn inhaled the fragrance of bayberry candles and fresh greenery to soothe her soul. Nora was busy running the cash register—no time for questions. Rosalyn joined her to bag customers' purchases as though she'd only slipped away for a bathroom break, while Loretta mingled among the ladies who were still shopping.

"I called the Grill N Skillet," Nora whispered as the next gal stepped up to the counter. "Seemed like a great day to have hot food delivered for lunch."

"Bless you," Rosalyn said softly. "That sounds so much better than the cold sandwich I brought with me this morning."

Even with the carols playing on the sound system and the shoppers' happy smiles, Rosalyn had to pretend she felt the season's cheer. Edith's remark about having a simple Christmas—being blessed with sisterly support that would get them through a holiday shattered by Dat's gambling— almost made her cry again. It was a good thing that just then her sister carried a stack of pottery pieces over to the work-table for a lady who was buying six place settings.

"I've taken the tags off these dishes," Loretta said, "so if you'll start wrapping them, I'll find a couple of sturdy boxes to pack them in."

Rosalyn nodded, grateful for a task that would allow her to focus on something other than customers. Over the past few weeks she'd wrapped so many plates, cups, and bowls with brown kraft paper that her hands worked while her mind wandered. The table sat beneath one of the speakers, so she couldn't help hearing the carol that was playing. It was an instrumental piece, but the words ran through her head.

Deck the halls with boughs of holly—

The happy song clashed with her grim mood, and it re-minded her of red candles, fresh greenery wreaths, and Mamm's Nativity scene. Maybe she should take the crèche over to Edith's place so they could all enjoy it—and so the holy family and the wise men wouldn't spend Christmas in an empty house.

'Tis the season to be jolly—

Rosalyn wrapped faster—anything to keep from thinking about the difficult Christmas ahead of her. She and her sisters faced some big decisions because Dat had left them with unpaid utility bills and a huge debt that would hang over Willow Ridge like a dark cloud for months to come.

Fa la la la la—

Would this song never end? The carol's gaiety reminded Rosalyn of her first date with Marcus—that picture-perfect winter night of gliding across snow-covered fields, and laughing over pizza. On that rarified evening she'd dared to dream that she and Marcus might become a couple.

But his tentative conversation and long silences after the members' meeting had sent a different message. She hadn't heard a word from him since their brief sleigh ride on Wednesday. Rosalyn pushed her thoughts of Marcus aside, glad that Loretta had come over to pack the wrapped pieces of pottery in the boxes she'd found.

"I'm amazed at how much stuff we're selling today," her sister remarked beneath the music and the customers' conversations. "We only have a few odd pieces of pottery left, and the quilted pot holders and place mats are all gone. You'd think folks had nowhere else to shop—"

"Ho ho ho! Lunch delivery!" a familiar female voice called out behind them.

"We were at the Grill N Skillet when Nora called, so we decided to save Savilla a delivery trip," a man chimed in. "That place is just as busy as this one."

Rosalyn turned to greet Rebecca and Wyatt. As she inhaled the aromas of warm barbecue and cheese coming from the boxes they carried, she was immediately struck by the glow on their faces—as though the world couldn't possibly get any happier now that they were engaged. "Probably best to put the food in Nora's office," she suggested. "We've got a lady waiting for these pottery pieces—"

"But you girls should eat your lunch as soon as you finish wrapping them," Nora insisted behind them. "I can't have my best elves keeling over from starvation."

Loretta's chuckle sounded a bit reserved. "You go first, sister," she suggested. "I can finish wrapping these dishes in a jiffy."

Rosalyn didn't have much appetite, so she hoped Rebecca's happiness would lift her spirits. When she stepped into the small office to set out the food, however, Wyatt's handsome face tightened.

He turned to her, lowering his voice. "You don't happen to know where Marcus made off to, do you?"

Rosalyn's heart stopped. She gripped the foil-wrapped pan of cheesy potatoes she'd been unwrapping. "Wh-what do you mean?"

Wyatt shrugged. "He left a note in his apartment that didn't tell me much. Must've driven away sometime Wednesday evening," he explained in a concerned voice. "I was sort of hoping he'd taken you with him, because that would at least explain—"

"Not that you're the kind of girl who would've ridden off with Marcus in his car," Rebecca put in quickly.

Rosalyn was aware that she was gaping, yet she couldn't gather any rational thoughts to answer the two people who were gazing so intently at her. It stung her to the core that despite the way Rebecca and Wyatt assumed Marcus had deep feelings for her, he hadn't even told her . . . goodbye.

First Dat and now Marcus. Why have both of them left me just days before Christmas? Rosalyn's throat burned and she turned away to hide her tears.

Rebecca grasped Rosalyn's shoulders. "I'm sorry, honey," she murmured. "We haven't shown any consideration for your feelings. It's obviously as big a surprise to you as it was to us."

"*Jah*, well—" Rosalyn shuddered as she let out a long sigh. "About half an hour ago Loretta and I watched Dat take off for parts unknown, too, so—I'm sorry I'm so upset—"

"Oh my word, you have every reason to be upset," Rebecca murmured as she hugged Rosalyn close. "I'm so sorry about your *dat*, Rosalyn. This is all very confusing."

"If you or your family need anything," Wyatt put in earnestly, "let me know how I can help. From what I've heard, your dad's left a lot of loose ends for you and your sisters to deal with."

Loretta stepped into the office with a worried look on her face. "I couldn't help hearing what you said about Marcus—"

"And you have no idea where he went?" Nora put in as she, too, came into the small room. "Why would Marcus leave, when he was doing so well at training your horses?"

Wyatt shook his head. "I wish I knew. He's progressed so much more than I ever expected, I was ready to take him on as a partner—to make him the manager of my Willow Ridge farm, with a pay raise and benefits so he could support a family," he said sadly. "I thought he was as comfortable working with me as I was with him."

Rosalyn blotted her face with her sleeve. She regretted what she was about to say, but she didn't see any way around it. "Nora, I really hate to leave you when you've got so many customers, but—"

"I totally understand why you don't feel like working anymore today—and you, too, Loretta," Nora put in quickly. "I do wish you'd eat some of this fine-smelling lunch before you go, though. It looks like Savilla sent us enough to feed a small army."

Loretta pondered the situation—and the fragrant containers of food. "I'd rather stay busy this afternoon, and think about all this stuff later," she said softly. "I'll eat a quick bite and get back to work."

Rosalyn shook her head as she took her coat and bonnet from the rack. "*Denki*, Nora, but my stomach's in knots. I'll pull myself together and be back to work tomorrow morning."

As she stepped out the back door, Rebecca was offering to help Nora for the rest of the day. Once outside, Rosalyn stood absolutely still, staring at the river and the mill, and then at Ira and Millie's modest white house and at the seemingly endless white plank fencing that marked Wyatt's horse farm on the other side of the river. The gray sky and snow-covered hills made a dreary backdrop for a winter landscape that suddenly seemed bleak and colorless. A gust of wind sent snowflakes and a few dead leaves skittering ahead of it.

Rosalyn shivered. She had no idea what to do.

Did Marcus leave because he was dissatisfied with his job, or with Willow Ridge? Or did he sneak off to avoid dealing with me?

As she started walking, Rosalyn recalled how Marcus had ridiculed this little town the day he'd arrived and how his dubious reputation had preceded him. Maybe it was for the best that he'd left town before he'd made her any promises—although he'd surely known he'd be breaking her heart. Bishop Tom and Preacher Ben would be disappointed that Marcus hadn't followed through with his plans to join the Old Order, too. But at least if he'd realized he preferred to live English, he hadn't taken his church vows and then broken them.

It's almost as though Marcus never came to town.

Rosalyn let out a humorless laugh as she headed toward the county highway. It was senseless to pretend that Marcus hadn't changed her life—hadn't given her such a heady sense of hope that she'd dared to believe she'd be a wife and a mother someday. A lot of what-ifs and if-onlys filled her troubled mind as her feet somehow placed themselves one in front of the other. She didn't stop walking until she was climbing the porch steps of the house where she and her sisters had lived with Dat.

Rosalyn reached for the doorknob and then drew back her hand. What would she accomplish by entering the empty house—especially when she was in such a negative frame of mind? After a moment she went inside anyway, figuring to rescue Mamm's Nativity scene.

The house felt eerily empty. Unnaturally silent.

She stood in the middle of the gloomy front room for several moments. It seemed like a good idea to check the entire house, to see if Dat had left them any unexpected surprises.

Except for a few dirty dishes, the kitchen appeared the same as when she'd last seen it, so she ventured down to the basement. The storeroom shelves were still lined with glass jars of vegetables and the freezer still held several packages of meat, so at least Dat hadn't made off with their winter's supply of food. Rosalyn's footsteps echoed as she crossed the concrete floor to the room where her father had worked on his clocks. She stepped into the shop only long enough to ascertain that all of his equipment and clocks were gone.

Rosalyn felt very uneasy entering Dat's shop—because he'd declared it forbidden territory, and because he'd gambled away so much money in this room while he'd pretended to be working. She hurried back up to the main level as though ghosts nipped at her heels, and then went upstairs to peek into the bedrooms.

Dat's closet was empty. The unmade bed—the stale scent of his abandonment—drove Rosalyn quickly down the hall, past the room Loretta and Drew had vacated and the smaller one that had been Edith's before she'd married Asa. At the end of the hall, Rosalyn stepped into her own bedroom and found it just as she'd left it.

Something hanging from the post of the dresser mirror drew her like a magnet. Marcus's faceless cornhusk angel gazed vacantly at her.

Rosalyn turned away, torn between leaving it and taking it. She'd become so upset by Dat's biting remarks that she'd hastily packed, not realizing she'd forgotten Marcus's angel. If she hung the little figure in her room at Edith's house, wouldn't she recall that Marcus—the love of her life—had abandoned her, every time she saw it?

With a sigh, Rosalyn lifted the cornhusk doll from the mirror post. "If ever I needed an angel, it's now," she whispered.

The angel rustled, as brittle and lifeless as an unanswered prayer, when Rosalyn tucked it into her coat pocket. A sense of desperate desolation filled the room, so she hurried downstairs. After she'd carefully laid the ceramic figurines of the holy family, the shepherds, the wise men, and the animals in the wooden shed of Mamm's manger scene, she lifted it carefully in both arms.

As she stepped out onto the front porch, Rosalyn vowed never to enter the house alone again. *Too many ghosts. Too much pain.*

Chapter Twenty-Six

As darkness fell on Christmas Eve, Rosalyn got caught up in the excitement of the crowd that was gathering at Preacher Ben's place. The men had gone to the barn to handle the animals while the women with young children were in Miriam's kitchen with an array of costumes for the pageant. As Rosalyn entered with Leroy, alongside Edith and Louisa, a happy pandemonium filled the large room.

"I get to be a wise man this year!" one of the boys called out.

"I wanna play with the sheeps!" another child cried.

"Mama, lookit! A hat like a donkey's head!"

"I'm gonna be an angel!"

Rosalyn held tightly to Leroy, who wanted to scramble around the kitchen table with the other kids. She couldn't help laughing with Edith, who appeared amazed at the noisy energy filling the room. Were these the same children who sat so quietly with their *mamms* and *dats* during church services?

Miriam lifted her little daughter Bethlehem from the fray. "It's time to listen, kids!" she called out. "Everyone gets a cookie from Teacher Alberta, and then we'll get you into your costumes. It's going to be a Christmas pageant like no other, what with all of you here to celebrate the birth of baby Jesus!"

When Alberta Zook took the foil from a big tray of cookies, the kids flocked over to claim one. The local teacher—Preacher Henry's cousin—seemed shy and reclusive when Rosalyn spoke with her at church, yet she took on a sparkle when her scholars surrounded her. "We've already discussed who gets to play which parts this year," she reminded them firmly. "No matter whether you're a shepherd or a wise man or an angel, we need you all to pay attention. We don't want anyone getting stepped on by a cow—"

"And we don't wanna step in cow *poop*!" Timmy Knepp interrupted.

"*Jah*, that, too," Alberta continued patiently. "You'll need to wear your coats under your costumes tonight. We've got wise men costumes over there," she said, pointing to where Lydia was standing. "Annie Mae's going to help the shepherds in this corner. Then you scholars can skedaddle while we dress the angels and lambs."

Rosalyn was impressed with the order that emerged from the earlier chaos. Soon Levi Zook and the Knepp twins, Joey and Josh, were wearing their fake beards and slipping into flowing robes of rich colors. Taylor and Brett Leitner were donning shortened men's bathrobes while Annie Mae tied headbands around the dish towels draped over young Sara and Timmy Knepp's heads. Sol and Lucy Brenneman—Seth and Mary's kids—were also dressing as shepherds as their *mamm* helped them.

Rebecca stepped in through the back door to see how the kids were progressing. She beamed as she looked around her mother's kitchen. "What do you think?" she asked Rosalyn and Edith with childlike excitement. "This is our third live Nativity, and everyone's really getting into the spirit."

"I've never seen the likes of a Nativity pageant," Rosalyn

replied. "And such costumes they have! They certainly don't look Plain."

"Our bishop in Roseville would never have allowed such an event," Edith remarked. "But it seems like a wonderful alternative to an evening at the schoolhouse."

"I found these costumes a couple years ago, when we realized there weren't enough scholars of an age to put on the usual Christmas Eve recitation program," Rebecca explained. "It's nothing short of magical, the way our pageant falls together and attracts so many folks from outside of town."

Miriam came over, smiling at her daughter. "Some of our success has to do with *Rebecca's* magic," she put in modestly. "Without her help, the pageant would consist of a few folks milling around out in the barn amongst the animals."

"Ah, but there would still be singing and celebration." Rebecca slipped an arm around her mother's shoulders and kissed her cheek. "Mamma, Wyatt and I went to church with Dad this morning, over in New Haven!" she said. "They made us feel really welcome—and most of them remembered my name even though I've not been there for a while."

"Why wouldn't they recall a bright and shining star like you, honey bug?" Miriam's face took on the glow of a Christmas candle. "I'm so happy to hear that. It's my fervent prayer that you and Wyatt will embrace whichever religious faith blesses your marriage all the days of your life together."

Rosalyn's heart swelled with warmth—and with memories of her own *mamm*. She missed her mother most of all during the holiday season, so she was eager to begin some new traditions during her first Christmas in Willow Ridge. The older kids made her chuckle as they commented on each other's costumes—and grabbed more cookies—until Teacher Alberta pointed them toward the door.

After the wise men and shepherds headed outside to the barn, some of the toddlers' *mamms* began to dress their children in loose white robes that tied in the front with big bows.

When Rosalyn saw Leroy doubtfully eyeing the sparkly silver circles that served as the angels' halos, she reached for a gray knitted cap.

"Leroy, we need a special donkey," she said. "Look at these awesome long ears! And the gray sweatshirt will fit right over your coat."

He nodded eagerly. "Donkey!" he repeated as he stroked the ears.

"And Louisa can be a lamb," Edith said as she chose a cream-colored sweatshirt and a hat with a lamb's nose and ears. "Looks like we have plenty of angels."

"Lambie!" the little girl cooed as she tweaked the ears on the cap. "Me a lambie!"

As Rosalyn fastened the knitted strap under Leroy's chin, she saw that Bethlehem Hooley; Josiah and Lena Witmer's son, Isaiah; and Rachel's daughter, Amelia, were being transformed into angels. Ella, the little Glick girl, stood absolutely still with her eyes closed as her *mamm* slipped a hat with a lamb's face on her head. It was the cutest sight Rosalyn had seen in a long time.

"Are these wee ones going to sit amongst the animals in the barn, too?" she asked. She had visions of Leroy getting bored and pestering the sheep—or the other little kids.

"They start out on hay bales alongside Mary and Joseph, or with the shepherds," Teacher Alberta explained. "After everyone sings a carol or two, the angels' parents usually circulate in the crowd with them to keep them occupied—and because everyone thinks they're adorable."

When the back door opened again, Rhoda and Andy Leitner entered with their little Aden. The baby was already bundled up in his coat with a pale blue blanket wrapped around him. Miriam held him while Rhoda put on Mary's blue gown and flowing headpiece. When Andy had tied the fabric belt of his simple brown robe, he took up a large carved walking stick.

"Ben and the other fellows have arranged the hay bales,

and the animals are settled in their places," he said, "so we're ready to start the pageant!"

"When everyone's in place, we'll sing 'Away in a Manger,'" Teacher Alberta instructed. "'Silent Night' will be next, and then we'll sing 'We Three Kings' as the cue for the wise men to come out of the barn and join the others."

The children's excitement was contagious, and as Rosalyn went outside, she was eager to watch the pageant unfold. She'd heard the story of the Nativity since she'd been Leroy and Louisa's age, yet she sensed this evening's rendering of Jesus's birth would breathe new life into it because it was being played out by people she knew—ordinary people, just as Mary and Joseph had been when they journeyed to Bethlehem to pay their taxes.

"Look, Leroy, there's one of Bishop Tom's cows by the barn door," she said as she pointed to it. "And those young mules belong to Ira."

"Daniel Kanagy brought the sheep in that pen," Edith put in as they headed for the barn. "And the little Shetland pony belongs to the Knepp kids."

Rosalyn couldn't help smiling at the animals tethered near the hay bales where Mary and Joseph were taking their seats with Aden. When she and Edith found a spot on a hay bale for the twins to sit, she saw that quite a crowd was gathering in the Hooleys' yard—folks from Willow Ridge, as well as people she'd never seen.

Rebecca jogged over to the barn. When she flipped a switch, everyone looked up with an *oh!*

Rosalyn sucked in her breath. High above them, a golden star sparkled in the night sky, basking serenely in the beam of a spotlight. In her rational mind, she knew it was a big, glittery balloon on a string—only a make-believe star—yet she couldn't stop gazing at it. A lump of emotion formed in her throat and she was filled with awe. After the events of the past week, her soul was eager to believe in miracles.

In her forlorn heart, hope blossomed. No matter what had happened recently in Willow Ridge and in her life, Christmas had come.

It's Christmas. In spite of everything, it's Christmas.

The wonder of the season enfolded her. The promise of the Christ Child lifted her spirits as the children sang "Away in a Manger" in their sweet young voices. As she drank in the simple beauty of the animals gathered around Mary, Joseph, and little Jesus, and the radiant faces of the children, Rosalyn felt transformed. She, too, was an innocent child again, unfazed by the harsh realities of adulthood.

"Silent Night" made her cry, but with tears of peace. The crowd was growing quite large, yet remained reverently quiet. The faces of men and women alike reflected the awe they were feeling in their hearts. When the wise men appeared to the tune of "We Three Kings," Rosalyn once again gazed up at the star.

You've blessed me with so many gifts, Lord, she prayed silently. *The light of Your star has shown me that my life is full and complete and meaningful. You knew this pageant was exactly what I needed, didn't You?*

On a hilltop outside of New Haven, Marcus stared through the windshield. "That can*not* be a star," he muttered. But he got out of his car to take a closer look.

It's probably part of that live Nativity in Willow Ridge. Just a show.

Yet in the stillness of the winter night, Marcus sensed that something much larger was taking place. That star had to be more than a mile away, yet it glowed like a beacon to attract anyone who was paying attention, looking for a way out of the darkness.

As a kid hearing the story, he'd wondered how those ancient wise men had known that the star over Bethlehem was a sign—and he'd had his doubts about three old guys trekking across the desert on camels, in search of the promised Messiah. They hadn't had a GPS system or any navigational guidance except their knowledge of astronomy, yet they'd followed the bright, special star on faith and found the stable where a tiny baby had been born.

Marcus laughed at the irony of it: with all his technology, he hadn't even made it out of Missouri. His transmission had gone out Wednesday night, just a couple of miles from Willow Ridge. Car repairs had eaten up his money and the delay had given him too much time to think. He knew he'd treated Rosalyn and Wyatt badly by leaving without a word, but now that he had wheels again, he still planned to escape the confinements Willow Ridge represented . . .

But maybe you should pass through for a look at that live Nativity before you hit the road. There'll be a crowd, so you can duck in and out without anyone spotting you.

Marcus gazed at the star a little longer. It was surely a large balloon with a spotlight focused on it—nothing magical or spiritual about it—yet its glow tugged at something deep inside him. He suspected Rebecca was behind this illusion, but he wondered how the star remained so high in the sky and so perfectly still without drifting or bobbing on the wind.

If you could explain everything, there'd be no need for miracles.

Marcus blinked. He'd heard a voice, yet he was alone on the roadside. He wasn't particularly in the mood for a miracle, nor was he sure he really believed in them. He was ready to roll—didn't know his destination, but he'd recognize it when he got there. He got back into his car, figuring to do a drive-by at the Hooley place and keep going.

Long before Marcus reached the Willow Ridge city limits, he spotted cars parked on both shoulders of the county highway. Considering that residents of Willow Ridge would walk or drive a buggy to the pageant, he was amazed at the number of English visitors.

Wow, if we could attract this many people to the auction—

Marcus shoved that thought out of his mind, because the auction wasn't on his radar screen anymore. He drove slowly, gawking at all the people who stood in Preacher Ben's barnyard—and stopping to allow several more to cross the road. At the Grill N Skillet corner, Sheriff Banks and Officer McClatchey were directing traffic onto the road that ran past Nora's store, so Marcus had no choice but to follow the traffic pattern.

When he spotted an empty space, he parked and hopped out of his car. The huge crowd guaranteed that he could step in for a closer look without anyone he knew spotting him. At this point, Marcus was too curious to leave without seeing what had attracted so many people.

Hey, it's just a small-town Christmas pageant. Why would anyone outside of Willow Ridge care about some farm animals and a few Amish kids singing Christmas carols?

Marcus made his way up Preacher Ben's driveway, engulfed by the crowd. He kept his head low when he caught sight of Asa carrying his little boy, who wore a big grin— and a cap with long donkey ears. As he stayed in the shadow of the Hooley house, the kids began singing a carol, and the whole crowd joined in.

"'Joy to the world! The Lord is come!'"

The sheer volume of the sound pressed Marcus against the house. When he peered toward the barn, Andy and Rhoda Leitner were standing in front of a Holstein cow, a Shetland pony, a couple of mules, and some sheep. They were singing at the top of their lungs along with several young shepherds in bathrobes, three short wise men in fake beards, folks in black hats and bonnets—and the entire crowd of English visitors.

Their happiness was so contagious that Marcus's heart began to beat rapidly.

"'Joy to the world! The Savior reigns!'"

Marcus thrummed with the power of music that rang so loudly around him, he couldn't hear himself think. The people of Willow Ridge had just been swindled out of the money in their aid fund, yet they were filled with the true joy of Christmas. Across the barnyard, Wyatt and Rebecca stood arm in arm, singing of a heavenly love that transcended even the feelings they shared. When Preacher Ben and Bishop Tom turned to face the crowd, they, too, were so caught up in the song that their bearded faces glowed with joy. All signs of their worry were gone, as though they'd never been dragged down by the undertow of Cornelius Riehl's treachery.

"'He rules the world with truth and grace!'"

Marcus rested against the house, overcome by the words and music. *Truth and grace.*

His Amish friends knew the awful truth about their errant deacon, yet they had the grace to celebrate Christmas and move forward into the New Year with hope and joy. Would it be such a difficult thing to live among people who could release their fears, along with the desperation that Riehl's betrayal had caused them? Where else would Marcus find such acceptance, from folks who'd endured his reckless attitude because they believed he could turn himself around?

Because they believed in you, *Hooley.*

When a bonneted young woman in the crowd turned sideways, Marcus forgot to breathe. Rosalyn was singing the song's last stanza, beaming at Louisa in her woolly white hat with little lamb ears on the top. The love they shared stunned him.

She could be looking at you with that love on her face, Hooley, but you messed her over—

As though she'd heard his thoughts, Rosalyn gazed full-on at Marcus.

The night went silent. The people were still singing, but he couldn't hear them.

Marcus clung to the house, bracing himself for Rosalyn's anger—for her scowl or her tears or a meltdown. By this time, she must know that he'd left town—that he'd run off and left *her*. There was no sense in trying to slink away, pretending he didn't see her, because Rosalyn's expression had nailed him in place. He couldn't move if he wanted to.

Her smile warmed him like the sun. Her face radiated a love and acceptance that turned his world upside down. She was making her way between the other folks to come talk to him.

"Marcus!" Rosalyn whispered beneath the noise of the crowd. "You came back! I prayed that you would."

Marcus's mouth dropped open. Rosalyn's simple declaration of faith took him totally by surprise . . . and he felt *good* about it. He didn't sense that she was trapping him, or laying on the guilt so he would stay. She was overjoyed to see him, and she'd believed he would come back to redeem himself.

Marcus let out the breath he'd been holding. "But I walked away from—from you and the whole church thing and—"

"We all get scared sometimes," Rosalyn interrupted with a shrug. "This is the best Christmas present ever, Marcus, that you've gotten over yourself and come back to Willow Ridge."

He almost smarted off at her, but her observation stopped him cold. *You've gotten over yourself.*

Marcus smiled. Wise woman that she was, Rosalyn had

him pegged. And she'd said nothing about taking up the relationship he'd left hanging—or any other expectations or conditions.

He suddenly realized that if Rosalyn loved him, and he loved her back, he'd never feel the need to run again. He could lead a productive life—he could have it *all*—if he accepted the faith she wanted to share with him.

Bless her, Rosalyn had risked everything to talk to him this way. Knowing how he tended to run from responsibility, she'd still approached him—rather than turning away to shield her heart from another loss. She could be whining about how he'd betrayed her feelings—how he'd led her on with quick, pretty words only to leave like a thief in the night.

But she was smiling at him, holding a little girl . . . making him wonder what it might be like if she were holding *his* child.

Around them, the crowd was dispersing, but Marcus focused on Rosalyn. He wished endearments and promises would roll off his tongue as effortlessly as they'd done for the other girls he'd thought he loved—but this woman didn't want his careless charm. Rosalyn deserved his honesty and his commitment to her, which implied that he would also commit himself to the Amish church.

"We, um, have a lot to talk about, Roz," he murmured.

"We do." Her gaze remained as steady as her smile.

Marcus raked his fingers through his hair, more nervous than he cared to be. "I—I have this urge to kiss you," he whispered, "but this is hardly the place—"

"I know a place—where we can talk," Rosalyn added with a wink.

Marcus gaped. When had this devout young woman become such a flirt? And when had she taken control of this conversation, and the future of their relationship?

He chuckled, at himself mostly. "Okay, so take me wherever you think we should—"

"Marcus! Welcome home, son." Wyatt clapped him on the back, smiling broadly. "Wasn't this live Nativity *something*? Who knew Willow Ridge would become *the* place to celebrate Christmas—to celebrate *everything*?"

Marcus began to laugh, gazing gratefully at Wyatt and Rebecca as a sense of warmth and rightness filled his heart. "Yeah," he agreed. "Who knew?"

Chapter Twenty-Seven

What are you thinking? Why are you bringing him to this cold, empty house?

Rosalyn gripped Marcus's gloved hand as they made their way through the snow to the back door. After they'd stepped into the mudroom, she quickly lit the lamp and headed into the kitchen. When she'd spotted him at the pageant her heart had kicked her into a higher gear, as though it sensed Marcus might turn tail again and never come back—unless she gave him a reason to stay. She'd made a daring suggestion when he'd wanted to kiss her, and she was determined to carry through with it. What did she have to lose—except her chance for happiness?

Marcus stood in the doorway, glancing into the flickering shadows. "So, won't your *dat* be coming back from the pageant pretty soon?"

Rosalyn fought back the fleeting image of her scowling father when he'd shooed her away. As she took Marcus's hands in hers, she found the strength to face this house and its ghosts. "He packed up and left town few days ago," she replied softly.

Marcus gripped her fingers. "*Seriously?* He skipped out

on his—? Wow." He exhaled in disbelief. "*Wow*. I—I'm sorry, Roz."

She sighed. "*Jah*, me too. But when you look at the big picture, are you really surprised? Dat was always the one dishing out the discipline, and it seems he's not much on taking it from other folks."

Suddenly Marcus was hugging her—not holding her close for the kiss he'd wanted, but to comfort her. To express his support. Rosalyn closed her eyes and leaned into him. Even in a chilly kitchen, with their winter coats on, this ranked as the most romantic, affectionate moment of her life and she intended to savor it.

"Will you be all right, Roz?"

With Marcus's arms around her, she felt safe and cherished—for the moment, anyway. Her life was as shiny as a star when Marcus was with her, but as bleak as a moonless winter night when he wasn't. "Once Edith, Loretta, and I realized that this whole mess was Dat's doing, and that we couldn't have done anything differently," she replied, "we agreed to let go of it—to let God handle it."

"That sounds like a *gut* plan." Marcus let out a short laugh. "Better than my way of doing things—which is to run off with no plan at all. Roz, I'm sorry I left you without—"

She placed a finger across his lips, determined that their time together wouldn't be spent making apologies. "I've wanted to run plenty of times in my life," she admitted as she held Marcus's gaze. "But as an obedient Amish daughter, I didn't feel I had that option. Truth be told, it's more like what Dat said. I didn't have the *gumption* to run."

Marcus's pale green eyes widened. "That's not true! You have more gumption than anyone I know," he protested. "Just making it from one day to the next with your father required more strength than most daughters ever have to call upon."

Rosalyn thrummed with his insight. It did her heart good to hear Marcus say that her troubled relationship with Dat wasn't normal . . . wasn't her fault.

She found a smile for him. "Well! This isn't what you had in mind to talk about when we left the pageant, ain't so?" she asked lightly. "How about if I cozy things up while you figure out what you wanted to say?"

Marcus blinked. Once again Roz had turned the tables on him, turned the conversation around with a sparkle in her eyes that kept him guessing. She was right, too. He had no desire to spend the evening talking about her father when there were so many more fascinating topics to explore—for starters, the fact that she'd brought him to a place where they'd be alone and unchaperoned.

As he hung their coats in the mudroom, Rosalyn put a pan of water on the stove. With quick efficiency she took mugs from the cupboard—and just as he moved toward her, she ducked into the unlit front room.

"Make yourself at home, Marcus," she called out.

He had to smile. Rosalyn was the picture of Plain domesticity, playing the hostess to hold him at bay.

But listen to what she's saying. She's talking about a home, Hooley, giving you all the right cues—if you have enough gumption *to follow through.*

The heating system hissed, which meant she'd turned up the thermostat. Rosalyn entered the kitchen with a platter that held three fat red candles nestled in fresh greenery. "We've had these pretty candles since before Mamm passed," she said as she set them on the table as a centerpiece. "We were always saving them for a special occasion, so it's time to light them, don't you think?"

He couldn't let that remark pass. "Oh, *jah*? What's the occasion?"

She struck a match. Her pretty face glowed in the candlelight she created as she lit the three wicks. "Well, Jesus has a birthday—and someone else in this room has one on Second Christmas, am I right?"

Marcus's mouth fell open. "How'd you know that?"

Rosalyn's smile turned playfully mysterious. "You told me—trying to convince me you weren't a mere *kid* when you invited me for our sleigh ride," she replied wistfully. "I made the mistake of calling you my boyfriend, but you got over it."

She had him there.

She has you, all right. Don't blow it.

"We'll start your party with some brownies and sugar cookies—but we'll have to wait for them to thaw," Rosalyn added as she went to the freezer. "If you play your cards right, I'll bake you a birthday cake and you can come over to Asa's place to celebrate Second Christmas with us."

"And if I don't?" Marcus challenged before he caught himself.

Rosalyn set a lidded pan on the counter, turning to hold his gaze. "Then we'll have a nice cake for dessert and you won't," she said with a shrug. "I suppose Miriam would bake you one if you dropped a hint—"

"I'll be there. With you."

The blush that crept into her cheeks told Marcus the time for teasing was over. He'd committed now—or he'd at least agreed to go along with her plans—and it would be the stupidest mistake of his life if he let Rosalyn down again. "*Denki* for remembering my birthday, and for already making it special," he murmured. "It's been a while since anybody baked me a cake."

She took her time setting goodies on a plate—probably giving him a chance to keep talking while he was on a roll.

"I—I have a confession about our first sleigh ride," he continued, hoping it was the right thing to do. "When I asked you to go out on that date, I wanted to ruffle your *dat*'s feathers—because I suspected he was hiding something."

Rosalyn did a pretty good job of masking her disappointment. "You were right, too," she whispered. "And without your help, we might not've learned the whole truth."

Marcus sighed. She probably wouldn't be such a good sport about the rest of his confession. "I, um, also asked you out to prove that I could lure you away from your straitlaced Old Order mind-set—so you'd spend time laughing and riding around with a bad apple like me, even though I knew your *dat* would get mad at you."

Rosalyn considered his words carefully. "I needed to laugh and ride around with you more than you know, Marcus," she whispered.

"But those were terrible, selfish reasons to spend time with you, Roz! It was a game to me," Marcus blurted. "But I had a wonderful time that evening and—and I want to court you, *please*. You believe the best about me when so many folks think there's nothing *gut* to see."

A smile teased at the corners of Rosalyn's lips. She poured hot water into two mugs and put them on the table. She took a canister of cocoa mix from the cabinet and brought it to the table with the cookies. She opened a drawer and removed two spoons. Just as these deliberate little stall tactics were driving Marcus to say something—*anything*, to end the maddening silence—Rosalyn sat down and gestured for him to take the seat beside her.

"When I look at you, Marcus," she said in a low voice, "I see a very capable horse trainer with cat-green eyes and killer dimples who's too handsome for his own *gut*—so attractive I can't believe he wants to be with *me*," she added humbly. "I also see a man who's sincerely interested in the welfare of Willow Ridge, a man with ideas and the energy to carry them out. But the thought of joining the Old Order makes him really, really nervous."

Marcus let out the breath he'd been holding. "You've got that right. I wish I could just take my vows without questioning—"

"But you *should* question!" Rosalyn insisted as she grabbed his hand. "Why do married men grow beards but never mustaches? Why must Amish women always go along with what their men say? Why is it so wrong to read the Bible for ourselves instead of believing that our bishop and preachers are the only ones who can interpret it?"

Rosalyn exhaled forcefully, as though her outburst had surprised her as much as it had him. "A lot of things about our faith bother me, Marcus, but I'm not supposed to question them," she said in a calmer voice. "I took my vows because it was the path I was expected to follow as an obedient daughter. You've spent some time on the English side of the fence, so be very sure you can live with the *Ordnung* before you commit yourself to it."

Marcus sensed it had taken every ounce of Rosalyn's courage to voice her frustrations about the Amish faith. She was handing him a ticket out, but when he gazed into her ardent brown eyes, he didn't want to sacrifice a lifetime of loving her for the sake of some unwritten man-made rules about Old Order religion. "Do you regret being Amish?" he asked softly.

Rosalyn appeared startled by his question, but she considered it. "It's what I know. The Amish faith gives me a framework to build a solid, stable life on," she replied. "I sometimes envy English women their conveniences and their independence, but I wouldn't last a day in their world. I don't know how I'd survive on my own."

Marcus cocked his head, amazed that she'd even thought

about these matters. "You could live English with me, Roz," he whispered. "I've got a *gut* job with Wyatt, and now that your *dat*'s skipped out, I'm sure your sisters would understand—would still love you—if you decided to leave the church."

"I'm not wired that way. I made my promise to God, and I intend to honor it."

Nodding, he studied the sturdy hand that held his. Rosalyn had answered in exactly the way he'd expected, without berating him for asking such a question. She'd stated her case, so he knew what his options were. He admired her even more—for her integrity, and for accepting her place in a world that tilted in favor of men and the rules they made.

Marcus stirred some hot chocolate mix into their hot water and placed a mug in front of her. "Shall we drink a toast?"

Rosalyn's eyes widened. "To what?"

He raised his mug, hoping he expressed his sentiments in a way that appealed to her. "Let's drink to our first Christmas Eve together, and to a Merry Christmas and a Happy New Year, shall we?"

She tapped her mug lightly against his and sipped her cocoa. "Now let's toast to your birthday, Marcus—and your best year ever," she proposed.

His pulse pounded harder as their mugs clinked again. Rosalyn was gazing at him as though she expected him to take another turn . . . until he finally asked the question that hovered unspoken between them.

Marcus grinned when something occurred to him. "When I mentioned courting you a few minutes ago, you didn't answer me, Roz."

"You didn't ask. You just said what you wanted—before you moved on to the part about other folks not seeing anything *gut* about you."

He set down his mug so he wouldn't drop it. *She nailed you again, Hooley. It was all about you.*

When Rosalyn raised her mug again to drink more cocoa, he had a feeling they'd play cat and mouse all evening unless he sent the game in a different direction. Why was this relationship such a challenge? Other girls had always—

She's not like the others. Rosalyn's genuine. She holds you accountable. Rather than hiding in denial, sweeping her emotions about her dat *and her religion under the rug, she's choosing to move on—and she'll take you with her, if you'll go.*

Marcus leaned forward and kissed her lightly on the lips. "Please, Roz, may I court you?" he whispered.

Her face glowed from more than the candlelight. "*Jah*, I'd like that, Marcus. More than anything."

"More than getting married?" he challenged before he caught himself. He really had to stop smarting off if she was to take him seriously.

Rosalyn laughed. When she teased his dimple with her fingertip, Marcus was afraid to move for fear he'd lose the moment and the endearing smile on her lovely face. "Some women say the courtship's the best part—all the fun of sleigh rides and picnics and such without the responsibilities of being a wife," she said lightly.

When her expression grew wistful to the point of appearing worried, however, Marcus sensed she'd hit a bump in her emotional road. Her hand dropped away, and he immediately missed the contact of her skin against his.

"Are you afraid I'll change my mind—run off again—if I get crosswise with Ben or Tom after I've joined the Amish church?"

Rosalyn shook her head, no longer meeting his gaze. "If we're confessing our deep, dark secrets, I'd be wrong not to mention mine."

Marcus's eyes widened. What could a sweet, sheltered

young woman like Roz be hiding? When she swiped at a tear, he got very concerned. She wasn't the type to gain his sympathy by crying.

"When I was young, my mother . . . well, she lost some babies—"

"I'm sorry," he murmured.

"—and she got to the point where she didn't want to go to bed at night, because . . . well, Dat . . ."

The fear and pain in Rosalyn's voice painted a picture of a father—a marriage—no daughter should ever find out about. No wonder she favored a never-ending engagement. But Marcus didn't intend to remain single and celibate, nor would he sleep in one room while his wife slept in another.

"I shouldn't even be talking about this private stuff—haven't told another soul," Rosalyn went on in a miserable rush. "But maybe you'll wish you weren't married to me when you find out that I don't want to . . ."

Marcus gently placed his hand on hers. "You don't want to be with a man? Because you're afraid?"

Rosalyn swallowed hard. Nodded.

How did he handle this? He'd heard that some mothers instilled a fear of pregnancy in their unwed daughters, but he sensed Rosalyn's *mamm* hadn't intentionally done that . . . partly because her sisters seemed to be such happy wives and their husbands always wore satisfied smiles.

But Loretta and Edith are younger. Maybe they didn't have a clue about their mother's sad predicament.

Marcus wished he were older and wiser—and he wished Nora were here. But Rosalyn had entrusted her deep fear to *him*, and he prayed he could come up with an appropriate answer—especially after some of his glib comments in the past. "After that crude remark I made about horses and women a while back, I'm amazed that you still tolerate me," he said ruefully. "I'm sorry I said that, Roz."

Rosalyn sniffled loudly, as though she hadn't heard

him. "You're my last chance, Marcus. It's not like guys are pounding down my door, so if I want a family—"

How had their Christmas Eve banter deteriorated into such a lament? Marcus shifted his chair so he could put his arm around her. "That is so not true, Roz! You're *my* last chance to become a decent human being—a guy worthy of the courtship you're allowing me," he pleaded.

He held her face in his hands and gazed into her sad brown eyes. "I don't know what to say to make you feel better about sex, but if we trust each other—if we love each other, and listen to each other—we can make a beautiful life together, Roz. Can you believe that?"

She nipped her lip, but bless her, she didn't look away. "I *want* to believe you, Marcus," she whispered. "I—I know you're nothing like Dat—"

"*Denki* for saying that," he put in. "Maybe that's where we start. Every marriage is different, so you're not doomed to repeat your poor *mamm*'s experience, Roz. I'd rather cut off both my hands than hurt you—or force myself on you. I'm not wired that way."

As Rosalyn held his gaze, Marcus dared to believe he saw a glimmer of hope in her eyes—the dawning of an understanding that would be the key to earning her trust. Her body relaxed. Her breathing returned to normal.

"What if we go for that long courtship you talked about— wait until a *year* from now to set our date, if you need to?" he asked softly. "I want you to love every part of what it'll mean to be married to me."

"A year's a long time—"

"For you, Roz, I'll wait," he assured her. "It'll give me time to save up money for a home and a family instead of expecting you to scrape by and make do, once you're my wife."

Rosalyn's brown eyes widened. "You're amazing, Marcus. There was a time I didn't think you could hold a serious conversation, but—well, here we are."

"*Jah*, here we are. Isn't that something?" He suddenly felt ecstatic about the way their evening—and their lives—were turning out. "We've got candlelight and cookies and Christmas Eve, and we've got each other. Pretty awesome, isn't it?"

When Rosalyn kissed him, Marcus had her answer.

Chapter Twenty-Eight

"Going once, going twice—*sold* for eight hundred dollars!" the auctioneer cried. "An Adam Wagler home remodeling project goes to those Detweiler brothers in the black hats!"

Rosalyn laughed along with everyone around her because about half the folks in Wyatt's big barn matched that description of Asa and Drew. "The auctioneer's having as *gut* a time as anybody," she remarked to Marcus. "And he's getting the bids up pretty high, too."

"That's Jude Shetler from Morning Star, and he's being assisted by Bram Kanagy—who grew up in Willow Ridge but lives outside of Cedar Creek now that he's married," Marcus explained. "Wyatt and I have attended their livestock auctions, so we asked them to handle this one. I hear they've donated their services today, and I suspect Bishop Vernon had something to do with that."

Rosalyn nodded. She didn't dwell on the fact that Dat was the reason the church district needed to raise so much money—especially because Bishop Tom and Preacher Ben were coming through the crowd, and they appeared to be in high spirits.

"Doing a little remodeling, Asa?" Ben teased. "Always a worthwhile project, keeping your Edith happy."

Asa laughed, glancing at Rosalyn and Marcus. "Truth be told, Drew and I are having the Riehl house repainted as our wedding gift to your cousin and his fiancée," he replied. "We're doing all we can to make an honest man out of Marcus and to convince him to stay in Willow Ridge."

"Rosalyn's way ahead of you!" Marcus shot back. He slung his arm loosely around her shoulders. "We're taking our time about tying the knot—but having the house spiffed up for us is a wonderful gift."

"Oh my," Rosalyn whispered. "I can't thank you enough. We asked Dat long ago if we could paint and put up new curtains, but he was having none of it."

Bishop Tom's smile fell a notch. When he'd learned that Dat had left town without fulfilling the obligations of his *bann*, Tom had explained to her and her sisters that their father was no longer a church member in good standing— and if he didn't return to make amends, the next step would be excommunicating him.

The bishop quickly resumed his positive attitude, however. "Cornelius put us under a dark cloud, but we're seeing the silver lining today," he said, gesturing at the crowd. "Look at the way every family and business in Willow Ridge—and in the towns hereabouts—have donated their time and some big-ticket items to the auction! We've pulled together for the common *gut*—"

"And with the way the sale's going," Preacher Ben put in, "I predict that our aid fund will be nearly restored to its former amount. It's the Lord's hand at work—along with Rebecca's advertising—bringing so many folks to bid on our items, too."

Bishop Tom nodded. "And I couldn't be happier about you two becoming a couple, by the way. Congratulations, kids."

Rosalyn felt her face turning red, yet she was glad their

news had been getting around town—mostly because Loretta and Edith couldn't keep it to themselves. It was gratifying that folks seemed genuinely pleased for her and Marcus, and that they didn't hold her father's mistakes against her.

"*Jah*, we Hooleys are calling Rosalyn a miracle worker." Ben's tone was teasing, but his smile told her he was deeply grateful. "It's the best sort of Christmas gift, to have a young man see the light—and it's coming from a star instead of a computer screen."

Rosalyn's eyes widened as she turned to Marcus. When they'd talked over the past week, he'd said he was gradually going to wean himself away from his electronics. "Have you already given up your iPad and cell phone?" she whispered.

Marcus's dimples deepened. "The auction seemed like a worthwhile cause to donate them to—"

"And over here, folks," Jude Shetler announced with his microphone, "we have a red Chevy for your consideration. It's got some miles on it and a touch of rust on the underbody—but it's also got a new transmission, so it'll be reliable transportation for a long while yet. Who'll start the bidding for me?"

Rosalyn's mouth dropped open. "You're selling your car now, too?"

Marcus seemed pleased that he'd caught her by surprise. "In for a dime, in for a dollar," he said as the auctioneer's chant filled the barn. "In my line of work, I'll always have access to fine horses, after all. Wyatt's already promised me a pair of his retired Thoroughbreds as my bonus for staying on—and for becoming his ranch manager."

"Glory be and hallelujah!" Preacher Ben crowed. "This calls for a trip to Cedar Creek to have James Graber fix you up with a new buggy, young man—my treat," he added. "It's a happy day, hearing that you're fully committing to the Old Order, when you could've gone a lot of other directions—or could've dragged your feet for a lot longer."

Rosalyn's thoughts were spinning after receiving so many surprises in the past few minutes. Christmas had been simple: she and her sisters hadn't exchanged gifts, and she and Marcus hadn't, either. Yet Marcus's transformation—his willingness to change so drastically, for *her*—was a gift she would treasure every day for the rest of her life. If he was giving up the English technology and conveniences that had meant so much to him sooner than he'd planned, maybe she could believe what he'd told her . . .

You're not doomed to repeat Mamm's experience.

Rosalyn smiled. She'd thought about Marcus's words several times over the past week and a half, as she'd gazed at the cornhusk angel he'd made for her.

You can be as happy as your sisters—or even happier! Give Marcus a chance—give him the intimacy he craves, when the time's right—and you might find out that today's surprises are nothing *compared to the delight he'll give you when you truly become one with him.*

And besides that, the little voice in her head added, *Marcus is so much cuter than your sisters' husbands.*

Rosalyn laughed out loud—and realized she'd have to explain her outburst. Before any of the men around her could comment, she grabbed Marcus's hand. "It's time for pie and coffee at the café, because I've been on my feet since early this morning, helping the ladies over there. I'll make it worth your while," she added as she flashed her best smile at him.

Asa, Drew, and Ben laughed and whistled, slapping Marcus's back—but he waved off their teasing as though hers was the only voice he could hear. When he and Rosalyn stepped outside the barn together, away from the excitement and noise of the auction, the relative silence of the winter day was soothing. Their boots crunched in the snow as they headed down Wyatt's lane.

"So what's really on your mind, Roz?" Marcus asked as

he tucked her arm beneath his elbow. "Sure as I'm about to join the church, you're not thinking about pie."

Rosalyn chuckled. Maybe it was best to just lay it all out, instead of trying to be clever. She stepped ahead and turned to face him.

"I love you, Marcus," she declared as she playfully held his gaze. "And I can't wait to be your wife—in every sense of the word. If you can turn over a new leaf, so can I, ain't so?"

The astonishment on his face—the joy—was an expression Rosalyn knew she'd remember forever. The way he grabbed her and kissed her was pretty memorable, too.

"You mean, like, you want to marry me *now*?" he asked in a hoarse whisper.

She thought about her options. "Well, you need to complete your instruction with Bishop Tom and take your vows in church—"

"I'm on it!"

"—and we might as well wait until you have that buggy from Ben, and the house is all fixed up, so we'll be a proper Amish couple," Rosalyn continued.

Marcus kissed her again, right there in the middle of the road. "You go get us a table at the Grill N Skillet, and I'll be there as soon as I tell Wagler he's going to paint our place before he does a lick of work for anybody else!"

Rosalyn watched Marcus dash toward the barn—and then he turned around and came back. He put his hands at her waist and effortlessly lifted her into the air, until she was giggling and squealing. When he set her down, he pulled her close.

"Roz, you didn't have to say that just for me—"

"Oh, I said it for *me*," she assured him. "When you told me I didn't have to be like my mother, you broke the spell of fear that she never intended to cast over me. You set me free with those words, Marcus."

He gazed at her as though she was the most beautiful,

most precious—and most amazing—woman he'd ever met. "I love you, too, Roz. You're my star—my guiding light," he said softly. "Nobody shines brighter than you."

Rosalyn's mouth opened but his eloquence had left her speechless.

Marcus kissed her again. "It's going to be so *gut* between us. You'll see!"

As he hurried toward the big red barn again, Rosalyn knew she'd been blessed beyond comprehension. This simple Christmas had been her best, because it had brought her love and joy that would last her lifetime.

Don't miss any of the
Simple Gifts novels by Charlotte Hubbard!

A SIMPLE VOW

Housed in a rustic red barn, the Simple Gifts crafts shop
celebrates the talents of the Amish of Willow Ridge—
and the faith that inspires them. For the acceptance
of simplicity opens the path to love.

As far as Edith Riehl is concerned, the baby twins thrust
suddenly into her arms are a heaven-sent gift. Unable to
conceive, she longs to be a mother with a home of her
own. She's going to abide by her promise to handsome Asa
Detweiler to take care of them while he looks for their real
father. And even if her domineering *dat* Cornelius refuses
to countenance Asa's suit, she can only pray the bachelor's
honesty and persistence will uncover the truth—even as
he's kindled an impossible hope for a love of her own . . .

Asa can't understand why anyone would think he would be
so dishonorable as to father babies and then abandon
them. He's determined to clear his name—but Edith's
caring ways also inspire him to help heal her wounded
spirit and earn her trust. In the face of heartbreaking
deception, he and Edith must find the strength to
understand, forgive . . . and claim their own hearts' joy.

A SIMPLE WISH

*The Amish residents of Willow Ridge share their talents
at the Simple Gifts crafts shop—and share the blessings
of faith, hard work, and love with their community—
even when family secrets bring unexpected challenges . . .*

Making rugs for Simple Gifts has taught Loretta Riehl
that an unassuming pattern can reveal surprising depth.
People, too, have a way of defying first impressions.
Drew Detweiler came to Willow Ridge under a cloud,
but the handsome craftsman has gained the community's
respect for his upholstery skills and commitment to
making amends for his mistakes. As her new
brother-in-law's twin, he's joining the family for
dinners and Sunday visits at the Riehl house, and
Loretta can't deny enjoying his attentions.

If only her *dat* were willing to let a little joy into his life.
Cornelius Riehl grows more stern with each passing day,
and Drew suspects there's more to his moods than missing
Loretta's late *mamm*. Hoping to fulfill Loretta's wish to
live in a peaceful, happy home again, Drew sets out to
learn the truth. It's a journey that will bring to light
painful realities—but also the chance to forge a
new, honest, and loving future together . . .

Connect with

Us

Visit us online at
KensingtonBooks.com
to read more from your favorite authors, see books
by series, view reading group guides, and more.

Join us on social media

for sneak peeks, chances to win books and prize packs,
and to share your thoughts with other readers.

facebook.com/kensingtonpublishing
twitter.com/kensingtonbooks

Tell us what you think!

To share your thoughts, submit a review,
or sign up for our eNewsletters, please visit:
KensingtonBooks.com/TellUs.

More by Bestselling Author
Hannah Howell